PERSIAN NIGHTS

Diane Johnson

FAWCETT CREST • NEW YORK

A Fawcett Crest Book
Published by Ballantine Books
Copyright © 1987 by Diane Johnson

Library of Congress Catalog Card Number: 86-46009

ISBN 0-449-21514-8

This edition published by arrangement with Alfred A. Knopf, Inc.

Manufactured in the United States of America

First Ballantine Books Edition: May 1988

PERSIAN NIGHTS
DIANE JOHNSON

"The best of her novels.... It has the unobtrusively good writing, the gripping readability, the tension of the others, but with a broader, more expansive canvas."

Rosemary Dinnage
The New York Review of Books

"Taut, compelling.... This is material for a tale of high adventure in a dangerous foreign setting; but novelist and screenwriter Diane Johnson... also explores a deeper level of human intrigue: one that has less to do with the suspenseful action than with its attendant moments of doubt and discovery."

Donne Raffat
The Los Angeles Times Book Review

"She portrays not only the unwitting victims, but those who victimize them, just as unwittingly .... *Persian Nights* is a quiet essay on the corrupting power of privilege—political, medical, national, sexual.... Her novel is funny, complex, well-ordered and most welcome."

Laura Furman
USA Today

"Johnson... has taken on a challenging and timely subject. She creates the scenes of political terror with an accomplished and sensitive eye.... All of this is rendered against a background so hauntingly sensuous, so exquisitely evocative, that one is tempted to make this same difficult journey into the strange and the sublime."

Brett Singer
The Philadelphia Inquirer

"Diane Johnson...is obsessed with two themes—reality and terror. *Persian Nights* is a deserving book...because of Diane Johnson's unique gift of narration and observation. The author has it all down perfectly, the mood and the look and the peculiar emotions."

Consuelo Baehr
Newsday

"With its theme of dislocated innocents abroad, the novel seeks to scrutinize the age-old struggle between the sexes by staging the battle against a stark moral and spiritual landscape....Johnson successfully captures the fears and ties of culture shock, particularly in the context of a country under siege."

Gail Caldwell
The Boston Globe

"[The] tension between the broad sweep of history and the minutiae perceived by individuals caught in its rush keeps *Persian Nights* holding steady....Johnson has found a middle ground between sensationalism and high seriousness. Chloe Fowler's good intentions provide a fascinating vantage point for the clash of irreconcilable cultures."

Paul Gray
Time

"Diane Johnson's lively new novel reminds us of *A Passage to India* with its lush foreign atmosphere and the way it ironically plays off inner lives against outer realities....A cleverly made, often funny and touching novel that jauntily needles all of us."

Alicia Metcalf Miller
The Cleveland Plain Dealer

"Johnson's fictions seem to find in . . . confrontations the truest test of human character. . . . Johnson plays expertly with the fine line between paranoia and real catastrophe. *Persian Nights* is an enjoyable read, and full of the kinds of lucid perceptions we expect from this author's heroines."

Jodi Daynard
Chicago Tribune

"*Persian Nights* reaffirms the novelist's eye for the smallest detail, but also a detective's and a political observer's. . . . Because Johnson doesn't tie things up neatly at the end, her story is saved from becoming merely a political thriller or a tiresome romance. It knows that those who play with fire are consumed by it."

Celia McGee
New York Magazine

"Diane Johnson specializes in an artful blend of high anxiety and deadpan humor. . . . In Johnson's fiction the sinister lurks just beneath the commonplace. . . . She infuses the labyrinthine plot with considerable suspense. In *Persian Nights* . . . Johnson has written a social and political satire."

Dorothy Wickenden
The New Republic

"*Persian Nights* is a novel of exquisite tension, and the author is always in control, balancing the work's formulaic structure against its undercurrent of hysteria."

Karen Rile
San Francisco Chronicle

Also by Diane Johnson:

Fiction

FAIR GAME

LOVING HANDS AT HOME

BURNING

LESSER LIVES

LYING LOW

THE SHADOW KNOWS*

Nonfiction

TERRORISTS AND NOVELISTS

DASHIELL HAMMETT: A LIFE*

EDWIN BROUN FRED: SCIENTIST,
ADMINISTRATOR, GENTLEMAN

*Published by Fawcett Books

For Alice Adams and Barbara Epstein

A Moment's Halt—a momentary taste
Of BEING from the Well amid the Waste—
And Lo!—the phantom Caravan has reach'd
The NOTHING it set out from—Oh, make haste!

EDWARD FITZGERALD,
The Rubaiyat of Omar Khayyam

My lately acquired and rather artificial liking
for uprootings and travel fits in happily
with the peaceful fatalism natural to the
bourgeoise that I am.

COLETTE, *The Vagabond*

Acknowledgments

My great thanks to those who have helped me with this—to Robert Gottlieb, whose suggestion began it; to Dr. Hibbard Williams, whom I consulted about the Shah; to Dr. John Murray; to Terry and Iraj Alborzian for their help verifying the Iranian details, and Dorothy Ladd for her help with the manuscript.

Quotations are from the Koran, the poetry of Matthew Arnold, and the *Rubaiyat of Omar Khayyam* translated by Edward FitzGerald.

Persian Nights

Chapter One

THE ARRIVAL

Wake! For the Sun, who scatter'd into flight
The Stars before him from the Field of Night
Drives Night along with them from Heav'n, and strikes
The Sultan's Turret with a Shaft of Light

"They're talking about you," said Abbas Mowlavi, noticing Chloe Fowler's glance behind him along the road, where the shrouded women peered at her, the whites of their eyes gleaming balefully out of the shadows of their veils. The veiled figures seemed to Chloe menacing, like the silhouettes of vultures, and there was menace in the unfamiliar cadence of the murmuring voices.

"What do they say?"

"They are saying only that it is interesting that the American woman has arrived alone." He had been surprised himself to find, at the airport, only Mrs. Fowler, not Dr. Fowler too.

"My husband . . . in a few days," murmured Chloe, pulling at her collar. "An emergency—he . . ." She was conscious of her bare arms.

"They admire your pretty dress," said Abbas. "They admire your shoes. I'm sorry for this delay about the key. You must be tired."

"A little," Chloe said, her head swimming with tiredness, for she had come from San Francisco, through New York, on to London, on to Tehran, with no sleep and inconvenient delays on the planes. A fragrance of night-blooming plants rose around them in the dusk. The women swayed in their black shrouds as if to move, but did not move. Cleaning women, kitchen women from Azami Hospital, tired after the day.

Chloe was hungry and wished that Dr. Mowlavi would suggest dinner. He, however, was thinking she would be too

3

delicately jangled by travel to eat, would want to rest. Her
wrists were delicate. She and Abbas were standing on the steps
of a two-story house made of cement blocks, Villa Two. Her
hair was the expensive red-gold you saw here only among
women who had gone to school in France—the Empress and
her friends, for instance—and on the American wives. Mrs.
Fowler's hair did not look dyed, but you couldn't tell in the
dusk. He could not tell the color of her eyes, for she still wore,
in the dusk, her sunglasses. The women behind him had the
opinion, which he didn't translate, that her hair was the hair of
a slut.

The house, Villa Two, was ugly. Through the window
Chloe could see the hall, lit by a bare bulb on a cord, like a
cell, suggesting torture, walls of cement like a dungeon. She
had been reading about Iranian torture. Her apartment presumably would be up the stairs and cozier. Someone had been sent
for the key.

"It's the eve of a holiday here. That's why people have gone
away. Tomorrow you have to stay outdoors all day." He
smiled, embarrassed by all this waiting. He was handsome in
the style of Greeks and Italians, not a style Chloe liked, gold
chains, unbuttoned shirt, hairy chest.

An emaciated old man with sideways eyes brought the key
and scuttled away without helping with Chloe's bags. These
Abbas gathered up, opening the door with his shoulder so
Chloe could go in first. He did not immediately understand her
recoil, hand to mouth and shocked look around at him. By the
time he had stepped in and smelled it too she had regained her
composed manner. It was the urine of cats. He did not see how
cats could get in here, but the smell was in the hall rug, putrid
stench of cat piss. The help was careless here, he muttered;
Hossein had left a window open somewhere. He told Chloe
Fowler to go quickly up the stairs.

The strong smell jolted Chloe like smelling salts out of her
fatigue, into a shocked awareness of her situation, and of how
unwise it had been, how simply silly, to have come on alone,
and of how she must go back immediately, tomorrow, regard-
less. Starved and frightened, she felt she must go back. Abbas
opened the apartment door with the second key. He was used
to the place; it was where American visitors always stayed, and

he didn't really see it any more, though he saw the way her eyes widened. She was tired, he was sure, he said. He showed her where the kitchen was and left her, would see her tomorrow.

The door shut after Abbas Mowlavi but even so the stench from the hall enveloped her. As she looked around in the twilight, the details of the room collected themselves repellently, reminding her of pictures she had seen of mental institutions—bare brown linoleum floor, a thick-armed chair of oak too heavy to pick up and fling at an attendant, its seat covered in green and yellow plaid, two army cots covered with bleak khaki blankets, a dresser and table of Hollywood blond. On the wall a poster of Isfahan showed a beautiful mosque covered in cerulean tiles, as beautiful as she had imagined. In her dreams of Persia she had imagined brasses and rich cushions, intricate tracery screens. Here were heavy metal-rimmed windows, which cranked open stiffly. She struggled with the crank. She was baffled. Famous visiting surgeons were usually housed in luxury—that was her husband Jeffrey, of course, not Chloe, but she was accustomed to the perquisites of his life.

She was shocked that they would treat him so, and then, in spite of her exhaustion, she was embarrassed by her easy American expectation of comfort; wasn't this a developing nation, weren't they here to help? Ostensibly. Her own reasons were more complex and she hadn't examined them in detail. She opened her suitcase. She wished for some dinner. She put her underwear in the top drawer, emotions of indignation and humility contending. It occurred to her that if the bathroom was clean she would be all right, almost happy. If it was not clean she would clean it, like a good American sport. She made her way to look. It did not seem clean, it did not seem dirty, but the bulb was dim, and she didn't want to look closely enough to know for sure. She felt a swoon of sleepiness.

Out the window, through the shabby trees, the lights of other windows. In some lighted room nearby would be Hugh Monroe, with whom she had half begun a love affair. But he wouldn't have expected them tonight. Their meeting tomorrow would be casual, a handshake, overseen by the innocent company of their Iranian hosts and American colleagues. So nice to see you again. Her pleasure in imagining herself in Hugh's arms almost took the chill off this terrible room. They had not seen each other for several months, and she hoped he would feel that the temporary absence of Jeffrey was a piece of good luck instead of, for instance, a responsibility, for Chloe had observed before that men behave differently to a woman when they are not protected from her by her husband.

She falls asleep stupefied under the thin blankets on the rickety camp bed, and then awakens in darkness, not knowing how much later, to sounds so hideous and uncanny that they had leaked into her dreams as a harrowing nightmare of humans being torn to shreds—sinners rent by demons—and her husband Jeffrey's voice saying, gleefully, "You're crazy to go there, a woman alone," although he had said nothing of the kind, and had, in fact, insisted supportively. The shrieks, howls, cries persist, actual, under her window. Animals in their anguish sounding human. Where is she? She breaks into a sweat of panic, entangled by one foot in a torn sheet. She twists, stifles a scream, thinking of shackles and torture. Awake, she untangles her foot; the ideas of Islamic demons quiet, her shudders quiet.

She hates to put her foot on the cement floor—new ideas, of terrible gyms, basements, hookworm, but she creeps over to the window. Moonlit white shapes rush in the shrubbery, baying, snarling wantonly, chasing and tearing. Dogs, it seemed, or it could be wolves—she is near-sighted—but she had never heard of wolves in Iran. She believes in a rational explanation for everything, and so tries to think now of a rational explanation for a pack of wolves under her window. Fearfully, she gets her distance glasses from her purse and peers through them at the dogs, or maybe they are jackals. They are horrible, scrawny and fanged, with tattered fur and broken tails.

Now she is chilly, despite the warm breeze, a scent on it of the pleasant, night-blooming flower. She lies down again on the cot and tries to remember her dream, tries to reassure herself that the human cries had not been real cries of someone, perhaps, attacked by savage dogs, a fate whose horror was not to be compared to the trivial inconvenience of her own situation. Yet her mind keeps drifting to her situation, to its implausibility. On the way here she had kept emphasizing to herself its reasonableness, but now she cannot escape a true view of it as rather reckless. The jackals have moved away. Faint baying farther off.

"Why don't you go on?" Jeffrey had said, and she, foolishly as she now believed, had agreed, arguing vaguely that she felt an obligation to the museum, which had given her a small but important grant, to go through with the project. I feel an obligation to other women, she had also said. Women who got grants and then didn't follow through because their husbands changed their plans or the kids got measles—she didn't approve of them, considered that they gave womankind a bad name and prevented others from getting grants and jobs. Luckily none of her children had come down with anything to complicate this already complicated departure. If they had, she might have stayed home. Then too there was the matter of Hugh Monroe.

Astonishing how any implausible course of action begins to seem plausible the minute you begin it, write the first letter, mail the first application, stop off one noon for the visas, each step connected reasonably and at no far distance from the last, the reach or sweep of the whole invisible around the bend. Here she was but not, strangely, Jeffrey. She gets up again, finds her sweater in her suitcase, and goes in to clean the bathroom.

Chapter Two

BROKEN DREAMS

Then she slept again. When she next woke up, it seemed late in the morning—bright sun struggled in at the dirty glass and someone pounded on the door, communicating panic and ideas of fire. When she realized there was no fire, she leapt up, ashamed to be sleeping so late, whatever time it was. It could be Hugh at the door. She called out and sped around finding her robe and patting her tangled hair in the bathroom mirror.

It was a stranger at the door, an Iranian man, portly and dark, his chin thuggishly blue but his smile attractive and his round balding forehead open and nice. He wore a light suit. She couldn't tell the meaning of his smile, but her disappointment that he wasn't Hugh must have shown on her face, for the smile shrank.

"Mrs. Fowler? I am Dr. Asghari, Mohammed Asghari. I have met your husband once, at the meetings in Boston. I understand he is not here yet?"

"Not yet," admitted Chloe.

"I hope everything is all right here? Your journey was safely performed?"

"Thank you, yes," said Chloe, seeing that he was not the right person to grab and drag in and berate about her living quarters. But you would think he could smell the cat smell. He had, himself, a pleasant, old-fashioned odor of bay rum.

"Today is the last day of Now-Ruz," said Dr. Asghari, "a holiday where we must not stay indoors, it is bad luck. We stay outdoors until nightfall, and then when we go back in, the house is invested with good luck.''

"I'm sorry," said Chloe. "I just woke up. I was awakened in the night, and tired after the trip, and—what time is it?"

"Seven o'clock. I am just on my way to the clinic, but I stopped to invite you to our house—a picnic in our garden, more properly, where you will meet others, and meet my wife, also, who wants to make you welcome."

"That's very kind." Could he smell nothing? Peering past her into the room, he did not seem any more surprised than the man last night had been at the ugly furniture, the odor, the bleakness of the atmosphere.

"Is there anything we can do to help you settle in?"

"I think I should buy some coffee and things," Chloe said, now conscious once more of being hungry. "Will the shops be open?"

Closed, he was afraid, on the holiday, but here were the directions to his house. He thrust a piece of paper toward her, nodded, and took his leave.

Chloe shut the door after him and turned to the room. It was as ugly as it had seemed the night before in the dim light, offensive furniture upholstered in green plaid, and mismatched chairs of molded plywood. But it was clean enough, and large enough. She could buy things to beautify it, wonderful Persian vases, brass lamps. This thought lifted her resilient spirits. Meantime she would be pleased to stay outdoors all day. The yellow-tiled bathroom, now shining clean, was actually quite all right.

It was only now that she remembered that the kitchen was not in here, in the apartment itself, but in the hall, where it was intended to be shared by other residents of Villa Two. Her hopes rose that she might find something left in there to eat. Keeping her door carefully ajar, she crept out into the reeking hallway and into the kitchen, a filthy room covered with crumbs and heaped with unwashed dishes, though the complete absence of any food made this puzzling. Stuck to the walls with Scotch tape were various messages and bits of kitchen lore, in English, exasperated in tone: "Washer works on 3 only. Keep cold water tap closed almost all the way or else. Doesn't spin dry. Good luck." There was something

reassuring about the good American fellow feeling that had
motivated these admonitions, but they might have left
something to eat. But there was nothing whatever edible
except some lumpy sugar in the sugar bowl. Chloe sucked on
it and went back to her room.

She set her watch to five after seven. What time did the bad
luck start? Perhaps it had started already and this was it. Or
perhaps it only affected you if you were Iranian. She began to
unpack. One dress in yellow cotton was not too wrinkled, so
she put it on and went outside.

In the morning sunlight, Azami Compound appeared much
as it had been described to Jeffrey and her by one or two of
Jeffrey's colleagues—a large walled assemblage of hospital
buildings and dwellings where nurses and doctors lived, many
of them foreigners invited by the medical school to lecture and
advise for a few weeks or months. The Iranian doctors, mostly
Western-trained, were conscious of needing help with their
project to establish a first-rate medical school in Shiraz, and
they had no problem recruiting, by the promise of air fare and
quarters to stay in, a number of leading doctors, usually
American or English, from among the ones at any given time
who were restless, divorcing, eager for a vacation, or wishing
to see the remarkable ruins at Persepolis. It was therefore
dependable that there would be, in Shiraz, at any one time, a
contingent of well-known doctors who would already have met
on the circuit of international meetings they all attended or
conducted, and Chloe could feel perfectly at home as the wife
of Jeffrey Fowler, professor of surgery and member in good
standing of this medical jet set.

Her building, Villa Two, stood just inside the high walls of
the compound, so she had seen nothing of the grounds the
night before beyond what lay between her window and the
wall. Now she saw that behind and beyond Villa Two were
other residences and outbuildings, and, in front, the large
gates through which they had driven last night, now shut
fast, though a small door at the side of the gates was open,
and people were passing through and walking along the road.
She sat on the broad cement steps of Villa Two to watch
them.

An impression she had had in the dusk last night of exotic

foliage and strange blooms was now corrected—here were bougainvillaea, geraniums, and clumps of iris, and she found it disappointing that they were flowers she could grow perfectly well in California. The grass of the lawn was coarse and grew in clumps, and the corner of the yard where the dogs had been last night was now strewn with rubble and bones. But a light, fresh wind supported her spirits, and the sun was delightfully warm for so early in the morning, warming the pink stucco wall of her new home. Among familiar sounds of birds and insects were other sounds, strange enough to reassure her that she was abroad and far away; her ear could find deep voices calling in an unfamiliar language outside the walls, a bell somewhere. Even the sound of the automobiles was not American-sounding. She could hear that the cars did not proceed along as they did at home but made a racket of untuned engines, of heavy feet on accelerators, slipping clutches, horns, horns, horns. This reassured her. She wanted strangeness, a feeling of being far from home.

The people walking slowly along the road in front of Villa Two seemed scarcely to glance at her, though it was hard to tell about eyes behind veils. She thought the women were pretty in their wrappings, most in black, but some in floating pastel nylon, as if they were twisted up in parachutes, carrying purses. She wondered if she might without incurring bad luck go inside and get her half-written letters to her children.

She had begun letters already, during the four-hour wait at Heathrow. She and Jeffrey had fallen into silence, the long flight from California behind them, in which they had already conducted the conversation of a busy couple in forced companionship, reviewing the household matters they had had no time for, and managing, in the interest of the long journey still ahead of them, to avoid recriminations and criticism on a variety of touchy subjects—things undone, details of child rearing, delayed decisions about the plumbing. Chloe did not say, though she had often thought, that if only Jeffrey would take the children out on some sort of expedition on Saturday afternoons, she could use the time to do some of the things that needed doing around the house. Jeffrey did not say, as he so often did, that if she were more punctilious about certain housekeeping things then the atmosphere would be generally more harmonious and he'd feel like doing more around the house. Maybe they should go ahead with a new sprinkler system, though in principle Chloe, home in the mornings, could take care of the sprinkling. Sara would finish the school year at her present, even though not wonderful, school. A few other things settled, a few deferred again. Second thoughts— maybe instead of the sprinkler system, the priority thing was the roof.

Their lassitude, the drinks on the plane, rendered the waiting nearly bearable. They settled to their books.

Chloe was reading, with horrified fascination, a book about the torture of Iranian political dissidents. It was luridly well-written. The author was a poet. It described people being hung upside down until they were paralyzed. Then there were the usual things—fingernails, electric shocks to the genitals. They had a machine on which the victim, strapped as to a stake, was rotated like a chicken on a spit, being flogged the while. If you were a doctor you were morally neutral, you could go to a country like this because the poor people needed medicine under any regime. But if you were a wife were you more, or less, morally neutral? Would the Iranian authorities search her bags and take this book away from her at the airport?

The harrowing allegations and descriptions renewed her excitement at the prospect of their trip. Chloe put the book down and asked Jeffrey for change to buy a magazine. She noticed for the first time how the place reeked of tobacco.

"You forget how the English smoke," Chloe said. "It's disgusting."

"They don't believe it causes cancer. That seems to be an American belief."

Chloe bought a *Country Life*, an *International Herald Tribune* for Jeffrey, and twenty postcards, and took them back to their post. She had just settled her feet comfortably on the cigarette-strewn table and written the words "Dearest Sara and Max," when a voice spoke loudly into the smoky air of the transit lounge: "Dr. Fowler, Dr. Jeffrey Fowler, please contact the TWA representative, desk eight."

She and Jeffrey stared at each other. Perhaps they'd left

something on the plane? They looked at their carry-ons, their coats. "Oh, God, the children," cried Chloe. Before they even got there.

Jeffrey was on his feet, alert and frightened equally of coming bad news and the possibility of an anxiety fit from Chloe, who was inclined to them when away from her children, in proportion to the extent she expected to enjoy herself. Enjoying herself, she suffered from insomnia and could be rather bad company, writhing and tossing with maternal guilt and now, as it was to be an unprecedented four weeks before their children joined them, she would have to be trebly reassured. He insisted that she sit there with their stuff while he answered the page, and she, subdued by her apprehensions, obeyed him. She tried to look again at the pages of *Country Life*. It was full of images of ideal domesticity, thatched cottages, flowers, cows in pens. "Here we are in England," she wrote on the card. It showed a guard in a busby.

As he came into view, Jeffrey waved his hands in a calming way, to cut short at a distance any fears of the worst. The worst had not happened, said the referee's gesture, "safe," of his hands. At the same time, his face was grim and glaring, wearing an expression usually directed at her, of irritation and outrage at something she'd done, or, more usually, hadn't done, so that now she thought she must not have done something. But what?

"That dumb bastard," Jeffrey was saying, shaking his head. "I've been telling him all along, the son of a bitch."

"What? Who?" cried Chloe.

"It's bad-news Henry. He's had an accident in his fucking hang glider."

Chloe relaxed. Only Henry. Henry was Jeffrey's colleague, and of course they were very fond of him. He and Jeffrey collaborated on research, applied for grants together, and shared a private practice.

"Dead?" she asked.

"The extent of his injuries still unknown. Serious injuries. He's in a coma and he can't move."

Normal pity began to stir in Chloe. "Poor Henry, how awful."

"I've told him a million times," said Jeffrey. No doubt he had too, thought Chloe, for Jeffrey never failed to tell people when they were behaving stupidly or dangerously. Poor Henry.

"Will he live?" asked Chloe. Jeffrey shrugged. The details, in their transmission from one TWA desk to another, had become abridged, obscured.

They sat, murmuring sympathy, dismay. Then Jeffrey seemed to be saying he would have to return. Go back to California. She hadn't grasped that implication. Turn around and go back to California. Their patients, their research, all left in Henry's capable hands, which could no longer move. Chloe saw the logic but was dumbstruck all the same. Their pounds of luggage checked through to Shiraz, Iran, all those hours behind them on the plane, the farewells, her mother installed with the children, the satisfaction of everybody—it had appeared—to see them go.

"Until we find out what's what," said Jeffrey.

"Oh," was all Chloe could say, "I can't bear it. What could you do for Henry, anyway?"

"Of course *you* don't need to come back," Jeffrey said, astonishingly. She would later try to remember the exact expression of his face. "In fact, you shouldn't. It's expensive, the kids'll just get upset all over again. You should go on."

"The kids weren't at all upset," snapped Chloe. "They thought it was nice we were going. Of course they didn't really understand how long we'd be gone." Her guilty panic rose. The children were to join them when their school was out. Even so, she had not been apart from them for such a long time as this.

"It makes perfect sense. You can just go on as planned, they're expecting us, the place'll be ready, there'll be someone to meet us, Farmani or Asghari—no problem. I'll find out what's going on, do what needs to be done, and join you as soon as I can."

Like going back, going on seemed a terrible idea. It was like being stuck in a hole in a fence. Venturing into an unknown Middle Eastern country, a woman alone? "It'll be all right," Jeffrey pointed out. "The Rothblatts will be there—you know them—and Hugh Monroe, and many other Americans."

"What'll the kids think, if you come back and I don't?" Chloe objected. The children had been brave, had even feigned indifference at having to stay behind with a rotation of grandmothers until their school was out, when they would travel with Chloe's mother to join their parents for an educational trip to Tehran and the Caspian. As she said this, she acknowledged to herself that in some ways it would be a relief to know that the responsible Jeff would be home to oversee things, even if only for a week or two longer. She'd been uncomfortable with the arrangements, agreeing on the one hand that it would be good for her and Jeff to get away together for a while, afraid on the other that their mothers would not really be equal to the difficulties of two lively children for such a long time.

Also, though she hated to admit it, she was afraid of going to such a place by herself. She knew, in the name of independence, female liberation, confidence, this fear must be mastered. And there was the final, secret reason, that it was slightly too propitious, being alone in the same distant city with Hugh Monroe. This was the kind of gift of fate only the unwary would accept without inspecting the underside; Chloe was a little in love with Hugh Monroe.

"I can't possibly go by myself," she said firmly.

"Chloe! That's more than a thousand dollars down the drain. Be sensible."

Jeffrey was persuasive. "We can't afford for us both to go back, and there's no point in it either." Nervously she allowed herself to be packed along to the Air Iran boarding lounge by a grim Jeffrey, whose real emotions were not clear to her. Maybe he was just being nice.

"Are you *sure* you don't want me to come?" she kept saying, always expecting to surprise a glint of relief at the offer, but receiving no clue at all to his feelings if they were different from those he was expressing. It really appeared that Jeffrey believed it was more sensible for him to go back to San Francisco, her to go on to Iran, probably for the exact reasons stated: expense, disruption. The Tehran plane was loading.

"I'll be there soon," he said, kissing her. "A week, two at most. The prognosis of these things is usually evident in a few days. It's just a question of doing whatever has to be done in the office and lab." There was something in Jeffrey, she reminded herself, that loved a heroic role.

On the plane she had been reassured, for it was full of

women traveling alone or with clusters of children and packages. Some were fashionably dressed in Western clothes and
carried snakeskin purses from Mapin & Webb; others con-
cealed themselves in the black veils of the Middle East. The
recirculating air of the plane wafted odors of musky oils and
strange perfumes.

Chapter Three

NOW-RUZ

Now the New Year reviving old Desires,
The thoughtful Soul to Solitude retires.

Chloe was a housewife, conscious of being un-fashionable in this, but active and happy at home, only occasionally discontented, fond of sewing and of her children, fond of solitude yet gregarious, and perhaps too confident of her own powers of rational discrimination. She was, she was apt to say, the most unliberated woman she knew, but this statement was a form of vanity; it was simply that she was out of step with the discontents other women she knew seemed to be experiencing. Also, she usually did just what she wanted. The child of unreproachful parents, she had seldom believed that her actions would affect others.

Fortunately, her activities were largely harmless—affairs of the heart, reading, and an array of somewhat Victorian handi-works; she was, as far as she knew, the last woman her age alive in the world who could tat. She did not feel constrained by either rules or fashions—did not feel, for example, on the one hand that it was necessary to be faithful to your husband, or on the other that if you were not you had to get divorced. Though she felt sympathy for the plights and despair of others, she had no real feeling for the restlessness and anxiety of many of her women friends, as they arrived in their mid-thirties and looked around for lifework, meaning financial independence or emotional lives of revived fascination. She was more interested in abstractions—in political writing or art history—and this last occupied what time she spent outside her home. At present she was a docent at the San Francisco

17

Art Museum and gave lectures on Chinese porcelain from
Sung to Ming, a subject she had worked up with the museum
staff.

Her friends were apt to find her too opinionated and her
views eccentric, but to look at she was soft and pretty, not at
all like someone with views. She continued to smile her bright,
pretty smile even while she was saying something combative or
horrible, a habit carried over from her days as a little child
beauty. But she was not, luckily, a monster of self-satisfaction
because she didn't think about herself much, though she tried,
when she did remember, to work against her own faults, some
of which she knew to be laziness, timidity, and absentmind-
edness, by keeping busy, daring to do things that scared her,
and writing things down. But mostly she drifted along, happily
enough, interested in the world around her and in the world
inside the large stack of books on her night stand. Men usually
liked her, because she was small, pretty, and intelligent, but
some did not like in a woman her slightly preoccupied air of
self-sufficiency.

"I know what it is about you," a psychiatrist, a colleague of
Jeffrey's, had told her at a party. "Free libido."

"That sounds too promiscuous," she objected.

"A kind of unchanneled life force. I'm speaking as a
Jungian. I guess I mean that something about you suggests that
you aren't really taken." He had smiled hopefully.

"Oh—I suppose I haven't found my métier," Chloe had
conceded, smiling into his eyes, changing the subject in the
way she had learned was reliable. "What about you?" Excited
by her refusal to discuss herself, he had called her for weeks,
truly not what she had intended.

And now here she was in Iran, very jet-lagged. As she
rested and wrote, the morning seemed to pass quickly. She
wrote the children a proper letter, describing the airplane
flight, and also two postcards apiece, ahead; one, which
showed Anne Hathaway's cottage, on which she described
Now-Ruz, and a picture of Buckingham Palace, on which she
simply said how much she missed them. She wondered about
the mail.

She realized she had dozed a little in the sun. And she found
she had a companion. Under the bushes at the corner of the

yard, where the dogs had gathered last night, amid the litter of bones she could see a small creature, a puppy—rather an ordinary-looking one with short beige coat and cute little face—probably hidden there by his mother and forbidden to go out, for he remained crouched under the foliage when he had seen Chloe. Perhaps she had frightened him by stretching out her hand. She smiled at him, and watched him from time to time, and saw his bright little eyes watching her back with, she thought, some rapport.

Then she was startled to see, a little distance from this bush, an old man lying full-length under another clump of bushes! She thought it was the old man who had brought the key, now lying on his face, with his arms over his head. He lay so still she became afraid to look, had heard that in some countries people die outside in the open air and their dead bodies are collected from time to time by carts.

He still had not moved when, at eleven, skirting what could be his corpse, she prepared to go along to Dr. Asghari's picnic. Following the directions sketched on the paper, she followed the road in front of her villa, Villa Two, past a big house on the left. If this were a military enclosure, that would be the general's house, and the rest would be the houses of majors and top sergeants—smaller cement-block houses with bikes and trikes in the carports, and everywhere lovely vines entwining eaves and walls, and here or there somebody with a talent for gardening had embellished his paradise with roses or peonies.

She tried to take everything in. She felt a kind of rapture to see that no matter where you were in the world, you were there, same style of clouds up above, same ants and pebbles underfoot, and you didn't feel odd. There must be ants in China. It was said there were no flies there. There were flies here. How pleasant just to wander along a strange road in a strange land, smiling back at the people sitting in their yards smiling at her.

A dozen or so people stood on the lawn of the Asgharis' bungalow or on the long cement porch. They were not all, to Chloe's rapid glance, Iranian—one woman with a mouse-brown permanent, a couple who from some quality of pinkness about them might be either British or American. A young

American woman doctor, Dr. Fay. The Iranians had long
sideburns, and the handsome, square-jawed look of the lovers
and warriors painted on Persian tiles. No sign of Hugh
Monroe.

The mouse-brown curls proved to be her hostess, Heidi
Asghari, an Englishwoman, who greeted Chloe warmly and
drew her into groups of people who smiled and shook her
hand. Chloe was charmed by the beauty of their dark eyes,
fine aquiline features. The men had high domed foreheads and
curly hair. One woman had a name like moonlight—
Noosheen. Chloe made an effort to remember the difficult and
unfamiliar names—Pari, Ravi. Of the faces she recognized
only Mohammed Asghari, whom she had met that morning,
and Abbas, whose last name began with M, the man from last
night.

Abbas had been helping Heidi Asghari carry a cooler of
soft drinks to the porch and was thinking, for the hundred-
thousandth time, that it does not hurt to die from drowning,
and then, because he could not help it, the reverie went on,
what about the minutes before you die, what about the fear,
sinking through the slimy water, knowing, resisting, hoping,
struggling. He was thinking of his dead wife, who had been
alive at the time of Now-Ruz last year, and now was dead,
trying to save their baby from drowning. She would have
been thinking of the baby, he could not imagine that she
would have had other thoughts, although they say it is given
to you to have a million thoughts all at once, of your whole
life, and in that case, as the brown waters took her over, had
she thought of him? Or of what? Why did he care especially
today? His thoughts were interrupted by seeing Heidi greet
Mrs. Fowler, the new American wife who had come in
advance of her husband. She was explaining about how she
came to be alone.

Chloe found that her situation sounded plausible to the
others: Dr. Fowler, unfortunately delayed in America, would
arrive as soon as possible; in the meantime, bound by the
circumstances of her grant from the San Francisco Art Museum
and the university at Shiraz, Chloe herself had thought it best
to come on schedule. She and Jeffrey had thought it best that

she come on schedule. Her journey had been uneventful. Her quarters were satisfactory.

Here, though, Chloe found she could not be persuasive. Her quarters were certainly not satisfactory but horrible, and these people, who lived in the pretty bungalows amid hibiscuses, were probably not aware of the state the place had fallen into, and would know whom to call to fix things, and would not wish, so evidently kind were they, that she or anyone be uncomfortable. She awaited a chance to mention her plight, perhaps to the Englishwoman, Heidi Asghari.

Pretty Noosheen—Mrs. Ardeshir—was sympathetic, but not much help, when Chloe had an opportunity to confide in her about the state of Villa Two. "I know it is not very nice," she said. "We, the wives, put those posters in there, and some cushions, to make it better, but it is true, it is still not nice, especially coming from America." She loved America, she said. The Ardeshirs had lived in Cleveland for nearly two years, and she would have been willing to discuss Cleveland at length.

"It is much more beautiful here," Chloe said firmly. "I have never seen such roses."

How kind they all are, how welcoming. Perhaps they are always delighted at newcomers. Do they feel confined within the walls of the Azami Compound? But on this lawn, under these trees, one does not feel enclosed but delightfully breeze-blown, outdoors, free. Far away from America. Chloe helps Heidi and the other women lay the cloths on the long picnic tables, weighting the corners with apples and cans of Pepsi, and, improbably, a bowl of goldfish. Chloe feels a moment of disappointment to see that they would have hot dogs and potato chips. You might be in America, this might be the Fourth of July, except for the addition of candles and a mirror. "It's a tradition," Heidi explains.

They sit on aluminum lawn chairs with plastic webbing, familiar. In the garden familiar flowers bloom but are called differently, strangely. "Here is the Jesus flower, and the Moses," say the Iranians.

She must visit Isfahan, they say. Heidi promises to take her to the bazaar. She and Dr. Fowler must take a few days to visit Persepolis, city of ancient Persia, and in a few weeks they can view the migration of the nomadic tribesmen with their flocks to the mountains to the north from the lower pastures near Abadan, where they had spent the winter. In a manner wonderfully kind, Dr. Ardeshir, the elderly husband of the pretty Noosheen, lays out a conscientious sightseeing program for them—the pink couple, the Hendersons and Junie Fay and Chloe, and Dr. Fowler when he arrives, for they promise not to keep their foreign benefactors at work every moment in the hospital or lecture room. "We are pleased to have visitors and wish them to see everything of the wonders here. The tomb of Cyrus! The footsteps of Alexander the Great!"

"Yes, I've been reading my Persian history," the conscientious Chloe assures him.

Hot dogs, potato salad, a plate of salami, hard-boiled eggs, yogurt. Chloe looks in vain for something Iranian, though the salad of rice and chick-peas has a distant savor of mint. Starved as she is, she tries to eat in a ladylike way and not wolf everything down in the manner of a starving person. She forces herself to eat calmly. Dr. Asghari brings wine, and begins to pour. She watches anxiously when it appears that he will skip the ladies, or pour them only tiny drinks. She notices that Noosheen puts her hand over her glass. Chloe does not.

"Iranian wine is not bad, you'll find. Our vineyards are young, planted only in the last decade—a project encouraged by the Shah, but the wine will become, I think, an important agriculture for Iran. An export."

"Was there no wine before?" Chloe asks. "The ancients must have had wine—I'm thinking of Omar."

Dr. Ardeshir intones a line in Persian: " 'A Jug of Wine, a Loaf of Bread—and Thou.' But you of course have a very fine translation of this poem, 'The Rubaiyat.' "

"Yes, one poem everyone knows."

"In Persia we revere poets."

Chloe sighs. Would they notice if she were to ask, very casually, did they know Hugh Monroe, was he here? Would that be thought odd?

"You must visit the beautiful tombs of the poets of Shiraz. This is a place eminently poetic," says Dr. Ardeshir.

Perhaps Hugh is at some other Now-Ruz gathering, even nearby, or with other Americans, sightseeing on this day off, or perhaps he is at the hospital seeing to patients while the Iranian doctors celebrate the holiday. Endure the holiday. The afternoon wears on. People had set up on their lawns like refugees to wait out the day.

"Abbas Mowlavi is so brave," whispers Heidi to Chloe as the ladies clear away the plates. "It must be so hard for him. This time last year he had a wife, a child, and then the tragedy. Just a few months ago, but he goes on. They drowned, a freakish thing. How could one go on?"

The dessert is a sumptuous plate of melon and grapes. When the places have been cleared and paper plates burnt in the barbecue, Mohammed Asghari brings cards and poker chips and the company sits around the picnic tables to play a game which someone explains to Chloe. They empty their pockets of money.

"You will need some money, Mrs. Fowler," Abbas Mowlavi tells her, and puts a stack of coins in front of her. "I'll stake you." Everyone pushes money around the table and laughs. They count in a strange way. "Panj," "heft," Chloe's turns pass safely when she makes simple choices, her stack of coins dwindles and grows. They almost fail to notice dusk, but at last someone does, with a cry, and everyone rises to take the picnic things indoors. The men carry the chairs and fold away the umbrellas. Chloe gives Abbas his money back. He counts it and returns a handful of coins to her.

"I could not consent to profit from your luck," he says, smiling.

"Dr. Monroe," Chloe suddenly says to the company, her cheeks warming. "We have a friend, Hugh Monroe, who we thought might be here now."

A silence. Abbas Mowlavi glanced at Mohammed Asghari. "We expected him before this," Mohammed said.

Dr. Asghari raised his brows. "I have heard something only last night, that Dr. Monroe is detained in Tehran."

"Detained?" cried Chloe, in spite of her wish to seem indifferent.

"By the authorities."

"Arrested?" Heidi Asghari asked.

"No, no, something about his visa."

"That could take weeks. I hope he's at the Hilton at least," said Heidi.

"We are not exactly sure where he is," said Mohammed.

Chapter Four

NEW FRIENDS

The dogs came in the night again, but now, her second night in Iran, they didn't terrify her for more than an instant. She lay awake, wondering what time it was in California, that she should feel so wide awake now, but she did not let the instant of terror spread and spill over into night fears about whether the children were all right, or whether Hugh Monroe was in trouble in Tehran, or about why she was here, a million miles from where she should be, in a grim room, on a rickety cot. Though the possibilities for a sleepless night were rich, she did not give in to them, and went to sleep again.

Now, in the morning, she had many things to occupy her. She would have to go to the bank, buy food, clean the hallways and kitchen, throw out the urine-stained rugs, and repair the torn screen where the cats were getting in. Heidi Asghari had kindly offered to show her where the shops and bank were, and she arrived as planned at ten. Noosheen Ardeshir was with her. Chloe was reassured to have been found by two such agreeable women already. She resolved in future to be more attentive to the wives of foreign doctors who came to San Francisco.

The city of Shiraz, which lay outside the walls of the Azami Compound, consisted of old walled houses glimpsed across green courtyards, modern apartment buildings and new villas built of cement blocks. Everything had a leached and dusty aspect, but though the flowers struggled to bloom in the desert

25

air, they bloomed. Water had been brought, she was told, in
sophisticated viaducts by the ancient Persians.

People hurried along the street, intent and Western-looking,
the men in dark suits or trousers and loose shirts, the women in
print dresses that might have come from Penney's or Sears.
Many were veiled, but many were not, or wore their hair
tucked up in sheer nylon scarves, olive cheeks bright with
rouge. Some women wore gypsy clothes of wild colors, with
many beads and petticoats, and had hard, sunburnt faces.
These were the tribal women who lived in the desert to the
south and kept goats and camels and made rugs.

Chloe liked the undulation of the Persian lettering on the
signs, like melted letters or dream words. Sometimes words
were written in English as well as Farsi. The bank was called
Bank Melli Iran. Here she cashed some traveler's checks, just
as easily as you might cash them in London. From the wall of
the bank, the visage of the Shah stared down, much as the
Queen smiles down in London. "In America no one smiles
down on you," Chloe observed.

"Oh yes, the President often does," Noosheen objected.
Chloe had never noticed that. "And George Washington often
does."

With each reassuring sign that it was well within her power
to conduct a regular, comfortable life here, and with each new
charming and exotic sight, Chloe's spirits rose. There was a
little supermarket, full of recognizable products by Procter &
Gamble or Nestlé, and with other products of mysterious
allure. She bought a beautiful tin of tea with golden camels on
it, and a bottle of skin cream, which showed a ravishing
woman hidden behind her veil, promising some Cleopatran
secret.

They were riding in Heidi's small car, in which she
fearlessly barged in among other cars, taxis, donkey carts,
horses, camels, people walking in the street. Chloe was too
fascinated to be fearful. Horns blew all around, it appeared
from mere exuberance, at the challenges to manhood that, as
the driver of a motor vehicle, one constantly met. Horns
sounded forth from rushing taxis, from encumbered cars,
drivers especially maddened by being stuck behind animal
carts, from innumerable buses in faded colors, which hurtled

from block to block, stopping with screeches, passengers swaying unperturbed. The drivers of animal carts most stirred Chloe's heart, so disappointed did they look, so affronted by unkind destiny, their little sons tucked up beside them, aware, by the look of their wide, disappointed eyes, of the humiliation of their fathers, a sorrow that would be theirs too if no miracle intervened to put them in charge, in due time, of a motor vehicle.

Heidi drove her on a quick tour of the principal sights of Shiraz—the university, the bazaar, the tombs of Hafez and Sa'adi, mosques, a fortress—so that Chloe would know how to find them and look at them properly at her leisure. They saw the beautiful rose garden at the summer villa of the Shah, and a bit of the ancient viaduct.

"The water is safe to drink," Heidi, noticing Chloe's interest in the water system, assured her.

"There is the building where I study," Noosheen said as they passed the university. "That is where you will be also. I began my studies in Cleveland, but I continue them here. English literature."

"That's wonderful," Chloe said.

Noosheen continued, "And in fact I have cherished a wish to ask you something—but I am almost embarrassed."

"Of course, anything," Chloe said.

"I told Noosheen you certainly wouldn't mind," Heidi said.

"It's about my senior thesis. It's not exactly what I chose, but anyway it's my subject, and I find it is really difficult. If I could just talk to you about it."

"*I'm* completely hopeless at literature," Heidi said. "I was a nurse."

"But what's the subject?" Chloe asked.

"Well, I'm studying Matthew Arnold's masterpiece 'Empedocles on Etna,' and his other poetry as well, of course, but I am writing about 'Empedocles,' and Heidi said you wouldn't mind talking to me about it, or perhaps when I begin to write you might read what I have written, to tell me if it's too stupid or if I missed the point. If we could just have some little chats about Matthew Arnold, that would help me so much."

Chloe, feeling fraudulent, agreed. But she cautioned that she had read very little Victorian poetry. At first "Empedocles" struck her as a strange subject for a young Iranian wife, but upon reflection she saw that for Noosheen to read Arnold was no stranger than for her to read Hafez and Sa'adi, which she intended to do, and Noosheen was reading Arnold in the original, after all, which is more than she, Chloe, was going to do of Sa'adi and Hafez. In the long run, the symmetry of the situation was appealing, and it was arranged between them that Noosheen would visit her, or invite her to tea, and they would discuss the poetry of Arnold, Hafez, and Sa'adi. Chloe felt lucky to have a role already, and a chance to get acquainted with an Iranian woman.

Also, she admired Noosheen—thought her beautiful in a way, though she lightened her hair and would have looked better with the heavy, dark hair that most Iranian women had. She had large brown eyes, like the eyes of an icon or one of those charming people painted on tombs, and a dainty figure, smaller even than Chloe, who was not a large woman. And Noosheen was infinitely more graceful, or so it seemed to Chloe, who felt rather clumsy and American and somehow oversized beside her. Noosheen wore stockings and high-heeled shoes. It wouldn't have occurred to Chloe to put on stockings and high-heeled shoes to grocery shop. Noosheen had a baby and a child of two, and her husband, Bahram Ardeshir, was the head of pathology at Azami Hospital.

Heidi Asghari's children were in school, and had to be picked up, so she and Noosheen dropped Chloe and her groceries at Villa Two. Satisfied and encouraged, Chloe climbed the stairs, put her groceries away, and set to work at cleaning the disgusting kitchen. Her anger at whoever it was who ought to take care of this place renewed itself, not that she thought of herself as being above cleaning kitchens. The oven was beyond cleaning, in fact, though she made some headway on the stove. Just at the moment that the steel wool fragmented to rusty bits beneath her hand, she was startled at a voice behind her, from the hallway: "Mrs. Fowler?" A deep Iranian voice, surprising from the small man in white doctor's coat, stethoscope in pocket. Something authoritative in his manner swelled her indignation at the state of the kitchen, as if he were the person who ought to do something.

"I am Dr. Farmani, director of Azami Hospital. In the past,

I have received many letters from your husband. I am sorry about his delay. Is everything all right?''

"As you see," Chloe began, in a rush of relief at having found someone at last to help, "the place is a terrible mess, really; it's really very disagreeable finding oneself in such a place, it's certainly not very welcoming or cheerful. I expect you didn't realize . . ."

"The man Hossein comes each day. You must tell him what you want him to do," Dr. Farmani said. He had a mustache and beard like a sultan, and little booted feet. His eyes, Chloe thought, were cold and hard, devoid of sympathy for her labor. She stood before him, steel wool pricking her fingers.

"I wanted particularly to ask you," he said. Chloe squeezed out the wet rag and hung it over the faucet.

"The horrible smell in the hall is in those rugs," she said. "Cats."

"It is said you are acquainted with Dr. Monroe, Hugh Monroe," he said.

"Well—slightly," she said warily, half-afraid he had seen into her heart, or imagining, though it was preposterous, that Jeffrey had written him. Watch and see how my wife gets on with Hugh Monroe.

"Dr. Asghari has heard he is detained in Tehran. Is that right?"

"I only know what Dr. Asghari said," Chloe said. "On account of some problem with his visa? They said it might take several days?"

"Do you by any chance know if—I want to help if I can— do you know if Dr. Monroe travels on a diplomatic passport?"

"No, of course not, he's a physician," Chloe said. "I mean, I would doubt it."

Dr. Farmani seemed to mistrust her. He peered at her eyes. "It is a matter of knowing whom to get in touch with. If I knew . . ."

"I would think just a plain passport, like Jeffrey's or mine."

"Physicians sometimes undertake additional missions, as emissaries or couriers—anyone might. Dr. Monroe travels widely, I understand?"

"Many doctors do. My husband does. They lecture, they are invited . . ."

"Dr. Monroe has been to Moscow, Edinburgh, Geneva."

"Well, I don't know anything about his schedule. Why are you asking me?" Why was he? She was embarrassed by her own cross tone. Then she was struck by another worrying idea. "Are you concerned about him? Is there a problem?"

"No, no, I'm sure he will be along in a few days," said Dr. Farmani, his tone dismissive, unconvincing. "If you have anything for him, I could probably arrange to get it to him." She must have looked puzzled, truly mystified, for now he turned away.

It seemed to him her eyes were wary, her appearance, clutching a dishrag, not convincing; she was wearing what appeared to be a Paris dress, anyway a pretty dress. A woman alone—was it indeed Mrs. Fowler at all? How would one know? Who had met her? Abbas Mowlavi had been in California, and had met Fowler but not the wife. She looked, it was true, like an American doctor's wife—same dyed hair. But of course they would choose someone who looked the part.

He had thought they would send a medical person, someone who would snoop around the hospital, not just someone to hang about in the compound. We will see what she does, he thought, and we will see what happens when Monroe arrives, and when they do I will watch both of them. His stomach crawled anxiously at the thought of Monroe reputedly in Tehran, talking to whom? He had the feeling that forces were being brought down on Azami, he knew not why, and Westerners with falsely smiling faces, people down from Tehran, this woman with her camera lying there unabashedly on the kitchen counter, and, although wearing a wedding ring, no husband.

"Ah, well," he said, "goodbye for the moment. I only thought to stop and ask in case."

"I'm sorry," Chloe said, but could not resist adding, in a rush, "I suppose it's silly, but anyone would be upset, being put in such a dirty place, it's not just me. . . ."

"You Americans are fastidious, it is well known," he said with a smile that stretched his little mustache into a line over his teeth.

Chloe listened to the tap of his boots down the stairs, muffled as he stepped on each horrible rug, ringing against the cement, then the clack of the front door downstairs. After a few moments, she followed him, dragging the horrible rugs down the stairs, across the foyer and out into the yard.

She sat on the steps for a few moments in the twilight, wondering about this strange visit, and about Hugh. He did travel a lot—he spoke of adventures in the Himalayas and so on. He was romantic and went diving in the Caribbean, skied in the Alps. Perhaps he did have diplomatic missions, special charges. Came, she had heard, from a family prominent in Washington. His accent was attractively eastern. She quite liked the idea of Hugh's being some sort of diplomat, not a CIA agent, of course—they were some sort of comedy team who never could get it straight about which thing to blow up. She watched the approach of Hossein, the man who supposedly cleaned and took care around the place, as he kicked at the puppy, which had crept out from its bush. She was horrified but not surprised at this unthinking brutality. Luckily the puppy scuttled out of the way.

He would not kill a dog, Hossein was thinking, now that he had been to Mecca. It was he who used to kill them, without enthusiasm, because he was told and paid to, but now he would not do that work, and no one else had been found to do it, and there were more dogs than ever around the compound, as there were more people in the world—like, even, the number of daughters of his brother—Hossein had no wife of his own— and half-grown curs, as thin as his own arm.

The new woman was sitting on the steps, a gold chain around her wrist. The rugs from the hallway were thrown about in the yard, and so must be dragged in again and put neatly in place. She was watching him, without expression. Did she think he would not take the rugs in again?

Chapter Five

NOT AT HOME

Yon rising Moon that looks for us again—
How oft hereafter will she wax and wane;
How oft hereafter rising look for us
Through this same Garden—and for <u>one</u> in vain!

Outside the western wall of the Azami Compound, the dry bed of a river, no more really than a broad ditch, bisected the city of Shiraz. Across the river lay some kind of military base from which, at intervals during the day, harsh amplified commands drifted on the air, at times competing with the drone of prayers. In the mornings, reveille was played on this public address system—fortunately not too early—and Chloe would lie on her cot, listening to the notes of the bugle, reviewing, as was her nature, the satisfactions before the dissatisfactions of her situation.

She was satisfied that, if they could not be with her, the children at least were safely with Jeffrey—as well as her mother and the babysitter; and that she still had not received a panicked call or telegram. When she and Jeffrey were traveling together, she could be shattered at any moment by the mere thought of calamities at home.

But Jeffrey would be there to deal with things for another week or so. The dissatisfactions were her ugly room, and that she was alone here, which was merely strange. She had married young; she had hardly ever, her whole life long, been alone.

She unwound her ankles from the sheet, which seemed to shred further each night. Last night she had not heard the dogs at all. It was rather pleasant to wake alone, she thought, free of the reproachful groans of another person clinging to sleep. She had planned a simple daily routine: coffee, hot and strong, and a few pistachio nuts, then an hour with *Teach Yourself Farsi*, which she had begun to study in California. She had not made much progress, but was resolved to be more diligent, and enjoyed tracing the squiggly lines that served as letters. She had already learned the numbers, and the coins—rials and tooman—and after her lesson she would walk to the grocery store, trying to identify numbers and parts of words in signs along the way. She could already write "Coca-Cola," because this sign was everywhere, and at the store had tried saying, "Khoda hafez," which was supposed to mean goodbye but had not produced a response. At the store they gave you your small change in aspirin or gum, your choice. She always chose aspirin. Today she planned to buy some vegetables and some meat, with which to attempt some Iranian dishes when Hugh arrived. If this was only to be an interlude in her life, she wanted it to be an interlude of sweetness and simplicity, walking, cooking, making love with Hugh Monroe, and avoiding the automobile.

Chloe knew that she should soon present herself at the university, to begin her work on Sassanian pottery. She had corresponded with a Mrs. Reza in the department of archaeology, and was expected, but she procrastinated another day. One problem was the telephone, with which to call for an appointment. The phone stood on a stool outside the kitchen and occasionally emitted a shrill white sound when you picked up the receiver; but she had no notion at all how to make it work, or whether, although she had written perfectly in English, Mrs. Reza would be prepared to speak English.

Also, since the university was some distance away, she would probably have to take a taxi. The taxis had been explained to her. You got in with other people, strangers already in the taxi, and paid your share. This was daunting—she was unsure of the fares and of whether the driver would understand her. The taxis themselves were frightening, small, dented Peykans, draped in photos, lurching forward before the lights had turned, trinkets flapping, drivers cursing. Heidi Asghari had explained that the drivers were more used to driving camels than cars, and you had to curse camels to get them to move.

She decided to get a feel for the distances involved by

walking first to the bazaar, which was no more than a mile or
so away, at the other end of the long main street. Along the
way she passed various office buildings and consulates—there
was the American consulate, eagle peeling dispiritedly. A
department store. A lot of record shops and banks, T-shirt
stalls, and shops with soccer balls in the windows. A cinema,
a pizza parlor—it might have been Europe but for the exotic
spicy smell of the air, and the drifting veils and the quite
chaotic upheavals of the pavements, and the strange ditch,
called the jube, that ran along the curbings, a menace to wheels
and ankles alike. Chloe walked slowly, savoring the rich
strangeness. The heroes and heroines of Iranian films stared at
her with big dark eyes from posters on walls, the actresses
gleaming with gold ornaments.

Most of the shops were shut. Perhaps this was another
special day, or a long weekend. Though she had read that
Western women could not walk alone in the Middle East,
Chloe found that no one here bothered her or looked askance.
The men kept their glances strictly to themselves, and the
women's bolder stares did not seem unfriendly. It was a relief
that an American woman was not regarded with dislike or
disapproval. Chloe was used to foreign travel and to the civility
of foreigners, but, as an American, was always aware that she
might, by her category—she hoped not by her actions—incur
incivility. On their travels, she and Jeffrey were always careful
not to speak in loud American voices, or wear bright colors, or
make scenes. They dreaded being taken for Americans.

She continued to be fascinated at the idea of veils. There
seemed to be no rule about them; some women didn't wear
them, some wore them tightly pulled around them. She thought
it would be awful to have to shroud yourself as if there were
something indecent about you, and yet it was exciting too to
think that the mere sight of you could stir improper desire, and
interesting to wonder if Iranian men were so inflammable they
could not look at you. Or else it was all just habit and the
libidos of men are the same the world around and these women
were not really ashamed of their faces. How do you find out?
Though she could see them, even touch them, she regretted
that she could never know or understand them, as they moved
behind their barrier of Farsi, their minds elsewhere, on the

washing or on saffron-scented dishes for their families' suppers. She watched a tiny girl, bouncing a ball with one hand, with her other hand clutching her tiny shroud around her, while her brother climbed along a railing, holding on safely with both hands. Chloe thought of Noosheen, whom she was expecting at Villa Two at two—had Noosheen grown up one-handed?

When Noosheen came, despite the warm day, she was wearing a schoolgirl outfit of skirt and sweater, as if she had costumed herself from Western movies about college life, or perhaps these were her Cleveland clothes. She had brought the collected works of Matthew Arnold for Chloe to brush up on before they began their talks in earnest. Chloe admired her passion for learning. Like Chloe, she had two children, though she was only twenty-four, and had been married four years, two of them spent in Cleveland. It must be hard, with such young children, to keep her English up and continue to study and learn.

Chloe made iced tea and carried it outside. They sat in the garden between her villa and Villa One on two aluminum chairs. "My room is much too ugly to sit in," said Chloe firmly. Today Noosheen was more sympathetic to Chloe's complaints about Villa Two and about the methods of Hossein, who so far had appeared each day at about noon and would push his wide, damp, greasy mop around the floor. Chloe didn't say that she did not like his jagged brown teeth and the feverish sidelong glance of his eyes. But Noosheen was familiar with the general problem of Villa Two, for other American wives had complained. The thing to do, she advised, was to speak to Linda Farmani, wife of Vahid Farmani, the hospital doctor.

"I have already met him," Chloe said. The Farmanis, Noosheen told her, lived in Villa One, and as she and Chloe were now sitting virtually in the garden of Villa One, they could call on her here and now. Noosheen jumped up.

"She is American," she said. "Vahid Farmani met her when he went to Los Angeles. He did a fellowship at UCLA. I think she was an airline stewardess."

Chloe was surprised, hearing this, that a fellow American

woman would not have looked in on her before now. She and
Noosheen approached Villa One and knocked on the door.
They were told by a taciturn servant that Mrs. Farmani was
lying down. This seemed odd to Chloe, who never napped.
Perhaps she was ill or pregnant, or perhaps it was a colonial
affectation of some kind, or the queerly enervating life of a
foreign land, the loss of normal American vitality. When
Noosheen had left, Chloe herself was nearly overtaken by
lassitude, but perhaps, she told herself, this was not owing to
the foreignness of Iran, or even to jet lag, so much as to the
poetry of Matthew Arnold, which she sat reading in the garden
awhile longer, with, as she caught herself from time to time, a
wonderful blankness of mind.

Linda Farmani, watching from her upstairs window, was
thinking that the new American woman was just the type she
didn't like. Visiting Americans believed you had to entertain
them just because you were American yourself. Well, she
would have her to tea or something, let her see the beautiful
house, its tracery screens like the lace curtains of Detroit,
where she had grown up, improving by their intricate patterns
the features of the crude world. Linda imagined that she of all
her friends left behind in Detroit had the finest house, not in a
style any of them could have imagined. Her mother still
imagined that she lived in a tent—this despite photos and
letters, and even a visit, during which she was overcome by fits
of sighs whenever she saw a woman in a veil. More wore the
veil then. Back in Detroit, Linda's mother had been afraid she
would marry a Jew, or a Catholic; a Moslem had never entered
her thoughts. This still filled Linda with glee.

Noosheen Ardeshir, arriving home, clapped her hands for
Ayah, and felt grateful that she came so promptly and with a
pleasant smile, not ugly and lowering like the brows of so
many servant girls. You saw the angry ones in other people's
houses, looking with straightforward hate at the woman they
worked for. Others seemed so modest, eyes downcast, wearing
chador, right from the country, then the minute you're out they

slap the baby and date soldiers. They all wanted to go to Tehran to train as secretaries. Margaret Yoganadoost's girl had scalded the baby, seemingly an accident.

Noosheen's ayah was Indian, from Lahore, where Noosheen's father, a diplomat, lived, and where Noosheen herself had lived awhile before her marriage. All agreed that an Indian servant girl was much more willing and quick, just the thing while the children were young. And Noosheen's house in Azami Compound was small but even so bigger than most, with Western furniture to dust. Mama and Papa had sent Ayah to her from Lahore on the train. She now slept on the back porch, where if they had one the washing machine would go; then they would have to think of somewhere else to put her. This little porch had seemed to Ayah huge and cozy; her eyes had widened. She had shown all her small dark teeth smiling happily. Noosheen sometimes, having been in the United States, felt a little anxious about the chilly porch, the foam mattress on the floor. An Iranian girl would complain. In America you would have many things, for instance a washer and dryer, to take Ayah's place—gadgets that did not defect or object. All of life was such a puzzle, or, in the words of Matthew Arnold's poem:

> *And on earth we wander, groping, reeling;*
> *Powers stir in us, stir and disappear.*
> *Ah! And he, who placed our master-feeling,*
> *Failed to place that master-feeling clear.*

In the early evening after a solitary supper of pistachio nuts and boiled rice, Chloe ventures outside to the garden again, to sit on a cement bench placed at the intersection of the paths to Villa One and Villa Two. She plans to think about her situation, but the powers of enchantment in the dark Persian garden make it difficult to think deeply or make decisions. She is in any case always more given to idle reflections than to purposive thought. She can hear a fountain. The idea of an early, solitary evening is at once agreeable and dull, but she knows the sensation of dullness will pass. It is more a matter of calming down and learning to lead a life whose natural pace is in harmony with the natural rhythms of the mind, instead of, as in America, life outrunning thought, heedless and rushing.

In America she has her children, her part-time job at the museum, philanthropic activities, wifedom, books piling up to be read, the dog needing to go to the groomer, the toaster to be repaired, the cleaning to be picked up—she has the normal life of an American woman, which she herself does not object to as strongly as some of her friends do. But she agrees that it is too fast-paced.

Especially if you try to have an affair. Nothing trivial or sordid, of course—her model is Colette, or European life in general, so civilized, where people don't divorce, just conduct affairs of the heart discreetly, with the toaster being dropped off at the repairman in an efficient way, not the havoc of American divorce, the chaos of abandoned children and objects and unrepaired toasters. Toasters partake of material life, that is the nature of material life, and Chloe does not disapprove of it, does not despise objects. She thinks of them as having emanations, or animation, or life.

Tonight she feels a little worried about Hugh. This morning she had felt almost irritated at him, an irritation born of some female insecurity, some doubt, to do with herself, that he was really coming, or that he had allowed himself in some way to be arrested and thrown into an Iranian prison rather than see her, or had cooled off and now looked back on their furtive, charming exchanges as squalid and compromising, or had fallen in love, since she last saw him, with someone more suitable—unmarried, younger.

Then she had told herself she was relieved in a perverse way that he was delayed, felt she deserved to pay some penance for the happiness of being alone in a strange land. To have Jeffrey absent and Hugh there suggested gratification altogether too smoothly arranged, as if by an especially malicious destiny planning ugly surprises. With Hugh not there she could pay in advance for anticipated pleasures, pay by uncertainty, solitude, and serious study, in a land hostile to women, far from her children, in an ugly room. What destiny could then begrudge her just a little fling?

But tonight she worries about Hugh. The Iranians themselves thought him arrested, though of course by mistake. Still you read about mistakes, usually in Turkey or Mexico, an innocent traveler carrying a package for someone, or buying an artifact from an urchin, then, at the border, charges of drugs or theft, and not all the efforts of the U.S. State Department can get you out again, young people wasting their youth, released only years later, staring and white-headed, broken, with rotted teeth.

She is thinking of this now in the darkness, and looking at a quantity of geraniums set out in little terra cotta pots on the terrace of the grand house, just visible in the soft light from a window. It would be nice to have a flower in her room in Villa Two. Villa One had plenty. Villa One had charming windows that were shaped like arches, and instead of shutters it had delicate screens. Far away the barking of the dogs began.

Chloe wonders where the dogs go in the daytime. Were they all, like the puppy, under bushes someplace? Or does each dog have a respectable daytime life as watchdog to a family? All at once she misses her children with a special intensity, and she misses Jeffrey. She will go inside and write to them. It occurs to her to slip one of the pots of geraniums under her arm and steal it for her room. The Farmanis will never miss it.

Darling kids, So far I have seen people
riding on: goats, donkeys, camels, and horses,
besides cars etc. Love to Dad. See you in a few weeks.
XX Mom

Chapter Six

OLD FRIENDS

And this first Summer month that brings the Rose
Shall take Jamshyd and Kaikobad away.

Well, let it take them! What have we to do
With Kaikobad the Great, or Kaikhosru?
Let Zal and Rustum bluster as they will
Or Hatim call to Supper—heed not you.

Her apprehensions about meeting the archaeologists at Shiraz University were still intensified by her fears of the taxis, so though it was far she finally decided to walk. She had letters of introduction to Mrs. Reza and to a Mr. Farmanpour, letters which, although she was too polite to read them, she imagined described her as a serious person, perhaps even as a real archaeologist, though she was only a conscientious amateur who had read and worked up the subjects, and had majored in art history in college, and volunteered at the museum. She imagined that her lack of real expertise would be only too apparent to the genuine archaeologists, who, however, welcomed her warmly, appeared to look forward to discussing their subject with her, offered her a study cubicle in the library, and invited her to visit the great ongoing work at Persepolis and the fields of shards that lay on the way.

Mrs. Reza took her to the library, a reassuringly familiar structure, with books in English, a Library of Congress catalog, a microfilm reader, and *Time* magazine and the *New York Review of Books* in battered bundles in the periodical room.

"As you see," said Mrs. Reza, "we are quite a modern university. You have the right to use the library at any time.

You will find in it your *Atlantic*, your *Good Housekeeping*, your *New York Times*.''

Chloe thanked her. She was watching a student, head demurely scarved, nunlike, gaze vacantly into an English edition of *Middlemarch*. All the books were in English. How odd it was. The oddness was reflected on the knitted brows of the young olive faces. Several of the young women wore those little head scarves, not exactly veils but with their hair neatly invisible. She remarked on this to Mrs. Reza as they walked across the quadrangle toward the archaeology building again. The fortitude with which some women throw aside the veil, the prudence with which others proceed. Is it their families? Do the men in Iran prefer that the women continue or discard the veil?

''The veil? The veil?'' cried Mrs. Reza. ''There is no veil. The Shah has outlawed it. It is over, the vestige of a bygone day.'' Chloe, who had been struck by the large numbers of veiled women, wondered at this but did not argue. Perhaps Mrs. Reza was speaking only of the university, where, indeed, no one was veiled.

When she had thanked Mrs. Reza and Mr. Farmanpour again and left them, Chloe went back to the library and checked out some books, serious works on Persian history, pottery, tombs, and a biographical study of Matthew Arnold, and, though they were heavy, began the long walk home, carrying them in her string grocery bag.

The Azami Compound, as she drew near it, already felt familiar and homelike, and she a part of it, the wife of Jeffrey Fowler, well-known thoracic surgeon soon to arrive, so she wasn't particularly surprised, just startled, to hear a man's voice calling her name. She thought at first of Hugh, but it was not his voice. A taxi full of men had pulled to the side of the street near her, and someone was waving from within.

''Chloe! Chloe Fowler! Dick Rothblatt!''

His head struggled out past that of the man by the window, who also gazed at her behind a drooping mustache. Dick Rothblatt squirmed past the knees of his fellow passenger, fishing change from his pocket for the driver.

''Tooman. Tooman, rials . . . I heard you were coming over. I have trouble with their coins.'' He stretched his arm to peer at the coins in his palm, plucked out one or two. Dick

Rothblatt, familiar, short and rosy. The taxi was paid and drove on. Dick happily took her hand. "Friends in a strange land. I heard that Jeffrey isn't here yet?"

"I didn't know you were here already, Dick," Chloe said, piqued that no one had told her. She was happy to see him, not someone she knew well, just a dermatologist they knew from Princeton, but looking now like an adored old friend. She was surprised at her own pleasure. "How absolutely marvelous," she said twice.

"I've been here a couple of days. How do you like it?"

"I like it, it's lovely. I even love the music. I hate my room, though. We were told an apartment. Have you got an apartment? Jeffrey will die when he sees this place they've put us."

Dick laughed. "Mine is not deluxe. Sort of a duplex; there's an English neurologist and his wife on the other side. It's okay."

Chloe tried to think of the name of Dick's wife. "I'm at Villa Two, is that near you?"

"Villa Fourteen. Next to the ophthalmology building."

"You'll have to come see Villa Two," Chloe said.

Dick had been invited to Shiraz, he said, by Abbas Mowlavi, who was also a dermatologist. They had met during Abbas's fellowship year at Princeton. They talked of the terrible tragedy of his wife and baby.

"Did you ever meet them?"

"No, he married after he came back here. He has a brother in exile, in Paris, a radical. He has to watch his step."

"No one mentions the Shah here, pro or con. No one mentions politics at all."

"Definitely a no-no. Topic interdicted. Or the Savak drags you off in the night."

"There should be interdicted topics in America—jogging, relationships."

Dick took her string bag of books. His arm was strong and well muscled. His glasses were thick. He smelled of cologne. They walked along. Everything in this block was half-constructed, iron rods sticking out of cement-block walls, rusting and crumbling on every hand, abandoned. People squatted on rubble, eating or merely staring.

"They have a lot of good ideas here, then no follow-through. The same at the hospital, from what I've seen. Expensive machines, all broken.''

''I'm sure they're much better off without machines,'' Chloe said.

When she told him that she had not yet seen the hospital, Dick invited her along to see it and have lunch with him in the cafeteria.

''When's Jeff coming?'' he added. She understood the association of his ideas.

''It's a little uncertain. But meantime I had this project here—I work at the museum in San Francisco, you know, so I came on ahead. Sassanian pottery.'' This smoothly oiled statement was sounding more and more reasonable to her, especially now that she knew the names of the Shiraz archaeologists and had a cubby. ''They had a vast civilization. There are fields near here where shards just lie on the ground. You don't even have to dig.''

''Who were the Sassanians?'' he asked. Chloe told him as they walked, a pre-Islamic people who ruled from the third century to the seventh century A.D.

''I'm doing rugs,'' Dick said. ''Now there's a complicated subject. I did a lot of reading. I had no idea. Anyway, I plan to buy a few rugs; there'll never be a better time.''

They walked inside the gates of Azami Compound and across the green lawn, past Villa One toward the hospital. Amid beds of petunias and roses, families crouched, unwrapping packets of food—black-shrouded picnickers, men in nylon shirts and serge trousers. They all looked to Chloe too somber; probably they had someone in the hospital, or maybe they were waiting for tests. Here and there she saw the upended backside of someone at prayer, prayer rug spread out on the grass. Chloe had not been able to figure out what precipitated a fit of prayer, since people did not seem all to do it at the same time, despite the calls that could sometimes be heard on loudspeakers from minarets downtown. Chloe and Dick picked their way quietly, politely, unobtrusively.

The hospital was an exotic structure, Moorish and pink, and on the inside much like all hospitals, tiled, smelling of disinfectant. Carts and trundles stood in the halls along the wall. Same apologetic and weary expressions of the faces of people wandering along or waiting by the open clinic doors. Not for nothing were you called a patient.

Then a fierce woman impeded their way, hair streaming like a gypsy in an opera, stepping in front of them from her place along the wall. She thrust a baby girl at Dick. The child was covered with rosy spots. Chicken pox, Chloe thought. Dick pointed her up the stairs. His expression changed as they went on.

Chloe suddenly remembered the name of Dick's wife, "Marlene isn't with you?"

"Marla—Marla and I are getting a divorce," he said. "Nothing rancorous or anything. One of those things. After the kids went to college we just sort of found out who we were, as they say, and we weren't people who need to be married to each other."

"That's common at our stage, isn't it?" Chloe said, noting the marriage-counseled vocabulary.

Dick shrugged. It was only recently he had been prepared to admit, even to himself, that he had contributed to the failure of his marriage by the occasional affair with a nurse or woman medical student. Now that there were so many more of these, it was hard to avoid. Yet he could see Marla's objections and sympathize with them; his own views on marriage were perfectly traditional too. What he couldn't understand was her unwillingness to accept his apologies and repentance, his perfectly sincere intentions to start anew. They would be helped by the fact that Scott, David, and Ellen were off to college and out of the house.

Neither was he very interested in Marla, for they had been married for twenty years, but he had noticed some new quality of vehemence and independence that interested him, and he was generally interested in the subject of women, not just sexually or because he enjoyed their alert and tactful way of listening—the feeling they gave that you could tell them things you couldn't tell a man—but existentially, in their situation, which once you came to think of it had been a difficult one historically and still was.

He was a feminist. He played the violin. His parents had hoped he would be a musician, and he had kept up his skill to the extent of playing in a quartet, but medicine had always been his love. You had to be sensitive to be a dermatologist, and you had to like women—psychology was half the practice of dermatology, as he was always telling his residents. Energetic, likable, and a good psychologist—he was chairman of the department at Princeton, a post high enough and visible enough to please even his mother.

"This is the cafeteria," he told Chloe. "Just get a tray and get in line. Don't be put off by the food—it tastes better than it looks." They lined up behind others, nurses in veils, technicians, some sleekly dark in their white lab costumes, others rosy Westerners whose nasal drawls somehow floated above or through the low Iranian voices.

"So fuck you, I told him," said a voice.

"Tracheostomy," said another.

Chloe hesitated over the white rice, soft and steamy, and the lightly browned rice, so the man with the ladle gave her both. He smiled. "Chelo," he said. He ladled a stew of gravy and peas over her plate, and a man by his side gave her a small plate of iceberg lettuce and pale tomatoes in a small dish. Her heart lifted. She had not yet risen to the difficulties of the vegetable stand, where she would have to gesture and point, so the sight of tomatoes, however sickly, warmed her now. Dick didn't take one. He shook his head at the salad person. They found a table.

"Actually, I wouldn't," he told Chloe when she set her salad at her place. "They have a problem here. We've been seeing a few cases of typhoid."

"Heavens," Chloe said, rather excited at the notion of being imperiled by third-world diseases.

"The little girl in the hall just now, for instance, that could be typhoid, the spots."

"Good grief," said Chloe. She ate a leaf when Dick wasn't noticing; obviously perfectly OK lettuce.

They left the cafeteria and, in the corridor, met Abbas Mowlavi, who was hastening somewhere but stopped with a look of genuine pleasure to see them. His chin was cleft like the chin of a man in a bourbon ad.

"We were having lunch," Dick said. "Have you met Mrs. Fowler?"

"Yes, indeed. Hello, Mrs. Fowler. I meant to ask you over

here to lunch myself one day. I hope you are not too solitary in Villa Two? But you've found Dr. Rothblatt.''

"So surprising," Chloe murmured. "To meet an old friend. Walking along . . .''

"Well," said Abbas to Dick, "are you coming to my clinic this afternoon?'' Dick was. "I have promised to take Dick into the countryside tomorrow after work, and perhaps you would like to come too,'' Abbas suggested to Chloe, perhaps to atone for depriving her of her companion now.

Dick liked Abbas, thought him a forthright and gentlemanly guy and a good doctor, trained at Hammersmith, Princeton, and Johns Hopkins. You couldn't blame them when they got back here for missing the sight of a CAT scanner or a cobalt unit. Hard on them getting all that fancy Western training then nothing to do with it, though to be fair, Tehran did send them very up-to-date equipment. It was just they couldn't get the people to keep it running. People like Abbas must be dedicated patriots, otherwise they'd emigrate. They seemed genuinely to want to improve the health care of their nation. Dick found that exciting too. Here was a chance really to do things, something to be done, a need surpassing the mere acne and drug reactions you got at home in America. Here huge horrible things swelled up on people. Sometimes you had no idea what they could be. There were dire systemic complications of skin conditions which in the West would only be little cutaneous things. Here you could die of impetigo. Or typhoid. He didn't worry about the typhoid, exactly, since medicine was perfectly up to date here and people could be saved, and undoubtedly they had a public health department tracking down the pollution, the well or source. But they seemed strangely unconcerned all the same, Abbas as taciturn as the rest about a disease that in America, where it wouldn't happen anyway, would create a furor. These Iranian doctors had to contend with death more immediately than Americans did, even American doctors. We don't let it in until the last minute; here it might come stealing in any time.

Dick's heart tightened with sympathy for that poor mother in the hallway, now huddled against the clinic wall, her shawl around her, her brown face sunburnt to paper, her child cuddled in the shawl. The little girl was not going to die, of course; this mother had had the sense to bring her in. Would Marla know what to do if a child got typhoid? All she had ever done, measles, broken arms, was call him up at the hospital and scream hysterically. But she was not a good example of female anything, Marla, just a credulous, silly woman. He tried to pat this peasant mother pleasantly on the shoulder but she shrank from him. Abbas, coming over, smiled at this mistake. He held his arms out for the child, and said something to the nurse, who began to take the child from the woman. The child clung to her mother's shawl, then to the silver ornament around her neck. The nurse pried her little fingers from around it, and handed her to Abbas, who carried her away toward his office.

"Where do these people come from?" Dick asked.

"They come from right here, from the town," Abbas said, and, seeing surprise fleet across Dick's face, added, "From the old part of the city where the plumbing has not been modernized and wells are used."

"Then it shouldn't be hard to find the tainted well," Dick said.

Abbas did not reply so Dick dropped the subject. Dick had been advised not to pursue topics that Iranians seemed to want to drop. You never knew when something was politically sensitive.

Abbas's mind was not on the typhoid, rather on the impression once again that someone was using his laboratory in the night. Certain chemicals disarranged, a beaker rinsed and still drying in the rack, a length of rubber tubing coiled in the sink. Nothing alarming about all this but that it was done in the night—by some insomniac perhaps, perhaps someone doing something dangerous or something that had to be done right away to save a patient in mortal peril. He felt no need to decide which of these things it was, except to resent, if it was something illegal, that it was done in his laboratory, bringing a certain danger to himself. It was the kind of thing you watch—would it happen again? The hastily coiled tubing lay in the bottom of the sink like a poisonous snake ready to strike at the hand that reached for it.

His mind too was on Vahid Farmani, his eyes distracted, barking irrational commands, not listening about the typhoid, his mind on Tehran, animated by fear or ambition—you never knew, any more, whose fear, whose ambition—and he, Abbas, didn't want anything of either but only to treat the sick and be left alone. The Azami Compound was a worthy sort of ivory tower, indispensable to any regime. He considered whether to have the lock changed on his lab, or maybe ask Hossein to stay up and watch some night. Then he decided it was better not to notice anything, and anyway he told himself he didn't care.

Chapter Seven

TEA PARTY

And we, that now make merry in the Room
They left, and summer dresses in new bloom,
Ourselves must we beneath the Couch of Earth
Descend—ourselves to make a Couch—for whom?

As the wife of the chief of Azami Hospital, you of course gave tea, dispensed welcome. Linda Farmani in a few days rose to her duty and invited the new American woman to tea, though she didn't feel gracious toward her, probably because Chloe was here alone and therefore was taking up a disproportionate share of attention being fetched and called on. Linda also asked the other newcomers, who were, she read from the list Vahid had given her, a woman doctor, June Fay, an English couple named Henderson, a Dr. Rothblatt. The name of Dr. Monroe was crossed out. Linda invited, which was to say commanded, Heidi Asghari, Noosheen Ardeshir and Zareeneh Yazdi to come make conversation and help arrange the sweet rice cookies, and put bowls of pistachios around the room.

So far only the women had assembled, and the tea was not yet poured. Chloe was interested in the striking decoration of Linda Farmani's rooms, which were prettier than most of the interiors she had seen so far, all of which had contained rather too much and too large furniture, covered in lurid shades of red or green velvet. Chloe supposed it was just that Linda's rooms were more American, Linda being American, though the strangely large furniture and colors of turquoise and blue seemed Persian enough. There were little tables made of brass trays standing on racks, and white-painted trellises nailed onto the walls, and a coffee table of plate glass supported by wicker elephants, which, though Chloe did not like it at all, was nonetheless imposing.

49

When she commented on the decoration, Heidi Asghari told her that Linda was an interior decorator; she had made a business out of doing Persian-style interiors for the American wives of Grumman and Philco and the other corporations.

"They're afraid to go to the bazaar and they don't know where to find things for themselves. I think that Linda does pretty well out of it."

"Kind of Hollywood Persian," Chloe said. "Well, it isn't so bad," but she was torn between admiration for Linda's enterprise and scorn for someone who would profit from the plight of her dislocated sisters.

Linda Farmani herself was a thin woman, pretty but tense, with dark, sleepless-looking eyes. Her midwestern American accent surprised, for if she hadn't spoken, she might have seemed Iranian herself, dark hair twisted up, earrings of gold. She looked about forty, her husband Vahid about forty-five, and these two had to their surprise just produced a child, which was brought in for the ladies to see. Linda held it as if it were a sack of meat or a log—something inanimate and faintly awful. The baby was called Henry, reminding Chloe of their poor paralyzed friend. Chloe longed to hold Henry properly, and give the poor little thing some human comfort. He did not cry but stared up at his mother, whose glance at him was of panic, or fear.

"What a pity about your husband," Linda said to Chloe, with a grave expression, as if she had heard that Jeffrey was dead.

"Oh, he'll be here soon," Chloe said. "I expect to hear any day."

They were joined by the doctors, who arrived in a gang, faces reddened as if they had raced each other from the hospital. Here were Noosheen's husband Bahram Ardeshir; Heidi's husband Mohammed Asghari, Dick Rothblatt, Dr. Henderson, and some others. Chloe was shocked to think that it was this small brown old Bahram who was husband to the pretty Noosheen; she had not really matched them in her mind at the first meeting. The horrid Dr. Farmani, with no glint of recognition of her, greeted the others as if he hadn't been seeing them all day. People began to talk and pass the tea.

Chloe was brought a cup of tea by a tall, thin man, whose

air of aristocratic and elegant cruelty had attracted her notice
already. He was slightly balding and wore a dark green silk
scarf knotted at his throat. He introduced himself as Dr. Ali
Yazdi. His wife was Zareeneh, the tall voluptuous red-haired
woman, equally noticeable, who had opened the door for
Chloe. Her clothes were imprinted with the names of
designers, and she emanated a delicious designer scent. She
wore a diamond ring so huge it riveted the eye and compelled
the conclusion that it could not possibly be real. But she had
seemed rather nice, ushering Chloe upstairs to the party, and
clasping her hand with a brisk, mannish, American handshake.

"You have such a bewildered air, like a lovely lost child,"
said Dr. Yazdi.

"On the contrary I feel most at home, everyone is so
agreeable here," said Chloe, smiling her smile, forbearing to
add her complaints about Villa Two.

"It's a charming thing in a woman—forgive me if I speak
too personally, but I am a connoisseur—I say a lost, bewildered
look is charming, but of course we cannot let it remain. That
is what I am driving at. Have people shown you around? Have
you seen the tombs of our poets Hafez and Sa'adi?" He began
an enthusiastic description of these wonders.

"American women are luckier than we," Noosheen was
heard to say, in a voice suddenly audible, with a defiant glance
to her husband. Chloe had not heard the beginning of the
conversation. "They can go where they please, they have
passports of their own." Bahram gave a look around at the
others, confident of their sympathy for him arising from
Noosheen's combative tone. It did not seem polite, at this
point, to inquire why Iranian women couldn't travel, though
Chloe would have liked to know. Perhaps they had no
passports.

"I think the Iranian system is perfectly all right," said Linda
Farmani. "It's just a tradition," she explained to Chloe. "If
you have a green stamp you may come and go as you please,
but if you have a red one, your husband must sign before you
can travel."

"You have an American passport," Noosheen said. "Naturally you don't care."

"No, I don't. I have an Iranian passport with a red stamp," Linda said. The topic hung in the silence, no one willing to go on with it.

"Anyway, an American passport is not always such magic. Poor Dr. Monroe," she went on.

"I would guess the visa is the problem there," said Dr. Farmani. Chloe listened more carefully. But no one had any news or specific information about Hugh. A silence again. It often happened, Chloe had noticed, that a thickening, palpable and heavy, swelled over topics here, bringing them to a halt, and people had a habit of looking up or away, not like Americans, who always plunged on with topics, however awkward. But of course in America no one came and dragged you off in the night. Chloe found she had picked up an uncracked pistachio that she couldn't open, and so rolled it between her fingers, a hard little inedible lump. Passports did not seem an intrinsically dangerous topic so perhaps it was only a sore one.

"Noosheen is a Zoroastrian," Dr. Yazdi said in a whisper to Chloe. "But Bahram isn't. It used to be that Zoroastrians only married other Zoroastrians. Then they changed their views. The rumor is they thought they were getting rather inbred. Rather short and ugly." Dr. Yazdi lowered his voice. "And dark," he said.

"Noosheen is perfectly beautiful," Chloe said.

"Yes, isn't she?" Dr. Yazdi agreed.

Abbas Mowlavi joined the party late, still wearing a white hospital jacket, in which he looked darkly handsome, and it appeared to Chloe that Noosheen was very aware of that too. Noosheen followed Abbas with her large eyes, and smiled flirtatiously at him as she handed him a plate of the repellent gelatinous candy, whose flavor Chloe had not been able quite to identify. She put her piece in her saucer, with the uncracked nut.

It seemed obvious to Chloe that Noosheen and Abbas were attracted to each other, and it seemed natural as well, with her husband so old and thin and Abbas widowed. An unhappy marriage would explain her restlessness and her romantic ideas about American life, freedom and love Hollywood style. Chloe wondered if people had affairs in Iran. Probably not.

Now Chloe found herself standing near Dr. Farmani, who had been listening to the discussion of passports without offering any views himself. Chloe wondered if she dared continue the subject of Hugh. It was the others, after all, who had begun it.

"It's too bad you haven't found Dr. Monroe," she said. "Isn't he a specialist in infectious disease? He could be helpful with this terrible typhoid epidemic."

Dr. Farmani looked at her with an expression she did not understand. "There is no typhoid epidemic," he said. "We had a case which for a moment appeared to be typhoid. Of course we were concerned. But, after all, it was not."

Chloe had not heard this news. A relief, she said. Why did Dr. Farmani glare at her so?

"It would be most unlikely, typhoid, hardly more likely than in your Omaha, say, or Connecticut." His pride was clearly wounded, and Chloe blushed at her rudeness at seeming to imply that they were behind here or couldn't cope.

"Where are you from, Mrs. Fowler?" asked Linda Farmani, drawing near and fixing Chloe with a smile. Her husband walked away.

"San Francisco, California," Chloe said.

"It is so pretty there," Linda said, though she had seldom been there. San Franciscans were so stuck-up about the supposed beauty of their city, and its supposed good food, but in fact it had always been freezing and foggy when she'd been there, in midsummer at that, and she'd eaten terrible previously frozen fish. You always heard that it was pretty. Linda looked past Chloe and around at her room, the marble floor, the rugs. If she hadn't come out here she might never have discovered this flair she had for decoration, for making something beautiful against all odds. She was proud that their furniture had been chosen, like everyone else's in the compound, from the hospital stores, yet look at the difference.

"Where are you from? Your house is so lovely! It's nice of you to invite me to your party," Chloe recited politely.

"L.A., but I was born in Detroit," Linda said.

"It's awkward about Jeff. I know they were counting on him at the hospital," Chloe said.

"How many children do you have?" Linda asked. It was a

question Chloe had been asked so often in her life that she could not later remember the rest of this conversation, during which she reflected on the vulgarity of the wicker elephants.

Her real attention was directed to watching Noosheen and Abbas. A tea party was a pleasant thing, she thought. Perhaps in Iran flirtations were carried on at tea parties instead of cocktail parties, but life underneath is everywhere similar. There was Dick Rothblatt, wearing a tie, talking to the new young American woman, who was wearing a short skirt and high heels. The skirt too short, it seemed to Chloe, for Iran. She accepted more tea from Linda Farmani with a smile eager and festive.

Abbas, standing behind Noosheen's chair, was looking with new attention at a photograph in a silver frame standing on the glossy table: Linda and Vahid with the Shah and Shabanou. He had seen this photo a hundred times, a ceremonial photograph, taken when the Shah visited the hospital. It implied nothing about the political opinions of the Farmanis, yet it struck Abbas now with a kind of foreboding. Perhaps it was because of Vahid's recent strange behavior, his lack of interest in the typhoid epidemic, his refusal to discuss it, his peremptory commands on a number of issues affecting the hospital, eyes trained, it seemed, toward Tehran, in expectation perhaps of favor or reward. If you took the picture from its frame and looked on the back, what inscription would be written on it? Who was Savak in this room? Who was listening to every word, remembering the words? Someone, without doubt.

These thoughts were prompted by having seen in the street today the mother of Zev Zahdi, a young resident in obstetrics who had been imprisoned three months ago for crimes against the state. Mrs. Zahdi had looked at him and drawn up her veil and looked away, mistrusting him. There had been no point in asking her if she had news of Zev. Zev would turn up again, with scars or fingers broken, or he would never turn up. Abbas had stared at the woman, hoping to convey some unspoken message of sympathy and trustworthiness, hoping to convey the information that he was not afraid to look at her. Could Vahid look at her? But these were the people who would naturally be schooled in long, frank glances, a sympathetic softness of the eye, and they would look at her.

"I don't pretend to approve of everything the Shah does," Linda Farmani was saying, astonishing him, as if she could look into his thoughts. The perfect spy can look into your thoughts. Linda, he saw, was talking to others. When she spoke, she pronounced, impressively. Conversations dropped off elsewhere. She held forth, rather. Perhaps it was her very large bosom that made this seem so. She was unconcerned about the forbidden topic of the Shah. "His methods—well, really. But he's done more good than harm. I think the people realize that."

Though this was not Abbas's view he did not contradict her or pick up the discussion. Neither did anyone else. Abbas could if anyone—he was in a way protected by the outright defection of his brother, who now lived comfortably, safely, defiantly, in the beautiful Parisian suburb of Neuilly. No one would believe in the disloyalty of Abbas because no one would believe that someone with so dangerous a brother would dare be himself dangerous or disloyal. The brothers of renegades must keep to a course of orderly preoccupation with their own affairs. Abbas wondered if he would ever see Paris again. Paris was lost to him, his wife and child lost, brother lost, untroubled mind lost. He could enviously imagine his brother, Emir, eyes blazing with devotion to an old imam, eating a croissant, mind untroubled, while he, Abbas, was condemned to a mind tunneled with thoughts of worms and ashes, caring about nothing.

He thought, suddenly, looking at Noosheen, of how at university he and English fellows, or sometimes with a girl, went on the river, hearts untroubled. Then he thought of the feel of a pole as you sought the bottom and the slow push of the punt, and high English laughter. He had been happy then, and yet he had never liked the soft feel of the mud at the bottom of the river. Had that been the shadow of the future?

"Of course you could argue," Linda Farmani said, laughing, "that teaching them to drive doesn't really improve their lives. Costs them their lives more likely. But it's essential to their feeling of themselves as a modern nation."

"Spoken as a child of Detroit," said her husband.

"We have to have the cars, the TVs, the washing machines."

"It's true, I agree," said Noosheen.

Abbas turned to Noosheen—so small, pretty in her blue dress, it was hard to imagine her a mother. He had known her since childhood. He asked after her children.

"It's that he has bad advisers," Linda said to Chloe. "It's hard for an American to keep quiet about things. I just end up saying whatever I think. If they want to drag me off, let them."

"You Americans are very bent on your inalienable rights," said her husband, looking rather as if he wished she would be quiet. Chloe, sensing a family quarrel on the issue of free speech, asked about the flower-flavored candy.

"Bahram won't give me a green stamp for my passport," Noosheen said to Abbas. "Can you imagine that?"

"We are all Oriental despots at heart." Abbas smiled at her.

Chapter Eight

MORNING CHATS

After a week, despite her horrible room and no word at all from Hugh or Jeffrey, Chloe had begun to feel that colonial life, or whatever this could be called, was peculiarly agreeable. The other Americans, except for Linda Farmani, were friendly and interesting, and so were the golden-earringed Iranian wives, especially Noosheen Ardeshir. The social life was casual and constant; little parties drove out after the work day, with Heidi or Noosheen or Abbas Mowlavi, to view a tomb or monument. Women had servants and were thus free to visit or read. Roses bloomed everywhere. People dropped by—Chloe imagined it was like the life of an eighteenth-century village, say, in England, and quite unlike San Francisco, where you had a calendar and penciled things in.

Although she missed Sara and Max with painful emotion, it was somehow pleasant to be without Jeffrey. She loved him, of course, but he was a strenuous person to be around. He had the normal life of a surgeon—up at five-thirty, late ward rounds—and at dinnertime he was often snappish and preoccupied, and, in truth, a little autocratic—a well-known surgical defect of temperament. She could at least tease him about it. Chloe's absent-mindedness she knew irritated him, but otherwise he was proud of her, and happy to delegate to her the supervision of their family and cultural life—tickets for the ballet, opera, string quartets, and the occasional recital. She had once calculated to herself the amount of time it took to get one ticket: conversations with Jeffrey's secretary, waiting on hold at the various box offices, the inevitability of the need to exchange the night. Here there were no tickets to anything, and it seemed wonderful.

Here was a life that seemed natural, and she felt herself to be growing more inwardly calm when she hadn't even been aware of being tense. She tried to do the same thing each day at the same time, like a nun.

In the mornings Dick Rothblatt always stopped to see her after his jog, on his way to the Dermatology Clinic. They drank their coffee on the broad front steps in a spot where the early rays of sun struck through the light fog of the morning. This picnic out of doors seemed more discreet, as well as more pleasant, than asking Dick in to her terrible room. No doubt they seemed eccentric, two Americans having this public early-morning picnic, or perhaps they did not, for the Iranians themselves were forever spreading cloths or newspaper over any disagreeable section of pavement and sitting down on it to eat. The women passing by gazed round the corners of their veils to see what it was they ate.

Chloe would bring down toast, and afterward give the crusts to the puppy, with whom she was making some progress. He was waiting each morning, watchfully, within his bushy cave, and darted eagerly out when she tossed the crusts, although he still growled when she extended her hand. She had patted him once or twice as he ate, and once he had wagged his little tail, which ordinarily drooped in a churlish, distrustful way. She had named him Rustum, after the Persian warrior in Matthew Arnold's poem, which she had been reading in preparation for her talks with Noosheen.

As they breakfasted, Dick would confide his marital woes. Chloe saw he was someone who found it easy to confide in women, secure in his expectation of their interest. He had been accused, he said, out of the blue, or at least after intermittent quarrels he hadn't taken too seriously, by an unexpectedly bitter Marla, of neglecting her and particularly their children, by being too wrapped up in his work and hobbies. This was so common a complaint that he hadn't even taken it personally; wives were always accusing their husbands of neglect, in proportion to the success of the husband, or so he gathered from the elliptical remarks made by other husbands in the process of being divorced.

"I've never heard it directly discussed, but they blurt it out, you come upon them at funny hours in the hospital cafeteria. Having dinner at the hospital is a sure sign." He wished men felt more able to talk things over among themselves. Marla used to fill him in on the causes of other people's divorces. She had always figured it out, or even talked it over with the wife, and after she told him—"He's never home at all—he's gained all that weight—they haven't made love in nine years"— whatever it was, he could always sort of see the wife's point.

But not so easily in his own case. He knew he was wrapped up in his hobbies, but not to the neglect of anything else. He was interested in almost everything and had a lot of nervous energy to spend, and was also a perfectionist, was not content with his tennis game, his endurance, his salad dressing, his garden, his cellar, his car, even his stamp collection, which he had officially abandoned at the age of fourteen but still, passing the window of a philatelist, added to. He had other hobbies besides. He jogged, collected, practiced, read, much as he had done as a boy, and had been led to believe it was good to continue doing so. His parents had wanted him to be a well-rounded person with values. And he was.

Each morning Dick and Chloe watched the shrouded Iranian women, ample and slow, in their stately procession to the hospital, as patients or on visits. Chloe remembered Marla Rothblatt—tense and small, with a perfect figure maintained by incessant tennis, skin a little leathery. Did he miss her really?

"It's the story of my life to be at the wrong place at the right time," Dick said. "Here it's a time of my life I could be scoring like crazy and where am I but in a land of modest women." He had not mentioned, in his confessions to Chloe, his occasional infidelities.

"Is Marla seeing anyone?" Chloe asked this morning.

"Not now," Dick said. "I told her she should, I'd pay for it. I think if she got some help, she'd see things differently."

"I meant, does she have a boyfriend?" Chloe said.

"Oh, no," said Dick, looking shocked. "Her energy seems to be mostly into studying." His tone was disappointed, as if he would have preferred a human rival, something more tangible than the intellectual fascination of an M.A. in Social Welfare.

"I suppose, all those years of marriage, I was away a lot—I know it was hard on her. But now I could organize my life to spend more time with her. She could travel with me now that the kids are grown. This should have been the best time, now in our forties."

Chloe shrugged. "Resentments build up—you can't just wish them away."

"I'm not resentful," said Dick. "In Iran, did you know? They have arranged marriages. You think it only happens in India. But they all say it works as well as anything else. Usually Bahram Ardeshir, the pathologist? His wife is young and flaky. That's one mistake I wouldn't make, a woman under thirty, that's somebody's law." His glance at Chloe was so conspiratorial that Chloe, believing herself to look younger than her thirty-five, was offended. Dick, she supposed, was about forty-five. Did this mean that she counted in his view as someone his own age, or someone too young? He talked to her in any case like someone out of the running—but maybe this was because of his acquaintance with Jeffrey.

But she liked having Dick as a friend. His confidences acknowledged her womanhood, and if he was a man who expected women to be endlessly interested in him, Chloe actually was, had always found the marital problems of new friends more interesting than those of old friends, if only because she hadn't heard them as often.

For her part, she tried slyly to introduce the subject of Hugh Monroe. Should they be worried about him, be trying to find him? One heard of the intransigent bureaucracy here, newly elevated peasants who took the rules seriously, and there were rules about visas, bribes, forms. Perhaps Hugh had failed to bribe or to fill out a form? If they knew where he was, they could send money or whatever he needed. What did Dick think?

Dick had better luck than she with the telephone, and more sense of its ways, and made it work as far as the Hilton in Tehran, whence a faint, distant voice told them Hugh Monroe was not registered. Perhaps the Sheraton? The Intercontinental? But the phone would not work a second time.

"We could call the American Embassy," Dick said, "but I wouldn't worry. If he was in trouble, he would be in touch with them himself."

"I'm not worried," Chloe protested. "After all, what do we know about his travel plans? It's just that if he's in trouble—and that's what they heard—it had better be us who try to help, because no one else will." She had, after ten days, the sense that Iranians did not help each other.

When Dick had gone on to work, Chloe went to her apartment again and watered her plants. She had now stolen one each night, and was pleased with the cheerful and colorful effect on the window sills, though she did not like the slightly unpleasant odor of their leaves. Today she was expecting a visit from Noosheen, but planned to remain firm that they must meet outside in the garden, because of the ugliness of her quarters. And if the geraniums were discovered she planned to say what she thought: why should one villa have all those geraniums and this one none?

Chloe found that she had much more to say about Matthew Arnold than she could have guessed. She talked with authority about the self-disgust of Empedocles, and how he represented the ennui and spiritual desolation of the nineteenth century. "He is a symbol of Western man," she said, thinking to lead up to an interesting discussion of comparative zeitgeists.

"Was Matthew Arnold married?" Noosheen wondered.

"Oh yes. Though not much is known about his life. He hated biographies and destroyed all his papers."

"He was handsome," Noosheen said. "See the picture on the front. Blond. I think blond men are very attractive." She giggled at Chloe's blond hair. "Of course there are no blond Iranians."

"I think Iranian men are very handsome," Chloe politely said. "So dark and handsome." Of course they were also short, and she thought them too thin, and always gasping on cigarettes, and their mustaches were wrong. Some were tall and handsome, to be sure—Heidi's husband, Mohammed Asghari, in a portly sort of way, and Dr. Yazdi, and Abbas Mowlavi, certainly; but Noosheen's husband Bahram, who looked about sixty, was one of the small, attenuated kind, with deep, rabid eyes. Chloe wondered if Noosheen had ever loved him, or whether it was a loveless arranged thing, as Dick had said. Poor pretty Noosheen.

"It is so beautiful," cried Noosheen, reading "Dover Beach." "The man and the woman against all hollow change and worldliness. 'Ah, love, let us be true to one another.' I guess Matthew Arnold never came to Iran. Persian men are not ever like that. They are dreadful compared to American men, they only want you to sleep with them and keep house, you can't say a word. They believe they want you to be liberated, like the Empress—she studied architecture. But they don't, really."

Chloe supposed this would be true of third-world men generally, or perhaps of men generally. It must be hard for a young woman like Noosheen to have glimpsed compatible Western couples, liberated Western romance. To her surprise, tears had appeared in Noosheen's eyes. She fished in her bag and drew out the corner of a cloth, which Chloe realized was the corner of a veil, a chador. Noosheen dabbed at her eyes. It seemed natural to Chloe that Noosheen should be disappointed with husbands, having this older and doubtless conservative husband, and she with her good English, and she had probably read God knows what—Betty Friedan? or she might even have read *The Golden Notebook*.

"I am sorry," Noosheen said. "I know this conversation is not about poetry, but you are so kind. I feel you will understand. It is just that I am not in love with Bahram, my husband. In Cleveland I was, I think, but now that we are here he is like my father, not a very kind man, and he is too old for me."

"Maybe it's just readjustment; it takes some time to get settled," said Chloe, who had learned that to sympathize too strongly made people feel worse. Inwardly she felt herself passionately resent the horrid caresses of old Bahram. "How long have you been back in Iran?"

"My husband does not realize that a woman needs—needs"—she sniffed and mopped again at her eyes. "Excuse me. We were talking about ideals and abstractions. I know real life is not the same thing as literature."

She is intelligent, Chloe thought. Too bad for her. And consider that her whole glimpse of Western life had been in

Cleveland. What would she have concluded from Paris or San Francisco? What sort of life did you glimpse in Cleveland?

Noosheen asked Chloe what her husband was like. Chloe described Jeffrey: light-haired, not really tall but medium. A concerned father, sympathetic doctor—Chloe was conscious that she gave Jeffrey the benefit of the doubt on a few points. Noosheen persisted. Did he mind that she worked outside the home? Did he wish for many children? What was his mother like? Chloe answered these questions as neutrally as possible, but her sympathies were animated.

"Read 'Sohrab and Rustum' for next time," she advised, "since it's a Persian story. I'll be interested to hear what you think."

If Chloe had put a glossy sheen on Jeffrey, making him sound bland, affectionate, American, indulgent, blond into the bargain, she was recalled to a more lively sense of him by receiving a letter from him. Hossein laid it gravely on her pillow when he came at noontime to mop.

"Take this to the American woman," Dr. Farmani had told him, holding meanwhile the foreign letters like a fan before him, or cards, and plucking out the one for the American woman. Carrying it along, Hossein kicked at the cur that lurked outside Villa Two.

As usual, every day, the rugs from the hallway of Villa Two had been thrown by the American woman outside and so must be dragged in again and put neatly in the corridor halfway between this wall and that, the green in front, the red and yellow always in the upper passage.

The odor from the kitchen sickened him—the things she cooked in there, unholy and greasy, reeking of pork. He laid the woman's letter on her pillow and hurried away, dampened his mop at the sink and dragged it along to clean the steps. He could smell the perfume.

Chloe was almost frightened to have a letter already, afraid it bore some scary news, though she knew it could as easily be good news. Perhaps any news would give her this queasy moment of irritation, of reluctance to be reconnected to her own real life. But of course she did wonder when Jeffrey was coming, and longed for news of the children. She tore open the envelope. Jeffrey could not yet predict his arrival. Two weeks more, it would seem, at least, and poor Henry still unable to move a limb but most of the neurologists giving him at least some hope of arm movement. Chloe shuddered, read on. The children: "I took them to the dentist, and Sara had two cavities, Max three, and the dentist said he doubted they were being adequately supervised as regards their brushing. He agreed with me that children that age who have had fluoride treatments shouldn't be getting cavities unless from neglect, or too many sweets. I've asked you so many times to be more watchful about what they eat."

Chloe's despair was immediate. Her own teeth had required endless fillings before she was twelve. Her children had inherited this bad luck, this bad enamel. She did too supervise their brushing, that is, always told them to brush their teeth. It was true she did not stand over them night after night, but neither did Jeffrey; he would always make sure to have something better to do. Anyway they were good children and did brush their teeth; it was bad luck, bad heredity, her fault. She seethed, agonized. And how could she watch, every moment, what they ate? They were school-aged children, they went places without her. Why couldn't *he* watch what they ate? He took no responsibility—her fury rose, and the worrying vision of Sara and Max suffering dental pain.

From the fan of letters Vahid Farmani picked out the other letter from America and threw the rest on his desk. As he read, he was conscious that his throat had somehow sealed itself up with intimations of horror. It was only a letter from Dr. Fowler, University of California at San Francisco, yet his hand shook. He laid it down with the others, picked it up again, might want it for evidence, or maybe should destroy it unread, lest it be used as evidence. So sorry, was all it said, unaccountably, unavoidably delayed. "I do hope Mrs. Fowler can stay till my arrival . . . her project . . . we will appreciate your hospitality to her project undertaken in the same spirit of Iranian-American friendship. . . ." Though Dr. Jeffrey Fowler did not say so, Farmani guessed that this meant that Dr. Fowler was not coming at all. He breathed deeply, got a hold on his emotions, told himself this was lucky, this clarified matters, the better to put him on his guard.

For it was clear to him, obvious, a beacon of clarity, that

despite the many letters from him, there was no such person as Dr. Fowler. Or if there was, this letter was not from him. The real Dr. Fowler was perhaps even unaware that he was awaited in Iran, his name being used so that this woman could be planted here. The false Dr. Fowler of the letter obviously a member of the CIA or who knew which faction of what party, the woman their spy. Farmani read the letter several times, to be sure if he had understood it, studying it for clues to its origin, its motives. So sorry, not yet coming, please allow my wife to stay. That was clear, but clumsy. The CIA was always clumsy, that's how you knew they were behind it.

She will be expecting him to say, Oh, Mrs. Fowler, so sorry about your husband, of course you can stay. He will say nothing. Let her wonder if he's got the letter yet. Clumsy of them to put a woman spy in an Islamic country, or fiendishly clever, no, clumsy; you could follow their thinking: "These Muslims think so little of women it won't occur to them to take one seriously." But the CIA had forgotten that he, Dr. Vahid Farmani himself, had an American wife and knew to take them seriously. He resolved to take some measure—something to put the awful woman a little in his power.

The center of social life in the evenings, at least for the Americans, was the Cyrus Hotel on the edge of town, a large structure of cement and plastic turquoise panels, built by the Shah and run by the government to encourage tourism. There was thus a Western-style bar where people hung out like expatriates in a movie, and a restaurant, and a general air of adventure and camaraderie that attracted foreigners, and even the more Europeanized Iranians, like the Yazdis or Abbas. In contrast to an evening at the Cyrus, an evening at Villa Two was unendurably bleak, if only because the light bulbs were so dim, too dim to read by, and when she had asked for others, first of Hossein and then of Dr. Farmani, and was refused, she had bought one herself, and blown out all the lights in Villa Two and Villa Four as well. Chloe's experience with the light bulb was talked of at the Cyrus, and everyone had a story like that about his own quarters.

Besides the foreigners of Azami Hospital, the other people

who frequented the Cyrus bar were hotel guests, or Americans or Europeans who lived in Shiraz and worked for Grumman or Procter & Gamble, or Aramco people who came to Shiraz from Saudi Arabia for rest and relaxation. An R and R woman told Chloe that Shiraz was heaven compared to Saudi Arabia, where Saudi youths chase you in pickup trucks right into the American compound.

"Good grief," Chloe had gasped, "trying to kill you?"

"Not really. I don't think they would kill you. But they didn't use to come right into the compound."

"What can you do?"

"Myself, I carry a whip," the woman said.

With such interesting revelations to be had there, Chloe had taken quite unself-consciously to going to the Cyrus each night. Sometimes Dick Rothblatt or Junie Fay would come by for her, some nights she went alone.

One night someone tried to pick her up in the Cyrus bar. She sat drinking alone, too early for the others, feeling convincingly expatriated, and a man in a white suit sat down next to her, his frank American leer rather charming, until she heard the Texas accent. Still, she reserved judgment.

"Loyal Cooley is my name," he said. "Waco."

"Chloe Fowler. I'm from San Francisco."

"Like it here?"

"Yes, I love it," Chloe said, silently excepting her feelings for Villa Two.

"Of course, the poverty," he said.

"Well, yes."

"It isn't quite like it seems, though. These peasant women, they all of them have some gold, gold bracelets or whatever. I heard once how much gold is salted away in these Eyeranian villages."

"That's interesting," Chloe said. "What are you doing here?"

"Consultant," he said. "Consultant and barfly. I get enough of *them* during the day, Eyeranians."

"I'm waiting for some friends," Chloe said. "I'll introduce you."

"Much obliged," he said. "Have you tried to get opium yet?"

"Good grief," said Chloe. "No."

"The Shah runs the show," said Loyal Cooley. This casual mention of the Shah made Chloe's flesh creep. She had already absorbed the local reluctance to pronounce his name. Obviously this Texan is a narcotics peddler, she thought, or maybe he's a narc. She refused his offer to take her home.

Chapter Nine

THE BAZAAR

Some for the Glories of This World; and some
Sigh for the Prophet's Paradise to come;
Ah, take the Cash, and let the Credit go,
Nor heed the rumble of a distant Drum!

"This is my last cigarette," said Dick to Chloe at their morning coffee on her steps. As a dermatologist, Dick had not had to advise people to quit smoking—that was up to their internists. But, with the new evidence about skin wrinkling, it was going to be coming up in his own practice, and he was not the sort of hypocrite who would advise others to quit while still smoking himself. Also, he was persuaded by the evidence of heart attacks, cancer—good God, could there be any doubt? He was especially motivated now by looking at the Iranian men, all of them smoking, it seemed, all of the time. It was pathetic. Victims of U.S. tobacco interests, entrapped by their sad, limited notions of macho. In a way it was embarrassing to be a male smoker. Maybe it was really embarrassment that now stung him powerfully. All the same, quitting wasn't going to be easy.

He had plenty of female support, from Junie Fay, who said, "About time." She had contempt for the whole problem, and her contempt was something of a goad. Of course she didn't smoke, except grass. Chloe Fowler was much nicer and more understanding, even though she was a typical California health nut and didn't smoke either, and ate the typhoid salad.

"This is the cigarette I'll really miss, the first one in the morning with coffee," Dick said. "Luckily there are no bagels."

"You should just give up coffee for a few days," said Chloe in her practical way. "Days or even weeks. The thing is to break all the associations. The craving is just a matter of conditioned association. We'll switch to tea, like Iranians.'' How New York Dick is, she was thinking, or did she mean Jewish? since the jokes that characterized either of these conditions were more or less interchangeable, jokes about mothers or psychiatrists, or heartburn or bagels. Of course some people in California made psychiatrist jokes and mother jokes, but they were mostly from New York and Jewish. Even Dick had brought with him a supply of Tums, which he surreptitiously popped after even the blandest Iranian lunch; and a touch of spice would provoke him to say something like ''I suppose I'll pay for this later,'' indigestion forming a conventional part of his discourse, like ''hello.'' Chloe had never had indigestion except once during pregnancy, and believed you got it from being made conscious of it by an anxious, obsessed parent. She had carefully avoided all mention of digestion to her own children.

Dick's digestive lapses, whether regional or ethnic, were rare, no more than odd touches from time to time. Otherwise he was funny, courtly, and in an unexpected way attractive, for someone short with thick glasses—he was even sexy, because of the vitality with which he bounded around. Vitality was the secret to sex appeal—she wished she herself did not feel so the reverse of vital—so languid and growing stupider, it seemed to her, daily. Sometimes she caught herself thinking nothing at all, and would hurriedly think of her children, to atone.

''Give up coffee?'' Dick said, wondering how he was even going to get through the day, especially with Abbas smoking in front of him. He had broached the matter of quitting to Abbas, who merely shrugged and smiled his beautiful, melancholy smile, and said he knew he should. Bahram Ardeshir, the pathologist, had shown them the blackest, most horrible pair of lungs ever seen. They had belonged to a tribesman. ''They get it from building fires inside their tents,'' the Iranian doctors had explained, as if cigarettes had nothing to do with it. Dick fixed his mind on those black, horrible lungs and finished this last cigarette.

He was dawdling over his coffee, waiting for Junie to join them on an expedition to the bazaar. She was waiting a

discreet interval so that it wouldn't seem as if they had spent
the night together. In fact he had thought it unwise of her to
spend the night—the Hendersons in the adjoining apartment
could not help but in time become aware of her, though it
probably wouldn't matter to them. But, instead of going back
to her own apartment, Junie had fallen sound asleep,
exhausted from the horrors she had been discovering on the
OB-GYN service.

Dick was tired too, had slept badly after a marathon night.
Junie did not really like sex much, it seemed to him, but
always wanted to go on and on in case she might. He
wondered why it was his fate to love, as opposed merely to
sleep with, these tense and nearly inorgasmic women, why
condemned to toil to exhaustion for their apparently tepid and
infrequent pleasure when it must be just as easy to fall in love
with a cheerful, bouncy, normal enthusiast. Slyly he
wondered about Chloe Fowler. You simply could never tell.
He had slept with a lot of uncomplicatedly sensual women but
could never predict in advance. That these were not the ones
he fell in love with he supposed was a problem in himself,
some unconscious reluctance to find too much sexual
competence in his partner. Why this should be so, though, he
could not tell, nor did he think it was fair that it was he who
tossed and turned, while Junie slept soundly, just as if she had
enjoyed it. He had tossed and turned and worried that the
Shah had some sort of morals police who came and got you in
the night, and about how she was going to leave without being
seen in the morning.

Dick believed that Chloe did not realize about him and
Junie, with Junie being so much younger and so on, but Chloe
had put two and two together, easily, upon learning that Junie
had been a student on Dick's service at Princeton. It all
followed: Junie and Dick have an affair, it is the last straw for
poor Marla—who knows what else she has had to put up
with—and she throws Dick out. Probably Dick wants to
marry Junie but Junie isn't interested in commitment. To
Chloe's mind Junie, though she seemed perfectly nice, wore
her hair too long and wore too-short dresses of rayon acetate
printed with flowers. When she realized how it was with Dick
and Junie, Chloe felt a little betrayed, though she knew she

had no reason to, by Dick's having confided in her, all those complaints about poor Marla and other intimate revelations, and all the while withholding this one vital detail, no doubt because it diminished his right to complain about poor Marla. He didn't want to admit to being an errant husband screwing around, just like all other philandering middle-aged men. Was his heart broken about Marla as he seemed to say, or was he really in love with Junie, or what? It occurred to her that it was perhaps gallantry that prevented him from discussing Junie with her, an instinct, perfectly correct, that women of her age do not like to hear about men's affairs with girls in their twenties, even from men they aren't interested in themselves.

"They are the cruelest people I've ever seen," said Junie as the three of them were walked to the bazaar. "They do everything to women without anesthesia—childbirth, D&Cs, anything. They let them tear themselves up before they'll do an episiotomy. They do *those* without anesthesia. A woman in labor forty-two hours—a terrible breech position—they wouldn't let me do anything to help. Her screams! I might as well not be here, I can't help. I can't stand to see it. Women die in childbirth right here in the hospital. We've had seventeen maternal deaths! Boy, I sure am learning. Chauvinist bastards. They hate women here, the OB men as much as the rest."

"And nobody is doing anything about the typhoid," Dick put in. "Maybe it's the Latin temperament. Que sera sera."

"But this is not a Latin country," Chloe objected, "it's an Islamic country, riddled with inhibitions and taboos, and they believe in kismet."

"It's certainly taboo to mention the typhoid. I've been wondering if they've been instructed, by the Shah or someone, to, you know, *let it happen*. It's happening in the poorer quarters, naturally. There's also a food problem here, and a population problem. These despots . . . Hitler . . ."

"Oh, Dick, really. They probably are doing something, searching out the wells. They don't need to discuss it. Anyway, Hitler *built* hospitals, not that I'm defending Hitler, or the Shah either, they say he pushes drugs, but you shouldn't exaggerate." How impossible that Abbas Mowlavi, or the nice

Mohammed Asghari, or anyone she had met here would allow another human being to suffer or die of disease. That's why they stayed, to work for their people; otherwise they could go and practice in Cleveland or Cornwall. She reminded Dick of this.

"Stalin allowed millions of peasants to die of disease and starve," Dick repeated. And, of course, he had. He thought of the boy he had seen that morning, huddled all alone on the bench outside the Dermatology Clinic, reluctant to come in, but then the boy extended his arm, and running along the forearm was a terrible gash of festering black flesh. If you woke up, thought Dick, and found that on your arm you would die of fright; *an American would be dead of fright*. Perhaps the boy had been frightened; there was something in his gaze into the eyes of the doctor that had implored information. Was it a death gash, death flesh? This was a boy of fourteen.

"It's anthrax," Dick had said to Abbas. "I suppose?" He had never seen a case.

"Yes, we see it often. The boy is a handler of goat meat."

Abbas had reassured the boy in Farsi. The boy smiled a little and wiggled on his chair, life returning. Dick had smiled at him. But how many boys are there like this, he had thought, who don't come in?

Dick was in the process of buying a rug, and on an earlier visit had narrowed his choice down to several. As they approached the stall where the first was to be found, the owner scowled, then, recognizing Dick, smiled at them and waved them in. They stood at the edges of the rugs as he unfolded them and stared down into the gardens of flowers and shimmering red. Dick suddenly doubted that he could remember which one it was he had liked. "Meshed? Khorassan? Saruk?" the man intoned. "Sinneh?" A goaty odor of wool and ammonia stuffed their nostrils.

"Sinneh!" cried Dick, remembering the name. It was a beautiful rug of black and red, with tiny flowers and vines. "This one!"

"Oh, lovely," said Chloe politely, thinking how it was like being shown someone else's child—she had seen three she preferred in the pile. Dick, however, beamed down at this rug, and of course it was beautiful.

"This is of the wool of very young animals, that is why the exceptional quality. It is the practice in Sinneh, and note also the very fine knotting. Truly this is an admirable rug, and of course therefore very expensive."

"Obviously very expensive," they agreed. "Too expensive, I'm sure," Dick added, and made a feeble attempt at bargaining, which he had been told was obligatory.

"Don't you think you should get a silk rug? Those are the most valuable?" Junie said.

"Well, I hope to get one silk, one wool."

"There'll never be a better time," Junie agreed.

"Uh—there's one or two more I've seen down the way. I'd like to have another look," said Dick timidly, not looking forward to the prospect of barter and hoping the merchant would just follow him, if he left, lowering the price at each step. Chloe and Junie followed him with, it seemed to him, misplaced confidence in him and developing ideas of their own. The rug merchant shrugged and began to pile his rugs again. Dick and the ladies began to look in the next stall.

"Mikhaham yek qali," Dick had learned to say in all the stalls of the rug merchants of the bazaar. "It's beautiful," Dick said, "but too large. Too big? I've just got a small place. I'm divorcing, so I just have a small bachelor pad. Not that I don't plan to get a bigger place. In general houses and apartments in the U.S. are getting smaller." The next merchant, smiling and nodding with the appearance of great interest, had already begun to pull out another, smaller, from his myriad wares. Dick caught, though, a glance between Junie and Chloe, a nonspecific glance that told him he was embarrassing them or confirming some view they had of him, he didn't know what. "Of course, I know these are heirlooms, you pass them down for generations. I have a daughter and two sons, I suppose I should get three!" He took a deep breath and stopped himself. Why was he going on like this? He wasn't someone who babbled on to shopkeepers. Did he always do this? He remembered long conversations with the checkout girl at his grocery store in Princeton, though he would have said that was because she was pretty. Did Chloe and Junie talk about him, agree between them that he talked too much to shopkeepers? What an irritating idea. But now the man was spreading at his feet the carpet of carpets, unsurpassed. His smile of crooked brown tobacco-stained teeth leered friendship. It was surely a kindly feeling that had made him rifle his pile for the finest, the not-shown-to-everybody.

"That man didn't understand one word you were saying," Junie said, in such an exasperated way that Chloe could not have failed to guess their intimacy.

Now they were carrying a rug, huge and monumentally expensive, between them like a log, with Chloe putting her hands on its underside in a way meant to symbolize helpfulness and walking along sideways with it like a pallbearer. People seeing them coming leapt over the jube ditch and stood in the street to watch. They were silent. Dick liked to think their silence was a form of reverence for a magnificent rug going by.

In the gathering heat of the afternoon the merchants of the bazaar rolled down their metal shutters. Chloe imagined them asleep amid the rugs or sitting in darkness with glasses of tea. She and Dick and Junie took tea in the government tearoom, which remained open for tourists. Minted tea, though Dick glowered suspiciously at the leaves of mint, imagining where they had grown, in typhoid-infected water. Then they wandered to look at the craftsmen making lacquer boxes or wares of brass, condemned by the Shah's forward notions to a nine-to-five life within a restored precinct of the bazaar.

Dick kept admiring his rug, rolled and bound with string, its muted underside hardly disclosing the splendors of the pile side, a wonderful tangle of brambles and rhomboids and birds, admired by both Junie and Chloe Fowler. He thought of how Marla would feel, seeing it in his apartment. Marla would have the good taste to envy it.

It *would* be nice to buy a rug, Chloe was thinking. Judging from the prices, these rugs were not exactly cheap but nothing like at home. She tried to think of ways of getting money, or getting word to Jeffrey to bring extra money. Then she scolded herself; the materiality of her life was just what she wanted for a little time to escape. Austerity was the lesson of Villa Two, which she had thought she was already beginning to learn. But perhaps one for each of the children, as heirlooms?

At dusk, crossing the garden on her way to the Cyrus, she was conscious of the snuffling of the puppy, creeping closer to her dangling hand than he had dared before, his spindly tail twitching with the suspicion of an impulsive wag canceled midway through. He was the wariest puppy she had ever met. Perhaps this was a breed of dog unused to domestication; perhaps these dogs had run wild here for centuries.

In the big house, lights began to come on, rosy behind the wooden lattices. In one way, Chloe rather yearned to be inside Linda Farmani's lovely room, and at the same time she relished her feeling of exclusion, isolation, and anonymity. When Jeffrey came they would have to take their place in the little round of suppers that occupied families in Azami Compound. Really it was good for her to be on her own for a while.

She brought a subject up at the Cyrus that night: Why are we here? Why am *I* here? Dick Rothblatt didn't think in his case there was anything peculiar. The breakup with Marla had nothing to do with it. If they had been together, he would have brought her. She would have enjoyed it. Or maybe he had thought his affair with Junie would be a little less conspicuous in Iran than in Princeton—just till things got settled with Marla. His lawyer had hinted, actually, that if there was anything like that going on, it was well to be discreet. But mostly it seemed to him, as he now said aloud, that he had come to Iran because he wanted to see Persepolis. He was interested in antiquity and also in Islam. And—it just now occurred to him—he was interested to see if the dry desert air of the Middle East would cure the patches of psoriasis from which he suffered from time to time.

"Everybody is here for a reason but me," said Chloe. "I'm here by accident of marriage."

"Not really. There is no such thing as accident," said Dick.

"The Eyeranians aren't bad by and large," said the Texan, Loyal Cooley. "I never mind them." The other Americans exchanged glances. Loyal Cooley seemed to have traveled widely, and to have had a bad experience wherever he traveled. They were always relieved when no Iranians were present to hear Cooley's xenophobic diatribes.

"But where you don't want to mess around," Loyal

Cooley said, "is with these crypto-commies, these commie-nazis, like in East Germany. Nazis by nature and commies by training, that is the worst combination, real mean sons of bitches. I'm talking about the time I was driving from Yugoslavia to France. You can drive on the autoroute in East Germany but they warn you to stay on the autoroute; it's just a way through. So okay, but then I see a woman by the side of the road, and a flat, it's just natural to stop, so I stop. We fix the flat, okay, and I'm about to pull out when three carloads of police, soldiers, *federales*, whatever you call them, hem me in, force me back on the shoulder, make me get out, crack my head against the car, accidentally, while they verify who I am, where I'm going. Then they let me go, okay. But the really vindictive thing was they then made me wait nine hours at the border. I show them my papers, they tell me to wait my turn, they throw the papers at the bottom of an inactive pile and I sit there for nine fucking hours. That was my little punishment, see—'you vill do as you are told.'"

The company nodded in genuine sympathy. All the same, they hoped Loyal Cooley wouldn't be around every night. He had been there every night for a week so far. No one knew what he did: "consultant and barfly," he would always repeat. All his stories concerned times his life had been in peril.

"Didn't anything bad ever happen to you in Texas?" Chloe asked mischievously once.

"No, but well, you see, I know a lot of people in Texas."

When Cooley had gone to his room, Dick said, "In London they have *Guide to the Texas Gentry,* put out by the genealogical people, Burke's." The Americans all laughed.

"Someone told me they have more French furniture in Dallas than in France," said Chloe.

"Style *tous les Louis.*"

"You have to admit Tex-Mex food is good," Junie said.

"But it's the Mex that's good," said Dick.

Chloe walked home from the Cyrus with Dick and Junie, and said goodbye to them at her door.

When she went upstairs she noticed at once that someone had been in her room, moved things, left them faintly awry.

She didn't at first feel afraid. They could have been that way in the afternoon or at dusk; she might only just now have noticed. It could have been Hossein moving things to clean. Hurriedly she checked for her little wrapped flannel roll of jewelry and her camera, and found them. She had heard people who had been robbed describe their sense of violation and outrage although she didn't quite feel this, no doubt because it wasn't really her room. But she became uneasy all the same and looked carefully in the bathroom and under her cot. She opened the drawers of the bureau and looked in expectantly, looked again more carefully. Everything was there. On the table a sheaf of papers and xeroxes was scrambled and disarranged. It must be secret police looking for documents and disloyalty. It was what you expected in a police state. She told herself not to be shocked, and that there was no danger in having books about Sassanian glazes.

Then suddenly she felt unaccountably faint. She went to the bathroom and washed her face, then lay on her cot. It was fear—the blood rushes to your heart or stomach and leaves you feeling faint. Perhaps it was a routine thing, she told herself, that they come in and search your room. It could have been done this afternoon when she was at the bazaar. It would be the spies of the Shah, Savak; she had heard that they were everywhere and that you would not know which person was the spy. But she had also heard that you could always tell them, that they were perfectly evident, fooling only each other. But that was talking of professional spies. Her mind churned with questions of spies. In Iran, she supposed, you would have amateurs whose real interests lay elsewhere, recruited from necessity or self-interest into part-time informers, observers, assassins, perhaps. Abbas, Mohammed, even Heidi, who knew?

A new chill of fear welled up in her. Her lapis beads. Her favorite lapis beads, the only thing she had worth stealing. They had not been in her jewelry flannel but in the top drawer next to her passport, and, she was sure, would not be there now. Sick with dread, she flung herself at the drawer and tore it open. The beads were there, next to the passport. Elated, grateful, she snatched them up. Chill stone, yet for the moment most precious—valuable, a present from Jeffrey, old and favorite. She would have been literally sick to lose them, desolated, unable to continue. Grateful for this narrow escape, she put them on and warmed them against her throat with her hand, melting under their comforting weight and at the thought of what a close call it had been. Whoever it was might just as easily have tucked them into his pocket along with whatever else he was looking for. She got into bed again, breathing deeply with relief, and fell almost immediately asleep.

Chapter Ten

SHAHPUR'S CAVE

Into this Universe, and <u>Why</u> not knowing
Nor <u>Whence</u>, like Water willy-nilly flowing;
And out of it, as Wind along the Waste;
I know not <u>Whither</u>, willy-nilly blowing.

In the morning it had seemed almost not to have happened. She could imagine having moved things herself, she could almost account for all the disorder. Nothing was gone. With daylight, things are not frightening.

Today was the day of a drive and picnic at Shahpur's Cave at Nam-al-Rush. People had stopped asking Chloe about Jeffrey's arrival, but they still included her in these pleasant hospital outings, and her opinions, owing to her archaeological connections with Shiraz University, were sought when planning sight-seeing expeditions. People considerately took her down side roads to stare at ruins. She found it gratifying to have her least exclamation on the beauty of a fragment taken with special force. Luckily she hadn't been asked questions beyond her depth, and she tried to expiate a slight feeling of fraudulence by reading and study. It was her hard luck that she was finding Sassanian pots rather plain and boring, compared to the vivacious masterpieces of China, about which she lectured at the museum. But little by little, *faute de mieux*, her interest was growing.

Besides Jeffrey, people had in the last few days stopped mentioning Hugh Monroe, who had apparently come to seem, like Jeffrey, apocryphal or legendary, just someone who was coming sometime. But Chloe was afraid their silence on the subject of Hugh meant that they had some terrible news of him and were waiting to find out whether it was true.

"Or else they don't care," she had complained to Dick

Rothblatt. "Maybe they think that Americans are just capri-
cious and unreliable and don't turn up. Maybe it happens all
the time that people don't turn up. And meantime poor Hugh
Monroe languishes in some hideous Iranian prison."

The party assembled at Abbas Mowlavi's house. He drove
Chloe, Dick Rothblatt, and Heidi and Mohammed Asghari in
his BMW, while Ali Yazdi drove his wife Zareeneh, the
Hendersons, and Junie Fay in the hospital station wagon. Heidi
had confided to Chloe as they walked to Abbas's that she had
fears about his driving, and the likelihood that his recent
bereavement had made him reckless. "If he won't slow down,
we'll insist on getting out," she said. Now, however, they
were in the car, and Abbas was driving at a stately pace,
playing Mozart tapes. He had a huge tape deck and a horde of
tapes stored under the knees of Dick Rothblatt. Squeezed in the
back between the Asgharis, Chloe felt cozy and contented. In
America, she was thinking, if you had an expensive tape deck
like Abbas's in the car it would get stolen.

Abbas, suddenly prey to a feeling for Persian music, had
changed the tape. It was no more than a wish for the sweet,
energetic wail of a voice like Leila Midias. "My heart has
never known such sorrow, when will I again know happiness?
Return, oh happiness, to your unfortunate daughter; we will
drink together at the well." He was happy enough. Pleasant
company. Heidi and Mohammed were his oldest friends in the
world—they had been together at Oxford—and the new people
were agreeable, and the afternoon warm.

They had to pause at a small bridge to allow a party of
people on horses and mules to pass by driving sheep and goats
and camels and cows. These were a sort of gypsy people, as
nearly as Chloe could tell. The women wore gypsy clothes of
spangled nylon and embroidery, and glittered with paillettes of
brass. Their brown faces were smiling. Barefooted they
pranced alongside the animals, driving scattered children and
goats together in a flock, babies and lambs strapped to the
backs of pack animals, and the men in ragged pants walking
along, looms folded, tents folded, enormous chatter and
calling, and a waft of the odor of camels.

"In the days of the Shah—of the old Shah, the father of the
present king," said Mohammed, "it was forbidden to take a

picture of a camel. He had the idea that it made Iran appear backward.''

Chloe took out her Minox. "Would you say they are twenty feet away? Or is it infinity?''

"Those people are an infinity away,'' Abbas said, laughing.

"In a month,'' Heidi was explaining, "we won't even be able to cross the road here, it will be so crowded with the tribesmen and their flocks. It's pretty, the migration, it's something to see. I suppose that gypsies originated here. Does anyone know? The same clothes, the beautiful colorful dresses, and the women seem as free as birds. Of course they work very hard.''

"I believe that gypsies came from India,'' said Chloe.

"Yes, you must see the migration,'' Abbas said. "It's a busy time at the hospital. They drop people off when they go by and plan to stop by at the end of the summer to pick them up if they're still alive. Sometimes all our beds are full all summer with stranded old tribesmen. Often they die while the people are gone, and the families don't find out until they check back in the autumn.''

"Oh, how sad,'' said Chloe.

Abbas liked Rothblatt and Mrs. Fowler, liked their interest in Iran, their questions and smiles of appreciation. Some Americans seemed frightened or offended or critical, sat stiffly; some were reluctant to leave their quarters. Finally, he supposed, he was a traditional man and preferred the modest demeanor and domestic virtues of Iranian women, but there was something attractive about the best sort of American women, their curiosity and poise. The worst ones were all wrong—the terrible voices, the loud laughs. Chloe Fowler's voice was more like that of an Englishwoman's. At Oxford he had had affairs with English girls, who were alike in being stubborn and thick-ankled, but he had liked their high, musical voices, which rocked like little sailboats up and down with their musings. Mrs. Fowler's voice was somewhat lower-pitched. An American woman, he thought, listening to Leila Midias, probably could not sing an Iranian song.

Chloe had imagined that Shahpur's cave would be below ground, under a mountain, but instead it had to be entered at the top of a perpendicular formation of rocks, nearly a thousand meters high, to which it was necessary to ascend along a switchback path on foot or by means of donkeys, which were produced on every hand by a myriad of little boys who lived in a village at the foot and tended coolers of Pepsi-Cola for the occasional traveler. At different times, the caves had been the headquarters of Sassanian chieftains and a hideout for robbers, and a place of worship. Heidi, Zareeneh, and Mrs. Henderson were put up immediately on donkeys. Chloe, who hated riding, wavered between the horrible prospect of clinging for two hours to the bruising back of a donkey and of seeming rather ostentatiously fit, then chose the latter, despite the fearsome incline of the path and the sun, which had begun even now, at eleven, to broil. They were followed at a distance by the little boys on their donkeys, who seemed skeptical of their prowess and determined to be there when the moment came—as it quite soon did for Dr. Henderson—when the hikers would flag and require donkeys. It was really very steep, hot, rocky. Chloe, who had believed that women have more stamina than men, envied crossly the brisk steps of Abbas and Dick Rothblatt and Junie ahead of her. Dr. Yazdi and Mohammed came behind her, more slowly than she. For nearly an hour they toiled along the path, unable to converse and keep the pace at the same time, each more or less satisfied with his performance, the boys riding happily and carrying the picnic.

At the top, the path opened out onto a broad table of rock, like a stage, and at the rear of this stage, forty feet above them, was an overhang of rock. Standing on the stage, stretching up to touch the rock ceiling, stood a colossus of stone, armless but huge, which had been invisible from below because of the angle of the cliffs. They walked amazed around the giant feet, the Iranians patting them fondly as if here was a pleasant, long-lost household god. They debated whether to picnic before or after the descent into the caves.

"In any event," said Chloe, "I'm not going into the caves."

"Do you suffer from claustrophobia?" asked Dr. Yazdi.

"A little," she apologized. It was just that the mouth of the caves, a stairway of wettish rock leading down into invisible blackness, looked appalling to her. This must be claustrophobia. She felt she could not make herself descend those steps, down which the others so blithely gazed in anticipation.

"The boys from the village have flashlights and lead the way," he said.

"Nonetheless," she said.

"Perhaps you are thinking of the Marabar caves, and Miss Quested. Remember Miss Quested?" said Dr. Yazdi.

Chloe, not thinking of books, said that she didn't know a Miss Quested, and Dr. Yazdi laughed with pleasure at catching her lacking in knowledge of her own literature. *"Passage to India,"* he whispered, leaning intimately toward her ear. "When Miss Quested, finding herself alone with Dr. Aziz, imagines she has been molested. Or is molested. It is never quite clear."

"It's been years since I read it," Chloe said. His smile, sympathetic or triumphant—she could not tell which—broadened.

"I'll stay up here with you. I have been down in the caves before," he said. "We can spread out the picnic." While the others filed along out of sight into the interior of the earth, they unfolded a cloth and began to spread the contents of the drinks cooler that had been carried up by the donkeys. She did not quite like the way his hand brushed over hers as they smoothed the cloth on the dusty rock floor. "My idea is to read the great Persian poets while I'm here," she said. "Sa'adi, Hafez. It is a very rich tradition." Her chatter filled the silence.

"Yes," said Dr. Yazdi, "the classical days of Persian poetry were very rich. Both narrative poetry and love poetry, but mostly a distinctive genre of philosophical, meditative love poetry. The manuscripts, which were often illustrated, are great treasures in themselves."

"Yes, I imagine."

"My father was a collector, in a small way. Some are extremely curious," he said.

"I'd love to see them sometime," Chloe said. "Persian miniatures . . . museums . . . so beautiful." She moved away, with a great display of business with her camera, to try to photograph the valley below, leaving Dr. Yazdi to finish putting the paper plates around.

Chloe managed, by earnest photography, to keep conversa-

tion with Dr. Yazdi brisk and general. She found something
alarming in his intimate manner, insinuating that they shared
the same hobbies or beliefs. His manner to others appeared
different, even rather aloof. He spoke English like a German in
a play. Certainly, she admitted, he was well read. But there
was something oily and familiar about him. Perhaps *he* was the
Savak agent.

"They have been gone a long time," he remarked, after
numberless minutes during which they gazed at the Iranian
plain and commented on the birds that darted among the rocks
below. "Excuse me, I will walk a little way along the path."
Chloe continued to sit, watching him walk to the edge of the
chasm and peer into it. She was again thankful she had not
gone down. Then it was as if Dr. Yazdi had conjured up
spectral music from the bowels of the earth, for she began to
hear eerie singing coming forth from the bottom of the cave.

"It is the singing of the cave boys," he called to her. "They
guide the party along the path by means of their song. Isn't it
pretty?" And it did seem to Chloe the prettiest music she had
ever heard, the little boy voices, the strange Persian melody,
cadences as in a call to prayer, the words—who knew, but
surely words about safety, carefulness, returning to the light.

Now, beneath the sweet voices of the singing boys, they
came to hear the rising, agitated sound of adult voices,
speaking loudly, an occasional shout. First emerged the little
boys with flashlights; then Heidi, Zareeneh, and Mrs. Henderson tottered into the daylight, their terrified faces belying the
beauty of the song. The little boys, too, now broke and ran to
Dr. Yazdi, shouting and waving their flashlights, and casting
frightened glances behind them down the stairs. Chloe's first
thought was that something had happened to the stout Dr.
Henderson. She could not understand the agitated conversation
in Farsi, but Heidi cried, "Quick, hurry, quick," and Yazdi
hurried to her. Chloe found herself running too.

"Something really terrible," Heidi was saying. "A
wounded man down there, terribly battered. We've come up to
get a blanket and Ali Yazdi to help."

The boys danced excitedly at the mouth of the cave, waiting
for Dr. Yazdi. Yazdi efficiently negotiated from a donkey boy

his sturdy cloak and saddle blanket. Carrying these, he followed the boys.

"What did you see?" Chloe asked Heidi, who swayed in a greenish, faint way.

"I couldn't see much," Heidi said. "One of the little boys caught a glimpse of a foot by the light of his torch, then this arm sticking out at a grotesque angle, and then, as the men investigated, a groan. The person is still alive, a man, and they're going to bring him up. I suppose he fell or something. Horrible. It could happen all too easily, someone going in there alone or in the dark. That's why the little cave boys."

"How awful," said Chloe, although she knew herself to be less horrified than poor Heidi, whose face was very white and moist with shock. So too Zareeneh Yazdi, who sat, shuddering, on a rock.

"They think it's a Westerner by his shoes," Mrs. Henderson said, causing Chloe suddenly to fear that it was Hugh, and that this was why he hadn't called or come. Her stomach crawled; she fought off the idea because it was ridiculous. They were miles from Tehran, and there were thousands of non-Iranians in Iran, and millions of Iranians wearing Western shoes. Dr. Yazdi probably was. Probably they were all, in her party, wearing Western shoes. The chill of terror lodged between her shoulder blades, irrational, immovable. She breathed deeply through it.

"People don't realize how dangerous," said Zareeneh. "These were bandit caves in olden days; this is where they put their victims—murdered them and dropped the bodies down."

"Dragged them all this way up," marveled Heidi.

"Made them walk up, then killed them. Our nurses used to tell us that if we weren't good . . ."

"I thought these were holy caves," Heidi said.

They were surprised after only a few moments to see some activity at the bottom of the steps, but it proved to be Junie Fay, whom Chloe had forgotten. She had stayed below with the other doctors but now approached, wrinkling her nose in disgust.

"Ick," she said. "Trauma is not my thing. It takes a certain type."

"What's happening?" cried the other women.

"Well, they're carrying him out; he's barely alive. We'll be able to tell more when we can look at him in the light."

The song of the cave boys, before so high and sweet, now seemed to the ears of those waiting above to have an operatic dirgelike quality, a little company bringing up their dead from the underworld. Despite themselves, the five women moved toward the top of the path and peered down, soon to see the tiny sparkles of the flashlights, then the faces of the boys, then the doctors, carrying something slung in a blanket, a wrapped shape that swayed unpleasantly. Once at the top they laid it on the ground and unwrapped the bloodied face of a man, barely alive, his tongue sticking horribly out of his mouth, and a hoarse sound rasping from him as he breathed. Dick and Dr. Henderson in English, Abbas and Ali Yazdi in rapid Farsi discussed what steps to take. Heidi had poured water but the doctors waved her away.

"No telling how long he's been down there," said Dick.

Abbas had begun giving directions to the donkey boys, who leapt alertly forward, preparing their animals to carry the man. Dr. Henderson was listening with his ear to the man's chest, his fingers clutching his wrist.

"He's very very weak," he said. "Exposure. There don't look to be any wounds."

"Lacerations," said the doctors. "Superficial? Heart attack? Concussion?" They muttered among themselves as they lifted him onto a donkey, gingerly, draped like a saddlebag, face down over the saddle, and tried to pad his face comfortably against the jiggling ride. His eyes suddenly opened and looked around him in terror. Then they fluttered shut, and he groaned.

"We're going to help you," Dick told him, walking alongside as the donkey lurched away. "Everything is going to be all right." The party set off. Chloe, looking around behind her up at the cliff, saw the little cave boys, watching them and drinking the Pepsi they had brought for the picnic and left behind.

"Dear me, what a pity," said Heidi suddenly to her fellow Englishwoman, Mrs. Henderson. "What a sad ending to our outing."

"Yes, dear me," said Mrs. Henderson.

From time to time Chloe looked ahead, with mingled curiosity and dread, to where the moribund figure flopped against the thigh of the donkey. A dying man is an inconvenience on a picnic. Dr. Yazdi pushed by the women and hurried off down the trail, saying he would get the car and be waiting with the engine running at the bottom. They would rush the man to the hospital. It made Chloe somewhat anxious to reflect that though this was a party of six doctors, not one of them appeared to have done anything to help the man. They were doing no more than anyone could do. You preferred to think that doctors could do miracles, but of course they cannot.

At the bottom, with all haste they laid the poor man on the cloak stretched out in the back of the station wagon. Junie and Dick crawled in beside him and crouched over him during the ride. Chloe and Zareeneh sat in front with Dr. Yazdi while Abbas drove the other car. They hastened along the gravelly road. Too energetic speculation was curtailed by ideas of seemliness, in case he was, in his coma, able to hear them. A too-intrepid hiker, they imagined, venturing down there without a flashlight, or with weak batteries. Chloe could not take her eyes off his bloodied hair, of a light brown color, slightly curly, and soft like the hair of a child. Junie stroked the hair off his forehead, and his eyes flickered open.

"I don't like the sound of his breathing," she whispered.

"Pardon!" said the man indistinctly.

"Shhh, shhh," said Junie, holding his wrist.

"He might have been looking for something," Chloe said. "Archaeological, I mean. He could be a scholar or spelunker."

"Oh," cried Junie, "I think this is it." She leaned forward, listening at his lips. She shook him a little. "This is really frustrating. Can't you hurry?"

The car was hurtling along the road at a speed far faster than safe. Zareeneh and Chloe both clutched the dashboard.

"Yeah, I think he's gone," said Dick surprisedly. "Well, the poor bastard." He and Junie began to thump on the chest of the man, who in fact looked the same as he had moments before. But gradually to Chloe's eyes an indefinable deadness seemed to solidify him, even his torn trousers and his socks.

Junie pressed her mouth to his dead mouth in a terrible
embrace, which Chloe realized was really resuscitation, but
Dick shook his head. Whatever had happened could not be
reversed. Gradually they sighed and sat up, and arranged the
cloths around him. Chloe saw Junie wipe her eyes. Dr. Yazdi
drove as fast as before.

Dick wondered if he wanted a cigarette. If he was ever going
to backslide, this would be the logical time. He wanted a
cigarette, but it was a pallid inclination, not a violent craving,
and could be resisted; it was like sex, sometimes, or like
looking in a store window at something you thought you
wanted. Just a stir. He was pleased. It was no more than
looking in the L. L. Bean catalogue, or Orvis at the most.

Presently Junie, who had been staring bitterly at the dead
man, crawled toward the front seat, to his feet, and began to
pull at his shoestrings. It seemed a bit late.

"Torture," she said. "It's just a hunch. You often find
something on the soles of the feet."

It seemed to Chloe that a flicker of dismay crossed Ali
Yazdi's features. Perhaps he was offended that torture was the
first thing foreigners in Iran would think of, the way
Americans are offended when Europeans go on and on about
mugging.

Junie had taken off the shoe, a new crepe-soled shoe, and
was pulling off the sock, Dick watching with an expression of
revulsion exactly reflecting Chloe's feelings. Zareeneh Yazdi,
who had never ceased to shudder, buried her face in her hands,
but Chloe couldn't help but look. The sole of his foot was pale
as alabaster, untouched, untortured. Junie began nevertheless
to tear off the other sock. She flung it crossly away. Dick
recovered both socks and put them in his pocket. Junie put the
shoes back on the dead feet.

"The police. Clues. Don't you watch cop shows?" They
laughed, but uncomfortably, wondering if there were police of
the regular sort here. You only thought of secret police
knocking in the night, but of course there must also be ordinary
police to deal with the ordinary matters of murder, traffic
accidents, wife beating. The laughter and the thought of
television eased the oddness, the sadness, strangeness.

The two autos arrived at Abbas's house, whence they had

started. It was now late afternoon. They alighted and stood around irresolutely. It seemed wrong to say goodbye and shuffle off to do something else; all seemed to feel that by mere presence they could somehow dignify this unexpected event, or that they would be needed by the police, or something. Perhaps others were as reluctant as Chloe to return to a solitary apartment to meditate on the unexpected way that death can appear at a picnic and take you away.

Abbas Mowlavi's idea, and Ali Yazdi agreed with him, was to take the body to the Pathology Department, to determine there the cause of death, meantime notifying the police. Ali Yazdi went off to find orderlies to carry the body. But evidently he encountered Vahid Farmani on the way, for he was back in no time, looking exasperated, accompanied by Vahid, who was shouting in great agitation and wringing his hands in violent distress, almost as if he knew the man, though he did not even glance at him. Vahid shouted in Farsi, and Ali and Abbas answered in more reasonable tones, but the others understood none of it. Presently Ali, looking angry, pulled the station wagon into Abbas's carport, with the dead stranger still inside. Vahid Farmani, coming a little to himself, looked at the English speakers and explained, with unconvincing calm, "It has nothing to do with this hospital; the correct thing to do is to take him immediately to the police. Perhaps you could all— not the ladies—go along. Dr. Henderson, Dr. Rothblatt, you, Abbas, of course."

He rushed off. The men piled into the Volvo and drove off to the police station without goodbyes. Zareeneh Yazdi excused herself too. Heidi, Mrs. Henderson, Junie, and Chloe, shaken and eager to talk, decided to go have a drink in the bar of the Hotel Cyrus. Later, writing her postcards in the dim night light of Villa Two, Chloe put only that she had been on a picnic and had a chance to ride a donkey. Could Jeffrey read between the lines her agitated spirit?

Not too much longer before we are all together. Love to Dad and you both.

Mom

Chapter Eleven

THE LOAN

Perplext no more with Human or Divine,
To-morrow's tangle to the winds resign,
And lose your fingers in the tresses of
Thy Cypress-slender Minister of Wine.

The dogs in the night seemed close under her window. She woke with a pang of worry about her family, then Rustum, then Hugh, and then lay awake turning over the strange events of the day with a dawning fearfulness on her own behalf. Until now she had felt safe, even well cared for, in Shiraz, but it was as if she had been injected with some poison of new apprehensiveness, which she could feel proceed through her body like hemlock. At home, after a near miss with the car, after an instant on a swaying stepladder, she had felt fear in a rush and then righted herself, but this fear was systemic, settling over her like a new condition: she was not at home here, but far away where the rules and ideas were not the same and no one was especially designated to look out for her, and people came into your room, and if you died you might be put down in a cave.

The shoes of the dead stranger remained in her memory, clear, especially poignant. Brand new, some kind of Hush Puppies. Why was there something especially poignant about shoes? Shoes are symbols of life and hope. If you knew you were going to die you would not buy yourself a new pair of shoes. When but in choosing new shoes are you ever so legitimately self-absorbed, moving your toes inside them, feeling the stiff, resisting backs, wondering how you will look in them? She thought of the poor little Iranian men she had seen in the bazaar, with their wild, hunted eyes; she imagined them standing at stalls wondering how they would look in new shoes. Every poor person—maybe not in Africa—sometime has a new pair of shoes. When you die your shoes remain; they represent you. You must always have neat, well-tended shoes; her mother had told her this, she had told her children. Even now they had begun to be careful of their shoes. In a foreign land you might die—in a cave, in the river, like the wife and baby of Abbas, or like the women at the hospital when Junie Fay could not save them. Where was Hugh?

Of course she had not really believed Iran would be a foreign land. She saw the deficiency in her imagination, that she had not been able to imagine with sufficient intensity the alien condition. A well-traveled American with no anxieties about hotels, headwaiters, planes—her imagination had provided her with no more than a benign region of camels, and mosques, and well-run hospitals of the American kind.

Even the difficulties—she thought of her outrage at the state of the kitchen, the rugs—had not seemed beyond the power of an indignant woman who was in the right, a woman with standards that no one could seriously question. She had assumed she could put things right, as always. Now she saw that this presumption was naïve, limited, unimaginative, and wrong. She felt her own foolishness. Tears of pity for the poor dead man came to her eyes, and at the same time a feeling of gladness that these correct sensations of fright and humbleness had come to her in time. She was cured of her American presumptions. This was all good for her. What had the man in the cave thought, realizing he was going to die so far away in Iran? This is real, she thought with a shiver. I am not at home here.

Noosheen, in the morning, by the mysterious process that served in the absence of what Chloe considered working telephones, had already heard the news. She had heard it from Heidi. They drank tea in the morning sun in the garden. Geraniums, dry in their pots, bloomed charmingly, and the world recovered something of its normal aspect.

"It must have been horrible for poor Abbas," Noosheen remarked. "I should think such a thing would make him think of the past—you know," talking as usual, Chloe noticed, of "poor Abbas," though when Chloe saw him he always appeared to be smiling and relaxed, addressing himself to some practical matter in the present and not romantically harrowed by his recent tragedy. But Chloe could see how Noosheen might imagine in him some attractive melancholy, especially when compared to the mundane, elderly Bahram. Chloe encouraged Noosheen to talk about Abbas, which she always seemed eager to do, elaborating on his brilliance, the excellence of his education, the bravery with which he had faced sorrow. "He is my true brother. I have always thought of him as my own brother," she said. Chloe thought it must be hard for a young woman like Noosheen, finding herself on the cusp of social change, aware that elsewhere in the world—America, for instance—women had lovers, divorces, married for love, to be herself disposed of in the old-fashioned way. Noosheen told about her marriage. Bahram, a widower, friend of her parents, had paid them a formal visit, almost as if he were another, new person, to ask for her hand. "It was very exciting at the time," Noosheen said. "Ah well. I cannot stay long today. I have a new washing woman, and I cannot bear her, so after I dropped the children and the nurse in the park I came here. The washing woman looks at me with scorn because I am so Westernized, I know, but the pity is I am not so Western I do not mind the stares of certain old women. I suppose they remind me of my grandmother. My mother is a perfectly modern woman in most ways."

"Old women always try to make young ones feel guilty," Chloe said. "We must remember to never do that when we get old."

"If I had a washing machine I think I could control my life much better," Noosheen said. "Another woman to deal with, it's just too much. An ordinary Maytag, like any American woman, it's not much to ask."

They proceeded to talk of "Empedocles on Etna," and Chloe marveled at the shapeless property of poetry: it was like a big sack, to hold whatever it was you were thinking of.

> *The weary man, the banished citizen,*
> *Whose banishment is not his greatest ill,*
> *Whose weariness no energy can reach,*

> *And for whose hurt courage is not the cure—*
> *What should I do with life and living more?*

This made her think of the dead man in the cave, or even of
herself, of course, except for not being a man. Noosheen had
been caught by other lines, sometimes puzzling ones. When
they came upon the lines

> *But the solitude oppresses thy votary!*
> *The jars of men reach him not in thy valley—*

she looked at Chloe with the faintest suggestion of confusion,
as if to ask what are the jars of men? When Chloe told her—
noises, rude interruptions—it seemed to her that Noosheen
pinkened a little. Goodness knew what she had thought men's
jars were.

> *And we shall be the strangers of the world,*
> *And they will be our lords, as they are now;*
> *And keep us prisoners of our consciousness,*
> *And never let us clasp and feel the All*
> *But through their forms, and modes, and stifling veils.*
> *And we shall be unsatisfied as now;*
> *And we shall feel the agony of thirst,*
> *The ineffable longing for the life of life*
> *Baffled for ever . . .*

At the mention of veils, Noosheen cried out, "How true,
how true!" Earnestly, in the warm sunlight, they discussed
pessimism. As she was about to leave Noosheen said pessi-
mistically, "Once you get used to an automatic washer, it's
hard to go back."

Noosheen's visit, as welcome as always, today afforded relief
from the fears of the night and memories of yesterday, or
perhaps it was the poetry that had made Chloe feel better. Here
was an ordinary day, an ordinary visit from a woman friend,
tea, lawn chairs, problems of love and laundry. When
Noosheen had gone, Chloe piled the cups on the steps for

Hossein to carry up when he came at noon, and she went along to the shops to buy her groceries. This was always enjoyable; because it involved transactions with real Iranians, she was left with the feeling that she became each day more in touch with the life of Iran.

Chloe was sorry to be cut off from the real Iranians, to whom she could never speak, yet she could peer into their lives—the mother sitting on the ground unwrapping meat and handing it around to the children, the men staring into distance, holding their beads, sitting on the benches in Azami Compound, waiting outside the hospital; or the crisp little nurses in their white half-veils, or the typists coming out of the office buildings at the university, in bright clothes and gold earrings, swaying in high heels. She would have liked to be a friend of one of these families and visit them and see into their house: what phonograph records did they have, what did they talk about; what did the taxi driver say, going home at the end of the day? Or Hossein? Did he talk to his wife? Did he berate her or laugh with her? The women talked and chatted in the bazaar, the men muttered and smoked, glaring out of their stalls, people dozed in the sunny noon hour, or sat unmoving on their haunches at the edge of the road. Some thin, tormented souls were chained to opium.

When she got back to Villa Two, she lingered outside to make sure Hossein had finished her room, then took her milk and eggs up to the refrigerator. It was not so much that she dreaded to meet him as her feeling that he dreaded to meet her. His eyes always slid away from her, burning strangely. Today he had gone, but he had brought the mail and laid it as always on the pillow of her cot, an odd gesture of intimacy from a person who never looked at her directly.

On top a letter bearing an Iranian stamp, in an elegant envelope of thin paper with flowers of blue and gilt surrounding the name of the Hotel Shah Abbas in Isfahan. She knew the writing to be Hugh Monroe's, though she was not sure what he wrote like. Despite her excitement, she opened the envelope with great care, thinking that she could put the beautiful envelope up on her wall.

A note. Her eye went to the signature. Hugh.

Dear Jeff and Chloe:
   I plan to be here in Isfahan this weekend, at this
hotel. As everyone says you must see Isfahan, that
goes for you too. I'll make you a reservation, and hope
you can come up after work on Thursday night, or
even on Friday, if Allah permits the planes to fly then.
                                        Best, Hugh

That was all. She looked at the envelope with a sense of deep
anticlimax. No explanation of his absence, no special clever
between-the-lines hint of his fondness for her. Nonetheless, joy
and relief welled up in her, and then a start of alarm when she
realized that Friday was yesterday, and that Hugh would have
given up on them. She prepared to rush to the airline office,
then remembered it would be closed until four. She paced in
frustration.

"Chloe, are you home?" Dick Rothblatt called outside her
window. She peeked out and waved, and he headed up her
stairs. He was coming from the American consulate, he said,
where he had been at the insistence of Vahid Farmani, to see
about the dead body.

"Because I'm an American—though Abbas came too—
Vahid thinks I speak for dead Americans wherever they turn
up."

"*Was* he an American? Do they know who it was?"

"They don't know. The police thought he was. They'd have
nothing to do with him. Then we went to the Consulate and the
American consul took fingerprints, but he said he was quite
sure he wasn't American. Who knows? There were no labels in
his clothes. And his haircut—what did you think?"

"Have you had lunch? Would you like something?"

"Well—sure. We could go eat at the hospital."

"I have hardboiled eggs. I could make egg salad."

"I'd have a beer?"

"Wine? I like the wine here."

"Fine. The funny thing was Vahid. He was on the phone to
the consulate shouting at them—'It has nothing to do with us.
Leave Azami out of it. It has nothing to do with Azami'—you
got to thinking, Jesus Christ, maybe it does."

"Vahid has a hard life—crazy American doctors, dead bodies," said Chloe, her tone expressing her dislike of Vahid.

"The epidemic is getting worse. Three people have died. In the olden days hundreds of people would have died."

"I must have misunderstood him," Chloe said, thinking that Dr. Farmani had told her there was no typhoid.

"This really is a dump," Dick said, looking around at Chloe's room. The remark surprised her. She had thought she was making some headway, and had sewed a red and green pillowcase out of a flowered fabric from the bazaar, to put over her pillow during the day, and the rest of the piece was draped over the sofa like a slipcover.

"I could give you my rug, you know, loan it to you. I'm getting another one; I've about decided on that Sinneh."

"That would be wonderful," Chloe said, seeing that Dick's rug would add a lot to the room.

"Sure, I'll bring it over later," he said, realizing, though too late, that Junie might be a little irked. He did not feel that Junie was very aesthetic-minded. Her taste was not equal to Marla's, whose keen glance dismissed a hemline, a color, and told him what he needed to know or think about someone's dress, not that she was so damned infallible, but she knew more than Junie, who, after all, had more important matters on her mind. Junie surely wouldn't feel the lack of the rug, temporarily, but she might take offense anyway, as if this were in some way a pass at Chloe Fowler or—he reached nearer the truth of his intuition—as if this were a gesture of affection to Chloe standing in for Marla—Chloe another legal wife, like Marla, whose whims took precedence over those of unmarried women. Dick did not always, he knew, understand women so accurately. Usually they accused him of not understanding, or of being not understanding, which they explained was not the same thing but equally his crime. But he knew he had got to the truth of Junie's probable reaction.

And of course he had got to like Chloe, for her own sake. It was interesting how you seldom got to know the wives of your colleagues. He had always thought of her as a pretty appendage to Jeffrey Fowler, whom he thought a stiffish but pleasant surgeon, more intellectual and less of a fool than most surgeons. Whereas she was really herself, a rather odd woman whose views were often the categorical opposite of Junie's. She was an extremist, vehement like Junie, maybe all women were. He believed that vehemence was sometimes a substitute for sense. Chloe announced once that she was an anti-vivisectionist. That was funny from a woman whose husband did medical research. Once she had remarked that frigidity was a moral defect, a symptom of selfish egotism, and Dick had felt mildly defensive on Junie's behalf.

"I don't know," he said, "haven't you ever just had an inept lover? Sometimes it's just an inept lover."

"I don't think I have," said Chloe, "but maybe I'm just too easily pleased."

Dick had thought that, although this was good news from Chloe's point of view, from a man's point of view you would never know whether you had specially pleased her. You liked to think that you had specially given someone pleasure that another had not, that you were the best lover. He thought of the poem by Browning, read in—my God, high school—where the husband killed the duchess who smiled at everyone.

How could you tell about frigidity anyway? If they scrunched up their eyes and groaned a little how could you tell? Maybe other men could tell. Women told him he was good, except Marla, who only told him when he wasn't good, and Junie, who never bothered to dissemble. How could you tell? It was a subject he had never heard discussed. If only men discussed sex more, the way women do. He had always been shocked at the things Marla told him she had heard from, or told, her women friends, things no man would mention. Anyway, Junie, even if slightly frigid, was not a selfish egotist as Chloe would have it.

What he had liked about Junie, when she was a medical student in dermatology, was her scorn for dermatology, her need for more dynamic afflictions, her restless competence, as if mere boils and rashes couldn't calm her. This was secretly the way Dick sometimes felt himself, although he told himself and her that if she got beyond the prevailing hospital population of drug reactions and mild dermatitises she would see the interest in your lupus, your pemphigus, your jungle rot. But she had gone on to OB-GYN, become a resident there, then chief resident, and he never saw her except in the doctors' dining room, where he remembered her, a cute kid.

Then he had gone down to the OB service to consult about a baby born with thrush so severe it appeared to have been dipped in oatmeal, the very look of it had scared her, and her fright, in turn, had been endearing; her eyes grew large and tearful whenever she looked at the pitiful, itchy little thing or thought of how the mother would feel to see it. After this, they had coffee occasionally, and he began to confide in her. It was at a shaky point in his marriage, he was having a battle over space with the chest service, and was suffering a painful tear of the achilles tendon (tennis).

"My roommate's gone this weekend," she had pointed out one afternoon late, meeting him in the elevator. They exchanged an unmistakable look. "I'll fix you some supper at my place." The roommate, the chief surgical resident, was a man, which he only found out later.

She had grabbed for his cock the minute they were in the door of her apartment, and they'd made it, him wearing his cast, and then gone back to the hospital together later to look at their patients. Quite a large proportion of the residents and interns were women these days, which did have this terrific advantage. Both he and Junie had got to really like, or love, each other besides. He remembered she had actually made the supper too, smoked salmon and cream on pasta, after they had made love and ward rounds.

If Junie complained that the rug was gone, he would point out to her the real source of her objections—jealousy of Marla; meantime he went over to his apartment, rolled the rug, and carried it back to Villa Two, where it did improve Chloe's room a hell of a lot. Dick thought Chloe was being very brave about Jeff's absence; it was now a couple of weeks she had been here alone.

It was only after he had gone that Chloe, looking with satisfaction at the room, which seemed livelier and improved beyond measure by the rug, saw on her pillow another letter, this from Jeffrey.

> I just thought you would want to know the results
> of my conference with Max's summer-school teacher.
> He is behind in math, for one thing, but more alarm-
> ing to me was her feeling that he is a lonesome little

boy, who needs more hugging and physical reassurance. She says she takes him on her lap almost every
day, whenever she can. I had strong feeling she thinks
of him as virtually a neglected child. Of course I know
you don't neglect him, but you can imagine how she
received my information that his mother was in Iran!

He was not sure when he could fly out. More later. Love,
Jeff. Irked beyond measure, Chloe flung the letter on the
bureau and hurried out to try to buy her airline ticket to Isfahan.

Chapter Twelve

DIRTY LAUNDRY

> *A Hair perhaps divides the False and True;*
> *Yes; and a single Alif were the clue—*
> *Could you but find it—to the Treasure-house,*
> *And peradventure to The Master too.*

Getting to Isfahan was perfectly simple, many flights daily, pay with your Amex. Chloe wavered about whether to wait until morning or take a flight that night at seven, knowing it would be more sensible to wait till morning, when if Hugh was not there, or if she was unable to get a hotel room, she could nonetheless look around Isfahan and come back. But it was hard to think of passing a lonely evening in the silence of Villa Two, or even at the Cyrus, when she might be with Hugh; and after all the Shah Abbas was probably a perfectly straightforward hotel, state-owned like the Cyrus, where they spoke English and tourism was encouraged. The mysteries of a taxi in Isfahan were the most she had to fear. Isfahan was after all not a cave. She booked for the night flight and went back to Villa Two to throw her things together. In the taxi to the airport she remembered that she should have put some food out for Rustum. She was not sure he could forage for himself now that she had been providing, and feared that he had been spoiled by civilization.

It was exciting to see Shiraz drop away below, proof that, wherever you are, you needn't stay there. The city looked small and dignified in the twilight, a tiny green patch on the wide brown plain. You could not have said it was Persia or anywhere else, it was just the world. She had the pleasant sense of competence that goes with travel.

Once buckled in, she could reflect upon her situation with Hugh. Arriving without Jeffrey would make it perfectly clear that she meant to go through with something they had only spoken of hypothetically, in the course of some impassioned kissing—an illicit weekend, something so relatively hard to arrange in America, in their respective situations, that it had the glamour of the unattainable. Chloe, and, she trusted, Hugh too, hadn't given up hope of some furtive embraces, maybe at a medical meeting, but unfortunately, because Jeffrey was a surgeon and Hugh an internist, they didn't often go to the same ones. Now the delightful presence of opportunity filled her with happiness and desire, and some misgivings too in case Hugh was not quite ready to have this sprung on him. But what kind of man, in that case, would he be?

Next to her a plump Iranian businessman who said to call him Teddy, and whose necktie was Gucci, told her to look below them, as they approached Isfahan, at the moonscape of brown mounds, like elaborate tunnels, pushing up the earth of the desert.

"Those are the qanats," he said, "tunnels that draw off the moisture of the desert to water the town. They are a mystery that no one has ever understood except the builders of the qanats; it is an age-old secret."

"How wonderful," said Chloe. How wonderful that there are still marvels, strange races of qanat builders. It meant that your own life could become strange.

In Isfahan, with great equanimity, she commanded a taxi and pronounced the name of the hotel. Driving through the streets, she could almost feel she wouldn't mind if Hugh was not there, it was so beautiful, so fabled and fanciful, the cobbled streets, arched porches, mosques. The voices called from minarets. The dusk promised wonders in tomorrow's sunshine of azure and cerulean tile, resplendent domes of shining blue. The shapes of the arches bespoke a confusion of successions, some for the better, some for the worse, of Achaemenians, Sassanians, Macedonians, and Mongols. Over the city, the lights had begun to go on. Chloe exclaimed in pleasure and anticipation. The taxi driver told her in good English that the tallest tower in the huge mosque behind them had once been entirely filled up, by the bloody Tamburlaine, with human skulls.

The Hotel Shah Abbas, built from a palace of the great Shah, was so beautiful, vast, and sumptuous that Chloe at once decided to stay a day or two whether Hugh was there or not. It was funny to imagine Jeffrey getting a huge Amex bill with lots of charges for caviar. She had expected there would be more caviar in Iran than there had been. Well, so far there hadn't been any.

She asked for Dr. Monroe, was given his room number, and motioned toward the house phone. But he was not in his room. She settled, not discontentedly, in the beautiful lobby to wait and watch the other guests, rich-looking tourists with smart luggage, the sight of whom affected her with a sort of pleasurable trance. She tried not to think directly of the happiness of seeing Hugh, but rather let the prospect warm her obliquely. Two women with cameras sat near her speaking French. Within the interior courtyard, visible through the long windows, fountains splashed at either end of a magnificent longwater. A scent of jasmine everywhere.

Hugh came in almost immediately. The Frenchwomen, whom Chloe was watching, saw him, and, following their appreciative glance, Chloe saw him, a handsome man, not in jail or dead, walking in, carrying a plastic bag, looking tall and Western in his pink oxford-cloth shirt. Her idea of the scale of men's size had altered slightly since she had been in Iran so that he seemed huge. She half rose, gave a little wave, and was seen by him. He approached, smiling the formal, delighted smile of someone who discovers a friend in a hotel lobby.

He kissed her cheek. "You got my letter. I was afraid you wouldn't."

"Yes," Chloe said.

"Where's Jeff?"

Chloe grinned. Hugh was astounded, disbelieving, but looked sincerely jubilant when she told him. Jeffrey somehow in America, Chloe here alone, with him. Chloe watched his expression for signs of discomfort but it was impeccably of happiness.

"I booked a room for you and Jeffrey," Hugh said. "But of course it'd be nicer if we stayed together." He led her toward the elevator, past the desk. Despite her intention of going straight to bed with him, with no priggish demur, she felt herself blush, mind floundering around after a perky remark.

Hugh's expression was perfect, not leering or knowing. "Shall I say we won't want it?" he asked.

She heard herself laugh nervously. It was scary going to bed with someone for the first time. The urgency, something clumsy always sure to happen. The possibility of disappointment on either side. She stole a glance at the size of his hands. Strong, manly large hands. She imagined her own body creased with red puckers caused by the elastic in her bra and pantyhose, or wrinkled with cellulite.

"My wife has arrived, but not Dr. Fowler, so he won't be needing his room," said Hugh to the man at the desk. At the elevator he held her back so that another couple could get in and ascend alone. She wished she were perfect, unmarked. Moist sensations of desire. In the elevator Hugh kissed her very ardently. When a couple got in at the mezzanine, they got off and walked the second flight to Hugh's room, so they could clutch each other rapturously in the passages.

He carried her across the threshold of his room.

"This is it, then," he said, smiling at her. She smiled too. Harmless adventure, was her thought. It will make me a better wife. Where has he been these past two weeks?

He began to kiss her and to unbutton her blouse. "Beautiful Chloe," he sighed. Chloe bloomed under his touch. Really, not making love for two weeks, it was bad for you, she wasn't used to it, you needed a man's attention. His chest was hairy and broad. He took off his glasses. It was going to be easy. It was going to go forward smoothly. What was behind it, this wish to have a particular person inside you? It will be terrible if we fall in love, thought Chloe, rapturously clasping him with her knees as he entered her. Her heart overflowed with love and sensation.

Their passion was enhanced by the uncertainty of their situation, by the separation, and by the tracery shadows falling softly through the drawn screen and the musical sound of splashing water in the courtyard below. It was even nice that there was no artificial air-conditioning, thought Chloe, lying contentedly, but warmly sticky, in Hugh's arms. It was the more exotic, the more Persian, the more meriting this unlikely trip. It was the sort of night to look back on, when you were an old woman, as a perfect one, and a perfect evening is more, she imagined, than many people have their whole lives long. She couldn't remember ever, with Jeffrey, having this powerful intimation of the beauty of love-making, and of its connection to the antiquity of the world. Chloe stroked Hugh's large, sunburned back. His hair was fair; he must burn easily. How she loved him. There was also the fun of having got away with something. She realized that she had not really thought of her children all day. I am not happy, I am not lucky, she told herself, lying, for fear that happiness and luck would bring down something bad on them. On the wall a little picture bordered in flowers showed a warrior on a white horse riding toward them waving his sword, and ladies under a tree laughing.

Hugh was Chloe's second-and-a-half affair. She prided herself on being immune to or above matters of erotic fashion, as propounded, for instance, in ladies' magazines, which seemed indeed to affect her friends, who were now becoming lesbians, looking romantically at boys of seventeen, or speaking of the new chastity. She thought of herself as old-fashioned; that is, she had reservations about divorce, and certainly did not believe in open marriage, and did believe in adultery of the old-fashioned scary sneaking-around kind. She saw that it could easily happen to you that you might fall in love with someone or want someone to whom you weren't married, and that this was a well-known pitfall of life, or perhaps a reward for taking seriously the responsibilities of adulthood. So she had been pleased to have this happen to her very pleasantly and so far without consequence. The only problem she foresaw with Hugh was that she could fall seriously in love with him, but she felt protected by the fact of his living in Rochester, New York.

Their natural affinity and sympathy had become gradually apparent during his sabbatical in San Francisco, when they found themselves laughing at the same things, ordering the same things in restaurants, once or twice a glint of sympathy from Hugh when Jeffrey behaved like Jeffrey in some especially boring way, usually by announcing just as others were going off to hear the balalaikas in the square that he and Chloe were tired and going home. Hint of a glance from Hugh, nothing indiscreet, nothing tactlessly critical, for Chloe was a loyal wife, in a way. Just a note of fellow feeling. Then she was seized by terrible gloom when his sabbatical was nearly over, and found herself looking around rooms for him at parties where they both might be. Alone together once or twice on strolls around gardens, they fell into amazed embraces. After her involvement with Hugh, Chloe became, she felt, more beautiful, and much nicer to Jeffrey. But then Hugh had gone back to his usual life as a professor of medicine in Rochester. He had been married twice, she had heard, though he had only mentioned once, and was recently divorced. She didn't really know him very well.

"Now," said Chloe—for they were hungry, were dressing, were going to go down—"Why didn't you call? Everyone in Shiraz thinks you've been arrested. I would say they were frantic, but they seemed rather sanguine, I thought. I was afraid to death. 'Detained,' they said. Dick Rothblatt and I tried calling various hotels. Well—were you arrested?"

"I didn't realize people were worrying," he said blithely. They had found an invitation in their room:

Dear Guest:
Welcome to Shah Abbas Hotel. You have been one of us since only a few days or a few hours. I will be pleased to meet you tonight between 6pm and 7pm at a business cocktail on your honor. Certainly, you will meet other hotel guests which might be an opportunity for a new deal!
Sincerely yours, The Management

"Certainly we should check this out," said Hugh.

At one end of the lobby, in a lounge off the bar, they found a number of foreigners in various groups, sipping very small cocktails presented from trays by circling waiters, and the management, a dark, bowing man, shook their hands. In another mood perhaps they would step forward and speak to the French ladies, or to the businessmen in their ties. As it was, they wanted only to talk to each other. Chloe again brought up the subject of Hugh's absence, feeling, as she complained to him, her resentments rise, as at a found child. She'd been so worried.

"I thought you were in jail; we all did. We called the Hilton—Dick Rothblatt and I—and we spoke to the American consul in Shiraz—he was supposed to be checking." But Hugh only laughed to hear of all this concern. He hadn't sent word because he didn't know they were worrying.

"But it was indeed trouble with my visa. I had to go back to London and wait for one. I'd forgotten to get one. I arrived with no visa, and they wouldn't let me in. I telephoned Guz Mohadim at the Tehran medical school to see if anyone could do anything and no one could. I had to turn around and go back to London—one good thing, Pan Am had to pay—some rule because they had forgotten to ask me if I had a visa. Otherwise I would have been out seven hundred bucks into the bargain."

"It's funny you didn't go to Tel Aviv, or someplace closer than London."

"You had to go back to where you came from."

"You'd been in London?"

"For a few days," Hugh said. "And never once thought of looking to see if I had an Iranian visa."

Hugh was quixotic, Chloe had observed before. Maybe that was why he had been divorced twice, once more than was normal for people their age. Quixotic, mysterious.

Would revelations, intimacies, emerge in the unexpected companionship of days or weeks relatively free of concern about being caught? Chloe felt a little worried about that. An affair might owe its charm to the excitement of agreeable danger. Also, she had so little to reveal, she believed. She felt inwardly ordinary and uncomplicated and was afraid that her plain personality would not support intimacy. Surrounded suddenly by the complicated beauty of the Persian décor, and by the mystery of Hugh, she felt herself to have no reserve of mystery, no temperament sufficient to intrigue others, no self-consciousness or demands. The demands of demanding beauties, she had noticed, were usually met, but she never had any. She could hardly, for example, demand fidelity from Jeffrey, even if he had been inclined to infidelity, which he was not. His vices were his work and his woodshop. Even as a child she had wondered at films where the pregnant woman experiences a craving for pickles and makes the man jump up and go out in the night. During her pregnancies she wouldn't have dreamed of bothering poor Jeffrey, who worked much harder than she did, but what was worse, she had experienced no unusual cravings. She regretted this curse of reasonableness, and longed to be, but knew she could never be, flamboyant.

Hugh's very blitheness was part of his mystery, for two divorces, if that was true, hinted at complications of character, of intriguing difficulties, though in the long run she hoped nothing really sinister, like parsimony or an overwhelming affection for his mother. For the moment it was enough to be in a splendid hotel with this handsome man, to lie, later, in his arms again. The catch of being his wife would be that other women would always be chasing him, maybe just as she had. Had she? She allowed herself, as they stood side by side in the cocktail reception, smiling and greeting others, to enjoy the idea that other people would believe them to be husband and wife.

They had dinner in the hotel dining room. In Hugh's opinion the dinner was not very good, but it was wonderful to Chloe, which showed how her standards had changed in the two weeks she'd been in Iran. They had caviar, which was splendid, but it was brought with thick slices of some American sort of white bread like Wonder bread; Hugh grumbled. Maybe he was a person who fussed at his wives about their cooking?

They had coffee in the garden. The dome of a mosque was reflected in the moonlit long garden pool. Little lanterns bobbed over the heads of the French tourists at other tables. "Très jolie, jolie, jolie," was murmured everywhere. Then they went again to their room, which smelt of sex, like caviar, to enjoy each other again.

When they had sunk into the sleep of the love satisfied, entwined as Persian flowers, they were startled by knocking at their door. They dragged themselves awake. Hugh pulled his trousers on and opened the door. Chloe cowered, indiscriminately fearing a variety of things—morals police, Jeffrey, a fire in the corridor.

An Iranian man in a turtleneck sweater, thuggish-looking but somehow familiar, thrust into the room, with a furtive glance backward down the corridor. Robbery, Savak?

"Hey," said Hugh, backing away. "What do you want?"

"You were in the restaurant tonight," said the man, his tone accusing.

"What of it?" said Hugh, his indignation growing as his head cleared. "Get out of here."

The man pulled a paper out of his inside pocket. "You signed this check?" He confronted Hugh with the dinner check.

"Yes, of course. There."

"Yes, but see, you signed it in red."

"For God's sake," said Hugh. "What of it? My pen was red."

"Red, sir, that is not legal. I think the American Express would not pay."

"Of course they would pay. Give it to me, give me your pen." Irascibly he snatched the check and scribbled his name again. Yes, it was their waiter, Chloe recognized him now. He didn't move.

"Also you did not give a tip," he said.

"Certainly I did," said Hugh, looking at the check again. "There."

"That is the hotel, the hotel keep that," said the man.

"It says 'Waiter.' That's for you. American Express pays that too." Hugh frowned and zipped his fly.

"Yes, but the hotel doesn't give. You pay a cash tip . . . ."

Now they could hear that it was desperation in his voice; it was not the voice of a swindler. Hugh snatched bills from the dresser. "Here. Please go," he said. The man was thin and anxious.

He stared at the money in his hand. He seemed to wish to complain of it, then his shoulders lowered, an expression of relief and chagrin crossed his face. He shrugged and stepped backward out the door.

"I never thought we would get to spend a whole night together," murmured Chloe to Hugh when he was back in bed. She wrapped her arms contentedly around him, but Hugh thrashed about, eyes open, disturbed. "The poor bastard. The hotel takes the tip and all. Did you see his clothes?" he said. It crossed Chloe's mind that she must be growing callous; had not noticed the man's poor clothes, his thinness.

* * *

In the morning, hand in hand, Chloe and Hugh wander in the streets. The great Shah Abbas had made the wonders of Isfahan to glorify himself and God in that order. They are stunned by the worldly beauty of the palace, the mosques, the school for holy study now partly converted into their hotel, the polo field where Chloe and Hugh can imagine ancient Persians in rich raiment at their games, and along the edges of the bazaar merchants then as now crouched over wares; calling to one another. Isfahan—so Chloe had read—had been taken by Achaemenids, and Sassanids, and Arabs, and Mongols, Safavids and Greeks, tribes from everywhere, vainglorious leaders, bloody scenes. She and Hugh feel daunted by the evident superiority of this panoply to their own short and skimpy history of sickly pilgrims and a few covered wagons going west. From Omar Khayyam to Sweet Betsy from Pike. In this wall, on that turret, in that grave lie the ornaments of Cyrus and Darius, Alexander the Great, Suleiman the Turk who had eluded the Crusaders, Tamburlaine, Genghis, and numberless other khans. Vainglorious Shah Abbas, to dress his city in such richness of decoration, such intricacy of carving, such fanciful surface, such yellows and blue. The water of the long pools reflects God; flowers bloom untended, as in Paradise.

Hugh Monroe and Chloe, conscientious sightseers, trudge for miles in the dusty streets, ravished by admiration, Chloe clutching her Minox. People stare, friendly enough. "Ciao," call the little boys. A woman says of Hugh "too tall." Chloe photographs, along a wall of the bazaar, a row of plows painted blue. She buys a tile, and plans to put it on the wall of her room. She thinks of painting the wall of her room, or at least the door, this sacred turquoise they use here.

The effects of the beauty—its properties elevating to the spirits and glorifying to God—are somewhat diminished in Chloe's view by the sight of men with machine guns everywhere, and this seems ill-advised too in view of the Shah's expressed wish to encourage tourism.

The Shah probably doesn't realize how this militarism looks. In France, Chloe had never liked the hordes of police around the Place de la Concorde either. Probably it is just that if you were a nice American, you had learned in the sixties—she proposed this to Hugh—to be jittery of police, because you had run up against them on peace marches. This had happened to her, calm and law-abiding though she was, and it had turned her against police.

She had been visiting Alice, her sister, in Los Angeles, and they had gone on a peace march, along with all Alice's friends and the people where she worked. Alice was a lab technician. The idea had been to walk along to the hotel where Lyndon Johnson was staying, chanting, "Hey, hey, LBJ, how many kids did you kill today?" Thousands of people walking from the park near Pico to Century Boulevard chanting, and the day was sunny, so lots of people had begun with a picnic, as they had—Alice and her two kids aged about one and five then. Chloe told Hugh about it.

"In the park Cassius Clay—I suppose he was called Muhammad Ali by then—gave a speech and fired everyone up," she said. A lot of doctors and nurses from the hospital where Alice worked, housewives, kids, hippies, some old people. People sang or carried radios, they carried their picnic baskets, carried toddlers who got grumpy along the way.

"I was carrying Sam, he was about one year old, and my sister was with Dana, who was five," Chloe said. "We noticed that police were lining up along the curb, we thought to keep order and protect the President, whatever, but all at once as we walked these police began pressing in at either side of us. Even then it never occurred to me they would hurt us. I had thought until then that policemen were always there to help you. It's amazing how hard it is to see what's plain. But we never expect this kind of thing. I suppose Americans are kind of innocent.

"The police began to press forward, sort of compressing us, so that you could hardly step without elbowing the person next to you, and I still didn't catch on that this is a technique of crowd control they use when they think a crowd is dangerous. Us! A bunch of lab techs and their sisters and tiny children! But luckily I did feel uncomfortable, and the baby began to cry, I thought from being jostled, so I decided to get out of the march. I looked toward the sidewalk, planning to step out of line, and saw that the policemen now had their arms interlocked, fencing us in, so I said, 'Excuse me, officer, but I want to take this baby over there,' and he looked surprised and dropped his arm—I remember so clearly his expression of surprise, and I stepped out, and looked back to call to Alice that we were over there, and saw them beginning to club the people. They clubbed my sister, my little niece, clubbed all the people as they were walking along singing. And this was America, in California! I stood on the grassy parking strip at the edge of the street and watched people being clubbed, these long batons rising and falling, like the baton of a conductor, and people screaming. I thought I could hear my sister's screams.'' Chloe could feel the rush of indignation she always felt when she told this story.

"Those were horrible times," Hugh agreed. His expression to her was tender.

"That's when I realized," said Chloe, "that, you know, they can't tell the difference. They can't tell the difference between a peaceful, nice person and a dangerous one. They didn't even try. I've never trusted them since then. A lot of people are cynical now."

"The policeman is our friend," said Hugh with an ambiguous note of mockery in his voice.

Here the great domes of gleaming blue and gold ornamented the Persian sky. Birds swept among the minarets; the walls were a dream of flowered tracery. The modest black wrappings of the women winding their way along seemed to Chloe a proper response to such beauty, the contrition of humble humanity, so transitory and plain. She tried to imagine the happy state of mind of the tile makers who painted the millions of flowers on the tiles, their brushes dipped in the enchanted azure, and of the architects dreaming these shapes and snowy walls and the long pooled gardens mirroring them.

They had a seven o'clock plane to Shiraz, and so went back to the hotel in the late afternoon to make love and nap and pack. It was Chloe who did the packing, like a wife. Hugh lay on the bed, slightly glazed-looking; like Mars in the Bellini painting, Chloe thought, conscious of her own deficiencies as Venus. She was always lively and invigorated by love-making. She threw her few things into her little duffel bag.

Into Hugh's neat case, open on the luggage rack, she put the things he had carefully arranged in the top drawer of the

bureau: black socks, white boxer shorts, three identical silk
ties. How tidy he was. Would she do this packing for Jeffrey?
Of course. She liked making things fit into suitcases, liked
being ready to go, liked to go. Hugh's shirts in their plastic
wrap from the laundry. An odd detail struck her. "Royal
Hilton Tehran" it said on the little paper strap around their
middles. Hugh, sleepily watching her, did not notice her notice
this, or did not mind. Hugh had had nine shirts done at the
Hilton in Tehran, yet he said he had not been in Tehran.

Chapter Thirteen

AN UNMARKED GRAVE

*Why, if the Soul can fling the Dust aside
And naked on the Air of Heaven ride,
Were't not a Shame—were't not a Shame for him
In this clay carcass crippled to abide?*

Farmani tried to control his fury, his panic, at the stupidity of Abbas and Yazdi and Rothblatt to involve Azami Hospital in this business of the dead man, which was fated, he was sure, to be a danger to them all: Azami doctors mixed up in the death of an American, police, inquiries, people down from Tehran, accusations of muddle, perhaps even some sinister real connection between them— between the dead man and who?

Abbas. No, Yazdi. No, Abbas. It was no coincidence, either, it seemed to him, that Mrs. Fowler had been along when they found him. He had tried to question Abbas, discreetly: "How was it you all went to the caves today?"

"I don't know. I try to make sure they get around to see things."

"Why the caves? Think, Abbas."

"Mrs. Fowler, I think. She has a guidebook."

"Ah," said Vahid Farmani, hardly surprised, but with a renewed sense of dread and helplessness at his lack of ability to dislodge or expose Mrs. Fowler from her oh-so-convenient perch. "Dr. Fowler is taking a long time to arrive, don't you think?" he remarked.

"Yes, poor woman. It can't be easy for her. But she evidently has a resourceful good nature."

"Evidently," said Vahid. "I don't know, Abbas. These people come here but they're just slumming. They're fascinated

113

to see how sick people can get, it's patronizing, they're just interested in our diseases.''

"They are always helpful. Always new techniques, suggestions,'' said Abbas. "More than that, somebody for us to talk to, professionally. Don't you feel the need of that?''

"No, I think Americans are bad news,'' said Vahid.

Linda Farmani derided Vahid's fears. He said she could never imagine consequences. She had no imagination, he said. She had no imagination, maybe, she said, but she had an eye for concrete detail. She pronounced Chloe Fowler perfect—perfectly what she was. "Your basic docent.''

Vahid had no picture of a basic docent, no understanding of American social types, though he understood something about the doctors. "And a docent can't be a spy?''

"Oh, of course.'' Linda laughed, liking, in a way, the idea of the conceited Mrs. Fowler a spy. Linda did not believe that they had anything to fear at Azami, from spies or from Tehran either, because there was no problem as long as you weren't political, and they weren't. It was kids, students, who got into trouble, which was very sad and horrible, or once in a while you heard of a woman arrested, but rarely. The danger was not from the Shah, in any case, but from the people around him, and, even more than them, it was the locals—the jailers, the informers, people with private grudges and small ambitions, enacting personal dramas of revenge or policy. Middle-class bureaucrats like Vahid and her were at once too high and too low and too old to be at risk. The other American wives shared her view of the political situation here, and the English wives too. Even so, they did not discuss the beliefs of their husbands, if they knew them. Cloaked in Americanness, Englishness, they voiced only their own opinions, and their right to have them.

"Leendaah,'' Vahid's mother called her. She always pronounced her name like that, like the name of a harem girl, or the sound of a moan. Vahid's mother had white streaks in her hair that went straight back like the wings of a statue, and her burning brown eyes seemed ringed in white in her muddy skin. She wore only black. Iranians when you met them in Los Angeles were just these dark, attractive men. Someone fixed you up with one, or you met them in a bar or at a party. Real estate had been a good way to meet them, they were already buying houses, that was ten years ago, that's how she met Vahid, he came with a friend who was looking at a house. Dark, attractive, doctors, you didn't exactly picture them against a background of camels and roses and the black shadows under the arches of the sun-painted porches. Certainly you didn't imagine their mothers, the furious brown eyes, gray widow's peak, black veil.

"*I'll* never wear the chador," she had told Vahid.

"Certainly not," he had agreed. "I would not want my wife to take the chador." He had been shocked to think she might wear one. Yet his mother wore chador. She sighed. Eventually you didn't notice them one way or another.

Rejected by the police and the American consul, Dick and Abbas had driven back to Azami with the body still in the station wagon. "Look, let's just put him in the morgue," Dick said. "Vahid won't even know, unless he goes over there. We'll put a sheet over him and tell the attendants something."

Abbas thought about it, then shook his head. "No. It's— how to explain it. These days, around here, if someone asks you not to do something you respect his reasons. You can't always know, he can't always tell you his reasons. It's best to interfere as little as possible."

"What possible difference could it make?"

"Apparently it does make some difference."

"We can't just leave him here. It's—it's hot." He wondered if they had embalmers in Iran, and what they did with bodies. It was obvious they would have to do something quickly. Abbas agreed.

"We may have to bury him," he said. "Then they could dig him up if it was necessary."

Dick shuddered at this repulsive idea, this slightly absurd idea of going somewhere and digging a clandestine grave. For the moment they did nothing, hoping the police would change their minds, the American consul would change his mind,

someone would call or come to collect him. They had
Dermatology Clinic and rounds. "We could dump him.
Downtown. Let someone else find him," said Dick.

"He's already been found, remember. The police know he
exists. What would be the use?"

"Oh, I don't know," Dick said crossly; the thing was too
idiotic. "Then *they* would have to deal with him."

"I am afraid he is ours," Abbas said.

At nightfall, lacking another idea, Dick and Abbas drove the
body out of town, somewhere to the north, sixty kilometers or
so, Abbas driving and Dick looking restlessly out the window
for places, deserted roads, ruins. In the vast, open landscape,
it seemed to him that anyone could see them from anywhere,
for miles. Perhaps Abbas had a destination in mind. He turned
off on a small road, then onto the sand and toward a large rock
formation in the middle distance.

Abbas had brought a shovel from his garden shed. They
should have brought two shovels. While Abbas dug, Dick
scooped the loosened sand that slid back into the hole. "This
is not happening," Dick said. He became preoccupied with the
stubborn tendency of sand to erase human effort, rippling down
into piles, filling the hole again. He tried not to think of the
man, stiff by now, but of a strange consistency. When the hole
was nearly waist deep, Dick began to feel funny standing in it.
He thought of films of people digging their own graves. Then
they shot you as you stood in the hole, or beat you to death with
your shovel and pitched the dirt over you. He climbed out.

"Isn't it big enough? We can put rocks over it."

Abbas considered. "Maybe." They stood gazing into the
grave.

"But what are we going to say we did with him?" Dick said.
"To Yazdi and Chloe and whoever."

"Well, we'll just tell them. We aren't hiding him, we're
preserving him," Abbas said. Dick hoped they wouldn't ask,
would assume the police had taken him, that he was being
buried decently somewhere, had been claimed.

"We should take his watch and things," Dick said, "to
identify him, if anyone should turn up."

"Yes, you are right," Abbas said. "There was a ring."

They lifted the blanket. Dick mentally stiffened himself to

look. At first glance there was nothing more horrible than before except the blood dried blackly now on the poor devil's face, and one eyelid had fluttered unnervingly up; the whole face was perhaps swollen. At touching him, though, Dick's stomach turned over, and he had to step back to master his nausea, for the hand was soft. He heard himself breathing hard; bitter spit trickled between his teeth. Then he took the watch, a gold watch with an incongruous Indian turquoise band. It was Abbas who took the ring off, cursing in Farsi the swollen fingers. Together they pulled the dead man out of the tailgate like bread out of an oven, nearly dropping the limp and heavy thing, and plopped him into his grave.

"We should have put the blanket down first for him to lie on," Abbas said.

"We can put it over him, to keep the sand out," Dick said. They spread the blanket again over the dead face. Who was he? Had he expected to die in Iran, to be buried alone in the desert, heaped with stones? What were the animals in this desert? What would dig at him? They built the rocks in a cairn-shaped mound.

"People will see it's a grave," Dick said.

Abbas shrugged. "The desert is full of graves."

"The desert is full of graves," he went on, in a moody tone that Dick found scary. "In archaic times, the old Zoroastrians laid the bodies out—up there, for instance—along a shelf of rock, for the birds to pick the bones, and then they put the bones into caves in the rocks. It is not unusual to find a little cave of old bones even now."

"That seems practical," Dick said. "A hell of a lot easier than digging a hole."

"It would have been simpler to sneak him into the morgue," Dick said again, on the way back.

"Vahid was really against it. I suppose he had his reasons. We never ask, as I said, the reasons." After a pause he said, "I think we just say nothing at all, until someone asks, then we explain what we have done."

"I think I should notify the American consul, just to cover our asses. We can tell them he's there when they want him."

"Provided they want him fairly soon."

Dick laughed but shivered, slightly exhilarated by this

macabre adventure, hiding a body. As a dermatologist he never saw dead people. Even as an intern he had always left the rooms before the last moments; left the last moments to the relatives. Also, he did not himself like to see that fading light, that cast of blue come over the white of the eye, the drop of saliva at the corner of the sagging mouth. That was why he had gone into dermatology.

"Let's have a beer at the Cyrus," Dick said.

Chapter Fourteen

THE RETURN

Chloe and Hugh took a taxi to the Isfahan airport. The little waiting room was jammed with a crush of enthusiastic French tourists clutching brown-paper-wrapped parcels, who were being boarded on a flight to Abadan. Then it was empty—a bare, deserted room, floored in brown linoleum, with a ticket desk at one end, and the inevitable knot of lingering guards and ancient men swaddled in rags, wearing caps, whose duty it was to clean. A picturesque Saudi swept through, flapping his white robes in a dash toward the tarmac, where a small plane for Tehran was ready. His three wives, glaring through their raccoon masks, watched with, it appeared, a certain detachment about whether the plane would wait for them, and then were herded, clinging, to the waiting plane.

The plane for Shiraz, they were told, would be two hours late. Looking at the handsome Hugh slumped next to her in the plastic chair, Chloe wondered if this feeling of solitude, of individual destiny, that overtakes you in an airport waiting room had not also accounted for her willingness to leave Jeffrey at Heathrow and journey on alone. She had felt herself to be alone already. Now Hugh's very self, of such immediate and intimate interest to her two hours ago, had seemed to recede into the body of an unrelated stranger, well-dressed and well-formed but of no consequence to her, not even an object of erotic curiosity. She was locked into a traveler's capsule, alone. As at Heathrow, Chloe bought postcards.

Hugh, after an interval of silence, opened his briefcase and began staring at medical reprints. "Here I am in this historic city," wrote Chloe. "I hope you are brushing your teeth."

Their reverie was interrupted by the American voice of a man they had seen earlier leaning against the ticket counter, and they had remarked his American appearance then—a compact, middle-aged man with short grayish hair and protuberant ears, which gave him a look of good nature. His air was friendly, like a figure on a television screen, his smile confident of the welcome of his fellow countrymen.

"Two hours? And this isn't unusual! Why do I turn up on time every time? Because someday, someday, Air Iran may take off on time." He spoke with a lazy southern drawl.

They smiled. Chloe was surprised at her own welcoming feeling, when ordinarily she would not wish to be talked to by a stranger in an airport. But now to meet another American seemed as nice as a present. This view seemed less marked in Hugh, who looked up with a start of impatience from his articles. But of course he hadn't been in Iran for two weeks. Or had he? She was not forgetting the shirts. Nine shirts, more than a week, if he changed every day, and most men could get two days out of a shirt.

The man handed them a business card, which Hugh read and handed to Chloe: Benjamin Brigante, U.S.A.F., Brig. Gen. Ret., Technical Consultant, Grumman Corporation. He extended his hand, which Hugh and Chloe in turn shook. Hugh half rose, politely. Chloe noticed with satisfaction that he had better manners than Jeffrey. They said their names.

"Going to Shiraz?"

They nodded.

"Me too. I've got to get back p.d.q. Though haste is relative here. You'll have noticed that. But they've crashed another of my airplanes. My beautiful F-14s. It is such a damn shame. I'm with Grumman—we make the things."

"An airplane crash?"

"This is the second one, and there'll be all kinds of hell to pay. Talking frankly, there's more hell to pay here when one goes down than in the U.S., never mind our so-called sanctity of life. I know, in the U.S., there's the wife, the kids, we get up a collection, somebody gets a medal, everyone feels bad, but basically we have plenty of airplanes. There's not such a lot of high-up paranoid handwringing as here. Here the higher-ups believe that planes shouldn't crash, period. When they do, heads will roll. And of course," his voice lowered, "here heads really do roll, so I guess that keeps things serious."

"Are you a pilot?" asked Chloe.

"Are you kidding? I wouldn't get into one of those things— Iranian maintenance. No way. Of course American-trained, but let me tell you these guys have no mechanical aptitude. None. We've been training them ourselves, back in Texas. We take 'em back there for sometimes four years, and when we send them back they still don't have the concept of preventive maintenance."

Chloe was beginning to feel uneasy about the forthcoming Air Iran journey back to Shiraz.

"The Iranian male, frankly, is not too bright. I don't know if it's the way they're brought up or what. The Iranian female, that's something else, she's alert, she's aggressive."

"Uh—won't you sit down?" said Hugh, hitching his chair to symbolize making room for General Brigante.

"Thanks," he said, sitting down. "And what are you folks doing? Vacation?"

"We're at the Azami Hospital in Shiraz," said Hugh.

"Azami, huh? You have some biochemists there, some hotshots?"

"Why?" asked Hugh. "I suppose."

"Just wondered. This is the second crash in a month. I think privately it's some kind of kamikaze thing. Pilots who think Allah will take them straight to Valhalla if they down a few of Sue's expensive aircraft. There's a lot of opposition to Sue's willful little ways."

"Sue?"

"We call her Sue, just to be on the prudent side. You know who I mean."

"Suicide pilots?" said Chloe, happily intrigued.

"Suicide or sabotage, I think. But, like I say, with Iranian

maintenance who can tell the difference? It's a question of
intention. The result's the same—either way, the damn things
crash.''

"But how awful for the pilot," said Chloe.

"Awful for you, too, if the thing falls on your house and,
actually, the pilots eject.''

After this, with General Brigante telling them horrifying but
entertaining stories about the Iranian Air Force, the time passed
quickly, though they felt more and more reluctant to get on the
Air Iran plane.

Chloe liked the general, despite his having been in the
military. When, eventually, they got back to Shiraz, he gave
them a ride to the compound in the Grumman car that awaited
him. Chloe wondered if you could get to be an American
general without a southern accent.

In the compound, there was a certain unease, for people had
noticed that Mrs. Fowler was not in Villa Two and had not
been there all weekend, a fact easily ascertainable from the
windows of Villa One, and noticed also by Hossein, who
confirmed Linda Farmani's observation, which she mentioned
to Vahid Farmani.

Vahid thought Chloe might be doing something over at the
airbase, might have met someone at the American Wives'
Club. It now occurred to him, for the first time, that her object
might not be the hospital itself so much as to watch the whole
Azami Compound, assessing the loyalties and sympathies of
all the people who lived and worked there. At this, he felt a
rush of hot dread, not to have seen before that a woman was
not an odd choice but was the very perfect choice for a spy,
could make herself the confidante of the other wives, be a
guest at the parties. It was the perfect situation for a spy, a
traitor, an agent, the perfect situation from which to learn
things, whatever there was to be learned. There was always
something to be learned.

Dick and Junie had thought it was funny when Chloe
wasn't around all weekend. Sunday night, after work, they
went to the Cyrus for drinks with Abbas Mowlavi, and there
fell in with a delightful guy, Richard Dare, an American

archaeologist working for the University of Chicago, and an expert on Persepolis, where he was stationed on a dig. This was good luck for Dick and Junie, because Dare offered to show them around when they came down to Persepolis, and they realized it would be a rare inside opportunity to see the great ruins with someone really knowledgeable. The date had not been fixed for the Persepolis expedition because the company had been awaiting Hugh Monroe and Jeffrey Fowler, but they were about to give them up and go without them.

"I plan to come too," said Abbas. "Like most of my countrymen, I'm badly educated in these wonders. It's always strangers and foreigners who must teach us, or who afford an excuse, at least, to learn."

Dare expected to be at Persepolis until the end of August, and said they could find him there any time. Dick hoped the guy would remember—tonight he might be just slightly in the bag. He was a pink-faced blond man wearing whites, a bit self-consciously tropical and colonial-looking, with the wide smile of a host, welcoming and bright, and an eye for Junie. He kept buying her vodkas. Perhaps it had been a while since he had seen an American woman. Dick noticed, rather to his annoyance, that Junie had adopted a rather silly, giggling manner, and said not a word about being a doctor.

Besides Dare, Junie also appeared to like Abbas. So for that matter did Dick, who found him melancholy but compatible, sweet-natured and empathetic with patients, which many Iranian doctors were not, and hard-working. And attractive. Dick had long since stopped being uneasy about his own attraction to good looks in other men. It was—it had been worked out—a wishful process of identification, an almost aesthetic response. Of course he would himself have liked to be a tallish, cleft-chinned dark beauty like Abbas; this was not a mysterious reaction, and Junie's reaction was not mysterious either. But plenty of women had assured Dick that he himself was attractive—they never said short—and praised his engaging smile, his dimples, and, in former days, his sandy hair, slightly grizzled now and thinner but not really thin to the extent that he had to resort, like some pathetic colleagues, to combing it into strange patterns, for instance up from the nape of the neck. In bed, he knew, had been told, he was a good performer.

He wondered if Abbas was getting any and what the Islamic recourse was for an unmarried man. What did you do? But the subject of women never came up. Abbas was friendly in an impersonal, international style; they had no sports team in common, did not read the same paper, had only medicine in which to find perfect collegial rapport, and now, of course, their guilty secret, their bond, the body in the desert.

Most important for Dick was that Abbas was a good doctor. Some Iranians he found boastful, thoughtless, and behind the times, though he also understood the practical difficulties they were up against and sympathized with their wish to use their elaborate Western training on something more serious than dysentery and malaria. Dick was not sympathetic to the wish of Vahid Farmani to have a CAT scanner. There were plenty of things they needed more. But he understood why Vahid wanted a CAT scanner, in order to go on feeling like a real doctor, not just a Peace Corps worker. Basically Dick respected doctors like Vahid and Abbas who wished to improve the health of all Iran.

Junie and Abbas were talking about skiing. "If you're ready to go home, Miss Fay, I'll walk you," Dick interrupted abruptly, and he was a little surprised when she said she was ready to go, as docile as a wife.

As they walked up to the Azami gates they came upon Chloe with, of all people, Hugh Monroe, who was carrying a suitcase.

"Look who I've found," Chloe said.

"Rothblatt! Hey!" said Hugh cheerfully, holding out his hand.

"Well!" said Dick. "At last! When did you get here?"

"Just now," said Hugh. "I don't even know where to go."

"He had no idea people were worried," said Chloe.

"This is June Fay, Hugh Monroe," said Dick. "Junie's in OB-GYN."

"How do you do?" said Hugh. It was a moment, it seemed to Chloe, when the four of them could have abandoned pretenses and gone off home in two pairs, promising never to tell. Instead they began an elaborate business of starting to shuffle off in four separate directions.

"Well, I'm going to roust out the Farmanis and find out where they've put me," Hugh said. "They weren't expecting me tonight."

"Let's go along together," said Dick, taking Junie and Chloe by their elbows. Hugh walked with them toward Villa One.

"What happened about the dead man?" asked Chloe as they walked.

"Well, it wasn't easy," Dick said. "Farmani wouldn't have it at Azami, so we took it to the police. But they wouldn't have it either. They said he wasn't an Iranian, it was a matter for the American consul."

"How amazing! Not a matter for the police!"

"Right. They just came out to the car, looked at the guy, discussed him in their unknown tongue, and shook their heads and went inside. So then we took him to the American consul, of course, a Mr. Collins, and he said it didn't look like an American to him and where would he put it anyway? This was all day Friday, Abbas and I and the body still in the hospital car. Finally I suggested we should just call the American embassy in Tehran and find out what to do, but no one would, Abbas included, and so I did, but they took Collins's line: How do you know he's American?"

"It's like the joke about the grandmother who died in Mexico," Chloe said, "and somebody stole the car as they were smuggling the body back. You must have hoped someone would steal the car."

"Are you sure he was American?" Hugh asked.

"No, not at all. His dying words—you couldn't tell. But he spoke English. 'Pardon' it sounded like."

"His clothes looked like American clothes," Chloe said. "He was wearing sort of Hush Puppies."

"Junie looked at his feet," Dick said to Hugh, "but she didn't look at the brand of shoes."

"You should have looked at them," Chloe said.

"Well, his feet had begun to swell; you couldn't get them off again," Dick said. It was easy enough for others, who were not there, to criticize.

"What did you do?" Hugh asked. "Smuggle him back into the morgue?"

Dick turned his head, and the light from a streetlamp gave him a momentary evasive glitter.

"Well, what else could we do?" Dick said, suddenly deciding not to tell them the rest.

"Where were you this weekend?" he asked Chloe.

"Digging," Chloe said. "Didn't I tell you? Like a real archaeologist." She'd thought of this on the plane.

"That must have been fun," said Dick.

Hugh dropped out at Villa One, to get the key to wherever it was he was supposed to stay. Dick and Junie dropped Chloe at her door. In the darkness they could hear Hugh apologizing to the Farmanis for the lateness of the hour. Then Dick walked Junie over to her place, and, because it was dark and no one was around, it seemed all right to steal inside for the night.

Chloe heard Hugh's careful discreet tap at the street door of Villa Two. How circumspect they all were! She stole along the corridor and down the stairs to admit him.

"Jesus Christ," he shouted in the night. Chloe heard the slap of his feet on the linoleum, the clatter of his cot.

"What's the matter?" she asked.

"What the hell is that?" He moved toward the window.

"Oh, the dogs," said Chloe, laying her head sleepily again on her pillow. "Some kind of wild dogs. They roam around at night."

"What a hellish noise. I don't remember that from before."

"You get used to it."

"You're used to it?" asked Hugh, astonished. After a few moments he came over to Chloe's cot and stroked her hair and drew her covers back. Then he crawled on top of her, for there was no room for two people to lie side by side.

"Just a little quickie, then I'm going to risk stealing out into the night, if I can escape the hell hounds. Now I'm awake," he said. Sleepily, amiably, Chloe parted her thighs.

*   *   *

Dick woke in the night again, thinking as he had last night, after he and Abbas had buried the dead man, that animals would dig at the grave. He wasn't sure what animals lived in the sparse desert, but he imagined wild jackals or cats, starved cats from the city, wandering out across the sand. He had dreamed and the dream was exactly the same as his waking picture of the scene, a dead hand stretching up, a fold of cloth, a voice feebly issuing forth, protesting the hungry slavering of the digging beast. He supposed he must have seen a movie of this scene, its details too predictable to have issued forth from the unconscious, unless the voice—as he suddenly realized—was his own, and the cloth was the hem of his own bathrobe, in which case who were the beasts? Did it have something to do with Marla? It seemed to him it did, and of course guilt feelings about that clandestine burying, and the fear of discovery. He had nothing to feel guilty about, though maybe they could have saved the guy if they had grasped what had happened to him. He always felt guilty if someone died.

But of course the animals were the dogs, the real dogs roaming the compound, now near his own window. He was not fond of animals, especially cats and dogs; that came from not having pets while growing up. He had insisted that his own children have pets—cats and dogs both, over Marla's objection. But he had never overcome a momentary tendency to flinch when the dogs ran up to greet him. He liked horses and cows, and other nice, majestic animals.

In the morning Chloe tied her belt around Rustum's neck and took him for a walk. People stared at her so oddly that she went back inside the compound, woman cruelly dragging small dog, the way people dragged goats and lambs here. He snarled and struggled. He was not going to be an attractive dog, she knew, but she grew fonder each day of his undistinguished color, his expression, perfectly expressive, of growing interest and trust. It was not just for food, either, that he came now when she called, for she was careful not to feed him every time but to vary the routine and assure that he was coming by the direction of his superego not from mere greediness.

When she saw Hugh that evening, he said, "There is no body in the morgue. I went in to look at the guy—in case—you

never know. But there was no one there at all. They take away
their dead almost immediately, these people, they don't leave
them in the hospital morgue, so there were no bodies there at
all.''

"Ugh," said Chloe, "why would you want to look at him?"
It seemed strange to her. Hugh made no answer.

Chapter Fifteen

PICNIC

Hugh, who had been a popular visitor a few years before, was welcomed back with enthusiasm by the wives as well as the doctors. It was remembered that he liked to play tennis, and Heidi Asghari lost no time in finding the net to the tennis court behind Villa Nine and organizing a picnic supper. Mohammed fixed the net and stamped down the scratched patches on the red clay surface, and Hugh rounded up players. The dead man in Shahpur's Cave was forgotten, or at least not mentioned.

Chloe, who did not play tennis, happily watched a game between Hugh and Abbas, two picturesquely handsome men, the one dark, the other fair, like athletes in a mural depicting international competition. She thought it possible that she loved Hugh because he was handsomer than Jeffrey, though Jeffrey of course was a nice-looking man. But no, it was not strictly looks—was not Hugh also better-natured, more deserving of love? Probably, being beautiful, he had always received love, and it was that which gave him his good disposition. Chloe basked in the sun with her sun hat over her face to prevent wrinkles, legs in tennis shorts outstretched, raising her head from time to time to watch the players.

In tennis whites, she had to admit, Abbas was even better-looking than Hugh, supremely handsome, with Hugh appearing, in comparison, a pinkish-beige color that was not so elegant, and turning pinker with each moment in the burning sun. In a few weeks, Heidi Asghari said, they would have to

129

play in the early mornings; it would be too hot at midday. Naturally Noosheen loved Abbas, thought Chloe admiringly. It was chemistry of an obvious kind.

Hugh was a better tennis player. He had played on his college team. Her heart warmed. She felt as she remembered having felt in high school, thrilled at any evidence of athletic prowess in boys. Those were her first premonitions of sex. Football players with their strong thighs and an aura of liniment clinging to them when you necked in the car after games. Now those boys would look too young to her, their necks too skinny. She watched the strong legs of Hugh and Abbas with a pleasant crawling feeling in her stomach. How strong, how graceful Hugh's forehand drives; a slight expression of pique on the face of Abbas, beneath his smile, at the ease with which Hugh Monroe sent balls spinning by him. She did not feel the tendrils and entails of marriage; her spirit floated free.

Abbas was thinking how off his game he was—he never played now; Americans were always playing. He'd have to make more of an effort, he thought, not to let his game go, though ordinarily there was no one much to play with at Azami. Monroe was as fast as the devil. He was conscious of Chloe Fowler watching them, and of how she leapt up to scurry after balls with the feigned energy of someone who isn't playing but wishes to look as if she might.

The Yazdis came with a net for the second court. Zareeneh Yazdi sat down near Chloe while Ali affixed it to its posts. Chloe was fascinated at the smoothness of her legs. At risk of seeming to stare, she found herself continually darting glances at this miracle of depilation, arms too, smooth as bronze, to go with the bronzed dark hair and sunglasses on which you could read the words Christian Dior along the temple. Chloe had read that men prefer women to be smooth because hair symbolizes masculinity, like Samson. She suddenly felt hairy and Western, though she certainly shaved her legs and underarms in the regular American way. A finger along her shin revealed the slightest prickliness. Abbas, on the court, began to hit the ball too hard much of the time, and she redoubled her efforts at fielding.

Dick Rothblatt and Junie Fay came along, looking rather a couple; Chloe wondered if the Iranians noticed this, and whether it mattered. Dick had still not acknowledged it, not really, to her. They carried their racquets and wore tennis clothes except for Dick's socks, which were black. He looked straight at Chloe, as if reading her mind, and said, "I forgot my tennis socks." Had she been staring snobbishly at his socks?

Something upsetting had happened in his life. He'd just gotten a letter. Chloe wondered if she would find a letter on her pillow when she got back to her room. It seemed as if letters always brought bad news.

"Marla has put the house up for sale."

"Shouldn't she? Isn't it hers?" asked Chloe. Junie rolled her eyes, informing her, by a cool glance, that Dick was irrational on the subject.

"Your kids are away—she probably doesn't want a big house to take care of," Chloe continued nonetheless, thinking that would be how she would feel.

"Well, they have to have someplace to go on their vacations," Dick said. "I didn't agree that she should have it so she could sell it. I was thinking of the kids, a home."

"Maybe—you know—bad memories. People have to start over, change, a fresh start," murmured Chloe.

"She would pick now to do it, with me here."

"I think it's completely logical," said Junie. "A house is a drag, she's busy, maybe she needs the money."

"She's a terrible businesswoman, she's bound to get screwed, she has no sense at all. And she would pick now."

"We're supposed to play," Junie said, waving at the Yazdis, who beckoned from the other side of the court. Hugh blistered a drive past Abbas; it was the end of their match. They shook hands, ceremoniously as at a tournament.

"She must have just been waiting till I was out of the country," Dick went on complaining as he walked with Junie out onto the court.

His game was stronger than Junie's. Though they were the same height, Dick was nimbler, fitter, and Junie was awkward. Marla, fifteen years older than Junie, was trim and a good tennis player. Her face floated before him, small and tanned, the tiniest bit leatherish, her pink lipstick and blue headband— these details were vividly present to his mind as Junie loped around next to him. He could imagine Marla selling the house to the tennis pro or some other gigolo; she had absolutely no idea of the value of money.

He and Junie by some miracle defeated the Yazdis, who were good players nonetheless. Then Hugh Monroe took a couple of games off Dick while the women spread the picnic, and they all sat under the trees drinking wine or beer and eating lamb sandwiches. Hugh Monroe, Dick noted regretfully, besides being fit and a good tennis player, was abstemious, stuck to beer pretty much, or the occasional glass of wine. Not that he, Dick, was a big boozer, but he found himself thinking about a drink from time to time, and at home he had a good cellar. Had had a good cellar. Left quite a bit of the good stuff for Marla, too. Would she think of moving the bottles from the cellar? He imagined some stranger wandering down behind the furnace, excitedly finding the well-stocked racks. He had in fact taken the 1959 Château Lafite-Rothschild and some other inspired purchases, but the stuff he left behind was by no means bad.

He had begun to keep a list of things like this he wanted to talk to Marla about, remind her about. When they first separated, she had been cooperative about details and telephoned to ask his advice. As she felt her way to independence she had stopped doing this, which was to be expected, but she now often quite irrationally resisted reasonable suggestions. So far he hadn't succeeded in getting through on the telephone, even from the Cyrus. He pictured a ring of real-estate agents in his cellar, turning over the labels, exclaiming, calling for a corkscrew.

Here they were drinking a perfectly pleasant white, grown somewhere around Persepolis. "They have some very nice whites in Egypt," he heard himself saying, even knowing Hugh was not too interested in wine, no more than most American doctors, "and the reds are okay, surprisingly enough. There's one called Pharaon. There's one called Omar Khayyam."

Then Hugh shocked everyone by bringing up politics, calmly observing that, although he had heard that unrest was increasing, things seemed to him on the whole the same, or better, than when he had visited Iran two years before. . . .

"People seem more prosperous, but less cheerful. That's how it seems walking down the street. And as to the peasants, the poor people we see at the hospital, they seem the same."

"They greatly resist change of any kind," said Ali Yazdi.

"Except the automobile," put in Chloe. "Obviously they love cars."

"So I imagine they will resist Marxism too," said Yazdi.

"Little kids eight or nine on motorcycles—it's scary," said Chloe.

"There are more soldiers," Hugh said. "Everywhere on the street, in Isfahan. Machine guns."

"Yes—I think there will be a revolution," Abbas said. The Yazdis, it seemed to Chloe, looked at him with masks concealing surprise.

"But isn't that good? The Shah is a monster. The torture," cried Junie.

"Yes, no one supports the Shah. His people are corrupt and cruel. He has tried to do things too quickly, without understanding, without any understanding—and yet . . ." He hesitated. How dark, how tragic, his eyes, thought Chloe. He could be a sheik in a movie.

"Well, then," Junie said.

"There will be terrible bloodshed, one can't want that. If the people could wait, if they would understand what prosperity can bring them. You've seen the air force, you've seen the police, the machine guns. The rebellion will not be a well-armed, well-organized fight, and so, of course, the Shah will be successful, and afterward more cruel, more watchful than ever." His voice became low and urgent.

"Uprisings succeed because of the will of the people. History is full of examples, the collective will, people without guns overpowering armed might, eventually," said Dick. He had the regular American view.

Abbas shrugged, imagining the short run, the shouting, wounded people, confusion. "People are very ignorant here still, very superstitious. I'd rather the Shah would change. There is more hope of making him change than of throwing him out."

"The world is always ruled by uniformed people and the rich, why expect Iran to be different?" agreed Ali Yazdi.

A company in tennis whites, at leisure amid the tangled thicket at the edge of the courts, bare legs in view, easy and laughing, while the peasants in question trudged by in their somber draperies. Chloe wondered if, when they uprose, these poor would fall upon Zareeneh Yazdi as well as upon an American woman.

"Of course," said Abbas, "it's always the middle class who suffer in the end."

Chloe wasn't so sure about that.

"And the intellectuals," said Yazdi. "Tell me, where do intellectuals rule?"

When the revolution comes, Abbas thought, and then interrupted his thought with the realization that he had not before fully, out loud, as it were, formulated this certainty: there would be a revolution. His next thought was to wonder— the idea just thrust itself in upon the larger preoccupation—if he should sell his BMW now or hold on to it. He believed, though not as strongly as Emir, his brother, that things must change here, so probably he should sell now. After a brief period of upheaval, then things would get better and you would still after all need a car, but in the meantime a BMW was kind of a conspicuous, capitalist car.

Chloe noticed now that Zareeneh Yazdi was wearing panty hose with her tennis dress; this accounted for the supernatural smoothness of her legs.

Chapter Sixteen

DAILY LIFE

> *Whether at Naishapur or Babylon,*
> *Whether the Cup with sweet or bitter run,*
> *The Wine of Life keeps oozing drop by drop*
> *The Leaves of Life keep falling one by one.*

Now that she belonged, however secretly, to Hugh, was part of a couple again, Chloe felt more than ever a part of Azami Hospital too. Being the appendage, even the secret one, of some man, was more natural to her than being an expert on Sassanian pottery. She supposed that anyone could see through her pretension of expertise on Sassanian pottery, but she continued to be taken seriously and to take it seriously herself, studying industriously, and appearing at the workshop at the university, where she was allowed to turn over cases full of shards, and had learned to delight in a trace of green glaze or the impress of a forked stick so charmingly evoking some disappeared potter now himself clay. Indeed, she had begun to love Sassanian pots.

She had surprised herself by having a gift for the painstaking work of fitting shards together. From a heap of fragments she could find matching bits with a facility that amazed the real archaeologists. She would find a bit, then the next bit; under her tweezer would grow the pattern, the form of the curve of a vessel lip. Perhaps it was practice, from childhood jigsaw puzzles. To her it was no harder than that. Yet the Iranian archaeologists marveled, assuring her it was an unusual talent. Chloe sat for hours with shards spread on the restoring table under a lamp, arranging them in piles. When an important restorer arrived, expected shortly from Tehran, she was to learn the technique of gluing them.

Sometimes, absorbed in her work, she would realize with a

quick start of surprise that she hadn't thought about her
children as she used to do, perhaps not all day. She had a
sense, new to her, of being separate from them, not "Sara's
mother," "Max's mother," so much as an expert on pots. At
such moments she would imagine that they had forgotten her
too, and thought of her as a dim abstraction, far away,
originator of postcards and fond sentiments from afar, that was
all.

She recognized that her pottery did not sound interesting to
doctors, involved as they were in dramas of life and death more
dire than those they were used to in America. They passed the
evenings in the Cyrus bar in shocked recital, if no Iranians
were present whose feelings might be hurt, of the preventable
medical horrors, the suffering, and the undoctorly treatment
their patients sometimes received. If an Iranian doctor joined
them, they became polite and emphasized the great strides. All
acknowledged that the good doctors—Abbas, Mohammed,
Vahid Farmani, and even Ali Yazdi—were models of dedica-
tion and compassion.

Chloe, being discreet, most often went to the Cyrus bar with
Junie, or with Junie and Dick, but never with Hugh, who
would come along alone, or, some evenings, go without her,
for a few beers and medical talk. In his specialty of infectious
diseases, he found much to occupy, interest, and distress him.
He was especially critical of the reluctance he sensed on the
part of Vahid Farmani to implement simple public-health
measures to control contagion.

"I've been talking to Vahid about a polio project during the
tribal migrations," he said. "You could administer the vaccine
as the people come through Shiraz. You could virtually stamp
it out. But he could care less."

"Prevention," said Dick Rothblatt. "You can't talk to them
about prevention. They think it's hopeless, I guess, and that
you'll never get people to take pills, or follow through, or
watch where their drinking water comes from. They could
clean up the water. The typhoid. But prevention doesn't
interest them at all."

"Ab-e-inja bad ast," said Chloe, using one of the phrases,
unusable until now, from *Teach Yourself Farsi*: "The water is

bad.'' She was delighted whenever she found a word that was the same in English and Farsi: *bad*, for example.

''One thing that bugs me,'' Dick Rothblatt said, ''among the many things, I mean, is the way they treat the poor patient. They talk right in front of him, in English, which he can't understand, and they never talk *to* him. They never tell him what's the matter with him or what's going on. When I make rounds, I make the resident stop and explain to the patient what we've just said, not that I can tell if that's what he's doing; sometimes the patients look more petrified after the resident talks to them.''

''You can die of fright,'' Chloe said.

''Yes, you can, absolutely,'' Dick agreed. ''It's their attitude. These are just peasants to them, or representatives of a disease. 'This is a liver,' they say. It's the attitude here I don't like.''

''Frankly, a lot of American doctors are like that too,'' Chloe said.

''I know it, but they're worse here,'' Dick said. ''The people are scared to death to go to the hospital.''

''American doctors are very bad that way,'' persisted Chloe. She felt that Dick and Hugh were themselves sometimes insensitive, if not to patients, then to the problems of Iranian doctors. Once they had been joined by a Dr. Gomez, young, fat, puffing with anxiousness, in the hospital cafeteria.

''Dr. Monroe, would you have a minute?''

''Of course,'' Hugh had said affably, though without rising. Dr. Gomez glanced at the chair next to him and nervously sat in it. Then he leaned so close to Hugh that Hugh instinctively leaned backward and scooted his chair an inch or two.

''I have a research project,'' said Dr. Gomez. ''Naturally it is not what I could hope if in the U.S., but I wonder if you can advise me regarding publication, and how I can get some funds maybe from the U.S. to continue. I can publish my preliminary results very soon, you see, and then perhaps attract some other funds.''

''What is the project?'' Hugh had asked politely, but Chloe had heard in his voice his lack of interest, and, days later, when she had asked him if he had looked in on Dr. Gomez, Hugh admitted he had forgotten.

"I have a hard time remembering their names," Dick confided. "It's really embarrassing. It's just that I never heard names like that before, so I have no associations with them."

"I try to think of a similar English word," Chloe said. "Noosheen, for instance, moonshine."

"But after you get used to the name it's just a name like Dick," Dick said. "Abbas, Mohammed, those are easy."

"Have you noticed that they get to looking more American, too? I mean, it's in one's head," said Hugh, laughing.

"Only the ones you know, though," Dick said.

Abbas Mowlavi joined them, as he often did in the evenings. Was it he, then, Chloe occasionally wondered, who was the agent for Savak? It seemed to Chloe that she was half in love with the entire company—Heidi, even Junie, though she was prickly and superior and looked down on ordinary housewives, not without reason. Even the English Hendersons, so pink-faced and owlish in their identical National Health spectacles, their clothes, in spite of their rather strong body odor, always so clean, freshly ironed it seemed by Mrs. Henderson. Chloe even liked General Ben, who was not someone who would ever come her way in America. Chloe liked the comical way he said things he must know perfectly well to be what people would expect of a wicked American general, though at times he spoke of gooks and Nam so unself-consciously she wondered if the proper view of matters was known to him. Chloe believed he had never met anyone who had been against the war, and that if he had he would have become something more sympathetic than a military officer.

The only one she didn't like was Loyal Cooley, the Texan, who hung around and bragged or complained. They all found his voice too loud, his stories too tall—the endless perils he had encountered on his travels outside of America, or for that matter outside of Texas, for bad things had befallen him in New York and San Diego, too. He was both a hawk and a racist, and told racist jokes.

"Black guy comes in for a vasectomy, all dressed up, white hat, fancy duds. 'Rastus, why you all dressed up?'—'If I's gonna be impo'tant, I's gonna look impo'tant!' " Chloe's ears had burned but the Iranian doctors had all laughed heartily. "What do you call a white guy with two blacks? 'Victim.' "

Once General Ben and Loyal Cooley had been going on embarrassingly about Nam and hound dogs, and football, and, as Chloe was withdrawing to talk to the Asgharis, she had heard Hugh join the conversation, under her very eyes transformed into an unrecognizable creature of another, inarticulate race, whose discourse was conducted in loud monosyllables concerning trout, and who knew what else if she and the other women hadn't been there.

"They had a linebacker then who was just a little guy, no more'n five ten," said General Ben, "could run forty yards in five seconds."

"That was Ernie Beatty," said Loyal Cooley, "only white guy on the team."

"Tennessee State," said Hugh.

"Heisman," said the general.

"Fractured ankle," said Loyal Cooley.

"Three suspensions that year," said Hugh.

"What do you call a white guy with five blacks?" said Loyal Cooley. "Five? A coach. Eight? Quarterback."

Poor Dick Rothblatt too seemed baffled by this unintelligible conversation, of a sort Chloe had been hearing all her life but which they perhaps did not have in New York, and certainly not in Iran. Chloe thought Hugh and the others rude to talk in sports shorthand in front of Iranians, gracious people who were making an effort to speak another language on topics of general interest. She was embarrassed. People would think Americans weren't capable of elaborate discourse on complicated subjects. In fact, in front of Iranians, she felt ashamed of her friends, seeing them as the braggart, the war-crazed general, and the dumb doctors with endless discourse on diseases but never books or cultivated subjects.

"Two thousand? Warden. Ten thousand? Postmaster general." The Americans laughed, ashamed of their laughter.

Tonight General Ben Brigante said to Dick, who was standing with Chloe and Junie at the bar, "Come sit down with me. I've been standing around all day," and he seized his glass of white wine and carried it to a table.

"I want to recruit you," he said. "As a spy, you could say."

"Me?"

"Yes, a spy should be someone like you, intelligent, watchful. You keep your eyes open. I've told you about the airplane crashes. We're quite sure it's somebody at Azami who is poisoning the fuel. We've found hospital chemicals, other things."

"If I were a saboteur," said Dick, uncertain how seriously to take this, "I wouldn't leave my chemicals around." He felt suddenly defensive of Azami Hospital.

"You wouldn't, I wouldn't, but these are Iranians. Or it could be the chemicals were left behind in a hurry."

Perhaps he was serious. He was often seen with Americans in uniform, or with Iranian officers. "Who wants them to crash?" Dick asked.

The general shrugged. "You could say anybody and you'd have a perfectly good chance of being right. There's Sue. If there's an uprising, Sue doesn't want her planes to fall into the hands of the rebels."

"You work for—Sue—don't you? Why can't you call him by his name?"

"Then there's the rebels themselves," the general went on. "When the moment comes, they want to have taken the planes out beforehand. Then there's the CIA. If there's a rebellion and Sue doesn't make it, then they don't want these planes falling into the hands of the Russians."

"Russians?" said Dick, who had not even thought of Russians.

"They're in the game. They always are. About the only people around here I'd say who want the F-14s in the air, besides me, because I don't like to see all that scrap metal out of what was once a beautiful airplane, are the Russians, because that's obviously who's going to wind up with them if there's a successful revolution."

"Complicated to understand," said Dick, confused but pleasantly excited at such strategic talk. "There are Russian spies here, then?"

The general looked meaningfully around the room.

"And the rebels," Dick went on. "Do they have spies? One

knows about the Shah's spies, of course. Who *are* the rebels, actually?"

"The leader is in Paris, an old mullah, but backed by the Russians, or that's what everybody says. Me, I'm not political. If you ask me, these people here have plenty to complain of. But I'm just doing my job, as Eichmann used to say, and that's to keep the airplanes flying, despite Iranian pilots and Iranian maintenance and all the other despites. I would really like to know who is getting chemicals from Azami."

"Why don't you just put guards around the planes?"

The general turned gloomy and stirred the ice cubes in his glass with the tip of his finger.

"I'm not sure whose side I'm on," said Dick. "I mean, I know I'm not on Sue's. I haven't given it any thought."

"Thoughtfulness is not required in a spy. Watchfulness, but not thoughtfulness."

"I'd hate to give myself airs, airs of thoughtfulness," Dick said. "All the same . . ."

"Keep your eyes open all the same," said General Ben, "though we may have seen the last of it for a while. Now that they know they can do it, they may decide to sit back and await the day."

"The day," said Dick. "Will it be soon?" He had suddenly thought of the strange disorder he had encountered in Abbas's laboratory some mornings.

"I doubt it," the general said.

"As far as I'm concerned," Loyal Cooley could be heard saying nearby, "French food is just caca. Not the food so much as the pretentious bull-caca that goes with it. The maître d'. The wine list. It used to be in Waco you went out to dinner, you ate, but now they tell you all the stuff they do to it—the sauce, the descriptions are as bad as the food, you can't tell what the food is anyway, they just pour cream and all that shit on it and put it under the broiler. It's that they want to impress you instead of feed you. Goddamnit, I go out to eat—to eat."

Chloe thought he overdid the simple-rube act. Probably CIA. He must think they were really stupid. She could not tell from General Ben's expression what he thought of Loyal Cooley.

It sometimes seemed to Dick that beneath Loyal's antic

façade lay a sentient being. At such times it was possible to imagine glints of watchful attention in his watery blue eyes.

"They mostly have English doctors here," he had remarked to Dick earlier. "Right? Like Dr. Henderson?"

"Henderson and a few others. Mostly Americans," Dick had said.

"Ever have Belgians or Frenchmen? It used to be that your educated Iranian spoke French, know that? Still that way in Egypt, your upper class didn't want anything to do with the English, which you certainly can't blame them."

"There was a Dutch radiologist when I came," Dick said.

"No French doctors?"

"I haven't met any," Dick said, stomach tightening. The man in the cave could have been a French doctor. Was Cooley looking for the man in the cave?

"Your Texans," said Ali Yazdi when Loyal Cooley had gone lurching drunkenly off toward his room, "are not as sympathetic as other Americans."

"The size of their belt buckles is inversely related to the size of their pricks," said General Ben. "Back east we have a joke: 'How do you find Texas?' Answer: 'You walk west until you smell it, then you walk south until you step in it.' " All the Americans laughed but not the Iranians.

"Florida," said Chloe scornfully when General Ben had left, "is entirely populated by senior citizens and dope pushers. And have you ever seen a picture of the Fontainebleau Hotel?"

Chapter Seventeen

FAMILIAR EVENINGS

> *Ah, my Beloved, fill the Cup that clears*
> *To-day of Past Regrets and Future Fears:*
> *To-morrow!—Why, To-morrow I may be*
> *Myself with Yesterday's Sev'n Thousand Years.*

At dusk, waiting for Junie after a long day, Dick falls asleep sitting in the hard bentwood chair in his apartment, and has the dream he has begun to have in the nights. In this dream, the dead man, a doctor, is walking toward him holding a leafy branch, which he sweeps before him like a broom. When he is near, the man looks at him and says, "You should have waited. I was getting better. I would have been all right if you had waited."

"We couldn't wait any longer," Dick says to him. "It's your own fault." Then the man thrusts the branch at Dick's eyes but a bird swoops down and wrests it from him. Then Dick sees that he himself is wearing a yellow butcher's apron, and that is the end of the dream.

After work, in the evenings, Abbas drives his car to a poor quarter of the city and walks the streets there, hoping to spy a well, in a courtyard or set into a wall, where the pollution might arise. He does not really expect to find it, but the exercise is calming. He thinks of the lines of the Koran: "He may bring forth those who believe and do righteous deeds from the shadows into the light." The doing of righteous deeds in shadow, that was all anybody could do now. Not that he was righteous or a believer.

Others may connive, hope—let them. It is one thing to flutter leaflets down from the sky and a lesser thing just to walk along the street hoping to spy something in the tilt of a drain, in the direction of a ditch, that could explain disease. It was bold in others to want to change hearts, inspirit hearts. He did not mistrust it—admired, even, the increasingly desperate and often horrible acts of the *mujahedin*.

Most of the time Abbas, because he has no wife, and various Americans have supper at the hospital, where the food is free, or sometimes the Americans eat at a restaurant Chloe thinks of as the Pepsi-Cola, because that is a sign she can read in Farsi. In the impossible kitchen at Villa Two she has tried her hand at some Persian dishes, but she couldn't manage the rice right, and was too shy to discuss with the butcher which cut of meat was which, though he spoke a little English. The cuts were unfamiliar, and they were all lamb, which she believed to be unhealthy, like all red meat.

"Persian food would be better for a little seasoning," she had confided her opinion to Heidi. "If it were more like Indian food, don't you think?"

"You're asking an Englishwoman about seasoning?" Heidi had laughed.

"Their buildings are so fancy but their food is so plain. What does it mean?"

"Poor people anywhere—do they have spices?" Heidi said. "In America? What spices do poor people use in America?"

"Well, I don't know. The same as anywhere. It depends on what kind of poor people you mean, black or Puerto Rican or what. In America, we don't really think of poor people as a single category with single habits," she said, wondering if this was true. "Garlic would be hardest to give up," she added.

"Persians don't use much garlic," said Heidi. "But they use rose water. I've never quite liked it."

"That must be it," said Chloe, tasting something funny in the rice.

They were eating at the Pepsi-Cola at tables of Formica, chrome chairs, linoleum of green and paste color, which she had grown accustomed to. Here you got a pretty good chelo kebab and fresh fish flown in from the gulf; it was ten times cheaper than the Cyrus, and everybody agreed that the food was as good. No wine. You drank tea or Pepsi-Cola. Chloe drank regular Pepsi now because they didn't have diet Pepsi. She could remember a time when she would have thought drinking regular would lead to death. The tea in Iran was strong as tonic. The doctors called it battery fluid. It was delicious, but if you drank too much of it you couldn't sleep, and she had passed a few sleepless nights staring at the mound of Hugh in the other cot.

Hugh chose most nights to stay with her on this second cot, rather than return to his own quarters, where he had at present a roommate, a snoring surgeon from North Carolina, to whom he had given, he said, no explanation for his absences. He would stay the night but then would steal out at dawn, with the first moan of prayer, when, fortunately, there seemed to be few faithful up to observe. He crept in at night, when the coast was clear, usually about ten. They were at a loss as to how to get him another key. Chloe had pretended to be afraid of losing hers, and asked for another from Dr. Farmani and been refused, and she had not found a locksmith, so for now Hugh was obliged to cough in the shrubbery beneath her window, she to steal down the steps to the front door. Hugh would scuttle inside at a moment when no one was passing by, which was easy enough after the front gates of the compound were shut for the night, an arrangement at once connubial and excitingly clandestine.

Hugh had adapted to connubial comfort without question and without analysis—a cheerful companion and ardent lover with no thought, it seemed, for the future. Perhaps he took domestic harmony for granted, was accustomed to find everywhere some nice woman in his life, arms extended, dinner ready, legs spread later. Chloe saw that she was just the nice woman of the moment; then they would go back to America and someone else would be the nice woman. And sometimes the nice woman would insist on marriage. Then he would marry her, because he was so cheerful and obliging, and then when she found out she was just a functionary, she would leave him; that must be the explanation for his two divorces.

She didn't mind being the nice woman, she told herself. For one thing, there was so much love-making. She had always kept secret her reverence for sex, which she believed she felt more keenly than other people but that it would, if expressed, be too easily mistaken for sexual boasting or sentimentality. What she felt was something akin to deep rapturous happiness and amazement that there were inexpressible forces that caused waves and atoms and emanations in her toward Hugh, or if not just him toward another handsome man. It was all very well to say "nature," of course, but what is nature? Whatever it was, she felt herself deeply, darkly, a part of it.

After a near disaster on Hugh's teetery cot, they had taken to love-making on the sofa, struggling awkwardly around the wooden arms or in a semi-sitting position, which Chloe secretly feared revealed the tops of their heads, to be seen by anybody walking by, head tops bobbing up and disappearing below the sill. And, when she thought about it, she found herself irritated that Hugh had not asked about contraception, simply taking for granted that she was doing what was necessary, just as she did at home, though that was not among the things she held against Jeffrey, whose offer of a vasectomy had horrified her, thinking as she had been that this would have the effect of controlling her life. As it was she wore an IUD.

She did not complain to Hugh about her life in California, or about Jeffrey, to whom she felt loyal in a way. Also, she was not able to formulate to herself just what it was about Jeffrey, or about Jeffrey and her, that wasn't perfectly harmonious, nothing you could say in a divorce court. But Jeffrey's crossness, his bad temper, contrasted so clearly with Hugh's cheerfulness and good humor that she found herself remembering more often than she liked certain passages with Jeffrey: once when he had turned the car around and driven them home, although they were all dressed for their outing, because the children had wrestled in the back seat. Once when he had been cutting salami and had brandished a butcher knife at her, and once when making love, during which the door had creaked and he had lifted his head and said harshly to her, "You didn't lock the goddamned door."

At the time she had laughed. To speak in such an angry tone to someone you are making love to! But it came back to her often. You wouldn't speak that way to a new lover, or to anyone you really loved. She felt that Hugh would not speak that way to anyone ever.

On the other hand there was something a trifle opaque about Hugh's radiant sweetness. If he had inner depths or torment they were not apparent. Vigorous, handsome, and intelligent. Lucky for him. Fortune had also favored him with an expensive watch, an elegant wallet of some lizard skin—these seemed to be his only possessions. Back home in his regular life he might for all she knew be a voracious collector of things, but she doubted it. He seemed indifferent to objects. When he took his shoes off at night he put them neatly against the wall, the toes pointing toward the wall, and hung his pants over the back of a chair. The socks in the shoes, the coat in the closet. When did he shine his shiny shoes, which did not seem to gather as hers did the dust of the Iranian streets?

There was no hint of an explanation for the nine shirts. She could never discuss his lie with him because she would seem demanding and proprietary. She was afraid to seem like that kind of woman, like a wife who would say, "Where have you been?"

She had tried once or twice to talk to Hugh about what they would do when they got back. She didn't have any ideas of her own—didn't want to break off their affair, but of course Jeffrey mustn't find out; would they go back to quick glimpses of each other at medical meetings, the occasional trip to San Francisco by Hugh to lecture? What would she do if Hugh suggested she divorce Jeffrey and marry him? This he did not seem likely to do at the moment, but who knew whether he would miss her when they got back to the U.S. again, immured in their lonely daily lives. His happiness now, his affectionate manner, his protestations of love, even, for he whispered "I love you" sometimes: were all these to end?

Chloe despised herself when she thought like this. She was going to go back to Jeffrey as had been planned all along, and would think of this as a lovely interlude and great good luck, but that was all. Would she really want to move to Rochester, New York? Hugh being fatherly to the children, taking them to Marineland—impossible to imagine, but then it was all impossible to imagine—America itself, representing itself to her imagination as a mélange of freeways and muggers—this must be the way foreigners think about it too—and her unweeded back garden and a stack of mail and unpaid bills and an appointment at the gynecologist and the dog for rabies booster, cats for feline distemper, children for tetanus and polio boosters, Pap smear, new transmission, rear brake linings, porcelain crowns. Such thoughts as these stimulated a rush of anxious maternity, and Chloe would write a long letter to the children full of lively description, injunction to goodness and cooperativeness; urgent desire to hug and kiss them and the happiness of seeing them and Grandma soon.

Chloe had come to understand Noosheen's passion for washing machines when the old machine in Villa Two gave out and she was obliged to wash things by hand in the laundry tub and drag them, pounds of sodden cotton, leaking up the stairs to the roof. She hadn't before appreciated the weight of wet clothes and could see why you would have to learn to carry them in a basket on your head. She had also come to enjoy hanging out the clothes. She had begun by flinging things haphazardly over the line, but now was putting things in neat groups, bras at one end, wind-filled breasts all pointing the same way, panties next to them. Now in the hot weather she never wore stockings. She had never accepted wash-and-wear clothing, but she had discovered that by stretching the skirts of her cotton dresses and smoothing the wet hems with her fingers, she didn't have to iron them. She pulled at the collars and plackets. She had not at first done Hugh's wash but really it seemed very little trouble to throw his socks and underwear into the water along with hers.

In other ways too her life with Hugh was like marriage. Some nights Hugh brought the *Herald Tribune* or London *Times,* and they sat reading, squinting under the dim bulb as the dogs gathered in the shrubbery and the last call to prayer went forth over the cricket sounds. Sometimes Hugh told her about being a boy in New England, making maple syrup. She was charmed at any individuating glimpse into his past. The evenings grew hotter, the nights hotter, the sounds blown about on a new wind from the desert. Like married people they exchanged hospital gossip. When Chloe told Hugh about Noosheen's unhappiness and aspirations, her studies, her dislike of her washing woman, her crush on Abbas, Hugh grew unaccountably impatient.

"Jesus Christ, Chloe, you encourage that silly young woman," he said.

"No, I don't encourage her, but I am sympathetic. She has no one else to talk to. Her family is away, she's very unhappy. . . ."

When you are overwrought, a calming mental exercise is to imagine yourself throwing away junk mail. You read the envelopes one by one and throw away unopened each thing that is addressed by means of a label stuck on. Father Henry's Boys' Village, the Christmas Pledge Drive, Save the Delta, Poets' Collective, Sea Gull Fund, kidneys, blood, lungs, heart, cancer, muscles, cysts, birth defects, brain damage. Some you save: unwanted children, starving children, baby seals. Envelopes for the starving stack up.

To think of the envelopes stacking up almost destroys the happiness of being far away, hanging up clothes on an Iranian rooftop, with nothing much to do, with a lover. It occurs to her that she is tasting some of the fun and power of being a man, being far away, on her own, working at something, sleeping with someone she won't mention to the person at home.

"Really," said Jeffrey in his next letter, "when you think how you'll be home in three weeks, it doesn't make sense for me to pack up and come now." At first surprised, Chloe found herself more or less indifferent to this news except for the disappointment to the children, who must have been looking forward to traveling to Iran and Rome, especially Sara, whom they had thought old enough to get something out of it. What had Jeffrey promised her instead?

Only three more weeks was the thing that struck at her heart. A period to happiness. But perhaps happiness does not exist without a sense of its limits. As they say too of life. Three weeks. It caught in her throat.

Jeffrey also wrote to Vahid Farmani that he wasn't coming after all. Vahid just showed the letter to Linda with a smirk. He was unsurprised. He knew it wasn't from the real Fowler anyway and was just a manifestation of the plan ticking away outside his control.

Hossein lies nights in the doorway of the Farmanis' kitchen, cool against the marble stoop, listening to the dogs, to the little tunes of radios flickering on the ear, thinking, though he is old, of having a woman, or thinking with disgust of women, of the American woman's washing, or of a house he knew where girls came in from the country. He no longer thinks of returning to his family in the country, in a village near Suse.

Chapter Eighteen

LOCAL COLOR

Ah, make the most of what we yet may spend,
Before we too into the Dust descend;
Dust into Dust, and under Dust, to lie,
Sans Wine, sans Song, sans Singer, and,—sans End!

The days passed. One Monday Abbas Mowlavi took Chloe, Junie, and Mrs. Henderson to a mosque. "Persons not conveniently dressed, not admitted," read the sign. "Any transgression will be denounced to the police." "*That* gives you pause," said Chloe.

Abbas had brought veils for them to wear. "You can rent them for a few tooman, outside the mosque, but I think it's not perhaps too nice," he explained. Chloe's veil was sprigged pink, those of Junie and Mrs. Henderson black. Chloe's veil held the faint scent of powder or perfume. She wondered if it had belonged to Abbas's wife, and whether he remembered her by this scent. If someone you loved died, you could keep the things that smelled of them. She'd never thought of this. But now the veils would smell of her and Mrs. Henderson.

In her veil she felt clumsy and kept dropping the ends. Abbas showed them how to wrap themselves, but he was no expert either. "You clamp it under your arm to start with, I think," he said. "Sometimes the other end they hold in their teeth." Chloe wondered how she looked. Mrs. Henderson's white hair and pink cheeks were all wrong. She looked like a rosy nun or elderly madonna wearing earrings of turquoise plastic. Junie was too tall and awkward. "In America this would be objected to, making the women cover themselves but not the men; there would be a class-action suit," Junie said as they took off their shoes.

The inside of the mosque was entirely covered in mirror, a

cathedral-size room in mirror mosaic. It seemed a worldly idea, for everywhere she looked she saw not Allah but a fragmented Chloe, pink-sprigged and manifold, amid the shimmering glass. In one corner stood the bier of a sacred person. Abbas explained he was the brother of an imam, and people kissed the mirrored bars of the cage that enclosed his coffin. Chloe saw a small woman in black, kissing the golden cage, her eyes tightly closed in passionate devotion. Chloe thought it was Noosheen, until she remembered that Noosheen was not a Muslim but a Zoroastrian. She wondered what sort of church the Zoroastrians had, and whether they wore veils. A heavy musky scent of incense, dusty rugs, and perhaps of bare feet, hung in the thick air. The effect on Chloe was oddly erotic. Chloe knew this place ought to be sacred, but when she breathed deeply the profane richness of the screens, the sultry burning of the lamps overhead, the sighs of prayer, she thought of harems. She thought of lounging here on cushions, with pistachio nuts and wine, voluptuous and indolent, waiting for Abbas. She the always-chosen, the nightly chosen, whispers, pleasure. The milk and wine of her breasts. The man would be Abbas—someone like Abbas—but in robes, in turban. The handsome men of the desert; to think that beneath their womanly skirts they were all equipped like men.

A wizened holy man, squinting and sour, glared at their clumsily draped faces. He knew them for Western women. Chloe shrank reverently over the tomb of a nephew of a prophet, absorbed in her imaginings.

Each day Chloe read a little of the Koran, a chapter a day, feeling no more interest in it than in the Bible, which it seemed to resemble, and which she had never read all the way through, just the Old Testament up to Leviticus, and the famous parts, studied in the Episcopalian Sunday school long ago. She knew she was illiterate in an essential cultural subject, but by toiling in the Koran, she told herself, she was in a way making up for her previous deficiency. In the Koran, the world was created by God in six days, and woman out of man, with this original pair being driven out of a garden; and there were characters named Lot or Abraham or Moses, so Mohammed had evidently read the Old Testament, and even, probably, the New.

Chloe did not know why she was not spiritual. She believed

in a general way that people should be spiritual, it was just that she was not. She hoped she might have natural piety. She would not scoff at God, or nature, or at the Koran, either. Indeed, while reading, she would fall into a mood of humble chagrin at her own spiritual failings, and feel the wish that something would seize her soul with faith or even with violent and emphatic skepticism. Instead she felt only the charm of the Day of Judgment:

> *Surely among delights*
> *Shall the righteous dwell,*
> *Seated on bridal couches they will gaze around;*
> *Thou shalt mark in their faces the brightness of delight;*
> *Choice sealed wine shall be given them to quaff. . . .*

A shiver of regret would seize her that she herself would undoubtedly be a victim of "The Inevitable."

"I suppose you are a Muslim," Chloe said to Abbas as they left the mosque.

"By birth. I am afraid I'm not very religious," Abbas said, apologetically and after a moment of pensiveness, like a fallen-away Catholic.

"I believe there are many similarities with Christianity," said Mrs. Henderson.

Abbas smiled. "Unlike Jesus, Mohammed was human. He was subject to human vulgarities, like desire and jealousy."

"I wish I could read Arabic. I would so like to read the Koran in the original," said Chloe politely.

"I believe there are some good translations," Abbas said. "How are you coming with your Farsi?"

"Not very well," she admitted. In fact it had been nearly a week since she had looked at the textbook, though she had learned to say *"Che qadr"* in the market.

"I think I need a teacher. The book isn't very satisfactory. I often have questions."

"For instance?"

"For instance, is there no word for 'please' or 'thank you'?"

Abbas laughed. "Probably you have got some old colonial book," he said.

Another day he took them to see the tomb of Cyrus, king of

the Achaemenians. This king once had lain in a sepulcher atop the rather desolate stone cairn they now beheld. Chloe, who had been put in charge of the guidebook, read out to the others: "According to Strabo this was inscribed 'Oh man, I am Cyrus who founded the Empire of the Persians and was king of Asia. Grudge me not therefore this monument.' "

Once, said the book, the funerary mausoleum had been decked with rich hangings, the body reposed in a sarcophagus of gold, the sarcophagus lay on a gold couch, and near it were arrayed various treasures of gold. Magi guarded the tomb, and lived nearby in fragrant gardens. The Americans viewed with satisfaction the desolation of the spot, the simple splendor of the enduring stone. Two Iranian men, their eyes leering out wildly from faces dark with dust, squatted in the shade afforded by the monument. Guards or perhaps just loungers, they motioned to the travelers that it was all right to climb the giant steps of the ziggurat and peer into the empty treasure chamber. Dutifully the Americans boosted each other up and stared into the stone cavity, empty except for a bit of plastic wrapper blown into one corner.

When they climbed down, the guards leapt up to lift the ladies down the last high step. With expressionless faces, their hands skimmed over Chloe's breasts, pressing furtively. Chloe glanced at Junie, whose pinkness suggested that this had happened to her too. Chloe pretended not to notice; she thought of laughing at the men, if only she could convey how she despised their little triumph over Christian women—women entirely indifferent to skinny little brown men who smelt of camel and tobacco and wore rags. As it was she said nothing, but she felt irritated and looked away, smiling her bright smile at her friends, as if she did not even see these functionaries. It now struck her that the Iranian women—Noosheen and Zareeneh Yazdi—had not climbed the monument. How stupid she felt herself, to mind what these poor men did, she who was so incalculably more fortunate.

Noosheen's husband Bahram had come along, though he rarely joined these sightseeing expeditions. Chloe was struck by how Noosheen walked before or behind him, and looked away when he looked at her. Perhaps they were having a quarrel. Bahram was the picture of a concerned husband, handing her in and out of cars and providing other attentions, like an old cuckold from Boccaccio or Chaucer, and Noosheen had just the same expression, under her expression of sweetness, of willfulness, a classical young wife. Chloe found these analogies comforting evidence of the consistency of human nature, any nation, any age. The Iranians are like us, she thought. Seeing Bahram, Chloe could better understand one of Noosheen's confidences: "I do not really like the act of love," she had said. "But I feel that I might if he were . . . different."

"Do you have an M.A.?" Noosheen asked Chloe now, as they walked back to the cars.

"No," Chloe admitted. Most of her friends did. She had always planned to get an M.A. but could never think in what.

"I hope to get mine," said Noosheen.

"In what?"

"Well—in English literature," Noosheen said, widening her eyes, a tremor of surprise in her voice that it was necessary to ask something so obvious. "English literature of the nineteenth century!" she added.

"Oh, of course," said Chloe, who had been thinking of being felt up by the horrid Iranians.

"Do you think I should?"

"Well, sure," said Chloe easily. "Victorian literature is wonderful."

"My husband doesn't want me to. It means a long period of study. First I must finish my B.A., that's another year to begin with. Then—it could be years. Also, would my degree be any good? I don't know if the teachers at Shiraz University are very qualified. I wanted to go to Wayne State. It was all fixed. But with perseverance it is possible to study here. Do you think I should?"

Chloe hoped this was only a rhetorical question, and that Noosheen was not seriously depending on her answer, for she had no idea what Noosheen should do. It seemed rather a useless specialty, Victorian literature, for someone living in Iran, although it would no doubt be a consolation in itself.

And, after all, a twentieth-century American was as remote as
an Iranian from people in a Dickens novel, neither having ever
seen a winkle or a verger or a dust heap. An M.A. in English
literature—why not?

"You can always teach," she said.

"Yes," Noosheen agreed, sounding dubious. Suddenly she
stopped and pointed toward the river bank ahead of them. Her
eyes had widened with, it seemed, a sudden rage. "Look, look
at that, look there!"

She was pointing to a spot among the stones where tribal
women, their wrappings tied back, strong brown arms wet, or
wading with skirts hitched up, wrestled wet cloths and beat
them on rocks. Doing the washing. Boxes of Tide near them in
baskets on the shore. It was picturesque and pretty.

"That, that is the real Iran," cried Noosheen, her voice
informed with a curious passion, her glance at her husband full
of irritable triumph.

They planned to return to their automobiles by a different
route, in order to see a little village that lay beyond the
monument. Dick strolled slowly behind the others, looking for
potsherds, mind idly dwelling on the dead man, on Marla and
the house, on whether things had been misplaced in the
laboratory yesterday. It was the house, for some reason, that
was uppermost in his mind this afternoon. He was remembering
how happy they had been when they moved in. After months
of looking, it had struck them both immediately as inevitably
theirs. Marla had called, with the realtor standing there, for
him to rush over. A big, lovely house, something the kids
could bring their kids back to, practically a mansion, and now
she wanted a condo.

He had fallen into the habit of keeping an eye out for
potsherds, at first intending to give them to Chloe, but now he
had got interested in them. It occurred to him that he had some
other little bits of pottery, picked up here and there—Mesa
Verde, Yellowstone—which with these might make a nice
collection; he could get them mounted.

This long road took them through a village of mud hovels,
roofed in straw. Women squatted before the hovels; goats
roamed in the dung and mud of the street. A trickle of water
wetted the dust. People looked at them without curiosity or

interest. A child smiled at them. Chloe liked, somehow, the acrid smell of meat cooking over a dung fire.

"*This* is the real Iran," said Abbas. "Most of the people still live like this. The tribal people, who move their flocks, live better than these villagers."

The children were thin; the little girls had ragged black shawls over their heads. Heaps of broken pots and rusting tubs of oil stood outside the doorways. Behind the houses, from somewhere they heard keening and wailing.

"Where are the men?" asked Hugh.

"In the fields. There is some agriculture here. Or they have gone to Tehran, hoping for work. The people don't want to work in the fields any more."

"What is the wailing?"

"Oh, a death or a funeral."

As the party stood, observing the life of the villagers as if it were a pageant, a play being shown to them by their Iranian guide, Dick's notice fell on a child propped against a rubble wall, a girl of eleven or twelve, whose arms had the appalling stick-like thinness of the starving, the wrists thicker than the bony limbs, wrists like bracelets of bone. Her eyes, staring and dull, saw Dick. The child's desiccation and lassitude were shocking. He had only seen starvation in photographs or films. Yet the villagers were cooking something, there was a smell of charred lamb. Illness, it must be. She was crouching silently, the head swaying slightly, as if she lacked the strength to hold it up. A dirty rag was wrapped around her shoulders, a child's veil. Women of the village walked by without noticing her. The Iranian doctors must notice. The dull eyes watched them.

"That child is sick," Dick Rothblatt said to Vahid.

"Yes," Vahid agreed. "She has the look of hepatitis."

"We should take her back with us," Chloe said, frightened that the child would die right now before them.

"In general the health of the peasants is very good," said Vahid Farmani.

"They suffer from easily preventable infections," Hugh disagreed.

"It's very discouraging. They must be educated first. Otherwise they don't take their medicines, they don't come back for follow-up care," said Farmani. They had begun to walk slowly along the rutted path between the hovels.

"The little girl!" Chloe cried.

"I could perhaps ask someone where her mother is," Abbas said, and called out to a woman near him. The woman answered him.

"Yes, they have given her up," Abbas said.

"At a certain point there is nothing one can do," Farmani explained. They were walking rapidly on.

"There are always incentives," Hugh said. "In every culture, even the most resistant, a way can be found to make people come in. And the people here are relatively advanced. You work with the tribal leader, or whomever it takes and you could stamp out these things."

"Yes, we have much to do," said Vahid, walking more quickly toward the road where they had left their cars. They were leaving the child; not even Dick or Junie looked back at her.

"But couldn't we help?" Chloe asked, her face white with indignation. This was the third-world lesson, of course she knew that, that you see some evidence of hopelessness, you confront the passive acceptance of death, you did what you could but it wasn't much, you had to get used to the whole bleak apparatus of reality. It was what was supposed to happen. She felt faint with anxiety.

"I'm trying to think of something to do," Dick assured her, but could not think what.

That night he had a dream that he was standing with a stick in his hand, a part of a tree, the leaves still on it, leafy and full, but with the stub end gnarled and bloody as if it had been wrested from its socket. He beat the man in the cave to death with it.

"Who was it that spoke," said Chloe to Hugh on the sofa that night, "of the deep, deep peace of the double bed, after the hurly-burly of the chaise longue?"

"It's true," Hugh agreed, "it'd be nice to have a double bed. A queen-size, while we're at it."

"Of course she was really talking about marriage," said Chloe, wishing suddenly to be married to Hugh.

Chapter Nineteen

NEWCOMERS

*O Thou, who didst with Pitfall and with Gin
Beset the Road I was to wander in,
Thou wilt not with Predestined Evil round
Enmesh, and then impute my Fall to Sin!*

The little dying girl haunted Chloe with feelings of shame and fear. There's little you can do, after all, to ward off evil and bring yourself some luck, even for her, a privileged woman; what chance for the little girl? Chloe always wore her lapis beads now, afraid to leave them in her drawer and comforted each morning by the tiny chill stones against her throat, then by the warmth her throat gave them, and the warmth of her fingers as she touched them. Lapis lazuli was supposed to bring out your character. If you were bad it made you worse, if good better, it intensified your qualities. But she could not see that any of her qualities were intensified. Was she worse or sillier than usual? It seemed to her that in some ways she was better—calmer and more agreeable to others, better unless you counted sleeping with Hugh Monroe as being bad.

She should have given the little girl something. Did anyone know whether inanimate objects might not really bring luck? Was there something about atoms? There was a theory: some blandishing and promising atoms collected together create a field, a force, and an object made of those atoms when worn had an effect. Chloe was pretty sure her lapis beads were lucky. She thought of the little girl in the village, with a brass disk on a chain around her neck. In documentaries about primitive tribes you saw the puny children decked in amulets put there by the frightened mothers. In Iran the poorest woman, in black shrouds, seemed to have a golden chain or charm, so there must be something in it. Down the centuries people believing in luck—could they all be wrong?

In the bazaar she bought a pair of tiny silver charms, old, set with glass and silver paper, clumsy and simple, but powerful-looking, and she planned to make her children wear them even though they would object.

She knew she'd gained weight. It was something in favor of the chador that you could be fat inside it and no one would see you. She knew she shouldn't care what people think. She was too vain to be happy fat in California but here it didn't matter. Hugh didn't seem to mind or notice a slight dimpling of her thighs, was never deterred in his always rather single-minded object by the increase of an inch around her waist. She wished you could wear veils in San Francisco.

Her friend Heidi wore head scarves when walking in the street. Chloe, tying a scarf over her own bright hair, saw it was true that one felt more comfortable. And she had strangely begun to feel uncomfortable with her upper arms bare. It was not that people stared, or that there was any objection to upper arms. The feeling, she recognized, came from within herself, presenting itself as a crawling sensation, as if you were in a draft above the elbows. It was really simpler, when you were just running out to the store, to evade the issue of being a Western woman, pale and fair, by putting on something long-sleeved, and a scarf. Chloe thought it was foolish of young women like Noosheen to want to lighten their fine, dark hair.

Her beads she always wore, and her wedding ring, of course, and the head scarf, and rather wished for a cloak or veil. If she wore her beads, that left only her camera worth stealing, so she had taken to leaving the door open for Hugh, or leaving the key under the mat where anyone would think to look. She had given up taking photographs. Sights found at first so ravishing, so voluptuously lacking in perpendiculars, so lavishly floral, vined, entwined, mirrored, filigreed, carved, inlaid, cushioned, screened, now appeared to her if not normal at least not so compellingly in need of being photographed. They seemed to be aspects of an enduring material world whose existence did not need to be confirmed in inept photos by American ladies. Indeed, it was a material world in process of amelioration, since everywhere the government had set people to refurbishing and polishing the lovely crumbling palaces and pavilions, and decayed corners of mosques.

The sociable and regular rhythm of Azami life was continuing despite disquieting rumors and disruptions. News of strikes in other towns reached them, and Chloe realized that the soldiers with machine guns she had seen in Isfahan had been there in expectation of some riot or insurgence. They had been, it appeared, prepared to kill their countrymen.

She, like the other Americans, though regretting these intimations of bloodshed, viewed them with equanimity, even approval. They had the regular American belief that tyrants must and will eventually fall. They didn't even mind the occasional manifestation of anti-Americanism. They didn't take it personally, and they were all leaving anyway. Chloe hated the thought that she had only three weeks left. Meantime, she did have something anti-American happen to her, startling her, if only for a moment.

The American Wives' Club met the third Thursday of the month, the English Wives' Club had a tea each Wednesday. On Wednesday nights the Iranian doctors had dinner in the Reza Café and went to the English-language films, as a way of keeping up their English and having a good time. On weekends the inevitable dinner party, sightseeing, tennis. Chloe liked the dinner parties best. Persian dinners were so pretty. At first they had surprised her. You are led into the other room, or a table is brought to the room where you are, all laid, a glorious buffet, with none of this shuffling dishes in and out from the kitchen that Chloe was used to and preferred until she came to see that the Arabian Nights fantasy way of presenting a meal was really better, as if a genie had waved it onto the table, though you knew, of course, that women had toiled over it. Chloe was not always invited to the dinner parties, though people always invited the attractive Dr. Monroe. Sometimes, for form's sake, he went. Chloe tried not to mind.

She knew that without Jeffrey she didn't really belong. As at summer camp, she was conscious of having to earn her place here. People, except for Linda Farmani, seemed to like her, but she was accustomed to being liked; a sympathetic listener, ready with toast and coffee, she made them comfortable. Listening to people and cooking for them were second nature to her, a reasonable price for the attention of others. Still, she was feeling slightly embarrassed, with all the hospitality she had received, not to have done more for others, and resolved to have something, perhaps a drinks party, or a little supper of her own. This inspired her to continue the refurbishment of her room, whose ugliness she had partly got used to, and she was grateful for the activity too to support her spirits, which, when she sat quietly, oppressed her with thoughts of the little village girl, and of all lame people and starving people, and of her own children, so unaccountably separated from her and far away.

She thinks Dick's rug looks wonderful in her room. She has put it in the center, where it can be seen from her chair or when she lies in her camp bed, and where it covered a worn spot on the linoleum. Any plain cell or tent can be thus transformed; you can carry your rug with you like a bedouin so that wherever you go will be beautiful. She sits on it amid the flowers and birds, protected, surrounded by the rich borders, and envies Dick his rug, and thinks how nice he is to forgo the pleasure and protection of his rug. She thinks of young women sitting by the rug loom, their eyes wet with strain, and being put out on the sand when their fingers grow too clumsy. Could that be true? Probably. Women are always expendable when they can no longer perform their duties. In America her life is safe because she can take the toaster and pick up the children from school. Here it is useless, without function. How strange, then, that it should be here that she feels full of purpose and calm.

She has a color in mind for her room, blue, something like lapis, but with more green in it, not a color you would paint anything in California except the bottom of a swimming pool, but the strong color they use here for window sashes and doors and porches. This color wards off evil. She buys the paint. She thinks it looks reassuring. She can see why it wards off evil. She paints the grayish plaster of the hallway, and then the door to her apartment, and then, encouraged, rather giddy with the success of this powerful measure, the outside door of Villa Two, let the Azami people remonstrate if they will. She loves this bright, uncanny color. She paints the window sills in the kitchen. Then she invites people to tea for the following day, and goes to the bazaar to buy pistachio cakes and tea.

It is here that she has the unsettling experience. Just walking along, not seeing, really, the women so invisible in their shrouds, when all at once one of them steps in front of her, impeding her passage along the sawdust hallway, and as rapidly as an executioner with a sword, the woman lays a finger along Chloe's throat. As delicate as a blade, as swift, then is gone. Chloe thinks for an instant that it has been an affectionate touch, a sisterly gesture of some kind, then that the woman had reached impulsively for her beads. Guiltily she realizes that she shouldn't wear them showing. Ostentation, so many women here with nothing, she ought to have realized that here was a gesture of hate or warning. It is disconcerting to be hated by another woman. Chloe did not think this had happened to her before. What had they seen in her heart? She tucks her beads inside her blouse.

Nearly everyone accepted her invitation. At first, the Iranians regarded General Ben with a certain reserve. He regaled the gathering with terrible anecdotes about Vietnam, embarrassing Chloe beyond speech. Why remind them that Americans had been the bullies of the world? How could General Ben not see that? Instead he said what Chloe had never actually heard anyone say, though of course she knew there were people who thought this: "We should have just gone in there with the nukes and got it over with." Of course, she reminded herself, it was not surprising that a general should be committed to military success. What was more surprising was that she continued to like General Ben, and even still more surprising that the Iranians also seemed, as he rattled on, to come to like him too, leaving Chloe alone in her dismay at his views. Noosheen sat next to him on Chloe's cot, sipping her tea and listening with unmoving eyes as he criticized Iranian customs.

"Of course women can escape," he was saying, "if they have money. They can get a forged exit visa or they can get themselves smuggled out through Afghanistan or Russia. A friend of mine helped a woman get out. An American woman married to an Iranian, no passport. The husband didn't want her to go. They put her in some rugs, like Cleopatra." He laughed. Noosheen clutched her cup. Chloe thought of the terrible situation of not being able to leave if you wanted to leave, a man, a marriage, a country. In America, what could stop you—if you had the money?

"They think of women as property," he said, "all these Arabs do. No offense, as the kids say."

"I'm not offended," Noosheen said. "I agree completely. Although, you know, we in Iran are not Arabs."

Nor did she seem offended when the talk ran on to the general subject of the modesty of Iranian women, and the conservatism of Iranian men on this point.

"I used to think that all the fuss that people make, in America, about how advertising exploits women and so on, I always thought people would do better to press for more important reforms, like reforming the child-support laws," Chloe was saying. "But now I've come to feel that there's something reassuring and nice about not always being greeted by huge billboard-sized breasts and so on."

"Actually they're all sex-mad here," Junie said sourly, "despite the purity of the billboards. The repression and mystery turn them into sex maniacs. It would be better to have dirty billboards." She put her cup on Chloe's tray, an inlaid tray of ivory and wood, of which the ivory was probably plastic, bought in the bazaar.

"Actually Iran is not an Arab country," Noosheen said.

"Actually I find them sexy, in a way," Dick said. "The veil is kind of erotic—the legs flashing by under the robes. They wear sexy stockings, some of them, have you noticed? Black mesh. High heels. Like a porn film."

"You hear that the whores in Tehran don't wear anything at all under the chador. Then they flash as the man comes by," said Chloe.

"Who told you that?" asked Linda Farmani.

"I heard it at the English Wives' Club," said Chloe, wondering if Linda had ever been invited to the English Wives' Club and whether she wanted to be.

"I didn't think they had whores in Iran," Dick said. "I never heard of any."

Chloe had invited Linda Farmani, who surprised her by coming, sitting with aplomb on the edge of Hugh's cot and seeming not to notice the wretchedness of the place, notwithstanding the improvements of which Chloe was so proud, and the considerable asset of Dick's rug.

"Foreigners often don't take things really seriously here, our laws, our customs," said Linda. "They think our rules don't apply. For instance, I'm sure that in California Mrs. Fowler would never snitch her neighbor's plants."

This was said with so affable a smile at General Ben, that Chloe almost for a moment didn't take offense; a shock only set in after a moment, when the talk had gone on to something else and no rejoinder was possible. Chloe resolved to explain herself to Linda later: I didn't think you'd miss them, she would say. Of course—wasn't that what thieves always did say? Her ears heated up. It came to her that no one had ever criticized her in public before. Moreover, she would not in California have stolen a neighbor's plants. What was becoming of her? Looking at the others, their smiles affectionate, the conversation turned to something else, she saw the moment had passed and that she was the only sufferer. What was becoming of her?

After the guests left, as Chloe stood at the kitchen sink, washing the cups, she observed an arrival. The apartment next to hers, whose occupants would share the kitchen, had been empty since she got there, but it now appeared that someone was coming to live in it. Chloe watched from the window, even pushing aside the screen to fold her arms along the warm window sill and lean out a little, the better to see. It was a taxi; a driver was carrying suitcases to the front steps. Vahid Farmani stood on the sidewalk and watched the luggage, and a man was helping a stout woman out of the back seat. Americans, by the look of their clothes. Following a wave of Farmani's hand, the two looked up at Villa Two. Chloe stared back at them with interest. The American woman was keeping both hands on the handle of her purse; probably she had carried a load of jewelry in her purse.

The three approached Villa Two and entered. Chloe reflected with satisfaction that the foyer was no longer the smelly place it had been when she had come, and enjoyed a pleasant sensation of philanthropic virtue. Footsteps on the stairs and the sound of the key in the lock across the hall, the door shutting after them, voices. Then Vahid telling them he would see them later. Chloe sighed. It was a nuisance to think of that fat woman in the kitchen wanting the coffeepot, and strange food in the fridge, and it would be harder for Hugh to slip in unseen. But did she even care who saw him?

It was nearly six o'clock. She thought she might walk over to the Cyrus. From the bathroom as she combed her hair she became aware of voices rising, drifting through the wall, indistinct but vehement. The woman was shouting.

She returned to her living room to wait. The knocking, as she half-expected, followed in a moment. Perhaps she was becoming psychic. The man's face was red and tired; he wore a tie clip.

"Excuse me. Harold Erdman. Is there a hotel in Shiraz, do you happen to know?"

"Oh, yes, it's called the Cyrus." She pronounced it as it was pronounced: Kurush, let them figure it out. Then she relented and said it the regular way. " 'Kurush,' we would say 'Cyrus.' "

"Thanks," he said, and went back inside his door again. Before long Chloe heard them bumping and carrying bags down the stairs again.

"I'm just going there now," she said as she passed them on the stairs. "Maybe you should come with me, and then send for your bags."

"You stay with the bags, I'll go fix the hotel," said Dr. Erdman to his wife. At this unlucky moment, Dr. Farmani himself strolled up with the Erdmans' key. Dr. Erdman stood rooted, embarrassed to be caught in flight, bags packed.

"Tell him we're not staying, Harold," said the voice of Mrs. Erdman from the upstairs window. Dr. Erdman glanced up toward the window in lieu of explanation. Dr. Farmani followed his gaze. The fat eyes of Mrs. Erdman glared at him, but she did not address him. The eyes of Dr. Farmani exchanged, for one instant, with Chloe, an enigmatic glance.

"Tell him filthy. What do they think we are?" shouted Mrs. Erdman.

Does Farmani think I've put them up to this? Chloe wondered. How good, how docile and polite she had been compared to Mrs. Erdman.

"More comfortable, perhaps, in a hotel," said Dr. Erdman to Dr. Farmani.

"They promised explicitly," shouted Mrs. Erdman. "Harold, somebody's lining his pockets out of this, put the Americans in here and pocket the hotel money, something like that."

Dr. Farmani glared at Chloe, as if she were the author of this scandalous rumor. "I don't know these people," she felt herself wanting to say, wishing to defend herself even to the horrid Dr. Farmani. "I don't even know these people"; her emotions a tangle of sympathy for Farmani, dislike of the Erdmans, embarrassment at their bad manners, and anger at them for not toughing it out as some other, more virtuous, people had. Dr. Farmani would not be thinking of this.

"If, of course, the hotel, more comfortable," he was saying.

"Since it's just a few days," Dr. Erdman was saying.

"Unhappily we have no financial arrangements for that," Dr. Farmani said.

"Oh, understood," said Dr. Erdman. "We'll take care of it ourselves. It'd be a help if you'd phone them."

"They speak English perfectly well," said Dr. Farmani haughtily. In spite of her dislike of him, Chloe applauded his hardness of heart toward the Erdmans.

Then, later at the Cyrus, there they were in the bar, bathed and cheerful, talking expansively about their sufferings in Villa Two. He was an otorhinolaryngologist from Johns Hopkins. They complained that the Cyrus was expensive, but they were only staying a week, had been in Egypt, and were going to the Philippines with this stopover in Iran.

"We thought it would be a good chance to buy some rugs," Dr. Erdman said. "I mentioned it to Farmani. He's going to write down for me the names of the good shops."

The Erdmans were further convinced that the Cyrus was

worth the extra expense when they heard Loyal Cooley's nightly discourse, tonight about a perilous trip he'd taken to some caves in Tunisia.

"Dysentery. Oh, hell, everybody had it, right from the first day. We got over worrying about it. We got expert. You only have one pair of jeans, you have to abandon shame. You got used to seeing someone just squat like a jackrabbit, same expression, sort of frantic fear, vulnerable, whip down the jeans. No rocks you can hide behind, remember this is the desert, you can see for miles. It makes a group close. In the silence, not a cricket, not an animal. Oh, they do have pit vipers. We killed two of them in camp. The bite of the pit viper's uniformly fatal. I had snake-venom antidote but no one else did. They all stuck close to me after they found out I had it.

"We walked fifteen hours a day. And this trip cost me thousands, besides. Out of eighteen people, only ten made it. It went from thirty-five, forty degrees in the morning to ninety in about two hours. Some people were really mad, paying all that money. Couldn't blame them. We made it, so it was worth it—wonderful caves. They hadn't realized how tough it would be, the tour leaders; this was their first time too."

Chloe looked around her, as usual, for a show of sly condemnatory glances from her friends but found in their countenances a certain opacity, a certain regional inscrutability, Dick looking, suddenly, very New York, the Erdmans Indianian—well, they were all Americans, including Loyal Cooley, including herself, and all were strangers.

"When I saw that base camp I knew that some of us were not gonna make it. Adversity says a lot about human nature. Right away I began saving my water. The second day I poured out my alcohol. I'd started out with a little alcohol, you know, thinking it would be nice at night. A pint of vodka poured out on the sand and it didn't even make a mark on the sand. If you had a granola bar it would have been worth two hundred dollars. We had eight people drop out in the first two days. One guy had a heart attack, one guy they thought had a stroke, one lady, really fat, had some problem with her leg. The others, heat exhaustion. Well, they should have screened these people. How could she climb on those huge fat legs?"

"Who was sponsoring this?" asked Mrs. Erdman.

"The Houston Art Museum."

"Did you see any cave paintings?" asked Chloe.

"Oh, sure, wonderful paintings, more beautiful than Lascaux, fifteen million years old. Or maybe fifteen thousand, anyway really great.

"Not a living creature except us, and the pit viper, and scorpions. If you heard something at night it was either a pit viper or somebody getting up with diarrhea. I was the most important guy in camp because I had the opium. I got it from my doctor, in case. Every night, you should have seen them line up, I put two drops of opium on their tongues. Even so there was diarrhea.

"Survival, that's the only thing on your mind. It's uplifting, in a way, just the simple thing of wondering where to put your foot next, when would you get some water. My wife didn't pour out her vodka. I could hear her in the dark, sneaking sips. One woman—somebody smelled chocolate on her breath— there was nearly a riot. But some people shared. That's human nature." All the travelers deeply sighed.

> Never mind, my darlings, you wouldn't like it here much and it's getting awfully hot. When I get home (soon!) we will start *diving lessons,* and what else you would like to do this summer, much more fun really.

She got a letter from Sara, which said,

> Dear Mom, Max broke my doll's dishes, he stepped on them.

Chapter Twenty

BLUE

The Ball no question makes of Ayes and Noes,
But Here or There as strikes the Player goes;
And He that tossed you down into the Field,
He knows about it all—HE knows—HE knows!

Dick one morning notices as he walks past Villa One on his way to the hospital an open door, a door that is usually closed. At the bottom of the house, and inside the doorway, he can see a wooden bench. This would not have attracted his eye or made an impression, except that during the split second of his perception, Hossein steps into his field of vision and squats on his haunches in the doorway, and Dick realizes with horror that this is where Hossein lives, in a dark, barely furnished room at the bottom of Villa One. Comes forth each morning and makes his ineffectual rounds in the various kitchens and bathrooms of the compound, maybe sleeps in there on the mud floor.

Does he have a family in there, does someone wash his shabby gray clothes? All the men he sees in Iran look somehow untended, shirts ironed as though by themselves; no female presence or care seems to attach to them. Not the doctors of course; their wives are as busy as American wives with children and parties and self-improvement. But the taxi driver, the man in the wagon—is this the price of female docility and seclusion that women revenge themselves by failing to nourish and tend? No wifely fingers on collar, at the knot of tie, a brush of shoulder, a pat. His heart taps more loudly for an instant at the thought of the pleasant but lost ministrations of American wives.

He is shaken anyway this morning by another harrowing night of dreams, ghastly guilt dreams of the staring body, hands stretching out of the grave to get him, exactly as if he had murdered the man. He supposes he feels guilty not to have saved him, or not to have made him a deathbed promise, or guilty to have let him go like that so uncomforted. He feels that these bad dreams do him credit, in a way, but he hates them. Last night he had brushed away the dust from the face of the corpse and it was the face of the little village girl.

On Wednesday, Chloe went with Heidi to the English Wives' Club tea. In the presence of her countrywomen, Heidi, usually natural and responsive, became reserved and polite, exclaiming over the tea in a high, official voice. Tea included "crisps," imported from England, which seemed to Chloe merely a form of inferior potato chip; and cucumber sandwiches, strangely spiced, and there were Iranian biscuits manufactured at a factory owned by the husband of Margaret, the oldest and most prosperous and therefore the dominant lady of this group. All the women smoked continuously, and were voracious for news of the outside world.

At her first visit they had asked Chloe all about California and also about Women's Lib, a subject remote from Iran, and also from England.

"Well," Chloe had said, "there've been great strides. Equal pay for equal work, and making sure women can advance in the job market, that kind of thing. I think they've accomplished a lot, even if they've put some people off with their methods. But the old bra-burning days are gone. I don't know—I can see that compared to here some of their goals might seem kind of frivolous."

"And what about the impotency problem?"

"The what?"

"Impotency? You read that Women's Lib has caused American men to be impotent."

"No, I never heard of that," Chloe said loyally.

"That's what they think in England," said Tina, laughing. They all laughed. English wives of sexy dark foreigners.

"Anyway," said Tina, "it's a man's problem."

"Impotency is not *our* problem," agreed the other ladies. Their accents varied by region and class. Chloe wondered if

they would know each other if they were all back in England.
And today there were two newcomers, one in fact Irish, called
Nora, and the other Australian, Betts: these two women
declared themselves resolved to keep their children speaking
English, ideas that were met with a kind of defeated scorn by
the real Englishwomen, mothers of little Farsi speakers. Chloe
privately believed that the Englishwomen would not have been
friends with Nora and Betts were they not all English-speakers
isolated here together. Nora was a bit religious-looking, Betts
peroxided and brisk, like an American but with the dreadful
Australian accent. Maybe they wouldn't have been friends with
Chloe either, a peroxided American. But here, now, they were
all sisters.

The talk today was of a terrible event in Abadan, the oil-
refining city to the south.

"But what has happened?" asked Chloe.

"This thing of the theatre in Abadan," they said. "Of the
people being burnt up in the theatre in Abadan."

Set afire, it was said, by religious fanatics who objected to
movies, and inside more than three hundred men were trapped
and died.

"If that's who really did it," said Heidi, with a significant
expression.

"Of course," said Tina, "they'd like nothing better than to
blame the fundamentalists. The government, I mean."

"Why not the fundamentalists? They don't care if you die,
you go to heaven. They are really bloodthirsty. Islam is
bloodthirsty, I mean, and these are fanatics."

"Yes," said Margaret, "you go right to Allah, so what does
it matter?"

"Whoever did it, they're all Iranians," Tina pointed out,
and this received nods of unsurprised assent. Chloe pressed
for details. She never saw a newspaper, had no radio. The
newspapers were in Farsi, after all, though you could walk
down to the Cyrus and get the *Herald Tribune;* it was just that
she had enjoyed not having a newspaper, and quite right, too,
if this was the horror it contained. The fumes, the flames, and
the doors had been locked. It was intended by the killers that
the poor men die—poor little thin men in rags watching a

movie. Her heart swelled. They had trimmed their mustaches and gone to die.

"I suppose things will really shut down now," said Margaret.

"They've sent troops to Abadan," Tina said.

"My God, how horrible," said Betts, lighting a cigarette. "Was it the mullahs or the Shah then?"

"It doesn't matter," Margaret snapped, "they're all Iranians."

"What does Mohammed say?" Chloe asked Heidi, as they drove back to the compound, and Heidi just shrugged. "What can anyone say?"

The English wives were gloomy about the future of Iran. The difference in mood among the American wives proved, Chloe supposed, a difference in American temperament—naturally more optimistic or naturally more self-centered—for the subject of Abadan did not come up on Thursday when she went to the American lunch. This was held in the garden of a Grumman wife and was an altogether larger and somewhat impersonal party. Rows of bridge chairs had been set up under the shade of the garden portico, and a projection screen suggested that there would be entertainment. Food was buffet style, with iced tea and lemonade; and a whole table of American PTA-style desserts—mainly chocolate cake and apple pie. Chloe looked around for Linda Farmani, who was not there, and was overjoyed to see Heidi and her English friend Tina, Englishwomen though they were. Chloe, relaxed by familiar faces, and then by the familiarity of the occasion, began to enjoy it and to hate it, the way she hated these things in California too.

"Linda Farmani did us," a woman told Chloe, speaking of her décor. "Well, you know, we have to do so much entertaining. It's practically like an embassy, so the company said we should go ahead. She has a wonderful feel for an Iranian look—well, adapted to what an American would like."

"Her own house is certainly pretty," said Chloe.

"I would never use a decorator at home. I think the décor should express the person. But here I wouldn't have known where to start, you know, where to get things, but she just barges into the bazaar, she hasn't an ounce of fear."

"I guess she speaks the language," Chloe said.

"Absolutely like a native. She gave us a rather wonderful raw-silk wall covering, then a lot of brass."

"It sounds lovely," said Chloe, politely.

First came announcements, then dues. The forthcoming meeting. Thanks to the program and refreshment committees. Announcements: "The only way to be sure the mail gets there is to send it in the pouch. Remember, everything goes in the pouch," a woman reminded them. Everyone nodded. The woman speaking, thin and tan, with white earrings, wearing a smart golf dress, was somehow familiar. Heidi and Tina watched it all with the appearance of interest and had come, they said, though they usually did not, because there would be an interesting speaker, someone who had begun life as a tribesman, riding the plains on a donkey, and was now Minister of Education of all Iran.

This interested Chloe also. You never met government officials in the U.S. because they were so far away. This man was accessible and nice, by the look of him—a portly, curly-haired man, dark-skinned and authoritative, being talked to in the doorway by the hostess and another woman. He carried a cassette of slides. He smiled beautifully and walked over to the lectern.

"I began here, in this village [slide]," said Mr. Khatem, "a son of a tribal man. My father had seven donkeys and a camel, and many goats. Therefore we were rich, yet I could not read, nor could my parents. Now families like mine can read. We have not tried, you see, to catch the children and put them into schools. No, the schools go along, along with the tribe, on trucks like these [slide]. They go to where the tribes rest in winter [slide] or here in summer, grazing [slide]. This is me with the Empress, that other woman is a friend of hers, also interested in education, and they have come, this is at Kaswin near Tehran."

Chloe saw a slide of two beautiful but artificial-looking women in white fox jackets shivering on a cold plain, surrounded by grinning children in colorful but ragged clothes, holding up slates.

Flocks of snowy sheep swarmed along a green hillside, mountains behind. A child with a shepherd crook.

A blackboard, with lovely lines of Persian writing across it, children sitting in front of it on stones, Mr. Khatem himself holding a pointer.

"Tribespeople dancing, made happy by literacy. This is my own tribe where I began, yet here I am today a respected and prosperous public servant, in a land where people can rise and prosper according to the wise provisions of our king."

The American ladies applauded with great enthusiasm and asked intelligent questions.

Heidi gave Chloe a lift home. They were driving in Heidi's Peykan, a nice little car; it seemed to Chloe more sensible than the huge American cars driven by the Grumman wives, or the Bell Helicopter wives, which you saw parked along the wide suburban streets of new villas out beyond the university.

First they dropped off Tina, then drove into the compound and into the driveway of Heidi's bungalow to the row of garages behind, where they were surprised to find Noosheen, sitting in her car outside her garage, huddled over the front seat as if in pain, the door open, but she immobile. Heidi and Chloe, astonished, saw that she was crying blue tears. Heidi rushed to her and embraced her, leaning clumsily in at the door of the car, and came away blue herself.

"What is it? What is it?" they cried. Noosheen, sobbing, extended her streaked blue arms.

"Good God, she's been inked," Heidi said. Chloe had heard of that—it happened occasionally that some religious fanatic would throw ink on an immodest woman or a foreign woman, or just someone without her head covered. They had heard of it happening at Abadan and in Tehran. It had not happened here, and why, anyway, should it happen to Noosheen? Chloe thought of the American wives with their Texan accents and their powder-blue golf dresses, uninked. Blots of black-blue dye stained Noosheen's simple cotton shirtwaist; her arm was blue where she had held it against her face. Heidi gathered her out of the car.

"I can't go home," Noosheen said. "I can't go in there. What if Bahram is home, or the washing woman?"

"Where did this happen?"

"In the bazaar."

She had come from her class in Victorian Poetry, and as she still had an hour before the ayah expected her home, she drove to the bazaar intending to buy some cases of Pepsi while she had her car nearby to carry it home in. She intended to patronize as usual the soft-drink vendor who kept a stall just inside the gates of the bazaar. When it happened, she herself was carrying a case of heavy tins, and the bazaar boy was following with three more on a cart, and they had reached the sidewalk outside the bazaar, walking to where she had parked near the main post office. They walked past the poor stalls arranged along the plastered wall outside the bazaar, the vendors of plastic shoes and T-shirts. The T-shirts said "Stanford University," she remembered, because the thought had just struck her that at Stanford University probably the study of Victorian poetry would be very advanced. Mounds of pistachio nuts, and scarves of magenta net, the strong smell of straw and dung—everything as usual. Two old women in black chador lurched along the sidewalk toward her in their overrun sandals, and a young man with narrow, burning eyes.

It was he who, stepping quickly forward, with a motion of his arm threw something at her. She had no moment to realize it was she whom he was attacking until she felt her face wet, the wetness on her dress, on her arm where she had flung it up. The cry was hers, and the pain in her ankle where the cans fell against it. Her eyes stung so that for a second she had feared acid. The old women tugged their veils and passed by. The man hurried away ahead of them, without looking back at Noosheen.

Stupefied, she blotted her face with her skirt. Her tears washed away the stinging. She limped toward her car, leaving the cans in the jube. The boy followed with the rest, avoiding her gaze. She rushed to get in her car, out of sight. There seemed to her to be a loudness all around her, the voices of people seeing her, speaking of her, but no one spoke to her. What could anyone say?

In the car, in her book bag, was a length of veil, to wear at the mosque or when visiting her aunts or for certain times when it was agreeable to wrap up in it. "The Iranian security blanket," she had called it, laughing with her friends. With her veil she now blotted her dress and wiped her face and arm. The blue dye, or ink, or whatever it was, trickled down her leg and into her shoe. It seemed viscous and horrible, like blood of a dying person; it puddled in the instep of her shoe. Her heart raced with the shock.

But why had this happened to her? This was something done to immodest women in provincial cities—in Abadan or Qum, perhaps—but not here in the university city of Shiraz, and she was not an immodest woman but a virtuous wife. The injustice only struck her now. But for an instant—was this true?—she had accepted that it had been intended for her, had known it was she who deserved it. This guilty feeling was now replaced by indignation, like a seed swelling in her belly.

A modest woman yet when ink stains you you think you deserve it, you think the punisher has looked into your heart. People looking at you think that too, that the thrower of ink has a secret way of knowing, that his hand is guided by the hand of Allah to the flighty, short-tempered mother, or to her who looks at men in a certain way, with certain thoughts. Bahram— she now realized—would think this. He would wonder what the punishers, avengers, fanatics knew. Bahram would not embrace a woman with blue limbs, perhaps would not even speak to her. The new fear, of Bahram's disapproval, animated her; she would have to get home and wash. Trembling, she started the car and drove to the compound, and as she parked, shaken, in the garage port, here were the comforting Heidi Asghari and Chloe Fowler, angels of sympathy and indignation. Heidi took her into her house to scrub her there.

Heidi had English towels, which were not American towels, she apologized, but better than Iranian towels, and she went to get them. Noosheen undressed, not worried by Chloe standing there, just in a hurry to get the inky clothes off. Out of her bra straps came her blue arms; the stuff had soaked through her dress onto her thighs. She had no pubic hair. Chloe tried not to stare but it did make a person look strange, statuelike. She could not tell if Noosheen was naturally this way or if she shaved herself. Chloe was not so conscious on herself of that little fat pad of flesh over the pubic bone.

Heidi called out that the bath was ready. They hoped the ink would wash off, but it was indelible, resistant, something invented by people who hate women enough to mark them, maybe to hurt them. Maybe in a slow way it burned into the flesh and could never be removed, or caused a toxic reaction from which later you died?

"Lemon, pumice," Heidi said.

"Peroxide," Chloe suggested.

Strangely enough, luckily, it came right out of clothes. Heidi reported this. Noosheen soaked, then got out and sat in her towel while Heidi ironed the dress dry. Noosheen's misery was mitigated by the kindness of Chloe and Heidi; she was not sure she could expect such kindness from any Iranian woman she knew here, certainly not Zareeneh or Soraya, though of course her old friends would be kind, and her mother, if only she were here. No men would be kind.

There had been women with the man who threw the ink. Were they with him or merely in front of him? Did they know what he was going to do, approve, cook up the stuff in their fireplaces to give to him to throw on her? There were mad people about. More and more mad people about, even people who had before been calm might drive their cars at you, or break your windows. Bodies lay in the jube, it was said, and were collected very early in the morning by the men who shoot the dogs. No one knew where they were taken; their families never knew. This stain didn't come off the skin. This American woman, this Englishwoman were, she knew, unaware of many things that were happening here in unhappy Iran.

Chapter Twenty-one

FALSE FRIENDS

*But helpless Pieces of the Game He plays
Upon this Chequer-board of Nights and Days;
Hither and thither moves, and checks, and slays,
And one by one back in the Closet lays.*

Whom Allah leads astray, no guide has he. In the days that followed, this text oppressed Noosheen, arriving unbidden in her consciousness from some childhood reading of the Koran. The shadow of blue was still visible on her skin. Although he had said nothing, Bahram must have seen it. Obviously she was in the category of people led astray, or this wouldn't have happened to her. She tried to calm herself, to think through the logic of the words: for if it was Allah leading you astray, you all the more had to think for yourself; it was no good looking to Him.

Then there were those who believed that your husband is His representative. If that was so, then it would be your husband leading you astray and you had better not follow him. No guide has she. On the other hand, if your husband was a loyal guide with your best interests at heart, it was he who went against the will of Allah, assuming it was Allah's wish to lead you astray. It was insoluble. Why would Allah wish to lead someone astray anyway? You would think that people went astray by themselves, to the dismay of Allah. But that was not what the text said. Her heart swelled with distaste for Allah, as well as for her husband, and father, and other old men.

And, if you are astray, how do you get back on the right path? Some sign alerts you, perhaps the ink. Then, is it up to you, or to your husband, or to Allah, to decide what to do next?

And can it be that things are true now, in the modern world, that have not always been true, for instance about the spirit of

women? Maybe women were subject, abject, deservedly low
in the time of the Prophet, but perhaps emerging along the line
of some divine plan so that now they were more free than in the
days of the Koran, more deserving of freedom, more the equal
of men than they had been back then. How else to explain the
denigrating tone of the Koran but that women had been
unworthy creatures back then? She thought of Empedocles,
alive before the time of the Koran and at a time when women
were highly regarded. Even so he had foreseen the hard times
that were coming for humankind.

The stain of blue must be to Bahram a sure indication of her
spiritual condition. It must pain him. He was in so many ways
a kind man, kind to her and the babies. She could imagine the
shock, the chill to his soul, a wife stained blue. Bahram always
too busy for badness, studying and helping the sick. She felt
his goodness to be as much a burden to her as badness would
be, if he were bad.

Sometimes, looking at her hands, her spirit would fire up
with indignation at the unfair stain, and then at other times it
would seem deserved.

On Sunday night, at the Cyrus, Dick sent a cable to Marla:

DELAY SELLING UNTIL RETURN MARKET CONSIDERATIONS UNWISE
IMPORTANT TO DISCUSS. LETTER FOLLOWS. DO NOT SELL
UNDERLINE. LOVE DICK.

In the late afternoon Wednesday, Dick borrowed the hospital
station wagon and drove northward out of Shiraz, hoping to
find the grave site. He half believed that the promptings of his
dreaming self should be attended to, that he would make some
discovery, or somehow at least allay this dreadful curse of
troubled sleep. Anyway he enjoyed driving, could think, away
from Junie, Abbas, Chloe, the rest, about things—about his
life. About how he had had no reply from Marla, though he
really preferred not to think about that, or he could think about
where his life was going, not a subject you ever wanted to zero
in on but could hope an inspired change of direction might waft

across your mind, some intimation of a future course he hadn't thought of before.

As soon as he was well beyond the outskirts of town, though, he knew he wouldn't be able to find the grave. The landscape was too strange, to his eye all undifferentiated rocks and plains. But he drove on in the hope that as he neared the allotted kilometers—they had traveled sixty-three or four—he would find something familiar, an outcropping of cliff like a stone visage stuck somewhere in his memory suddenly appearing to him. And it was true that as he neared the place they had turned off, the landscape assumed a kind of familiarity, born, he guessed, of his concentrating fears the other day. It, the dead man's grave, was somewhere around here. He drew off the road and into the field at the foot of one of the steep escarpments and parked. He got out of the car and circled round it, gazing up. He believed he remembered looking with Abbas at the same rock ledge above him though in fact the strata were all horizontal here, tilted in another direction. There was no sign of the grave.

There was something looming, forbidding, about the steepness. It was like finding yourself suddenly next to a very much taller person in a dark place; he had a sense of being looked down upon, perhaps watched. He saw no one. If the ancients had dragged the bodies of their dead to ledges like that, how had they got them up there, anyway? He studied the conjunctions of the rock, and, thinking that he could see a painful route, felt an impulse to climb it, with the idea too that from its height he might be able to spy the fresh grave below. The element of risk was appealing; if you fell, he thought as he grappled rock outcroppings and scrambled along, you would not be found. Only a couple of hundred feet, but of a daunting steepness.

Once he had gained the ledge he felt better, then unhappy looking down, and worse looking out to see the absolute, barren, wide landscape. Something about these open landscapes had always filled him with dread. He had first felt it in New Mexico, which he had always heard of as beautiful but found horrible in its scale and impersonality. New Mexicans doubtless felt daunted by the tall canyons of cities, the gloomy shadows of buildings.

He wondered if Zoroastrian bones had really been laid up here. This would be a place, all right, for vultures to help themselves, high enough so that humans could not disturb them, nor be disturbed by the disgusting spectacle. He studied the rubble of pebbles and roots—there were things that might be bones, might centuries ago have been bones, or might be the whitened roots of the gnarled shrubs that sprang from the rocks. He stood here for a quarter of an hour, mind empty of thoughts, a start of reluctance when he viewed the route of descent. Then he began to scramble down. There had been no grave. Perhaps this was the wrong place altogether. Without losing the sense that he had been sent, been intended to find the place, he headed toward Shiraz again. Like returning to the scene of the crime. Some inner prompting remained, but he drove back, and went directly to the Cyrus.

There he had a drink with Richard Dare, the archaeologist, who had reappeared in the Cyrus bar after a few days of absence; he had been at Persepolis at the dig. Dick, Junie, and the others had at last set the date for their great expedition to the famous ruin. Perhaps Dare would be there?

"Quite possible," Dare said. "If so, you must let me show you *my* Persepolis. I feel very proprietary about it by now." There were still depths, layers, boxcars of antiquities there, he said, awaiting the shovel, awaiting the expert from London or New York, awaiting the whim or dictate of the Shah.

"Though the Shah doesn't have any real feeling for the antiquities," Dare said. "He's interested in restoration, but it's the Islamic period that interests him. The tribesmen find things from the classical period and sell them to us. They know they're worth something." He lowered his voice. "Between us, I've managed to pick up some very nice things for myself. Some jewelry, several little heads. A necklace that's very very good."

This excited Dick's imagination. He liked the idea of owning a Persian antiquity, the jewels from a mummy—had they had mummies? He thought of the Queen of Sheba—where was Sheba? And of beautiful slave girls, and of how one's ability to imagine antiquity was entirely blighted by the movies you had seen as a child. But Richard Dare seemed to see the days of antiquity before him, and when he spoke of the beautiful carving of the friezes, his voice trembled.

He and Dare joined Chloe Fowler, Hugh Monroe, General Brigante, and the Texan, Loyal Cooley, in the dining room.

"When she heard what she'd been eating, she got mortally ill," Cooley was saying. "I didn't feel so hot myself, but hell, I figured I'd kept it down thus far. But it shows you the power of suggestion. They had to get a doctor."

"Mr. and Mrs. Cooley ate bats in China," Chloe told Dick, with a pleased expression.

"Well, I wish this were a, what, a hamburger," said Hugh of his plate of lamb and rice.

"A taco. A taco. I think about tacos all the time," Chloe said. "I don't even eat them that much at home."

"An egg cream," Dick said. "An egg cream is something I would never dream of drinking in America. I haven't had one since I was twelve. But it's true—the other day I found myself thinking about egg cream."

"What exactly is an egg cream?" Chloe asked.

It turned out that none of them knew what an egg cream was. Dick was astonished. An egg cream! A regular everyday thing. As he explained it, the others agreed it sounded more disgusting than it would taste.

"Your little friend Noosheen came to see me the other day," General Ben said to Chloe.

"Really?" Chloe was surprised. She wouldn't have known how to find General Ben, how had Noosheen known? "When? What about?"

"She wanted me to smuggle her into Afghanistan," said General Ben. "Remember our conversation? I guess she remembered every word."

"Poor Noosheen. But what did you say?" Inwardly Chloe was chagrined that she had not realized Noosheen was as desperate as that.

"I've heard of it done, as I said," said the general, "but I'm not myself personally in touch with the people—it would be tribesmen or merchants. I said I was afraid I wasn't her man."

"Oh, indeed," said Chloe. "I hope you didn't tell her husband, in some misguided impulse of male solidarity." She spoke vivaciously, wishing to protect Noosheen from being talked about, and to protect her own surprise. She began to prattle in a way that Dick thought of as her dumb blonde act.

She wasn't dumb but could genuinely seem so. That was very Californian. Their eyes glaze over, and they are thinking of exercise or drugs—Chloe not drugs, of course, yet she did take quantities of salad, despite his warnings. She had begun leaf by leaf but had now built up to huge platefuls of deadly lettuce and the rather pallid poison tomatoes, which Dick would rather die than risk. She had reported no difficulties, though it was possible she wouldn't report them. She was probably full of Waspy prudery about digestion. Once he had brought a girl home to dinner who was shocked when they passed out Tums after dinner. "It's not very complimentary to your Mom's cooking," she'd said. He'd never thought of it like that. They—that girl and probably Chloe—would rather die, probably, than hear stomachs mentioned.

"Which loyalty comes first?" Chloe asked. "Whom would you *betray* first—the fellow male, the fellow family member, or the fellow American?"

"Or the fellow doctor?" added Dick. "Or the personal friend?"

"Patriotic people turned their families in, in Nazi Germany," said General Ben. "Country comes before family."

"The mistress or the wife?" wondered Chloe.

"It would just depend on the circumstances," insisted Dick. "There are no fixed principles."

"I don't think I would betray anyone," said Hugh, with a manly seriousness that corrected any impression of self-satisfaction such a remark might have been thought to contain. "But it would be according to how well you knew them. The less well you knew them, the easier it would be."

"Are we talking about loyalty on principle or self-interest?" Dick asked.

"Men would usually betray people before abstractions," Chloe said. "It's a difference between them and women, or so people say," though she wasn't sure of it.

"Who would you trust more, your foreign mistress or a fellow American doctor?" asked Dick.

"The fellow American doctor," Hugh said, again very seriously.

The slight obtuseness of the usually intelligent Hugh on this subject served to focus in Chloe an emotion of anger at him that had been simmering. She was angry that he didn't realize she was angry, that he never spoke of the future or of Them. Hugh was mysterious. When she tried to imagine what he was thinking, he was opaque as a stone. Usually she liked that in someone else. She could always look into Jeffrey if she wanted to, but she did not want to. She had looked in once or twice and found only crossness and clutter—it had been like looking into someone else's purse at an apparatus of anxiety—toothpicks, scalp remedy, bus tickets, a letter from his mother.

But what maddened her now about Hugh was his incuriosity about her. She wished to be opened, inspected. Didn't he think it was odd that she was still here and Jeffrey wasn't? That she loved him and risked her marriage and stayed on in this strange land to sleep with him? Didn't he wonder how she and Jeffrey were getting along? What marital advice might he give her? But he accepted her like a beautiful present, and she had begun to see that he was used to getting wonderful presents. He must assume his needs were taken care of by right, so that his splendid altruism wouldn't be damaged.

Free of entanglements himself, did he imagine she was free of them? Did he imagine she just existed in what she stood up in, alone, like a statue or a sprite? Had he no sense of the dentists, parent-teacher associations, dog kennels, real-estate agents, aunts all standing in a circle around her, hemming her in and propping her up? Did he imagine she could just pop out and over, in some thrilling trajectory, all quotidian reality? He seemed to have no sense of her as a hemmed-in person, but perhaps, to be fair, that was a tribute to her free spirit, or a condition of this idyll. Or, more likely, he had no interest in her actual circumstances. Perhaps—the idea had occurred to her before—his wives had divorced him because he was so blithe, so uninvolved. Her face thinking of all this, in the dim restaurant light, had flushed a color she knew was becoming.

Dick Rothblatt's often mordant absorption in mundane materiality was more to her taste. She was sorry to see him so tormented about his house. It was hard for men, the way they lost their houses after they had put up all the shelves and painted—not that Jeffrey ever painted—but Dick had, she felt, and had paneled his study, and worked a long time on the kitchen and made a studio for Marla, in her painting phase.

 Something linked Dick and Hugh in her mind, though the
nature of their complicity eluded her—doctors together or men
together? Men believe each other before they believe women,
even women they love, as Hugh had just admitted. But Dick?
She had thought of telling him about Hugh's shirts, not with
any idea of disloyalty to Hugh but because Dick would be sure
to explain that there was an emergency laundry service at the
Tehran airport, or that she, Chloe, was blind; somehow he
would explain Hugh's lie.

 But then she had had a feeling, just like the feeling of
standing outside her parents' shut bedroom door, or looking at
the covers of certain books that would turn out to have
horrifying pictures or stories of death, the feeling of an
important shimmer, almost a hum, off the cover that told her
she ought not to press on with this inquiry. Perhaps Hugh and
Dick were up to something? Perhaps the CIA was involved?
Good-natured Hugh would never suspect that he was being
used; and he would do things for patriotic reasons, Dick
doubtless too. How surprising it was when people lied. It was
the last thing you expected.

After all, the mystery of the otherness of another is charming.
Chloe is not someone who wishes to possess all knowledge of
others. She considers that rude. But who can blame her if she
wishes just a little that someone would want to know all about
her; she would not tell, but it would be evidence that she was
interesting or desirable. On the other hand, she has friends with
jealous husbands who say, Tell me what you did, where you
went, what you are thinking. She would not really want that
attention. Is it not better to be alone, attentive, smiling, full of
love of an outwardly directed, disinterested, sort?

 Hugh never does ask about her. She wonders whether he
knows her maiden name. She sees it is quite possible that he
might want to marry her and would not have inquired about her
maiden name. He thinks of her as Chloe Fowler, which she is
really not, she is Chloe Linden. She, on the other hand, has
many times thought, but has never been able to say, "What
about your shirts?" How beautiful, she thinks, Hugh's cuff-

links, his exquisite watch with its alligator band—a Must of Cartier?

Dick is thinking of Junie's odd behavior that morning over the dead man's watch. She had spent the night—the Hendersons had gone to Isfahan. Getting up in the early dawn, she had taken the dead man's watch from the bureau and waved it at him. "Mind if I take this?"

"Why?" He wasn't sure she knew it belonged to the dead man. She might think it was his own—quite an elegant watch, Patek Philippe, with an incongruous band.

"Because I broke my band. How'm I going to get that fixed in Shiraz, Iran? Still, Iranian watchbands must break, there must be someone. I'll wear it just for today. Hmmm—nice watch!" She had gone off without coffee; there was a woman in labor she was anxious about. Dick, whose first clinic was not until nine, had lain in bed awhile longer, wondering whether there was any chance of Abbas seeing it on Junie's wrist. But she herself must have seen it on the dead man. Had there been other funny things about Junie's behavior? He remembered, slightly revolted and with new apprehension, the way she had stripped the shoes off the dead man. Maybe she'd been looking for some mark of identification she knew about. You heard that the CIA recruited young women from the Seven Sisters; that had been one of their main bases of recruitment. True, that had been in Marla's day; young women Junie's age were more leery of the CIA and the government generally. Junie's grandfather, though, had graduated from West Point, probably the whole family had a pro-military bias the CIA could prey on, something like that. How little he knew about Junie, really, beyond her fierce views, so apparently left-wing, so ardently feminist.

What if, now that they were in it together, he couldn't trust Abbas? Different rules obtain in a country where people are dragged off to be tortured and murdered. You couldn't blame them if they lied or evaded—but could you trust them? Someone like Abbas especially, with a tragedy in his life—that made for a certain burnt-out quality. If it came to an official inquiry, it would be every man for himself; he couldn't expect Abbas to stick his neck out. He could imagine Abbas saying to the authorities, "I think you'll find that Dr. Rothblatt knows something about the whereabouts of the body."

All at once Dick realized that Vahid Farmani didn't want the body there *because* he knew something about it. His hysteria was not owing to a mere antipathy to dead strangers, was not mere intransigence but *informed alarm*. There were funny goings-on, bodies, things moved, occasionally, in the laboratory overnight. Things known to Abbas, and Vahid Farmani. Vahid and Abbas in league, or else opposed to one another, making moves like chess players, without speaking of their deadly game. He himself, innocent Dick Rothblatt, drawn into it. His feeling was a mixture of fear and importance. Deadly games dignify life, even if you sensibly wish to avoid them. Chloe, he thought, looking at her, so pretty, so animated, came to life strangely in the evenings and often left the Cyrus precipitately, as if she had meetings to go to, strange doings in the darkness. She had not gone down in the cave, almost as if she had known what they'd find.

General Ben, who always had his car, drove them back to the compound. Chloe alit at Villa Two, called goodnight again to her companions, and climbed the steps to her apartment, where she hurried to wash and brush her teeth before Hugh came in. It was romantic to imagine him chivalrously hovering at the dark end of the path that ran between his bungalow and the Infertility Clinic. Tonight, having had perhaps a bit too much wine, she dozed a few moments under her lamp, waking only at the sound of his voice beneath her window. She started awake in the dim room. The low bulb of her lamp gathered insects through the riddled screen.

There was something strained and urgent in his voice. She hurried out into the hall and down the stairs. He tottered in. His face was gashed and swollen; blood drooled from a cut at the hairline and spilled onto his shirt. He smelt oddly of blood.

"My God!" cried Chloe. Had he fallen? Been hit by a car?

He said nothing but followed her up the stairs and swayed toward her armchair. Blood dripped off his fingers onto the linoleum floor. She thought of Noosheen and the ink. She rushed for one of the thin dishtowels Hossein left each day, and Hugh mopped at his face with it.

"My dear, what is it?"

"Somebody was in my apartment, going through my stuff." His voice, in contrast to his damaged face, was perfectly calm, normal. "He tried to run, I chased him—he got away easily in the dark. But then somebody grabbed me from behind. It had to have been a different person, waiting outside all along."

"Is it bad?" asked Chloe, mastering her stomach, for she was queasy about blood. It didn't appear to be too bad. Hugh got up and studied himself in the bathroom mirror. "Not too bad. It hurts."

"What did they want?"

"Evidently some medical records I was keeping, about a patient I saw. At least that's what's gone." He sat down again, seeming dazed and weakened.

"Do you think you should tell someone? Farmani? Abbas? Is it an Iranian patient? Were they Iranians?"

"No. I don't know." He was grim. "I only know I'm going to Tehran tomorrow and get this straightened out."

Ah, thought Chloe, Tehran. It obviously bore upon his absence, his being in Tehran when he said he wasn't. She wondered if she should mention that she had noticed his shirts.

"Ah—is it anything you can tell me about?" she asked.

"No. I'd tell you about it if I could," Hugh said, "but I promised I wouldn't tell anyone," and Chloe understood from her knowledge of Hugh's character that he would therefore not tell her. This was an irritating goody-goody side of him. You didn't tell anyone except your mistress, that was the way to look at it. You had to tell someone. An Eastern prep-school goody-goody, valuing secrecy and other male foolishness, without a doubt a CIA agent.

Chapter Twenty-two

DIVIDED LOYALTIES

The Moving Finger writes, and, having writ,
Moves on: nor all your Piety nor Wit
Shall lure it back to cancel half a Line,
Nor all your Tears wash out a Word of it.

The battered Hugh sleeps fitfully at her side. Chloe hardly sleeps, turning over certain matters in her mind about Hugh. Does he travel on a diplomatic passport, as Dr. Farmani had asked? He has been to Geneva, Moscow, Rangoon. Why? Nine shirts laundered at the Tehran Hilton when he said he was in London, and now someone has bashed his head in. Does someone do that out of the blue, except in America? Chloe tries to imagine reasons for the shirts, for the travels, but can't think of any except that Hugh is some kind of spy or emissary, mixed up in something, or maybe an international criminal mixed up with dope or diamonds or guns. Which would it be? What sort of criminal would the admirable and attractive Hugh be? Or what sort of patriot, for he had been to the best schools, the sort that prepare you for the CIA, or maybe he was a Russian spy, though that was more common in England. She hadn't heard of a person from a good American school being a Russian spy. In America, treason was more a proletarian thing.

But Hugh? So handsome and selfless, working long hours in Azami Hospital, full of genuine concern for Iranians, so cheerful and uncomplicated by nature, though cheerfulness could be a pose—all those divorces?

Should a woman stay with a spy? With a murderer or swindler? What is the cutoff point for loyalty? Her previous views had been categorical: a woman should not stay with a criminal. She disapproved of women who stayed with bad

190

men, saying, "My man right or wrong," and she thought it insulting to women to hold that they had no higher duty than the simple one of loyalty to some appointed master, like dogs, and were not supposed to make moral judgments or think. There were women who interested her, like ones who conceive babies on visits to prison. The idea overwhelmed Chloe with disgust.

Eva Braun! If you loved a bad man and stayed with him, you were just as bad, so she both wishes and does not wish to know what Hugh is up to. But she is sure he must be up to something or people wouldn't jump him in the night, and she is sure she isn't going to mention the nine shirts. She is conscious that she might have found these thoughts exciting a few weeks ago; now she is troubled. Perhaps it is her more active sense of Iran as a real place, her more careful way of seeing that the people are thin and frightened, their lives not to be tampered with by Americans but running along according to principles of individual destiny quite apart from hers, or Hugh's.

Hugh, his bruises livid by morning, took a cab for the airport, bent on Tehran, saying grimly that he would be back in the evening or the following morning. His mood, understandably, was angry. Chloe went early to the university to avoid the heat, which was daily becoming worse, too hot to walk in the midday. At the gates of the university, she was astonished to see soldiers silently putting students into trucks. Other students stood watching on the sidewalk, shaking their fists and muttering, but the scene was curiously listless, as if this were somehow between the acts of a play. "What does it mean?" Chloe asked of Mrs. Reza.

"Nothing," Mrs. Reza said. "When the weather is hot, the students are always like that. The police keep order; that is their job, after all."

In the evening she went, more from habit than from inclination, to the Cyrus. She, Abbas, Dick, and Junie had gone to the garden to avoid Loyal Cooley, who had been holding forth on international currency:

"The rial isn't too bad, as foreign money goes. At least you can spend it here and there in the Middle East. Try the zloty anyplace but Poland. I got stuck with about five hundred dollars' worth of zlotys once. You used to be able to spend them in East Germany; now even the East Germans won't take them. That's because of the Polish brassières.''

''Polish brassières?'' they murmured politely.

''The East Germans used to accept the zloty. Polish women used to come over into East Germany to get underwear, the East German bra was a lot better, you can imagine what the Polish is like and they would just take off their Polish bras and try to flush them away. That way they jammed up the plumbing, till the Germans had to stop letting them come over. Also shoes, they'd leave them in big piles in the street.''

The company sat hushed with wonder.

''Poles are incredibly anti-Semitic,'' said Dick after a time.

In the garden you could take a glass of tea after supper and enjoy the fragrant night, the lights strung over the long reflecting pool. Music drifted, barely heard, and crickets sang.

''What do you think—what is thought—of Beethoven here?'' said Chloe, as they listened to the notes of the Emperor Concerto on the public-address system.

''We revere Beethoven. I would give all our Iranian composers for him. We have poets, but we have no great composers.'' Abbas's voice oddly passionate.

''That can't be true,'' objected Chloe.

''Nonetheless.'' He smiled.

''What will become of the students?'' Chloe asked, talking of what she had seen that afternoon.

''Nothing.'' Abbas laughed. ''The jails are full, after all. Though I have noticed they are enlarging the garrison.''

When he had gone, Dick said to Chloe, ''He's attracted to you.'' He was interested in Chloe's reaction, whether she would seem pleased. He wondered if she was lonesome. He wondered if she would sleep with Abbas if he made a pass at her. ''He wouldn't do anything—he knows Jeffrey and so on—but just from the way he mentions you, always bringing you up.''

He watched her, but she didn't seem anything but politely complimented.

Chloe did wonder how Muslim men were in bed. Maybe they were terrific, intense, insatiable; you heard of men with harems who had to do it ten times a day. So many experiences are cut off from the life of a middle-class American housewife.

"You always think people are attracted to people," Junie said to Dick, crossly. "You seem to relate everything to sex. I think it's stupid."

Chloe supposed this would initiate a quarrel. Dick and Junie often quarreled, albeit on impersonal subjects, but in a personal way that made Chloe sure that everyone must know they were lovers.

"It's a view of life, all right," Dick said, pleasantly, not disposed to quarrel. He paid for their tea and they drifted off together into the street.

"It's the Islamic view of life, so prurient, so disgusting," Junie went on. "We had a girl—fourteen years old, beaten horribly by her bridegroom, because she hadn't done the thing with the sheep's blood. The whole concept of virginity is prurient and disgusting."

"Oh, I don't know," Chloe said, for the sake of argument. "Maybe it's more charming to lose your virginity with a lot of pomp and ceremony and sheep's blood and fear and general acknowledgment of your altered state, better than in the back of a car, I mean."

"I would think," Dick said.

"Or maybe men function better if they're a little bit pepped up by these lurid rituals of possession and virility," said Chloe.

"Now wait a minute," objected Dick.

"In Philadelphia—these were Saudis, not Iranians, but still—a guy killed his sister because she was sleeping with her boyfriend. And he got off. The jury just said, Well, it's their religion," said Junie.

Dick didn't want to be drawn into an argument with Junie, because Junie was contentious and inflexible. You could never win an argument because she would never yield a point, even when proven wrong. Sometimes bystanders were drawn in to adjudicate, as now, walking home from the Cyrus, when the discussion changed somehow, from whether most things were related to sex, to Freud and penis envy. Dick understood this quarrel to be symptomatic of a strain in his relationship with Junie, brought on to some extent by her increasing involvement with Iran. She stayed most nights now in her own quarters exhausted. Each day brought some obstetrical crisis, some opposition of her opinion to that of a benighted Iranian chauvinist, clashes, heartbreaking errors, maternal deaths. She had lost weight. Dick tried to comfort and cheer her, but she often fell asleep while he was making love to her.

When they had arrived, agreed to have this fling in Iran and avoiding talk of the future, a slight apprehension had existed on either part that the other would not be able to support the mood of light tenderness and professional camaraderie they hoped for. Dick, especially, feared that Junie would want to marry and have babies. He believed—he knew—that young professional women wanted as much as other women to marry, have babies, and, of course, why shouldn't they? He, however, was not ready to start up another family, for sure.

Junie feared that Dick would want to marry. That was Chloe's impression too. He was not a convincing bachelor. The regularity of his morning visits to her, for instance, his evident pleasure in the little domestic routine, his confident reliance on intelligent female companionship meant, Chloe supposed, that he would remarry momentarily, whether Junie or not was hard to guess. Their quarrels on trivial subjects seemed to contain a note of impatience.

"But there is no such thing as penis envy," Junie was saying. "Freud just thought there was because he thought his prick was such a fine thing everyone must want one. But everyone doesn't."

"It *is* hard to imagine having—you know—nothing down there," Dick pointed out, in defense of the fatherly fellow physician whose edicts had never seemed personally to impinge upon his life.

"Women don't have nothing," screamed Junie furiously. "They have something. Phenomenologically, something. They experience it as *something,* therefore do not feel the lack of the other thing."

"That's ridiculous," Dick said, teasing her along. "It's a well-established observation, penis envy."

"It is *something* there, just as much as your hand or your ear. Nothing would be if there were *nothing* there," Junie persisted.

"Look," said Dick, "my analyst was a Jungian, I don't even believe in Freud, it's just that it's so obvious."

"The trouble with doctors is that they never read anything," Chloe snapped.

Chloe dropped back a few steps, taken with sudden melancholy, and a recollection of the visage of the paralyzed little girl and her own strangeness. It was always at night, walking along a street or across a compound, that she most felt her strangeness. Inside the walled gardens people murmured, out of view, belonging here. A lightbulb strung on a cord hung over the black flowers. Chloe could imagine the moon on the long pools, but she couldn't see the pools or the dusty grass or the roses. The ditchlike jubes seemed to yawn and widen under the curbings. She crossed carefully at corners, clutching a male elbow. The few automobiles proceeded slowly, as if blinded, as if sleepy after dinner. The mad cacophony of the day was gone. No one lurked in the shadows, just some men coming out of the film, a young couple, the young woman wearing the tightly tucked scarf, students. Voices coming from the upstairs windows of a restaurant. No one was old.

She and the others were shut out from Iran by the thick walls, by the murmur of Persian words opaque to the ear. But it was peaceful to be shut out and to slip along the walls and through the windows going nowhere, going off to make love. It was nicer, Chloe thought, to be outside than in, for if you were inside your walled garden, it would be your garden and you'd have to weed it.

Gardenless, childless, husbandless, how strangely happy she was these days. If something happened to Jeffrey, and she was tempted to remarry instantly, assuming someone would have her, she hoped she would remember this happy, unencumbered feeling and think twice.

By thinking of Jeffrey, it is as if she has conjured up the letter she finds waiting on her pillow:

Dear Chloe,

I'm sorry not to have written for a week or so. I've been mulling this letter over in my mind. I've written Farmani, by the way, so he knows I'm not coming, but I suggested he let you stay on to finish your work at the university, since it's only a few more weeks.

Well, to get to the point, the situation between you and me. I guess we both know it hasn't been wonderful. I haven't known what to do about it, and I'm sure you haven't either, and when we try to talk about it, we never quite get to the point. I for one believe you can't really talk about these things. I mean, you can say I should be home more, and I can say clean up the house, and we can try to do whatever, but it isn't really getting at the problem. I know there are these routes—shrinks, counselors, therapists—but I don't think either of us has a lot of faith in that kind of thing. God knows we know enough people who've gone those routes.

The kids are fine, by the way, I should have said, and Henry is coming along—at least he's not a vegetable.

I guess I should come right out and say that I think we should get a divorce. I realize we've been in this holding pattern in part because I was unwilling to take the responsibility. I was unwilling to be the bad person, the one at fault. I kept hoping that you'd do something so I could blame it on you. But now I see that even though you aren't perfect, that's not the point, the point is not blaming the other person but facing up to your own behavior, not trying to maneuver the other person into a position of guilt. Now I'm able to do that. So: it's my fault, I accept the responsibility, everyone will say what a shit Jeffrey Fowler is, and that's okay with me. Of course I want to do what's fair for you and the kids in every way. Don't worry about the financial end of things.

I suppose it's obvious that there is somebody who has helped me understand all this—I don't mean a shrink. I mean that I'm in love with someone, and her support and love have made me see things much more clearly. I suppose you guessed that when I went so willingly back to California—I practically shoved you aboard that plane to Tehran. You must have been puzzled and scared, and I think you are a brave lady. I know that after these weeks there in Shiraz you will recognize that you are able to stand on your own two feet and

maybe you even prefer it. We'll talk about details
when you get back. I guess it's a little bit chicken to
write you like this, but it seemed worse to hit you
with it when you got home.

Chloe looks at the letter, first at its physical characteristics, as
if to see whether it is genuine. Then she reads it once more,
with a growing amazement that begins to swell into fury, as
though at a trick by which she is going to lose her neck.
Stunned and amused; amazed and angry. Enraged. She cannot
describe the pale, swooning sensation that seizes her. It is in a
way the letter she has hoped for, that she could never herself
write, and now can't bear.

   She sits down on her cot and reads it again. Yes, he had
almost shoved her onto the plane. She feels her throat
constricting, as if she were being choked. Duped. Tricked.
What a fool she is. Now she can see that he had plotted; now
she can see that he has been having an affair all along. With
whom, for heaven's sake? He'd be happy she had taken up
with Hugh. Maybe he'd even planned it—maybe Henry hadn't
had an accident at all, and it was all a pack of lies so that
Jeffrey could go home. Maybe Jeffrey and Hugh are in
collusion somehow. Take her, she's yours. Perhaps Jeffrey
wants her to have a little professional success—Sassanian
pottery—so that he won't have to support them. My wife the
archaeologist, he will say in court. Now she sees his plan. How
she hates the ignominy of her thoughts, but cannot change the
wild, vengeful, embarrassed emotions that tumble over each
other across her mind. What is the name of her principal
emotion? She seeks it—vainly—and then finds it: chagrin,
chagrin, chagrin, chagrin. She reads the letter over and over.

Chapter Twenty-three

TRAVELING LIGHT

Waste not your Hour, nor in the vain pursuit
Of This and That endeavour and dispute;
Better be jocund with the fruitful Grape
Than sadden after none, or bitter, Fruit.

When Chloe awoke in the morning, she lay enjoying as she did each morning the distant cries and military music, the dappled sun in the leaves outside the window, Rustum's little barks below the window—for he was now impatient to see her each morning when she came down to have coffee on the steps with Dick. Then the confusion of memories rushed in on her, of the battered Hugh, the students yesterday, and then Jeffrey's letter. Her emotions, as she crawled from her cot, were still those of astonishment and indignation. It seemed too treacherous a letter for even Jeffrey to have sent. You just didn't send such a letter to someone far away in isolated Iran, beyond discussions, beyond reproaches, beyond repentance. She searched her memory for signs of Jeffrey's having taken up with someone else and found none at all. It had seemed to her he was always home, except a little late for dinner a few nights, or gone for an hour on Sunday morning to check his research rats. She was almost admiring of Jeffrey, now, so cleverly had he got himself into whatever it was without her knowing it.

This morning it seemed to her that it was just that Jeffrey should leave her, or, if not just, inevitable, because of her affair with Hugh; female transgression was being paid for as usual. Down the centuries nothing had changed, and by some cosmic process, which operated evidently at great distances as easily as in San Francisco, as if by satellite, transgression in Iran affected the atomic structure, or would it be the chemical structure of Jeffrey's heart? So this freedom and happiness in Iran were not, after all, to come free of cost. She wasn't really surprised. She lay in her cot a few moments longer than usual, savoring these reflections with a kind of bitter interest. Perhaps she hadn't noticed what Jeffrey was up to because she hadn't cared. This thought was dismissed. Of course she loved Jeffrey, difficult as he was, and had no wish to change her orderly and secure life, which seemed, in the abstract and at this great distance, precious to her. And anyway Jeffrey would have changed his mind by the time she got back. Think of the children.

At this she was seized by the most violent fear: that Jeffrey meant to keep the children. His letter said nothing about them; he was with them while she was far away. She could imagine what he might say to a judge, about maternal desertion, maternal uncaring. She could imagine the satisfaction of his mother, who had never really liked her, it was borne upon her now—and would have suggested the strategy by which they meant to prevent Chloe from ever seeing them. . . . Thus her thoughts raved, out of control, and regained perspective only when she reminded herself that neither Jeffrey nor his mother would like to be in full-time charge of two young children.

But what about the new woman? Maybe she was intensely maternal? "The real mother off in Iran"—she could hear the things that could be said against her. This precipitated a fit of anxiety so intense she had to sit down and breathe deeply. Jeffrey, somebody who resisted taking the children to the park or the movies—was he now seized by proprietary paternal emotions he had never felt before? Was it an aspect of his anger at her? She remembered all the newspaper dramas she had ever read, about desperately warring parents stealing their children back and forth, hiding in motels, having to go and live under assumed names in Florida.

Chloe got a hold on herself. The reality would be that Jeffrey would take the children on weekends, if that. The reality would be that by the time she got home he would have thought twice, or forty times, about all this, and changed his mind.

She fortified herself with such rationalizations as she got up and made a pot of tea, battling a knot of fury and panic that seemed to have struck her painfully in the middle, like a fast tennis ball. She tried to will it or think it away. She didn't want to know anything about Jeffrey's sordid affair; she would never ask. She had no right to ask. Jeffrey was just acting this way because he was missing her. She was humiliated. She would say nothing of it, she decided, to Hugh or anyone else. She would say nothing and it would, as life problems often do, go away. She had never thought of herself as someone whose husband leaves her.

She took her tea and went out into the garden. It was too early for Dick, but the sun was already hot. Rustum rushed to her and licked her hand. The garden furniture had been moved around to the other side of Villa One, she had heard, for a reception there for some grand people down from Tehran—the Minister of Health, she had heard, and a party of courtiers who would stay in the summer palace. Without chairs, Chloe emulated the Iranian villagers and old men in the square. She had wondered how they bore it, such an odd posture, hunkered down on their haunches, arms resting on knees, chin resting on arms, but now she tried it and found it was perfectly comfortable. Probably also it correctly aligned your intestines or female organs to a more healthy position. This was the healthy position to give birth in, she had heard.

Crouching, she watched the early-morning activity along the road, women walking to the clinics, nurses in white, an ancient ambulance creeping among the people walking on the road. She was startled at the approach of one of the black-shrouded women; she often saw them glancing at her sunglasses, but none had ever approached her. It had always seemed to Chloe, when she came close enough to them in the bazaar to see the wrinkled eyes, the set squints, that they could prevent these signs of early aging if they would wear sunglasses themselves.

Now Chloe was startled to realize that the woman was Noosheen. She squatted down next to Chloe, drew the veil from her face, and gathered it around her shoulders.

"You see I am a chastened spirit now," she said. "I wear this now. I don't want it to happen again."

"Oh, it couldn't, could it?" Chloe said. "It wasn't you, it just happened to be you."

"It doesn't come off. Look." Noosheen extended an arm.

The blue stain turned her olive skin faintly green, like the arm of a mermaid.

"Bahram doesn't say anything. I don't know if he sees it— he doesn't really see *me*," she said. "But of course he must see. I don't know how to speak of it to him. I know what he must think."

"Well, he must be very angry at whoever would do such a thing," Chloe said soothingly. "Perhaps he thinks it's you who can't bear to speak of it."

"He is right, I can't bear to speak of it. But I know what he must think."

Chloe could not believe that the mild-looking Bahram could conceal excesses of brutality or mistrust. "I think you should discuss it. That's always the best thing, to bring things right out in the open." Oh, the irony of this advice. But she was sure it was good advice, and that things should be brought out in the open, except for things that mere politeness dictated you conceal. She would never reproach Jeffrey, for instance, for his rather puny physique, since he couldn't help it, though she had always believed he could improve it by working out and not smoking.

"I want to leave. I want to go to my parents," Noosheen said, and only now did Chloe detect the quaver of desperation that accounted for the rather deceptive calm in her voice. "I have been wanting to leave Bahram for a long time, but the only problem is my parents are in New Delhi, India."

"There must be something we could do to get the stain off. Salt and lemon juice," said Chloe.

"You must help me," Noosheen went on, in the same urgent voice, her eyes not meeting Chloe's but staring in a frightened way off into the middle distance.

"I know what you will say, but I have thought of all. My children, what will happen, what my life will be. Such thoughts are not easily arrived at. I have been tormented in the night four nights now, but I think many nights before that since we have come back to Iran. I want to leave my husband. I think that in time my parents will help me to have my children with me, because my father is an influential man, but now first I must leave Bahram, so that it will be done and none can dissuade me. Otherwise they will expend the same energy trying to dissuade me, naturally.''

Chloe would not pretend to try to dissuade her. Anyone would want to leave a dry old cross husband she had been forced to marry. The situation of arranged marriage, so romantically dreadful in fiction, appeared, in life, merely intolerable. Millions of women down the ages forced to sleep with old men they didn't love or desire. The situation had never really interested or affronted her before, but now it seemed intolerable. A young woman, so like herself but for the accident of being Iranian, should be able to marry the man she loved.

Or was this a stupid American notion, as so often claimed? She shuddered to think of the embraces of the desiccated Bahram, could almost imagine his tiny, dry cock between her own thighs, poking her. She thought of the affectionate glances between Abbas and Noosheen and could imagine Noosheen's beautiful body, blue like the body of a goddess in a miniature painting, entwined with Abbas in the act of love, his the heavy penis of a sultan, the two as one, emblem of sultry sexuality, in an arched pavilion cooled by the waving fans of servants who had been blinded so as not to behold this inspired copulation.

''Of course, I would help,'' she said impulsively, ''but I don't see how I can.'' And these words rang in her own ears mockingly, so typical of complacent American detachment, of superiority, of all the people who hadn't helped the Jews or been able really to believe in evil and death, political evil and death. Not that Noosheen was in danger of dying, but when a rational person comes to you and says they need help, when it is they themselves who have decided to overturn their lives, ought not a rich and comfortable American listen?

''I mean,'' Chloe said, ''tell me what to do.''

This appeared to stop Noosheen for a moment. Probably she had been expecting Chloe to know what to do. ''I need to go to India; that is where my father is. The problem is the passport. I do not have a green stamp for my passport. I have thought I could ask Bahram to sign my passport, say I am going on a visit to my mother and father, but he would suspect me, because it is not the season for visits, and the children are in school. Ordinarily I join my parents in Beirut or Athens for our holiday in September, when it is hottest here and also in India. I weighed whether to say perhaps that I was feeling ill and wished to see my mother, but that is the last time Bahram would send me to India, since the health care is better here, and he is a doctor, obviously. I also thought of saying it is my parents who are sick, or one of them, not both, but in that case it is Bahram they would call, and I cannot ask them to summon me, because they will not be in sympathy with this intention of mine to leave. So you see I have to leave first, then all will fall into place.''

''You could take my passport,'' Chloe said. The moment she said it, she saw the plausibility of the suggestion. They were nearly the same height. The only difference was the color of Noosheen's hair. Chloe had read in a spy novel that women can easily pass for one another. To the eye of a guard, women are interchangeable. ''Then I can go to the American consul and say my passport is lost or stolen. They will give me another,'' she went on.

Noosheen gaped at this bold and simple idea. ''How can you be sure they will give you another?''

''Well, it happens all the time. People are always losing their passports and having them stolen.'' She paused a moment for the notion to take hold. Yes, as she reviewed it: simple, bold, practicable.

''Let's go inside; let's look in a mirror,'' Noosheen said. They looked at their two faces in the mirror, looking nothing alike, yet who would see it? A further lightening of the hair . . . Chloe dropped the passport into Noosheen's purse.

''You can mail it back to me, in case I can't get another. What could be simpler? But you must act at once, because I'm supposed to go back myself, in two weeks.''

''I will, then, if you believe you can get another without difficulty,'' said Noosheen, with the firmness of the resolved and desperate. She embraced Chloe and rushed off to see about tickets and peroxide. She would come back in the afternoon to practice an American demeanor. Chloe's own heart raced with excitement.

She drank the rest of the tea in the pot, right down to the hot grounds, and stared out between the geraniums at the light shimmer of leaves in a rising breeze. It portended, perhaps, a change of weather, though it was only August, and the heat would endure for weeks yet. She did not know when the weather broke and changed here. It would be nice to see a storm.

She thought of her dresser drawer, now empty of passport. She sought a chill of terror, a sense of having done an irrevocable action, a *frisson* of importance or drama. But she was unable to produce any of these sensations, for she knew that for an American doctor's wife the loss of a passport is not the end. She had a not-unpleasant, abandoned feeling, the feeling of fatedness, kismet. Yes, this was the feeling she wanted, of pleasure to be rid of her passport, symbol of her earthly situation. Passportless and free, and unable to return to the United States.

This enabled her to see her gesture as a childish response to Jeffrey's intention to dump her. So what, I can't come home anyway, she was trying to say. The reality of Jeffrey's letter came back upon her.

It was important, she saw, to be the leaver, not the left. She must decide in her own mind to leave Jeffrey. You seldom get to do anything you believe in, for something you believe in, she thought. Life requires no decisions and no actions from a person like her. She thought of people in lifeboats, deciding which one to eat; she thought of polar expeditions, of herself rolled in a rug, crossing over into Afghanistan. If it came to that, it was reassuring to think that General Ben would undoubtedly find a rug merchant quickly enough for an American woman.

Regarding Jeffrey, it soon occurred to her that it was not reasonable to resent and fear the same action by another that one had been planning to take oneself. She was sure she had been planning, unconsciously, to leave Jeffrey. Of course it is more disagreeable to be rejected than to reject, but she saw that she ought to be grateful that both of them were of the same mind. It was lucky, really, that Jeffrey had someone else.

She did wonder, though, who it was, and she minded that although Jeffrey had someone she herself did not, not really, for she could not imagine herself proceeding directly to marry Hugh, however agreeable this interlude. Nor was she sure that Hugh would suggest it. This meant, she guessed, that she was not in love with Hugh; if she were she would now be delighted, whereas she was not exactly delighted, only relieved, now that the pique had worn off, and concerned for the children, though that was a little abstract and in her heart she didn't think they would be worse off without Jeffrey. They would be better off, she told herself. There would be plenty of time to worry about the house, the division of the furniture, and all the other distresses of divorce her friends had reported.

She did not seem to be able to summon, from some reserve of feeling, much emotion at all about this. How odd, in a crisis of life, this rather flat and apathetic uninterest. She wondered if she ever felt things enough. Too much? What *was* the appropriate amount of self-concern? She watched the old women in black, or the bright-skirted tribal women carrying water, and wondered if they ruled secretly in their houses and analyzed their emotions, or perhaps emotions came to them as headaches, or as death.

"For its own works lieth every soul in pledge," she read in the Koran. She wished it would rain. She liked to see wind come up and the sky darken, and the quickening of things, of laundry on the line. You never saw that in America, but here the things hung on washlines, and would twist and flap in a wind, and all the dogs cowering under bushes again, and the jubes would flood; she'd like to see that, with shoes and tin cans and paper and the tops of carrots all floating along in the rushing water of the jube. It would be disgusting.

"It's knocked the props out from under you," her mother would say, or she would say, "You have to have the props knocked out from under you before you can fly." How conventional I am, thought Chloe, filled with scorn for herself. I can live alone, and have affairs, and travel to foreign lands as long as I know I have a husband, but if I didn't I'd be scared. After all, wasn't it really Jeffrey's fault she did these things—ran off to Iran, slept with other men? If he were nicer or easier to be with . . . Chloe had always felt sorry for men. They seemed so forlorn and unprotected. But now she saw she was in Jeffrey's power, as Noosheen was in Bahram's power, and now, in the power of men, she felt afraid.

Later, at the Cyrus, she heard Loyal Cooley talk about the importance of passports. Her pulse quickened fearfully.

"I carry my passport and traveler's checks around my neck," he said. "I have a bag around my neck, I just put them in there, then I don't worry—you know me, I get drunk and wander around—this way I don't have to worry. Without a passport you've had it."

Dick had in his pocket a small box containing a necklace. He had bought it from Richard Dare, whose name, it had not escaped him, seemed entirely appropriate for an alter ego of himself—an adventurer, on digs, in foreign bars, perhaps not entirely trustworthy? Dick hadn't much liked the dealings. He loved the necklace. The necklace was not visibly valuable, contained no jewels or stones, was made of beads of clay, rather drab, in fact, in colors of cinder and brown, with eyes painted strangely on the sides, glaring up at the wearer. She would not have been a queen, said Richard Dare, but a serving woman, although beloved, valued of somebody. Mourned.

At times, at the hospital, when there was no one in his office, he could not resist taking it out to look at, though Dare had warned him against this, for it would be illegal for a foreigner to have an antiquity. No one saw.

"I think I'm going to leave Jeffrey," she said to Dick over white wine. "And Jeffrey thinks we should."

"Really?" exclaimed Dick, taken by surprise by this sudden confidence, this sign of restlessness in the restfully stable Chloe. "You've decided?" She nodded.

"Well, it's usually for the good," Dick said. "I was all for it when we did it. Though now sometimes I think it was a lot of trouble. We should have just been a little more tolerant."

He means Marla should have been more tolerant, thought Chloe.

"Yes, I've had some time to think," Chloe said. Looking her most radiant. "It helps to be away, to think. I'm very relieved," she said. "I know it's for the best," as if the whole thing had been her own idea. One has, after all, one's pride.

Chapter Twenty-four

CINQ À SEPT

You know, my Friends, with what a brave Carouse
I made a Second Marriage in my house;
Divorced old barren Reason from my Bed
And took the Daughter of the Vine to Spouse.

Chloe didn't go immediately to report the supposed loss of her passport; it was a day or two before she could bring herself to think seriously about her impulsive transaction with Noosheen, and when she did it was with misgiving and satisfaction both, imperfectly sorted. She was in a way happy without her passport, and she congratulated herself that women were free of the temperamental constraints that confine men to the rules and regulations of their own devising. Women did therefore dare things with passports that men would never have done. On the other hand, her misgivings grew. "I'm Chloe Fowler," she told the American consul, in the seedy consulate full of filing cases of wood-grained Formica. He had a middle-western accent, but wore Iranian clothes. "I left my passport in my room, I think. Anyway, it's gone. Or it could have been in my purse, though I wasn't conscious of anything else being missing, either from my room or from the purse." Her recollection of the time her room had been searched gave her now, she felt, an injured, convincing tone.

"You're saying that you've lost your passport?"

"Yes, I've looked everywhere, naturally, and it simply isn't there."

"Oh, Jesus," said the consul. "It's getting rough, you know. You heard what happened to your colleagues the Erdmans?" Chloe had heard that the Erdmans, though there so briefly, had bought sixteen rugs. "Some for their sons and daughters-in-law," Heidi had said, "ten for themselves."

"No."

"They overstayed their visa by four days, so they put him in jail for four days. Took him right off Pan Am in Tehran." Despite herself, Chloe giggled. "And what happened to her?"

"They sent her off without him. They take these things seriously here nowadays. They don't like us here, you know. Oh, the Shah likes us, your Iranian doctors, they like you, but the guy that stamps the passport, the guy that issues the visa, they don't like us, they drag their feet. Things take weeks, things get lost. If somebody flouts the law, they can lock them up or confiscate things."

"I'm supposed to go September 10. I have my ticket," Chloe said.

"I hope it isn't an excursion ticket," he said. "You might have to change it. It won't be anything getting the passport. I just telephone our embassy in Tehran. But then you have to get a duplicate residency visa from the Iranians. That's what could take some time."

Chloe composed herself and determined not to be rattled or frightened by this. She filled out the forms he gave her.

"Suppose it was stolen—can someone else use it?" she asked as she was leaving.

"Sure, if they look like you," he said.

Life so seldom requires action that Chloe was quite unused to the feeling that came over her now, at last, of having taken a rash action. It went to her head like drink; she was woozy with anxious qualms on Noosheen's behalf. Perhaps she was recklessly sending Noosheen into danger, apprehension, arrest. Perhaps she should have counseled her firmly to stay. I'm out of my depth, was her thought, directing the lives of others. At twilight, when she thought he would be home, she went to Abbas's to ask his advice, for he was bound, she felt, to have from his long acquaintance with the Ardeshirs a more balanced view of Noosheen's real situation and perhaps would advise her to ask for her passport back and counsel Noosheen in patience.

She was surprised, she could not have said why, to find him cutting roses at the side of his garage. "Come in," he said. "How nice to see you."

Rather formally, they sat in his living room, which had the

sort of wood and upholstered furniture of hospital issue you saw here, and pretty oil paintings of flowers and cups on tables. She explained her mission. She admitted that she had encouraged Noosheen to leave, but, intent on confession although she was, something at the last second prevented her from admitting that she had given away her passport, literally empowering Noosheen to flee. This was what she had intended to confess, but now it sounded too desperate, too silly, too dangerously meddlesome. This realization impeded her account. She faltered.

"Would you like some tea? Some sherry?"

"Not really," she said. She had nonetheless the feeling that there was something she wanted. The moment was slightly bleak, inhospitable because something was withheld. Perhaps he was angry or disapproving of the way she had busied herself with Noosheen's life. "I am so sure that Noosheen loves you," she said.

He laughed. "Oh, Noosheen. It's true Bahram is not perfect for her. I've known her since she was a child. However, she's not in love with me. I know her parents. She was a reckless, obstinate little girl who was famous for riding a bicycle off a bridge. You must ask her to tell you the story."

He had poured two glasses of sherry.

"You could help her," said Chloe, wishing more than ever to pass along the responsibility for a reckless child who dashed off bridges. His beautiful smile was princely in its indifference.

"But it's you I want," he said, handing her the little glass. This impulsive remark seemed to affect her.

Her eyes widened. She took the glass. She felt heat flash her face. How unexpected men are. How plausible an idea.

"You are mysterious to me," he went on. "It's partly that." She was beautiful; he liked her pale translucence and the increasing voluptuousness of her body. "If I made love to you I would solve you a little. But perhaps it's simpler than that."

"I guess it's always rather simple," Chloe said, laughing, feeling herself attracted to this proposition. It would be, in fact, perfectly simple. They could go in the bedroom this minute and take off their clothes.

And indeed why not? They simultaneously recognized that they were staring. Each shifted. Abbas half rose. His the dark beauty of the warlike Turks in paintings, the Ottomans, painted with their daggers, their brocades. He leaned across the table to kiss her. She, in leaning toward him, laid her hand on the thorned stems of the roses and gave a cry of pain. As in the fairy tale, a drop of blood sprang to her palm. They rushed to Abbas's bedroom.

Her generally anxious state of mind caused brief apprehensions to flit into her thoughts—the worry of getting undressed with someone for the first time—what he will see, and, almost worse, what you will see, for though you know what he will see, what you see may surprise or disappoint or throw you off stride, intimations beforehand notwithstanding, and then what if he reacted to the clear difference between the color of the hair on her head and her pubic hair, or that she had it at all—here she thought of Noosheen, but no, he had been to school in England, after all, it was just that she had never slept with a person from the Middle East, or, indeed, anywhere but America, though these kisses were quite recognizable, causing her to think she would devote her life to pleasure, to giving and receiving pleasure, like this.

As they moved toward the bed—neatly made, India Madras bedspread—she saw him see that she had noticed the picture on the bureau of a woman and baby. But he said nothing, and she was spared the awkwardness of "I'm sorry." She couldn't tell if the woman was beautiful. Of course she must have been. A year is not long, only a year. She wondered if he had slept with anyone since, and who. His embraces were not of the starved but of the bountiful, bestowing kind, even leisurely, a lot of foreplay, so that Chloe, who had always been bored by foreplay, hastened things along. Not too much, just until she was reassured that things were going to go forward, and that Abbas wasn't going to cry, "This is madness," and get to his feet.

Abbas whispered Persian words, delightfully unintelligible. She knew she ought to wriggle vivaciously in his embrace, but was captured by a sort of ecstatic languor, a heaviness previously unknown to her in this situation, so that she could barely lift her arms to stroke his back. Her arms and legs seemed not to belong to her; she was only a center. When, after the climax, he lay against her, she saw that she had pleased Abbas too.

"I suppose I meant for this to happen—hoped, I mean, unconsciously," she sighed later as they sorted themselves out from the jumble of shoes and clothing on Abbas's bedroom floor.

"I'm glad," said Abbas. "I naturally had not dared to hope—or hoped, perhaps, but scarcely dared to plan." They smiled at each other, and Chloe, who had thought herself in charge of the situation, being the American, now had intimations, unfathomable but reassuring, of centuries of dark gardens, Persian poems.

There were not going to be any odd Islamic consequences, whatever those would be. Abbas, a sophisticated man, more handsome than Hugh, really, in a way, she thought, and as good, but now a stranger again, making tea. How odd sexual passion is, coming on like a fit. Her head now clearer, her body calm and light again, she felt that her life was not over.

She returned to the subject of Noosheen, her unhappiness, her love. "I even wonder if I should have encouraged her in her academic ambitions. She asks my advice. I wondered what you think. . . ." This glowing olive color of Abbas more attractive than paler skin, his shaving lotion some regular Western brand she couldn't name. Rich people here tall, like Abbas, only the poor ones small, except Bahram, beautiful rugs here, a lot of electronic equipment, that BMW, Abbas must be rich and choose to live here and devote his life to the poor. He had pounced on her as smoothly as a leopard. He had seduced people before. Something purred in Chloe. She knew there is no such thing as seduction. Of course Noosheen loved him, how could she not?

"Oh. I have to go! I'm having dinner at the Asgharis'," she said. What would happen now? Nothing. She would leave, though the paths outside were now encumbered by nurses coming for the evening shift, workers leaving the hospital, in the air the call to prayer; she would be seen by all the industrious and righteous. Sensing her hesitation Abbas brought her a black veil. On it the soft scent of powder, perhaps that of Mrs. Henderson, worn at the mosque. Chloe wrapped herself in it, clumsily as before, pulling the front down over her hair. Romantic subterfuge. They laughed as she glided out unseen onto the path among the others.

In a veil no one sees you. You may speak to them, they to you, yet you remain unseen. Invisible even though the man in the donkey cart has to rein up as she steps distractedly in front of him; it is not she who impeded his course, just someone, a woman, unknown. Eyes do not look at her; she is impressed by the difference. Now she remembers that in America when you walk along the eyes of the people approaching you assess you. You see them look at your shoes, and you think, Is something the matter with my shoes? My stockings?

"Well, it was just fucking, it didn't mean a thing," she plans to say, like a man, if reproached. But who could reproach her? She is cheered and fortified in her renewed sense that she is her own woman to do with as she pleases. She would have liked to tell Junie Fay. Junie she is sure would be approving of such liberated behavior. But of course she won't tell anyone. Neither will Abbas. Will they do it again? Why not? Chloe's cheeks so glow with daring and happiness, walking home, that she is sure anyone could tell she is not a modest Iranian woman.

Some interesting gossip at dinner: Noosheen Ardeshir has disappeared. Her husband confided it to Mohammed; he has no idea where she is; he has telephoned her brother in Tehran. She could not have flown home to her parents because she has no passport. He is certain, he says, that it was because she was so unhappy to be back in Iran; he understands her perfectly. But he is worried—where can she be staying? He doesn't know the names of her friends. She might have met millions of people in her Victorian Poetry class. The nurse seems stupid with the baby, which cries constantly. Reported second hand, thus, stripped of the anxious tones of the husband, the account does not suggest what emotions underlie it. If a young woman disappears in America, you imagine a car accident, or murder. Noosheen lying in a coma in a strange hospital, or abduction, body buried in a shallow grave dug up by dogs. Chloe feels it is a credit to Iran that no one seems worried that Noosheen has met with foul play.

The Yazdis walk home with Chloe and the others. "You must come some evening and see my collection, I spoke of it,

I believe. The collection begun by my father of Persian miniatures," says Dr. Ali Yazdi to Chloe, taking her arm to help her across the jube. She feels the silk of his sleeve against her upper arm. His cologne. His wife is far behind them.

"I should like to very much," Chloe said. "I've seen some in the bazaar. And the little pictures painted on ivory. I am going to buy one of those."

"Mine of course are very rare. From only special dealers. Many ordinary ones have been bought by Western dealers, but the very special ones have remained in Iran. Some are very curious, you know."

"Really?" says Chloe politely, not understanding the significance of this word. Curious.

"Cunnilingus," says Dr. Yazdi, leaning toward her. The startled Chloe withdraws her elbow. She is not sure she has heard correctly.

"Fellatio," says Dr. Yazdi. "These distinctive contributions by Persia to the arts of love."

Astonished, Chloe says nothing.

"You know what I'm talking about, I suppose," says Dr. Yazdi intimately. She feels her cheeks burn like a Victorian's. "The arts, the refinements of love are discussed in the earliest Persian texts; some of the earliest of history," Dr. Yazdi said.

"Um," says Chloe, heart beating with surprise. He knows what she did in the afternoon, or it is because she is a woman alone. Dr. Yazdi would not speak to a woman with a husband of things like this. She sees how he, they, must see her, loose and free, alone. But of course in a Middle Eastern country so conventional about the status of women, of course she must seem fast and free. She thinks of Zareeneh Yazdi, soignée, smooth-legged, flying to London for shopping, what might she not do there in hotels with Englishmen? Or perhaps this is just the way Iranians talk about love?

Or perhaps it is known what she is up to with Hugh? With Abbas? Perhaps they think all American women are whores? This is the way you talk to a whore in Iran? Or else there are no whores in Iran. What do I care what Dr. Yazdi thinks? They know about me. Perhaps they will write to Jeffrey. Her heart races. The minute you are unprotected, the minute you are light, men can tell. Not just Islamic men, all men can tell, she thinks.

"Thank you, Dr. Yazdi," she says at the door of Villa Two. "You are all so kind. Goodnight. Goodnight."

Chapter Twenty-five

REMORSE

A Book of Verses underneath the Bough,
A Jug of Wine, a Loaf of Bread—and Thou
Beside me singing in the Wilderness—
Oh, Wilderness were Paradise enow!

She awoke with a feeling of remorse, like a stone. Usually her depressions were two days before her period, like everyone else's; now she woke with an Empedoclean weight upon her of dismay and embarrassment, head aching, faintly sick at her stomach. She groped along to the kitchen to make coffee, hoping Dick Rothblatt wouldn't come too early, and that only he, not Junie or Hugh, would turn up. She could somehow talk to Dick, even if she couldn't tell him the truth about this, and he always made her laugh. She was a silly, promiscuous woman, but he seemed to like her.

Her bleak mood did not escape the notice of anyone she saw throughout the day. She half-heard the monotone of her voice, its flatness. "I'm tired, I didn't sleep," she explained to those who asked. Even Mr. Farmanpour asked. It was curious, but her trance of remorse enhanced her ability to concentrate on the assemblage of shards, which she could ordinarily do only for an hour or two before her restless energy ("short attention span," a teacher had once said censoriously) drove her to something else. Now she sat four hours in the afternoon, in the hot light, despite the growing heat, picking at the bits with tiny tweezers, achieving another inch along the side of the huge terra cotta beaker she had been given to work on. At moments her thoughts drifted to what she had done. Defensive phrases tumbled one after another through her brain: a pleasant occasion, a handsome man, curiosity, pleasure, all very natural, following the natural instincts without hurting others,

216

people do odd things on vacation. I was only trying to help Noosheen.

In the evening, Hugh returned from Tehran. She was glad to see him. She loved him. Making love later would be pleasant. But he hadn't found out anything in Tehran, he said. The people he went to see wouldn't see him. He was grim when he spoke of it, his mood as heavy as she had seen in him. He looked like a wartime President, except that his eye and ear were still horrible vegetables, cabbages or plums. He planned to complain of his security to Vahid Farmani. "I don't like this feeling of being in a risky game I have no stakes in," he said. She didn't press for details, didn't care. Her curiosity was subdued, or in abeyance, or she had perhaps given in, when she had failed to mention the shirts way back then, to her own emotional and erotic needs; she had surrendered her right to ask. Perhaps she even liked the idea that Hugh was complicit in some large operation of power and interest. This was perhaps the secret of the allegiance of criminals' wives—whom she still despised in principle—this feeling of being connected to influence.

Hugh suggested dinner at the Reza Café. It was Wednesday night, so the Iranian doctors came in for pizza before the English-language film at Cinema Pars. Chloe was surprised that anyone could bear to go to the films, now that the men had been burned in Abadan. This theatre could be set on fire, too, the doors locked, as in Abadan, locked by fanatic killers so that the patrons would be sure to die.

Abbas was with the others. They came laughing up the stairs. His expression at seeing her was for a moment astonished, and she realized that this was the first time she had been seen alone with Hugh. Or perhaps he was astonished at Hugh's bruises. Then he joined in the greetings. His words to her communicated, but most discreetly, their bond. Chloe's heart pounded like a schoolgirl's. She felt her face warm. It occurred to her that given a few weeks—less—you could sleep with every man in this room, a small room like this, if you were a free woman on your own. Some, though, were not attractive.

She and Hugh went to the movie with the others. Chloe

watched the exits, breathing deeply, fearing to catch a warm burst of air or smoke. If the theatre was set on fire, she and the others, sitting in a small balcony, which cost more, could rush outside to the fire exit. Chloe longed for someone to try the door, to make sure it was unlocked, but no one did. She did not give in to her hysterical wish that someone try the door.

The film was *All the President's Men*, about Watergate. She would have thought it would not be allowed, but here was a whole theatre full of Iranians watching a film about the fall of a powerful leader. The audience was completely silent. Chloe thought their mood was fascination. Hugh thought it was on account of the complicated English and relatively slow action.

"It says something that they would allow a movie like that," Chloe remarked to Dr. Ali Yazdi afterward, as the Iranian doctors stood on the sidewalk, deciding where to go for coffee. Ali looked surprised at such a direct remark, its implied criticism of the Iranian political climate. Chloe saw that it sounded more critical than she had intended it to sound, and to just the wrong person, Dr. Yazdi, who, it seemed from his jewelry, would have good connections in Tehran.

"I mean you wouldn't think there would be much interest in American politics here," she said.

"Robert Redford is very popular here," he said.

Abbas gave a short laugh and walked away ahead of them. He was thinking that it had been a fascinating movie, two men able to accomplish so much within a framework of laws and immutable regulations and constitutions. To do something in Iran, you would have to be a lone assassin or a guerrilla. Though it was not his style of thing, he rather more admired the youngsters hiding in the mountains, or the little newspapers printed in secret by people who risked their lives. Woodward and Bernstein had not risked anything, certainly not their lives. Luckily it was not necessary to risk your life, if you were a doctor, to do good; you could do it under any regime.

"It will be hard, going back," Chloe said to Hugh, the lightness of her tone concealing her emotion, its nature unknown, like something hot swallowed, waiting for his word to dissolve it, some medical balm of a word from Hugh, though she didn't know what it could be. What would he say? What could he say but yes that it would be hard going back; this he said. But that was not what she had meant. Hard going back to separate lives, he in Rochester, New York, she in San Francisco. "Never seeing you," she explained, careful in her tone, though, to show she wasn't nagging or making an ultimatum. Just an observation. "I've got so used to you."

His look at her seemed prolonged, seemed more astute than she might have given him credit for. Perhaps he did think of her, have, that is, a theory about her character, or an understanding of her—perhaps she was more a subject than she had thought. But her glint of comprehension was only momentary and was perhaps imagined, the way sometimes the pictures in a gallery could seem to look at her with friendliness and understanding, if she wanted them to, "Pinky" or Mrs. Siddons seeming to say that you and she have a lot in common.

"I know," Hugh said. "I've been trying not to think of it."

"Should we think of it? Hugh?" cried Chloe.

"When we get back we will think of it, whether we ought to or not. Then we'll see. That's the real world, after all."

"Oh, I know," said Chloe, with a light, uncaring laugh, thinking that the world around women were hanging on the words of men, right as they spoke; how she despised it.

"I love your dynamite big cock," Chloe says later in bed, and a whole lot of other things like this, not her usual way of talking but men seemed to like it, compliments to their cocks and generally a loose way of speaking in women in hot moments, if the woman didn't talk that way usually. She herself thought it odd that they didn't think it was odd that a prim ladylike woman such as she should come out with these things, but that was the point. Predictably, Hugh grinned. Perhaps he wondered what had heated Chloe up these nights; she wondered herself.

One night thereafter Hugh confided that he had once seen a book called *The Arab Art of Love*, which extolled the external genitalia of women in terms that were unfamiliar to a Western man.

"Cucumbers, or melons," Hugh said. "Different shapes of fruit. Just bend over slightly," said Hugh to Chloe, who was standing with her back to him in her thin nightdress. Chloe obeyed, rather apprehensively. "Yes," said Hugh, "there is a kind of outline. Very exciting to Arabs," seeming, after a moment, rather excited himself.

"You are a pear, Chloe," said Hugh, which disappointed Chloe, rather, though pears were a perfectly nice fruit. It was not a part of yourself you ever saw.

In the days that followed, though no one spoke of Noosheen, she preyed horribly on Chloe's mind. She thought of Noosheen in flight; imagined her wrapped in chador, veil flowing behind her as she sped along a dirt road, or carrying a few belongings tied up in a cloth, or wearing smart Western clothes on a flight to London, using Chloe's passport, pulling her gold earrings, fidgeting anxiously in her seat, or hidden in a wagon, swaying along behind donkeys over the mountains, wherever the mountains were. Perhaps the silence of other people was out of consideration for Bahram, who continued to come to work, his manner subdued, and otherwise to behave as if no domestic crisis had entered his life. They heard that he was making inquiries and contacting people in Tehran. Heidi and Chloe discussed Noosheen, though Chloe did not confide her knowledge or her part. The two women were sympathetic. "She hasn't been happy since she got back here," Heidi said, and "You never know how Bahram is in private, I suppose. But Mohammed thinks the world of him. It's just a sad situation."

"It was the ink, I imagine," Chloe said. "It changed her. Made her feel blue." She began to laugh at her silly joke, then broke off in case Heidi should think she was cruel.

"At least no one thinks she's dead," Chloe observed. "In America, you would assume she was dead."

Regarding Abbas, the torments Chloe was experiencing on her own behalf were familiar to her from high school: the fear that she had made a fool of herself and would not be respected; adoration and desire in a provisional form, which could be switched to distaste and fury depending on developments; an attitude of wary waiting and a mood of heightened interest in the world itself, the noise of bees sounding loudly in her ears, the hibiscus and jasmine stronger, sensation, sensation. When she did see Abbas, each day usually, by lingering outside the hospital on her way back from the university, or when eating lunch with Dick and Junie, she analyzed her emotions afterward and found them to be affection and fascination. His demeanor was perfect, communicating affection and regard to her, and nothing to any bystander. They did not, however, find themselves again alone.

She had somehow exasperated Junie, who was never admiring of other women but now seemed especially impatient with Chloe, who couldn't think what she might have done in particular, though generally, Junie gave her to understand, she symbolized lightweight self-indulgence and indolence. Words erupted during one of their lunches, always before so friendly, in the Azami cafeteria.

Chloe had brought up Noosheen. "She should have some counseling," Dick said. "Someone to help her adjust to her reality situation. When they find her."

"Really, how can you say such a thing?" Chloe disagreed. "One thing good here at least is that they aren't ridden by psychiatrists. Not that I don't think people need someone to talk to, but she had people to talk to. Me for one. And she has poetry. That is what art is for, isn't it, to help people bear reality? They get on very well here without Freud."

"And without Jesus," Dick said. "At least they're spared Marx."

Chloe disagreed. "Maybe they could use Marx."

"That's ridiculous," said Dick. "Show me a Marxist society where the people are any better off than before."

"China," said Chloe.

"Do I want to go back?" said Dick suddenly. "Back to all that acne, all those medical students, all those little proto-right-wing, guaranteed-rich kids. Endless boils and liver spots. I don't know. Not really." Psychiatrists were another thing, though. He had continued to have his recurrent dream about the body in the desert. He supposed it really referred to his burying his father, but he would just like to have talked to Edelstein about it, about the idea that he was feeling so repaired in spirit these days because he had in some sense really buried his father.

"I know," Chloe said. "Here a person can really do

something.'' Junie gave a sharp laugh. Her face had grown thinner—like a fox's face, Chloe thought.

"That's a laugh, Chloe. What do *you* do anyway?'' she said. Chloe had no reply. Junie's remark, unexpectedly cruel, was nonetheless true. What does Chloe do? The others talked of other things in hasty voices.

Junie was right, she agreed, thinking about it later back in Villa Two. She doesn't blame Jeffrey for loving someone else. She is unworthy, unsatisfactory, a terrible wife, an absent mother, indifferent, untidy, indolent, unfaithful—who could blame him? She dreads his going around San Francisco telling the story of his marriage. Please let him not testify or confide in people. If she marries again she promises to undertake it more knowingly, more sincerely, to be better. Her mood is one of pity and sympathy for Jeffrey.

How would it be to marry Abbas and stay in Iran, of course sending for her children, who would benefit from an international upbringing and learn to speak Farsi? Funny to think of Sara wrapped in a little shawl, wearing little earrings; in California all she wanted to do was go to swimming practice. Max would have to go to school in England like Abbas; that would be better than the schools in California. They would have another baby. A letter to Jeffrey saying, "I'm not coming back; put the kids on the plane.'' What a relief to follow this line of thinking. Max and Sara arrive with little suitcases, a court order. Rice diet better for the teeth. What a relief to follow the line of thinking that began with Abbas's serious smile and intent expression of passion and understanding. She could make him happy.

Noosheen halfway across India by now. It was mysterious; no one spoke of it, because of Bahram. No police out searching. Private inquiries? Was he doing nothing to find her, to get her back? If he had appeared distressed, frantic, if there had been an outcry, Chloe would have confessed something to him, had prepared a half-confession in which she unwittingly might be able to reassure him, she without realizing . . . Chloe hopes Noosheen, who seemed so confused among the barriers and thickets of Arnold's verses, can manage trains and the lie at the border. Western clothes, sunglasses, a hat, it should be easy, if only she hadn't got sentimental and tried to take too many things with her. Iranian jewelry, photos, books in Farsi. Probably they search your bags.

"It's true, it'll be hard to think of you going back to be Jeffrey's wife," Hugh said suddenly from his cot in the darkness. "You are my wife."

"I'm an archaeologist in far-off Iran. I'm nobody's wife," said Chloe, distantly.

In the middle of the night she wondered if Abbas would try to see her again, and whether she wished it or not. In his sleep Hugh sighed. He slept in his T-shirt, nothing on the bottom. She got into his cot with him and crept close to his hairy, warm thighs. One of these days she would suck his cock. She had selfishly ignored his wistful hints. She would try to be a better person soon.

Chapter Twenty-six

OUTCAST

Indeed the Idols I have loved so long
Have done my credit in this World much wrong,
Have drown'd my Glory in a shallow Cup,
And sold my Reputation for a Song.

In the following days, Chloe continued in a preoccupied state of misery and happiness she recognized from her adolescence; how strange it seemed that the decades do not diminish the symptoms: slyly looking or hoping to get a glimpse of someone, practicing a bright, intimate, but perfectly respectable expression to wear when happening upon him. Chloe despised herself as she grimaced in the mirror, or turned her head to try to see more of herself. She would just like to try it with Abbas once or twice again, she told herself. Desire is irrational, transitory. Otherwise Hugh suited her perfectly, and her fondness for him grew. When she tried to recall herself to a sense of her real life, need for her children, impressions of the future, she could not.

Perhaps, she thought, her voluptuous languor was owing to the heat, which increasing by slow degrees each day had now become stifling at midday. The doctors and the students went about their ways, but Chloe found that she lay on her cot after lunch, aimlessly staring at the circling flies, watching for a stir of branches, hoping for a breeze so she could bring herself to go to the university. Villa Two, like other Iranian houses, it was explained to her, was constructed so that if a breeze arrived it would be drawn right into the apartments by means of the stairwell and a tower that came out on the roof. The trouble was that no breeze arrived. At noon, the stillness, the airlessness which descended, coincided with a mood of menace, the report of terrible events. Soldiers had shot some students in Qum.

If she woke at dawn when Hugh left, she would get up and walk with Rustum in the garden. This was the perfect time of day. Thus it was that she saw the arrest of Vahid Farmani by a party of soldiers or police.

The police saw her watching but paid no attention. Perhaps they did not think she understood what they were doing. The police were young, and wore starched, short-sleeved shirts, and they had big shoes that flopped li! clown shoes. But their faces were frantic and grim. They were pulling the reluctant Vahid out of his door, punching him brutally in the back, as she watched, and kicking gratuitously at his shins, like angry children. He uttered a thin cry and twisted his body around to look at Linda, who watched from the doorway in an old nightgown. Vahid Farmani was shouting at the soldiers and calling out to Linda in Farsi, so that the words ''Linda, Linda'' were all that Chloe's ears could discern.

At the end of the garden by the gate of the compound a black Peykan waited with two taxis. Vahid was thrust into a taxi, and all three cars backed rapidly out of the gates. As he turned in the back seat of the car, for a glimpse of his wife, his eyes met Chloe's. His had a resigned, mute, doglike look. Chloe stood, watching from the flowerbeds, and Linda in her doorway broke now into loud sobs. Chloe hesitated. It would seem unsisterly and cold to ignore the terror and misery of another American woman. Chloe crossed the garden and timidly approached Linda.

''What's happened?'' she asked. ''Can I help?''

Linda looked at her, astonished. ''You!'' she cried. Her hair was down over her bare shoulders, showing a strand or two of gray, and her eyes stared like the eyes of a madwoman.

''But what's happened?'' Chloe persisted. ''Why are they taking him?''

''I don't know why they are taking him. He is arrested. They never say why.'' She abandoned herself to a frenzy of weeping, head bent against the panels of her front door. ''He is dead,'' she said again and again. ''They'll kill him. I'll never see him again. That's how it is here. Don't you know anything?''

Suddenly she was calmer and looking searchingly at Chloe: ''Who did you tell?''

Tell? ''About what?'' Chloe asked, thinking back, trying to

think, whether she had in fact told, or said, something, whatever it could be, to someone, to endanger poor Dr. Farmani. Perhaps she had said something. Perhaps to Loyal Cooley, the Texan CIA agent, or to General Ben, who worked, after all, for the Shah. Misery assailed her. She could indeed have said something terrible about Dr. Farmani, about his cruelty in the matter of an extra key, or his unsympathetic attitude about the cleaning of Villa Two.

About the typhoid. It came to her. "I have certainly criticized his handling of the typhoid. But to whom, who am I?"

"Maybe that's it. Oh, who knows? I don't know everything," cried Linda, breaking again into tears. "Things go on."

Chloe, wildly examining her recollections, was moved to embrace Linda comfortingly. It was strange how she had not felt authorized to embrace the wretched Noosheen at a similar moment and yet could enfold Linda, who didn't even like her.

"I'm sure he'll be all right," she tried to say. "Perhaps it's just for questioning?"

This suggestion brought further wails from Linda. The torture, the broken limbs. "Go to hell, go to hell," she sobbed, and rushed into her house.

That evening the Americans who had heard the news congregated anxiously at the Cyrus, which seemed safe and neutral, like an airport lounge, international territory where police wouldn't come, and Chloe was made to recount in detail what she had seen befall Vahid and what Linda had said. It was already apparent that Ali Yazdi had taken over as head of the hospital.

"But what do you suppose he did?" Dick Rothblatt said.

"The typhoid," Chloe said, "probably."

"I always thought he was a Shah person," said Junie Fay. "He's really gone up in my estimation."

Dick hated to mention the body. The others appeared to have forgotten about it. To him it seemed clear it was Vahid's handling of the body that had brought on his doom. Either that, or by his refusal to have anything to do with the body he had been unable to prevent what he feared, that association with it would bring him or the hospital down. "It had nothing to do with Azami Hospital," he had cried of the body, but perhaps the authorities in Tehran had thought it did all the same.

Perhaps even now they were beating him, torturing him, putting electrodes on his penis, on the soles of his feet, saying, "What do you know about the disappearance of Mr. X.? Where is he?" And Vahid didn't know, only he, Dick, knew, and Abbas Mowlavi, unless Abbas had told Vahid. Perhaps they were in league. You had no way of knowing for sure. Perhaps he and Abbas had merely been doing Vahid's dirty work in disposing of the body. So Vahid either did or didn't know about where the body was. This was or it wasn't the question the torturers were asking him right now. His head spun.

"Farmani was trying to cover up the typhoid, and Yazdi let it out," Junie speculated.

"It could have something to do with the airplanes," Dick said. "General Brigante thinks someone gets chemicals from Azami to sabotage the airplanes."

"Vahid trusted Yazdi. They were close. He might have told him any of his fears, and then Yazdi turned him in," said Junie.

"Perhaps political crimes we know nothing about," said Mrs. Henderson. "I rather think that's more likely."

"Maybe he's been a member of the resistance for a long time. How would we know?" agreed Junie.

Dick felt terrible and responsible. It was surely something to do with the clumsy handling of the body situation. Vahid had been petrified with fear over it, and now, for that matter, since he and Abbas were implicated, they should all feel afraid.

"Maybe he's been embezzling, something like that," someone said.

"*I* think Dr. Yazdi denounced him to the authorities so he would get to be head of the hospital," said Chloe, motivated more by her dislike of Yazdi than from any intuition of this.

This interpretation struck the others. It comported with what they knew of Yazdi, of the authorities, of the social aspirations of both men, of human nature—all the bits of assent from everybody present, collected themselves into the official ex-

planation. It became, in everybody's mind, the explanation—
even Chloe's, for it sounded plausible to her too. She thought
of his folded silk scarves, Pierre Cardin.

Altogether there was nothing to be done. Like a blind chorus
the Americans commented, then they had drinks. Luckily, they
remarked, things did not really affect them because they were
all to leave soon anyway. But they had been noticing a new
insolence, a *lenteur*, in the service at the Cyrus—they all had
instances of it—and there were various stories about the
student uprising at the university, and Dr. Henderson, out
driving in the hospital station wagon, had seen heavy artillery
on the highway to Pasargadae.

Nonetheless they were surprised to hear from General Ben
later that night that he had advised Mrs. Brigante not to return
from Fort Lauderdale. They had not realized things had gone
so far. And the next day they heard that the Mitsubishi wives,
charming little creatures who took tiny steps and paused at the
jubes as at great ditches—they were all leaving, someone
worrying about their welfare back in Japan. Procter & Gamble
had its dependents on alert. Chloe thought of all the substantial
cement-block houses and pretty gardens in the American
section by the Shah's summer palace, with the long American
cars parked in front. She imagined the American wives rolling
down their metal shutters and fastening the grills. But she
could not imagine herself leaving. These alarms seemed
excessive. Life went on the same. The following day Dr. Ali
Yazdi instituted some organizational reforms at the hospital
and ordered a cobalt unit from West Germany.

The abrupt deposition and arrest of Vahid Farmani left a
void, a pall felt at the hospital immediately. The Americans
were indignant at the seeming calm of the Iranians, though they
understood that this Iranian appearance of uninterest, as if
Farmani had never existed, might be reticence rather than
callousness. Each had expected, however, that the Iranian
person closest to him would confide an attitude, a theory at
least. What had Farmani really done? Dick tried to bring the
matter up to Abbas, who would only say, "That's how it goes
here. It's deplorable, of course."

Abbas didn't know what Vahid had done. He'd been
surprised by the arrest. He thought—something told him—he

would try to sell his BMW after all, and he spoke to Jahlal Hakemi, a resident known to have money, and Hakemi was interested.

Linda Farmani abandoned herself to stormy weeping only for the remainder of the first day. She told herself she had to keep her wits about her; there were the hospital, baby Henry, things to do for Vahid. She asked herself whether she really believed she could outwit Vahid's enemies. She had lived in Iran for seven years; did she fear Iranians more or less than at first? Life is cheap to them, someone had said that; they are so cruel to each other. Yes, someone had said that, at the American Wives' Club, or in a book. A book by Pearl Buck, maybe, talking about the Chinese? Life is cheap and now they had Vahid's life, or maybe it was just a minor affair, maybe he'd be back soon. If she went back to America, all her years here, her pretty rooms, her speaking Farsi, none of this would matter; it would be as if she hadn't lived at all.

She thought it was she herself who had brought this down on Vahid because she was American. That made him more vulnerable; they hated an American wife here, even more than they hated an English wife, though she had never put herself forward or pushed. But she had made some mistake. What? Maybe only that she should have been nicer to Chloe Fowler. She herself was in no danger. American wives were not thrown into prison. But how horrible that she had odd thoughts, for instance to wonder if Vahid's salary would be paid if he didn't come back.

She dressed in somber navy blue, and tied a scarf on her hair, and went to the garrison where only a few months ago she had taken some American visitors named Nelson, to see the ancient structure. Back then she had thought nothing of the busy reconstructions they had seen. Now she wondered if they were building these new cells for prisoners. Maybe someone would tell her if Vahid was there, but no one did.

She went to the hospital. Here, in the familiar dining room, she openly wrung her hands and urged people to write letters to the Shah. Her large, purple-lidded brown eyes were ringed with dark, tragic shadows; her lips were swollen with her anxious way of catching them between her teeth.

Walking home, she came upon Chloe Fowler in the garden. She ground her teeth. Policy, policy, she told herself, and smiled at Chloe. The Yazdis had still not returned the garden furniture, so she squatted beside Chloe amid the remaining potted geraniums while Hossein resentfully swept and puttered at his garden duties, glaring at this unseemly commerce between Farmani's wife and the troublemaking foreign lady. Chloe was humbled to see Linda, humbled to think of the triviality of her own problems, mere matters of erotic choice, mere marital problems.

"I'm sure you didn't mean any harm," Linda said. "Try to think. Who have you talked to? What have you said?" Her voice was sweetly smooth.

"No one, honestly," said Chloe, defensively. "Except the people around the Cyrus—General Brigante? I did mention the typhoid. And conditions at Villa Two."

"I know, you were out to get him from the first," Linda suddenly cried, jumping to her feet. "That's what he said. But you were mistaken. My husband is not political. He never has been. Does it make you feel good to do something like this to an innocent person? Do you like to think of the sufferings of an innocent person, you meddlesome bitch—has it ever occurred to you you might be wrong?" She walked swiftly into her house, leaving Chloe amid the shards of a flowerpot that she toppled in her flight.

Chloe was shocked and stung to be accused, so unreasonably, of something as serious and alarming as bringing on the arrest of Vahid. She felt her face flame. There was something exciting, too, to think you could be imagined so wicked, mischievous, and powerful. Only another American woman would pay you that compliment. But she didn't really believe that a remark about Vahid's handling of the typhoid could cause him to be dragged off, or that Linda could really believe so either. Linda was evidently speaking in passion and terror, casting about for someone to blame. If it weren't so serious she would have thought it was silly.

She went for her groceries in the late afternoon, when the shadows made things cooler. As she walked home, she saw

Heidi Asghari coming toward her from the compound. Suddenly, Heidi turned and went into a shop. It was strange. Had Heidi not seen her? Chloe, passing the shop, saw that it was a toy shop. Heidi was inside gazing at the shelves. Chloe hesitated but did not go in.

At dusk, as she was dressing, the phone rang in the hall. This was such an infrequent event that it frightened her. The feeble ring seemed, at first, to be a pained cry from under the floor or a hallucination. The caller was Heidi. "I'm so sorry," she was saying, in a rushed voice, "it's a bother, but I'm afraid my dinner party's off, something's come up for Mohammed."

"Oh, that's too bad," Chloe said.

"Well, I'll do it again soon," Heidi said. "I'm sorry."

"Oh, me too," said Chloe, thinking that she had nothing to fix Hugh for supper.

"But I'm planning to go to Heidi's!" Hugh said later. "No one has told me not to. I left Mohammed just now and he said he would see me at eight."

Chloe could hardly realize what had happened. Heidi had uninvited only her. Could they all believe she had somehow been behind Vahid's arrest? She was astonished. As far as she knew, she had never in her life been unwelcome. She was at first too shocked to feel hurt, then she felt hurt and indignant.

"Ah," she said. "She means that the dinner party's off for me, then." She told Hugh about Linda's accusations.

"Shall I stay home with you?" asked Hugh solicitously. "I'll make some excuse."

"No, no," said Chloe at once. "Then they'll know we've talked. No."

But she waited up for him, asking eagerly as he tiptoed up the stairs, "Did anyone speak of me?"

"Of course not. I mean, no one speaks of anything. No one even spoke of Farmani."

"But they think I somehow put him away." Chloe couldn't help but laugh, though she knew it wasn't funny. The thought that her friend Heidi, or worse, Abbas, could think such a thing of her was nearly unbearable.

"Chloe," said Hugh, unlacing his shoes, "you *don't* always

think before you speak. You don't take them seriously here. You don't realize that their lives are at risk, their families. You just say whatever you think—I've heard you talk about the body, the epidemic, God knows what else. People here are good people, trying to do the best they can for Iran. They are in danger all the time.''

His tone was that of a man addressing a child. Tears of indignation shot to her eyes. As she was about to retort, she thought of Noosheen. She had had nothing to do with the arrest of Farmani, but she had certainly meddled in the life of Noosheen, who now, fleeing across unknown spaces, hiding in airport toilets, or landed penniless and desperate in India, or murdered by unscrupulous wife smugglers and her husband left grief-stricken, her babies deserted—this certainly was owing to Chloe's meddling. Chloe felt at this moment that she would sell herself to bring back Noosheen and get her own passport back, so she could leave this wretched country.

Still, just though Hugh's accusation of meddling might be, it was disloyal of him to rebuke her. He ought to stand behind her, she thought; he ought to believe in her. All at once her tears blinded her. She went into the bathroom.

''I'm glad it was a nice party,'' she said, in her bright, normal voice through the door. When she came out, Hugh went in. Chloe hurried to her cot and crawled in, and closed her eyes so that she would seem definitively asleep. But her heart was pounding with wakeful rage, and with an unfamiliar but unmistakable emotion—self-reproach. And fear. But with luck Hugh wouldn't find out about her part in the flight of Noosheen.

No Iranian now saw or spoke to her. Chloe tried not to think about it or to mind. It was unjust but just. She only hoped that Abbas did not believe with the others that she was a spy or informer. She would be leaving, she knew, in ten days, if her passport came. No doubt it would come. She would leave in ten days but this seemed a meaningless unit of time, neither long nor short. She did not intensify her activities and do the things she had been meaning to do. Hugh had offered to lend her money for a rug. She could go to the bazaar and look at rugs. She wanted to finish her large beaker, a late Elamite beaker from the second millennium, and see the nearby city of Pasargadae. But her energy, her will, seemed already departed.

Darling kids. To think I will see you soon! The hot weather here is really hot. You wouldn't like it. Love, Mom.

She worked at the university in the mornings, as if she had all the time in the world, and in the afternoons drifted or slept. She took to sitting on a bench near the hospital entrance, near the flowerbeds where people could be seen walking in and out or squatting amid the roses to picnic or whisper, sometimes to weep. Chloe had been married to a doctor for a dozen years, but was still frightened by hospitals, emblems of the menace and arbitrariness of fate. Try to think of them as places of healing, Jeffrey would say, but how can you, with this woman swaddled in blue sitting on the ground pressing her cloth against her wet eyes, swaying in her grief like a wind-shaken dahlia.

Chloe would think about that woman, would try to imagine her at home, what her cooking pots were like, whether she had a radio, a line of children eating soup of peas and rice. A husband with a thin mustache. Did they kiss? Did anyone kiss the old dried faces, kiss the old men with thin shoulders? It appeared not. People appeared to shiver. Chloe watched them unwrapping their sandwiches. Who kisses the old?

Now, when she imagined the life of others, it was their pain she imagined, their suffering, their fragility, never their happiness. Why? It was safer to be herself, a person formerly happy, usually happy. She tried to imagine the happiness of women, wiping the hands of her little boy, that one, the other wearing a gold bracelet. Sometimes women would buy beautiful things in the bazaar, or a new broom, and feel pleased. A new broom was what she needed in Villa Two.

She wished she could see inside the woman's house, see her kitchen, see her shoes, plastic shoes walked over at the heels, think her thoughts as she looked at her shoes. What if all her thoughts, every minute, were of misery and sorrow? Chloe thought of all the women she had seen in photos, trudging with water jars and burdens. What if their every thought was sorrowful, miserable? Was this even possible? Surely the most unhappy mind is distracted at times by mere perception; by the beautiful tree in bloom, of the grayish fuzz of moss along the bark and the radiant light through the petals.

She never took off her beads. She understood the men who stood staring on street corners, heads wrapped in dirty rags, fingering their strings of beads. A sensation of permanence—hard, significant objects, with poems and rules to go with each one, and the interest of Allah invested in each one, in each bead as in each sparrow.

One night Hugh frightened her a little, making love, kissing and sucking at her breast. It suddenly seemed to her when his teeth had closed around her nipple, that he would bite her. She stiffened and pushed him away, and he turned the attention of his fingers to other parts of her, his kisses gently to her throat. She did not tell him what she had for a moment felt afraid of.

One afternoon there was a knock on the door. Chloe opened it, and was surprised to see a woman standing there in a nylon peignoir, blue, trimmed with ribbons. She was sixtyish, blond and well preserved, face made up and powdered, pink lipstick, smiling.

"Yes?"

"Hello," said the woman. "I'm Sugar Dunham, from Chapel Hill. My husband Homer Dunham and I have just got here, and I was just changing, and I went out in the hall to go to the kitchen for a drink of water, and I'm afraid I've locked myself out. Do you by any chance have a key?"

"I'm sorry," Chloe said. "There's only one key. That's how it is here, only one key. Come in, I'm sorry." Sugar Dunham stepped inside and Chloe closed the door. Sugar looked around, noticing apparently with approval, or even envy, the rug, the geraniums, the cheerful turquoise border around the window. Chloe felt gratified at the surprise on this new woman's face.

"My husband will be back. They're showing him around. We're supposed to stay a month but I'm already having my doubts. This is really terrible, isn't it? How long have you been here?"

"Nearly seven weeks," said Chloe.

"*Seven weeks*," said Sugar Dunham, as if she couldn't believe it, "Oh, honey," she said.

"It isn't so terrible when you get used to it," Chloe said. She wished to explain how much worse it had been before, but this seemed like too much trouble. "Won't you sit down?"

Sugar Dunham sat on the sofa. She seemed to shudder as she looked at the cushion. Chloe had forgotten that Rustum was underneath the sofa. Unused to strangers, he snarled near Sugar Dunham's ankle. She looked around her in wild fear.

Chloe made her a cup of tea and talked to her about what sights to see: the garrison, the tombs of Hafez and Sa'adi. Dr. Dunham was brought back to Villa Two presently, by Ali Yazdi, who was able obligingly to send for a duplicate key to the Dunhams' room, as if nothing were simpler than a duplicate key.

Somewhat later, someone knocked again at her door, and it was again Sugar Dunham, now coiffed and wearing an expensive Pucci knit of chartreuse and turquoise.

"We're going to dinner with the Yazdis," she said. "But I have some time, and was wondering . . . "

"Come in," said Chloe.

Sugar was carrying a bottle. "I was wondering, honey— would you like some vodka?"

"Well, maybe," said Chloe. "Yes. Thank you. Sit down."

Sugar Dunham handed her the bottle and a plastic lime. "I always bring a little something when we travel," she said, sitting on Chloe's sofa, looking carefully first. "You'd be amazed how often it comes in handy. And now, I really want to know . . . "

"Sure," said Chloe.

"Tell me honestly . . . "

"Of course," said Chloe.

"Tell me honestly, honey, are you all right here?" Sugar Dunham's voice dropped confidentially. Chloe suddenly saw herself through Sugar's eyes—a fat, disheveled primitive, imprisoned two months in this dismal room, perhaps afraid to talk about it. Sugar's face was bright with concern. Chloe would have liked to say: No, I'm not all right. For some reason not. It's Hugh, Abbas, my husband, Jeffrey. I must go back. My life is no longer in my hands. I can't make it out. Also I don't care. Where are my children? Why should I be ostracized and criticized and enveloped in a mantle of gloom? Where is my passport? What have I done?

But the ingrained habit of reticence, or her imperfect understanding of her feelings, or simple lassitude, prevented her from speaking. She managed no more than a warm smile of thanks, appreciating the solicitude. But the kindness of the woman's tone brought her close, for the second time in recent days, to tears. She who never wept. Then her tears overflowed, like the tears of Linda Farmani, and became huge sobs, which Sugar Dunham regarded with attentive solicitude, proffering Kleenex.

"I don't know what's the matter with me," Chloe said. "I feel so confused."

"Well, my God, look around, who wouldn't," said Sugar Dunham. "Or it could be pre-menstrual syndrome."

Chapter Twenty-seven

PERSEPOLIS

The expedition to Persepolis, which they had all looked forward to as the summit of their enjoyment of Iran, was arranged for the weekend after the end of Ramadan, but it was shadowed by the growing mood of rumor and fear. One heard of further ugly incidents in the South—new riots; an American man killed by the side of the highway, apparently by robbers; two students beaten by an angry mob in Abadan. In Tehran the prime minister was changed. There was no word of the imprisoned Vahid Farmani, or of the vanished Noosheen.

As the day of the journey approached, they had word that in Tehran one hundred thousand people had demonstrated against the Shah. The confusion and anxiety that settled over the spirits of the Iranians further lowered the spirits of the Americans, though nothing was openly discussed between them. Neither did Hugh discuss his bruises, nor did he mention his trip to Tehran. Chloe wondered how he had explained his bruises to people.

The Hendersons had argued for postponing the Persepolis trip on account of the danger, but for the others, whose visits were soon to end, this would be the last weekend to see the great ruin—Chloe's airplane ticket was for the tenth of September, and Hugh and Dick were to leave the twelfth. So they went ahead with their plans. Rooms were booked in the Darius Hotel in Persepolis—one for Junie and Chloe, one for Dick and Hugh, one for Abbas and a newcomer, a Dr. Ames.

237

The Hendersons nervously elected a day trip, declaring themselves willing to drive back to Shiraz after *son et lumière*. The Americans believed this to be because of the expense. The Dunhams said they preferred to go along with the Hendersons, and with them it appeared to be a case of the known evil, Villa Two, over the unknown evil of an Iranian country hotel, of which they had depressing expectations even though they were assured it was deluxe. For a time it appeared that the Yazdis would come along. The Yazdis continued to socialize as usual. Chloe had been amazed at the docility with which the compound had accepted the ascendancy of Ali Yazdi, whom she believed to be a usurper and informer, and now, judging from his continual presence with one or another of the many foreign visitors, obviously the Savak agent. Though, when you came to think of it, Abbas was always with foreign visitors too. . . . She did not think about this too carefully. At the last minute, in any event, the Yazdis decided not to go.

Of course it didn't matter who was Savak and who wasn't, or what she thought, for soon she would leave. She foresaw clearly the form of her return to San Francisco: Jeffrey would pick her up at the airport. An ugly scene or two. He would have moved out already or be poised to do so—no emotion stirred when she thought like this—poised to move out as soon as she got there to be with the children. In the kitchen; exactly the same disorder in the knife drawer, exactly the same uncurtained window, and the blind that had fallen down still rolled in the corner waiting for someone to go buy new hooks to hang it by. The same thin sheets, cotton and polyester, the cotton after ten years mostly washed away, leaving them essentially polyester, nearly transparent in the center—pale vestiges of floral sprigs, designer sprigs, nearly washed away. Pillow cases unmatching, differently sprigged, different designer. You can never get the same kind when you go back to get more; the designs have changed. She hadn't known that or she would have stuck with white.

Had Jeffrey talked to the children, explained, prepared them? Or was he leaving that to her? Were they upset or calm?

Now she didn't care. When she thought of anything she thought of being in the movie theatre in Shiraz. What if the fire had started in Shiraz? She could imagine it licking round the curtains, smoldering in the chairs, could imagine the bodies of the thin desperate men stacked up like sticks by the doors. In this vision she and the others were in the balcony, in their reserved seats, from which they could escape, but they stood horrified, inhaling the smoke, watching the flare of stick bodies, which crackled as they burned like paper.

She did not know why this vision came again and again to her, not a dream, but a notion that came vividly into her head like a daydream, pictured, insistent.

They assembled early in the morning. "I'll get in back," Chloe told the others. As she was always the smallest, her seat was always in the back seat in the middle. June and Dick got in on either side. Hugh rode in front with Abbas, and the new doctor rode in the hospital station wagon with the Hendersons and Dunhams. On the way, they stopped to look at a wayside shrine that had been there, said a sign in French and English, since six hundred years before Christ. The shrine was devoted to Ahura Mazda, God of the Zoroastrians, who taught kindness and wisdom.

"Thank you, O Ahura Mazda, for beautiful Iran," said Chloe, and said, silently, as was her habit when visiting religious sites, a prayer for the long life and happiness of all those she loved. She excluded herself.

"Thank you, O Ahura Mazda, for my backhand," said Hugh aloud, whatever he said silently.

Chloe also wanted to stop on the way in the great fields where Mrs. Reza had told her shards lay on the surface, a museum of the history of simple daily lives of people who lived centuries ago on the desert near the city of Persepolis. Sure enough, bits of pottery lay on the ground beneath the low grassy clumps and weedy flowers. The short-sighted Chloe was obliged to crawl on hands and knees, peering intently at the roots. The others strolled, stopping occasionally to bring something up and show it to her. To them broken bits of pottery, to Chloe—for her studies had not been in vain—a matter of joy to find an example of early green glaze, or the even earlier unglazed, stick-incised conventional border, or the all-over-incised, glazed interior—it amused the others to see her face light up over a particularly good bit.

But they had to leave off at the approach of a soldier across the field, waving his arms censoriously. They put down their shards, but Chloe furtively thrust several of hers into her bra and pockets. Abbas called something reassuring to the man in Farsi and they returned to the car. The Hendersons, driving up just then, asked what they had been looking at but didn't get out of their car.

"Some broken bits of pottery for Chloe," Hugh said.

Dick had pocketed some shards too. He looked at Chloe. There was no question but that she was a little subdued these days. She was so pretty. He thought of giving her his necklace, when they got back. He himself would run the risk of smuggling it through Iranian customs; then in the airplane he would bring it out, or he would go to see her sometime in San Francisco and give it to her there. He had been thinking of giving it to Junie, but the truth was that Junie didn't care for jewelry, though she went on wearing the dead man's watch. He had even thought of giving it to Marla, or of keeping it for when Ellen graduated from college. But then he would think of how unreasonable Marla had been about the house, and of how Ellen always lost things. Chloe liked jewelry, and always wore a string of blue beads.

Further along the highway they stopped to relish their first glimpse of the magnificent ancient city, Persepolis at last, set high on an escarpment of sheer rock, a citadel of immense grandeur, lofty columns, and broad staircases visible even from here. They were stirred, as they had expected to be.

"Somehow, no matter how often I see it," Abbas said, "it is the most beautiful and moving sight."

"Magnificent," said the others. "Magnificent."

"Alexander the Great," said Sugar Dunham. "The horses, the panoply."

"This was Darius and Cyrus," her husband reminded her.

"Oh, sweetie, I know, it was Alexander who *burned it down*. It's just that I have more of an image of him," she apologized.

As they drew nearer, the company could see bright tents on

the plain at the foot of the walls of the tower in the city. These, erected for the Shah's millennial celebration, were surrounded by trees planted in orderly rows and were thriving on careful irrigation. In this encampment the rich and powerful and famous and curious had assembled for a lavish festivity organized a few years before to celebrate the thousandth year of the reign of the Pahlavi family. Abbas explained with a touch of irony that the festival had not been popular. Hungry people protested the vast expense. And the family of the Shah had not in fact ruled for a thousand years. Now, harmlessly deserted, the tent city looked pretty, and did not seem to symbolize the wickedness of monarchy or the poverty of the people so much as the transitory nature of all temporal power. The inevitable seedy cats strolled in and out of the deserted lanes and walks. Up close, the tents seemed to be of plastic laminate. Several dirty children crouched to watch, and their old grandmother, near them, adjusted her veil. Except for these people, the site was deserted. Above them, on the walls of the ruin, tourists could be seen, tiny as fleas.

The city of Persepolis itself also suggested transitory grandeur. They parked their cars on a strip of tarmac at the foot of the ancient wall, which, lower on this side, rose on the other to a height of forty feet. Near the parking lot, at the foot of a broad stone staircase, were a gate and tiny kiosk where tickets were sold, and old men hung around to volunteer as guides. Above them towered vast columns and strange plinths and capitals, and the stone heads of bulls. They hurried excitedly up the steps, steps wide enough for ceremonial visitors, for the entrance of princes, and the stones were worn low and smooth by the wheels of chariots and hooves of horses.

At the top, looking ahead, they saw acres of ruins, vast, deserted, elaborate, a surreal landscape of columns holding nothing, stairs leading nowhere, broken figures, blocks of stone. Sometimes these had been organized and numbered by archaeologists, whose neat notations could be seen. New paving stones here and there completed an antique design. Otherwise, they could imagine, Persepolis must look much as it had when people fled and the embers had cooled, two thousand years ago. Chloe had a *Guide Bleu*, in French, and Junie had Fodor. They stood at the top of the steps, turning their books round and round, trying to face the direction of the maps.

"À gauche, la porte de Xerxes; au centre, la plate-forme supportant les colonnes de l'Apadana," began Chloe.

"Oh, thanks a lot," said Junie, who had continued to be strangely brusque with Chloe. She strolled off in the opposite direction, followed after some hesitation by Hugh and Dick. Abbas walked back down the great staircase to look more closely at the friezes, and Chloe, wishing to follow the recommended route of her book and to take photographs, strolled off in her own direction, disappointed that Abbas had not come with her.

Alone, her melancholy mood prevailed. The mighty ruin dictated a certain historical perspective from which the troubles of modern Iran, to say nothing of one's personal fortune, lost immediacy, lost pang. But she still regretted that she would soon fit into the category, divorced woman, that she had always felt to be so disadvantageous, associated with poverty, quarrelsomeness, yearning, hard-up sexuality, general lack of dignity—modern pretenses notwithstanding—compared to married women and widows. She had always hated the idea of being divorced, but now, as it occurred to her, gazing at the Apadana, she didn't care.

Chloe guessed she was getting her period; she felt some discomfort. She hoped she wasn't getting a bladder infection. It wouldn't be surprising, all that love-making, and Hugh had wanted a few times recently to take her from behind, her on all fours, wasn't there a joke about that, psychiatrist telling you to change your marriage? But she couldn't remember what the joke was. From behind, so that he enters more deeply, making her have to pee right after, and now that familiar burning beginning, but anyway, all these doctors, she can easily get some sulfa. Not a good time for it to come on, in Persepolis, but endurable. Little infections, prospective troubles, had no interest.

They had only an hour or so to wander now, after which they would go to the check-in at the Hotel Darius, and then come back for the *son et lumière*. They would visit the city again in the morning, which, according to all authorities, was the best time to photograph the bas-reliefs. Chloe was happy to be alone, to wander among the stones, to enjoy her mood of philosophical gloom, her meditations upon transience, and to seek an imaginative transportation into dusty history, where Persepolis in all its splendor would somehow become actual to her. She found, though, that a truly elevated state did not develop. Perhaps she was too permanently dead, too flat, numbed by Villa Two or something. Nothing stirred, as she looked at the stones, except objective admiration, distant and practical. What fine immense columns, how handsome the vast stone steeds and guardian bulls, how delicate the carving of the coiffures of the immortals pictured upon the stairs. She thinks of Omar's lines,

> *How Sultan after Sultan with his Pomp*
> *Abode his destined Hour, and went his way.*

That these streets had been full of living people, walking along, hearts full, hearts pounding, should have struck her with its poignance, she knew, but she felt indifference. The pity of all this destruction should have struck her, rubble where magnificence had been. But it didn't make any difference, she thought, rebelliously, and it probably didn't make any difference if a bomb fell on, say, New York, beyond the immediate tragedy of death. What would be left anyhow in ten centuries? To lose Paris or San Francisco might be a pity, but even those—for she must sternly adhere to this line of thought, no sentimental reservations—even Paris and San Francisco made no difference to the universe, to history, to the bare ground that went on being. Even the bomb—what difference did it make?

What, anyway, does anything matter? What does anything mean? For it was all gone. These are the appropriate thoughts to have in such a place, she thought, with a touch of satisfaction at the proper cast of her thinking, at her emotions, which swelled and rose, unnamable, at the mute stones, the dumb faces in the carving, processions of ancients, each snail-like curl of beard as fresh as then, strong legs protruding from their little tunics, oxen with long horns, men carrying fish, figures marching in profile, their eyes looking straight out at Chloe.

Strolling up and down the staircases, craning her neck up at the immensely tall columns, inspecting the carvings was absorbing work and pleasure. In the distance Chloe could see the Hendersons wandering around. She was surprised to encounter Hugh, and to realize he'd been hanging back, tactfully, not liking to disturb her reverie. When she caught his eye, he stepped forward briskly with a "now that you've seen me" expression.

"Really something," he said.

"Amazing," she said.

"Does it make you sad?" he asked.

"I guess. Does it you? The idea is supposed to make us sad," said Chloe.

"Maybe us especially," said Hugh.

Chloe felt her eyes sting but could think of nothing to answer. Hugh put his arm around her shoulder and hugged her, and patted her bottom in the time-honored proprietary affectionate way.

This was seen by Dick Rothblatt from a distance, around a wall.

"Chloe and Hugh!" Dick said to Junie. The thought just struck him. Remembered scenes peeled backward across his mind, rewinding Chloe talking to Hugh, Hugh lingering on the dark path. Smiles. "Do you think they're making it?"

"Of course, obviously," said Junie.

"I didn't realize that," Dick said, baffled. Why should Marla or Junie—even Junie—find these things so obvious? Yet it was obvious, once you thought of it at all. He felt—what? Hurt, or strangely taken aback. Did he expect Chloe to have confided this? Well, yes, in a way, after some of the stuff he had told her. Or was it that he had thought there was something pure about Chloe—not that he respected purity, of course, that sexist, old-fashioned concept. Yet some women did seem to be . . . above sex, or to have it hidden away somewhere in their lives out of the prying view, like a lovely sachet in their stocking drawer.

He felt rather angry with Chloe.

"What makes you think so?" he said.

"Well, I don't know, no one thing," said Junie. "It's just so totally obvious."

"It's some female talent, noticing things," said Dick.

"She could be fucking everyone in the compound before you'd notice," Junie said.

Chapter Twenty-eight

SON ET LUMIÈRE

We are no other than a moving row
Of Magic Shadow-shapes that come and go
Round with the Sun-illumined Lantern held
In Midnight by the Master of the Show.

The party checked into the Darius. Their cases were taken to their rooms. Junie and Chloe, in theirs, took out their sweaters, in case it would grow cool at the *son et lumière,* and unpacked their toilet articles. To Chloe there was something restful about having a female roommate, and maybe Junie felt this too, for her manner, lately so hostile, seemed for a moment to melt. Looking together into the mirror, they combed their hair, and joined the others in the garden for a glass of tea. All at once a waiter told them to rise and hurry off, so as not to miss the vaunted spectacle of the sun setting over the columns, and over the tombs and distant hills. Obediently they left, their tea unfinished, and drove in their two cars to the parking lot by the gate of the city, and rushed toward the steps, alarmed by the growing redness of the sky. Junie clattered a tripod with her, and bore a heavy camera on her shoulder.

At the gate it appeared that a problem had arisen. They found the guards in the process of shuttering the ticket booth and locking the gates above. Abbas had a long conversation with them in Farsi, then returned to the others. "A difficulty," he said, "though perhaps not an insurmountable difficulty. They say they are planning to close, that they have had an order that there will be no performance tonight. My own opinion is that they just feel like closing, but I think this can be solved in the usual way." The Americans stared resentfully at the knot of guards, who stared back, it seemed with a trace of satisfaction at this power they had to thwart rich tourists. Abbas returned to talk to them. Moments passed. From the tone of the voices, the quarrel was bitter, even violent. Abbas shouted with the rest. Then, all at once, arms waved, smiles spread among the parties. Abbas smiled. Like a chorus, the Americans smiled too, bowed toward the guards, stirred.

"He's crossed the palms," Hugh said.

"He's getting them to open just for us; that can't be cheap," said Dick.

"The show will go on," Abbas said, smiling, as the guards neatly restored the "Open" sign and propped up in its wicket the notice of times of performances, prices, languages, and waved them in.

"Lazy fellows," said Abbas. "That's the trouble here, they have no interest in whether things work or not. They are thinking it is for them to decide whether to open or not. All is caprice and bribery in this country."

They were to view the spectacle from a wooden grandstand that had been erected in the courtyard of the great central palace, which they had learned from the guidebooks was called the Tripylon. There they settled themselves, with growing enjoyment, to wait for the dark. Chloe had forgotten her sweater in the car; Dick borrowed Abbas's keys and gallantly went back to get it.

They were awed by the splendid sense of having nearly to themselves this ancient and remarkable place, though in fact a few Iranian tourists had also profited from Abbas's negotiation and were scattered here and there in the grandstand. After the last pink, darkness fell as rapidly as a shutter. All at once the lights were extinguished, and a deep, amplified voice boomed in the darkness, in a rather British accent, "I am Cambyses, son of Cyrus the Great. It was I who chose this spot on which to build, to the glory of the Achaemenians, a sacred city of Pars." Drums boomed in the loudspeaker, and then the triumphal march from *Aïda*.

Then a light illumined the door of a tomb in the hill above them, and from there another voice returned: "I am Darius the

Great, son of Cambyses, and it was I who built the sacred city of Pars, to the glory of the King of Kings." Now, nearer to them, another door was lighted in the hillside.

"I, Xerxes, here built in my day, too, much that is beautiful, to the glory of the King of Kings, Ahura Mazda, to whom I prayed that the sun eternally shine on these palaces and on this kingdom," intoned a third voice.

Now they were again for an instant in blackness, and when the spotlights picked out the ruined columns nearer them, the great voices had taken on a tone of lament. "Oh, what, O Ahura Mazda," began Cambyses again, "have been our crimes that you have shaken down these walls which we erected to your glory?"

Chloe sighed contentedly to think of the desolation of history and the crimes of antiquity. Xerxes had, it seemed, destroyed the Acropolis in Greece, and it was this that brought down Alexander upon them, to destroy Persepolis in revenge. Living and dying by the sword. From the dark plain came the voice of Alexander, a brash tenor, boasting of his power, and of the beauty of his mistresses, and of his vengeful plan. "Give up, O Persepolis, your treasures. I have brought ten thousand mules and five thousand camels to carry them away," he crowed. The *William Tell* Overture swelled up.

Chloe, who had always scoffed at *son et lumière*s and thought them a silly genre of entertainment, thoroughly enjoyed the majesty of the lights and shadows on the great ruins, and the evocation of the kings who had built it, and the sense, momentarily reassuring, that this long and mighty history included her, and her friends, and the one or two Iranian tourists, and, somewhere, the projectionist and someone playing the tape. Her pleasure was a little diminished, though, by the discomfort in her middle, a menstrual feeling of urgency and pain.

"I, Darius, King of Kings, expect, O men of Asia, your tribute. Bring me, Kushia, your ivory; Putaya, your chariots; Zranka, your cattle; Arabians, your dromedaries, Skudians, your lances; Sagartians, your horses; Hindush, your vases; and Parthians, your camels.

"Bring me, Gandara, the great humped bull, Bactrians and Egyptians, cloth and animals, and, pointed-hat Scythians, bring me bracelets and trousers. You Ionians must bring bees and woolen skeins, and the Harauvatish the skins of lions. Cicilians, I will have from you your fine rams.

"Katpatuka, Haraiva, Babylonians, all, your tributes. Syrians, your cups and jewels, Susians, Armenians, Medes."

It occurred to Chloe that if Persepolis had been burned by the drunken soldiers of Alexander in 330 B.C. then it had been ruins ever since, ruins for two thousand years; and that all the Sassanians and khans and shahs and glorious kings thereafter had seen it as she was seeing it now, these cautionary and reproachful ruins, and Alexander himself was the last, before days of *son et lumière*, to see it ablaze with light.

At last, as the words seemed to retreat into the tomb, in the black hill beyond the illumined movements, the bare light bulbs above them went on, signifying the end of the performance. They stood, murmured, gathered their cameras and coats, and Chloe excused herself to go to the ladies' toilet at the foot of the stairs, saying to the others as she raced down the steps that she'd catch up to them.

The toilet was not as squalid as she had feared, though it was of the hole-in-the-ground variety. She'd gotten used to these. They always stank. As she squatted over the pit, the lights in the toilet went out, making it a bit complicated and precarious moving her feet. In the darkness the splash of her urine seemed very far below, down into archaeological strata where Achaemenians had peed. She thought she had gotten her period. She felt in her bag for a tampon.

She expected the lights to go back on, but they didn't. The place was relentlessly closing for the night. She expected the others to be waiting outside the lavatory door, but they were not. She could not even hear them. She stayed by the doorway until her eyes grew accustomed to the darkness.

For a moment she could see the amphitheatre steps but no farther. To the right was a path leading toward the entrance, or was the entrance the other way? She paused, knowing her own propensity for turning in the wrong direction. She was irritated that neither Hugh nor Dick had thought to wait for her.

She retraced her way up the steps again, to where they had been sitting, hoping to be able to see from the high seats the direction of the entrance. The silence was strange; it was the silence of the desert, with no mechanical sounds, no horns or calls, only small insects and somewhere an animal cry. She held tightly to the chain handrail, fearing to lose her footing in the dark and miss a step. She stopped at the row they had been sitting in, and from there, seeing nothing, she climbed to the top row of the bleachers, where she could get the best view. Where was the moon?

From here she could see that the entrance was below and to the left a few hundred yards. There was the top of the ticket kiosk, and a small light from within it illumined a few feet around it. She decided that the others had forgotten about her and were walking toward this entrance, or had gained it and left. They would in a moment remember her. If she kept her gaze fastened on the ticket kiosk, there was the gate through which they would pass. Or she could hurry after them, sure, now, of the direction. But the silence made her hesitate. Something new had happened but the darkness gave no clue at all about what it was.

She could call out. In the silence she would be heard for miles. She feared, oddly, to hear her own voice echo among the tremendous stones, like the deep fake voice of Darius over the loudspeaker. "I am the Queen," she could call. "You have forgotten me. Beware the curse of Alexander's Queen."

Now she could hear an alarming chorus of angry voices, shouts and muttering, male and female, in the direction of the entrance.

And now she did see people moving at the entrance. She put her bag on her shoulder and began to descend the steps. Then the after-image of what she had seen made her look again, straining her near-sighted eyes. She felt in her bag for her distance glasses. Bringing things into focus, she could see that the figures at the gate were guards, not her companions, and the lights came from headlights, shining from the darkness outside the walls. An impression of activity, different from the lethargic keepers and lounging guides who had clustered around the entrance when they had arrived. Where there had been dozing old men, now people strode briskly.

More men walked into the light. With surprise she saw that they carried guns, what looked like little machine guns. Four men stood a few feet apart in front of the stairs, like a net waiting to catch anyone who wanted to descend on them, and two more men, thumbing the shoulder straps of their guns, pushed into the darkness of the deserted city. These were not the guards, then, but police or soldiers. She heard her own gasp in the hushed air. The blackness was suddenly intimate and warm, as if she had been stuffed into a closet.

Now she hears voices again, mutterings, amplified by the stones, harsh commands, protests, nothing you could make out to be English or Farsi but a familiarity about the rhythm of objection, complaint, maybe the voices of Hugh or Dick, or the voluble Sugar Dunham, or the high voice of Mrs. Henderson. Then a woman's scream, sudden, like the false scream in a funhouse, but terrifying and sudden out of the blackness— Junie, if you could tell by a person's scream. Chloe feels herself grow more still, concentrating; she has to think now, and not do the wrong thing. Something is going on here.

It could be a turned ankle, a sudden fright, yet this is no time to seek simple obvious explanations, for there are people with guns down there, and sneaking, and screams. The best thing is not to move. If they had flashlights, they might see her up here, or maybe not even with flashlights, for she is high up. If this is nothing, the others will come and find her, and if it is something . . . But what can it be? Some people are born knowing about danger, others have to infer it imperfectly from second-hand data, TV, guns in films. This has a filmic aura of stealth and darkness. Her heart beats loudly. She doesn't know what is going on here but will wait and see. Her eyes are growing used to the dark.

Dick remembered Chloe had gone to the ladies' room and began walking back toward it to get her when the lights went out, so he instinctively turned back toward the safety and reassurance of the others, seeing, in an instant, before the scene was dispelled, a man pointing a gun at Abbas and Hugh, all of a sudden, by the gate. A man in blue jeans carrying a machine gun, Hugh throwing up his hands. Dick's eye and mind took this in, then it was gone. Hugh and Abbas dived off in opposite directions, ducking behind stones, Hugh with a curse. The man then indifferently waved the gun at Dick instead, motioning him closer. Dick stepped obediently closer, astounded. How had they dared defy a man with a machine gun? He supposed it was instinct, you do it without thinking, impulsively, and sometimes get shot, you leap at the throat of the intruder, you throw yourself into the water after the drowning person, and you drown.

What was happening? Why? The man pointed him along a dark stone aisle. Behind him he heard cries, shouts, a curse, Dr. Henderson, Mrs. Henderson, maybe Junie's voice among the others. Someone behind him had a flashlight, whose narrow beam illumined a frieze, conjuring a horde of staring stone Achaemenians watching Dick. Dick shuffled along, aware that someone else shuffled along behind him, another man, Iranian probably, wearing a suit. Probably he was the father of a family that had been at the *son et lumière*.

They found themselves being shoved into a wooden shed filled with picks and other excavation tools and various boxes, an assortment of objects momentarily visible in the light of the flashlight, before the door was slammed on them, and bolted. Dick's companion began irascible shouting in Farsi, and by the sound was feeling along the walls, tripping on things. Dick tried the door, which was fast. He threw his shoulder against it a few times. In the complete darkness, the frenzied activity of his companion was irritating. They needed thoughtful silence. "Ssshhh," he hissed at the man, "quiet, shhh." The man stopped.

Then from somewhere distant, Chloe or Junie screamed, or it could be Mrs. Henderson, anyway a woman, a fully articulated scream, a lunch whistle. This triggered a rush of frantic associations, soldiers, rape, Junie, attired in comic-book dress, ripped off the shoulder, skirt short almost to cunt, shrinking in a corner with horrified face as animal soldiers advance—why Junie not Chloe? But somehow Junie was more the type to get raped.

*   *   *

No further screams. Dick stumbled over a box of something, sat on it instead, settled straining to listen. His companion sighed rhythmically as if trying to control fear or weeping.

"Do you speak English?" Dick asked. Only sighs in answer. The darkness was solid. Now that he wasn't smoking he didn't carry matches.

He thought again of the way Hugh and Abbas had neatly jumped aside, as if without fear of getting shot, losing themselves instantly in the night and not being pursued. The gun was pointing at him alone, and at this man, but not at Hugh or Abbas. Perhaps at Junie or Chloe; just noticeably not at Hugh or Abbas, who had vanished as if at some signal. He sat silently, resenting his own docility, but what could he do but wait a little, see what developed? Each moment passed with excruciating deliberation, almost ticking, moments became hours, in the phrase.

He could hear no one nearby, but in the distance shouts from time to time, and engine noises, as if vehicles were drawing up below the ruins on the plain. Because of the strange acoustics of the place, he could not tell in what direction the people might be, how nearby, how many. Their captor had been Western, sandy-haired. He heard no women's voices.

His companion lit a match, lit a cigarette. Dick saw his face illumined, a middle-aged man with graying hair, mustache. His eyes had been looking at Dick, trying to see him in the dark. It showed a hell of a bad judgment to light up in here; who knew if there was dynamite or whatever. Dick shook his head, frowned, but the match had gone out. The glow of the man's cigarette grew and diminished with each breath.

"What time is it?" Dick asked. "Time? Watch?" Understood, evidently, for the man lit another match and leaned toward Dick. Dick thrust his wrist toward the man, and the man was showing Dick his own watch. Somewhere near eleven, it appeared, before he shook the match out. Then another match, held higher, revealed the space a foot or two around them. Plenty of tools with which to escape when they could, though the moment was clearly not yet propitious.

Chloe safe probably in the women's john, if she'd had the sense to stay in there, or else—had she too absented herself according to some plan? In the same way she had in fact

absented herself from the cave when the body of the man was
found there? The array of coincidences was troubling but his
suspicions lacked the crucial ingredients of explanation and
hypothesis. There was no plausible game for them all to be in.
It was all very well to say CIA, that catchall, you still had to
have a hypothesis, and anyway it was ridiculous, since she was
Jeffrey Fowler's wife, from San Francisco, which he knew for
a fact, he'd known them for years, Hugh Monroe too, though
her involvement with Hugh was new to him. There always had
been something a little elaborately romantic about Hugh; you
heard of him studying viruses in Borneo, or skiing glaciers
somewhere in July. He suddenly thought of Marla reading
about all this in the paper, a massacre at Persepolis, American
doctors die in dangerous drama—she would wonder what he
had been up to, what had been his game, and she would believe
he had had one.

His thoughts raced fitfully; it was like having insomnia,
night thoughts, waking ravings. He tried to slow them down,
tried to feel his way calmly toward an explanation.

They've put me in here separate from the others, Dick
thought. What do they want? It's something to do with the man
in the grave. Intimations of torture tightened his throat. Who had
betrayed them, he wondered. Abbas? or Hugh? The dreadful
explanation, further elaborated, presented itself. It was no accident but by design that he found himself alone in this hut,
except for this unexplained fellow. The others marched off
together, he himself singled out in this isolation. Their captors
would be coming back to get him, to make him confess his part
in the murder of the man in the grave, or in the cover-up of the
murder. Dick struggled with this unreasonable paranoia. He had
not killed the man. A party of men would hardly need to invade
Persepolis in order to seize Dick Rothblatt. He knew it was just
his tendency to feel guilty. He told himself to stop it. He wished
the man would decide to smoke another cigarette, but probably,
with crafty prudence, the fellow had decided to cut down, in case
they were in for a long imprisonment.

The invaders had not been Iranian, could have been American or anything else Western—he had not heard them speak—
so they were not the Shah's secret police, say, or a troop of
rebels. They had to be here looking for someone or some-

thing—Hugh? Abbas? But it would have been simpler to find either of those two back at the Azami Compound. The guns bespoke a belligerent or illicit intent. The only other tourists were this man and his family; except for them and a few guards and guides there had been no one here.

Now the man, sitting in the dark, tugged at Dick's coat, pressed the pack of cigarettes into Dick's hand. Dick hesitated, desire and fear contending, expanding his trachea. Fear of his own nature. If ever he was going to relapse this would be the time, wouldn't it? The smell in the shed was of dirt and stone.

"Thanks," he heard himself say, and grabbed one urgently.

Chloe tries to figure this out, tries to review in an orderly way the possibilities, as if it were a secret that would yield itself up to reason, if you started at A, like Mr. Ramsay. Junie had screamed. The others had vanished silently, either captured by or in league with the armed men. It made no sense to imagine that armed men pursuing them would have to besiege all Persepolis to catch them, when they could wait until later and catch them in their hotel, or on the road tomorrow. They were therefore in league. But with whom? Abbas? Dick and Hugh? One of these but not the others? What had Persepolis to do with it?

She thinks of once, when she was a child of what—three? four?—and wandered off at the fair, at the Indian show, and was lost in the fairground. She had sat right down where she was, and waited, knowing they would find her, and didn't budge, even when she heard her name over the loudspeaker. Chloe Linden, Chloe Linden, said the immense amplified voice. She had huddled under a picnic table and waited and sure enough they came and found her, and that is what she would do now, just stay put until rescued.

Now, minutes or hours—stretched long meaningless rubber-band units of time—however long later the sound of a shot. The idea of gunfire there all the time was now actual, but startling all the same to Chloe huddled on the grandstand seat, tucked away up above, thinking she could see the prowling figures stalking through the ruins, see their lights at least, hear the heavy rumblings of their purpose, whatever it was. One shot, then silence afterward, a deepening and serious silence, filled with new ideas of menace, retaliation. Who had they shot at? At Hugh or who? Why?

Chloe, frightened by the gunshot, sits stiffly by her post high up above, able to track the little lights wending in and out among the stones. She is cold, though it is a hot night. She is forgotten about, no one is looking for her, the thing is to sit still and unseen. She wonders if Junie has been captured. Who are they? She can imagine that perhaps since this afternoon America is at war with Iran and these people have come to capture them, but it makes no sense to imagine, as she fleetingly had, that Abbas has led them into a trap here, since they all could have been arrested quite easily in the Azami Compound, as Vahid Farmani had been; there was no need to pursue them crazily through the night. She thinks with guilty alarm of the contraband potsherds in her purse.

The invaders are busy. Flashlights, ropes, muttered consultations, shouts. Once she hears two men drawing near the bleachers, never looking up, say in plain English, "It'll take a winch, whatever he thinks." When they move on, she takes from her purse her black veil, brought to wear in case of going to see a holy sight, and wraps herself, to be warmer and more invisible during the night. If they come near, she will ditch the potsherds behind the bleacher seat. Despite her willed intention not to think terrifying or sad thoughts, her imagination develops the scene in which her children are told of her death, and fears come about their motherless adolescence. Her longing for her children is an idea, almost, that it is they who could rescue her, were they only here; had she not so wickedly left them.

Chapter Twenty-nine

PLUNDERERS

Although it must be warm, it seemed cold. This was fear, she guessed, compared to which she hadn't ever been afraid before, not like this. It was a matter of trying to calm yourself down, trying to think what to do, trying to breathe. What would she do when it got light in the morning and they could see her? She'd better have a plan, better line up a place to hide in out of sight when it got light, in case they would shoot her because she was up here watching, even though she couldn't see anything.

She was sure there had been gunfire. Had there been enough to shoot all the others? Surely not, she thought, only a shot or two, not enough to execute her friends by, so they must be all right. As she thought lurid thoughts of execution, she was aware of a kind of hum produced by her own body, the toxins of fear producing a chemical hum, and her throat was dry so that she could hardly swallow, and she had an ache in the places at either side of the base of her throat, just where a killer would put his hands. She might be overlooked by accident, like the Filipino nurse who hid under the sofa. Killers with their adrenaline, their toxins surging, they too make mistakes and overlook people hiding.

If anyone came, or when it grew morning, she could lie right here in a kind of trough formed between the topmost seat of the bleachers and the supporting wall behind it by some cement buttresses. Or maybe she should crawl in it now so as not to risk attracting any attention if it were to grow light. For how

257

long had she sat here, anyway hours, mesmerized by the silence and by fear? Half expecting a bullet to split her skull as she moved, she eased herself over the backrest of the seats and lay on her side full-length behind the seat, half in the trough, her arms pinned oddly to her sides by the narrowness of the space. She lay, shivering in the hot night.

Then she was unable to keep lying there, pinned in like that where if they came she couldn't run; she could imagine them suddenly standing over her pointing guns down at her head, and now she was no longer cold but wet with hot sweat, her steamy panic building till she had to move. This was how it happened—you sat still until you couldn't bear it then bolted like a rabbit right into the sights of the police rifles, snipers waiting for you, knowing when you can't bear it a moment longer, and they were right she couldn't lie still, not in this position on her side looking up where she would see their faces as they pointed their guns.

She thought of the photographs of the men standing in a ring around the little boy in Warsaw, pointing their guns at him. She thought of the photograph of the man being shot by the Vietnamese general, of the expression on his face, of pain and disgust.

She had to climb out of this tight place. She was sweating, that was why she was cold, and she thought she could feel blood trickle down her leg. She moved slowly along the row and crouched at the top of the stairs, keeping low, but she could bolt down the stairs if someone should approach through the open space in front of the grandstand, or she could run along the top row if someone came up the stairs.

Anyway, the thought came to her, you have to save yourself; no one is going to come and save you.

With the first light coming in through an aperture between the roof and walls of the shed, Dick could see that this was a flimsy structure with no actual windows and no bolt on the inside, so that although they couldn't get out, anyone could come in unless they could concoct some sort of barricade from the kegs and timbers stacked along the wall. Dick listened alertly for clues about what was going on outside. He heard no voices, no gunshots. Then the silence was broken by the noise of an airplane close overhead, a drone as loud as doomsday, then sputtering to silence somewhere close by. He tried to see out the crack between the eaves, and when he couldn't, he was boosted by the Iranian, whom he could now see was a man in his forties, graying, in a neat business suit, with nothing about him otherwise to provide a clue to his condition. This man had subsided passively onto what looked like a keg of plaster, disconsolate head drooping toward his knees, one hand clutching worry beads, but now he jumped alertly up when it appeared he could help Dick look out. He did not himself seem to wish to see, though he could have by standing on his keg, but instead hung back and watched Dick for signs of understanding or plan. Outside, there was nothing to be seen except an empty vista of stones.

Dick threw his shoulder a few times heavily against the door, as he had done at first, and found it as solid as before, but not so solid they couldn't ram it open with one of the boards stacked in the corner. Then he realized it would be simple and quieter to pry the door off its rather loose hinges, and looked around for an implement.

At the same moment, almost as if it had yielded to his shoulder, the bolt slid and the door opened a crack, then decisively, and Hugh Monroe peered in. Dick felt a moment of alarm, as if Hugh were the captor.

"Quick," said Hugh. "Quiet." He stepped inside, and pulled the door shut behind him. He spoke in a whisper.

"What's going on?" cried Dick.

Hugh glared around the dark shed. Except for the bruises on the side of his face, the ones that had been there already, he appeared unhurt, normal, even rested. Dick stared, trying to quell his odd suspicions.

"Where were you?" asked Dick.

"There are some people, they could be Americans, an airplane, and a lot of Iranians with uniforms. But they aren't the army. It's hard to see. It looks like something being unloaded. I think they rounded everybody up last night and they must have put them in the museum; that's the only structure except this, and there's a guard outside it. Some of their people are walking around, but I think we can keep out of sight. I don't think they've hurt anyone.''

"How did they miss you?'' Dick asked.

"Well, I was looking around for Chloe. They never saw me.''

"Did you see Chloe?'' Dick asked.

"No.''

Dick remembered the sudden way Chloe had grabbed her purse and streaked down the stairs.

"They didn't expect anyone to be here last night.'' This suddenly came to him. "The place was closed. Abbas got them to open it.''

"Well, that's right,'' Hugh said. "A bunch of American tourists weren't in the plan. Let's get out of here.'' Dick found himself following Hugh cautiously out the shed door, half wondering if Hugh would deliver him into the hands of the captors. The Iranian man stepped out behind them, then stepped back in again, and stood in the doorway peering after them as they crept along the path that led to the main staircase, he hoped not into a trap.

It became clearer to him, as he thought of it, that Hugh must be involved here; it would explain his bruised face, his confident demeanor on the path ahead, his accurate knowledge of Dick's place of imprisonment. The Iranian man had had the sense to see that he was safer inside. But Dick felt quick-witted, equal to this, whatever it was. From the path he could see their cars parked below on the desert, amid other vehicles brought there in the night, a rabble of old trucks and a van, men loading boxes into the trucks.

Distant, in the other direction, was the airplane Dick had heard, some kind of light cargo plane with the belly open, and people running up and down ladders. He and Hugh hid behind the monumental protoma of a horse's head and watched. Boxes were being unloaded; men carried them to the trucks, passing things out of the hold, wobbling on the ladder, and handing and hoisting things in. Now they could see that a huge stone head, massively heavy, was being dragged along the sand, festooned with ropes. Near the trucks, the Iranians were opening one of the boxes and taking out guns.

They'll never get that head in there, thought Dick, feeling an abstract interest in the effort; but the plane had some sort of winch, and inhaled the giant artifact in moments. They could now see that the pile of rubble near the plane was entirely heads and limbs of giant rams and sphinx-like gods, stone figures entire or broken bits of cornice or column, all to be carried away, and more objects were being lowered from the walls of Persepolis by ropes to the sand below.

Chloe with the arrival of the dawn could dimly see her watch, and calculate an end to this terror, estimate the distance from here to there, figure out what was going on. She could gaze out. She could see. It appeared that a party of men had sealed off Persepolis and now with the dawn could be seen making their way among the ruins. Some were wearing ordinary clothes, carrying guns, and some were in military outfits—dark men, apparently Iranians. They did not seem bent on rape and vengeance and they were carrying archaeological artifacts. It grew lighter. She reasoned that if she could get from here into an enclosed space—say the museum, where the others must be, or the women's bathroom again, or the little plywood projectionist's booth suspended at the other side of the courtyard—she would be safer. Slowly, recklessly, she climbed down the bleacher steps.

At the foot of the steps she paused, mesmerized by the sound of voices approaching—American voices. At first she thought it must be Dick and Hugh. All the same she shrank into a shadow. Then—it was with a kind of horrified calm—she saw that the American walking toward her, with others, briskly striding across the Queen's courtyard, was Richard Dare. Richard Dare, the shifty archaeologist; she had never liked him. She stood frozen in an attitude of female passivity, sculptural and invisible. Dare turned around and looked in her direction, as if remembering that he had seen someone there, but she stood motionless, and, although she was full in his view, he did not see her. What came to her mind was a comedy movie, where Jerry Lewis or someone like that wearing women's clothes walks through carrying a mop or bucket and no one sees him. That must have become part of her unconscious knowledge, that if you cling to a bucket, or wear a veil or widow black, no one sees you.

All at once her elbow was gripped firmly from behind. She gasped and turned. Abbas pulled her further into the doorway behind them. He shook his head for silence; they waited till Dare's steps disappeared. Then Abbas led her around the periphery of the courtyard, apparently thinking, as she had, of the projectionist's shack on the other side, where one could unseen watch events. Chloe's mind warmed with relief and apprehension at the same time. Was she saved or captured? They hastened up the ladder and inside.

On the plywood wall of the projection booth, Chloe saw a plan of Persepolis with the toilets and gates indicated, and the exits. She saw where they were, where she had been. From this vantage, Abbas looked out the peephole beside the spotlight lens.

"What do you see?" she whispered.

"I'm not sure. Iranians, Americans. I think guns—it seems the Americans are gun runners. The Iranians, therefore, would be . . ."

He turned, and smiled his melancholy smile, as if it did not matter. "Rebels, perhaps."

"Will they hurt us?" Chloe asked.

"We'll stay out of the way."

She shivered, as if thawing out. "It was frightening, last night. Through the long night."

"Yes," he said. Presently he added, "Have you ever passed a night like that, in danger, in the dark?"

"No."

"No. An unusual experience. There are better ways to spend the night."

Not an arch or flirtatious remark, just a statement of fact.

"Yes," Chloe felt her blood speed up with inappropriate longing. Could they not discuss this? When but in danger did one need comforting embraces? He was looking out the peephole again.

"I can see Monroe and Rothblatt," he said. He drew back so Chloe could see Dick and Hugh, lying on their bellies behind a mound. Hugh was crawling up it to peer over the top.

Chloe could now see what she could not before, and what Hugh would see when he got to the top of the mound: statues and artifacts being loaded into the airplane she had heard, now taxied up under the walls of the city, open at the underside, surrounded by men loading and carrying, intent upon the difficulties of managing huge objects of stone.

Abbas pushed her rather abruptly away from the peephole and looked again, as if the significance of what he had seen before had just struck him.

"My God," he said. "Look. They're loading the statues."

It looked that way to Chloe too.

"It makes sense! That's why the guards were bribed to close last night, so these people could come in and loot the treasures of Persepolis!" His voice trembled.

"It's Richard Dare," she said. "I saw him."

"A harmless archaeologist, bringing guns."

"I don't see the guns," said Chloe.

"Over there. Those crates of guns, loading on the trucks."

"Oh, yes."

"My God, my God," said Abbas, "I wonder what I can do? This can't be permitted. They don't understand, they are ignorant peasant boys, the stones mean nothing to them, they have given them away!"

His dismay intensified, along with a feeling of moral correctness that verified it; he was right to feel this patriotic, this admirable dismay. Foremothers shrouded in veils murmured from the sky, a sort of spectacle of ancients with jugs on their heads approving his indignation, ancients on their horses, with long white beards, tents stretching out into the desert, camels all around, and dancing people, joyous in his release from some self-preoccupation, some tense and Western inwardness. Here was something he could do something about. It would be just a very small act at that, to notify the authorities, or the resistance, or anyone who could come in here and stop this. It was not so very much to do.

Shahs, imams, all were as transient as himself, but the stones of Persepolis were Persia, and that Persia was something to him after all. Mere people, mere factions—he would have preferred to stay in London but he'd come back to Iran, for the sick people, or maybe he had come back to save these stones.

He felt the exhilaration of righteous action. He would alert the military post behind the Darius. A pleasant feeling of desperation and justification swept over him, seized his being, transported him. Chloe Fowler's eyes watched him, dark with fear.

"Perhaps I can talk to them," Abbas explained. "They don't understand. They are young, they know nothing."

"The soldiers?" asked Chloe, to whom it did not seem possible that he could imagine stopping this elaborate spectacle below, for which all these trucks, airplane, guns, ropes, and dozens of men had been marshalled. How could he?

"Or I could telephone somewhere. The police—the army . . ." his voice grew excited, distracted, his accent grew strongly Iranian.

Below them, as they watched Hugh achieve the crest of the mound, they saw Richard Dare materialize from the opposite, invisible side.

"In it, all together!" Abbas shouted.

"Oh, shhh," cried Chloe, "they'll find us here. Abbas!"

"Chloe. I'm going to do something."

"No, please stay," she said.

"Stay here, this is safe. I'll come back." He touched her shoulder, and then was climbing down the ladder. She watched him run along the edge of the courtyard, off toward the staircase of Apadana. She wanted to scream after him but did not.

Abbas ran through the ruins toward his countrymen loading guns. Indignation and loyalty rocketed through his blood. Whatever happened, it must not happen that these treasures be stolen. "For whatever good works ye send on before you for your own behalf, ye shall find with God."

Richard Dare pointed his gun at Dick and Hugh. They stood, aghast, Dare as astonished as they. Richard Dare! What was he doing here and why had he raised his gun? Perhaps they could for an instant have grabbed him, but had not. Now it appeared that he would shoot them, but he did not. He, like Dick and Hugh, was all at once distracted by a fleet of off-track vehicles approaching directly across the sand from the direction of the

Darius. These could be seen to be four military-type vehicles, which parked at some distance from the airplane. Soldiers leapt out, carrying machine guns, and rushed, firing, toward the plane; rescue, perhaps, or reinforcement. Other men rushed, like warriors of antiquity, toward the high platform of Persepolis itself. Dick saw the distant figure of Abbas Mowlavi running toward them, waving his arms. Dick and Hugh exchanged a fraction of a glance, expressive of their shared moment's impulse to run after Abbas, to rescue, to help, like good Americans. The moment passed.

"Believe me, if we don't get this stuff out of here, these crazy spicks will blow it up themselves," said Richard Dare, in an apologetic tone, turning back. He turned again and was waving his gun at the advancing men. He fired aimlessly at them, and turned again to Dick and Hugh.

Dick saw him bring the gun up again. It was shocking to see someone you knew transformed with greed and purpose, not even recognizing you, or recognizing you and determining to shoot you, having passed ordinary limits of compunction, civility, conscience, raising his gun right at someone he used to drink in the Cyrus with. Panic electrified Dick's spine; he suddenly broke and ran. He spun around the corner and ran on weak legs, stumbling down the ceremonial staircase, expecting a bullet between his shoulders, but not waiting for it. The noise of his feet clattering, stumbling, plastic heel taps economically nailed to his shoes now ringing through all Persepolis.

Chapter Thirty

THE WHISPER

Oh threats of Hell and Hopes of Paradise!
One thing at least is certain—this Life flies;
One thing is certain and the rest is Lies;
The Flower that once has blown for ever dies.

Dick flattened himself against the wall of the Apadana stairway. The sun poised above him between the columns like the flame on a candle, and a bird flew across the sky. The sky was deepening blue, as if he were down in a well, and the sound of shooting, far off, echoed. No one had followed; Hugh was not with him. He crouched, wondering what to do, analyzing with growing acumen the sounds, direction, changes, chances. He could hear men calling to each other, the crack of rock falling—a rope broken, a stone leg lost—all this in the distance. He was relatively calm. It was better to be under the open sky than in the prison hut. Dare and his people would be off and he was not sure what he had to fear from the Iranians, the recipients of the guns. He tried to find a comfortable position, squatting like this, but his quads ached however he bent.

Now to the sounds in the distance were added the sounds of other trucks, or cars maybe, shouts, wilder cries, wails winding up, and now bursts of gunfire from automatic weapons. Sweat trickled down his sides from under his arms. If you were out long in this sun, you would die. He retreated farther down the stairs, into the shadow where the sand stank of urine or damp.

The implications of the new situation frightened him again, fighters coming into the ruins, not just down on the desert by the plane, people perhaps attempting to hide, as he himself was hiding, from the machine guns. Whose machine guns? His fear was growing customary to him, an alternate state from which he could retreat for a moment and re-enter with wits sharpened. He had changed his shoes for dinner last night. He wished he had kept his Nikes on.

Shooting, wild cries in Farsi, a shout repeated over and over. The clear probability that the fighting was coming closer. He wondered where the construction shack was and whether he could get back there. Still he stayed motionless, his mind reviewing like crossword clues the possible explanations, without caring which fitted. The military could rescue them if they could avoid being shot first. Maybe someone at the Darius had seen the plane, or maybe the Darius was seized, maybe it was a war starting up. He shifted, half stood to give his knees a change. He had been in college during the Korean War, then he had gone to medical school, and by then was too old for Vietnam. He had missed all the wars and battles. He was surprised at how prepared, adroit, clear-minded he felt. On the wall of stone a carved warrior dragged two prisoners along by their hair, their eyes glaring backward at him, their expression after all these centuries still alive with baleful disappointment. Probably their actual bones lay somewhere here, out on the plain amid the shards or deeply buried now after how many centuries, twenty-two centuries, two eons or rather millennia.

Unfolding below Chloe, as if she were meant to film it from her projection booth, a drama of battle, men scurrying over and around the stones and troughs, retreating from the ramparts of the ruin, leaping, crouching, standing up behind a fallen stone to fire at other soldiers below on the plain, whose numbers, in a little trail, like ants, streamed toward the ceremonial staircase. There are more shouts than bursts of gunfire, strange long wails and yelps. The men call to each other harshly, and those who have no guns wave their arms. All are Iranians, looking small and dark in the distance. The man at the museum door has disappeared. From the desert, the immense belches of the airplane engine starting up nearly drown the nearer noises and pale the shots to little pops of harmless sound. On the plain, near the trucks, a few fallen men, as tiny as sticks, lie on the ground. Near her, quite near now, at the circumference of the courtyard of the Tripylon, new men are hiding or creeping along. They are approaching the museum, meaning perhaps to go in and shoot the people inside. Chloe stares, unmoving, at their progress.

She cannot tell the ones from the others; who is shooting whom? All are dressed in khaki pants or jeans, they wear short-sleeved shirts of white or khaki, but it is not the white shirts against the khaki shirts; sometimes these are huddled together, and shout at another man climbing a wall. The men arriving in an ant stream are soldiers but some have taken off their military coats. She sees a man take aim with a gun and fire, and another man falls. Each wears a white shirt. They are so cruel to each other. She is seeing death before her eyes and she can believe it. It is clear.

Her heart beats faster. Can they see her? What would they do to her if they could? Pull her out? Horrible gang rapes, your insides get torn up then they have to kill you to hide you from Amnesty International, make you disappear, make you drink some kind of acid, she'd read about that, but that had been the Philippines, or was it Argentina? Latin America worse than Islam, what was it about Latin America? Was it the Spanish? Was it Catholicism? Was there something in Islam, some mediating tenet of the Koran that kept them from being as cruel as Latin Americans, or were they just differently cruel, the cruelest people always Spanish-speaking, or maybe Portuguese, but why? Speaking English doesn't save you from being cruel either, though, look at Ireland. There you couldn't help thinking worse of them because they spoke English, hence could help being cruel and stupid, were they worse than the Latins whose heritage cruelty was? Islam too a heritage of cruelty, cutting off limbs, plucking out eyes, towers filled with the skulls of the slaughtered. Try to think of a country not brutal and horrible, some islands somewhere maybe, or Egypt, or she'd thought America, until Vietnam, American soldiers raped women there and murdered them, you read about it, how could you admire America after that? Hire a veteran? What a joke, how could you hire a veteran after that? American soldiers speaking English, too.

Suddenly, just below her, from somewhere, a young man in military dress scuttles along the perimeter of the amphitheatre, his eyes rolling to see each way, like lighthouse eyes under the brim of his military hat. If she had a gun she could shoot him from here, only she doesn't, doesn't know how to shoot, doesn't know if he is an enemy or Persepolis guard. He has a rifle, which he drags behind him so that it makes a trail in the dust. He is clutching it by the barrel; even she sees he's going to shoot himself in the side. He could pull it to his shoulder in seconds and shoot her if she moved a muscle to alert him. His eyes rove the stones, looking for the tops of heads, or round mouths of guns. Chloe can see that he is very young, a teenager, eyes boggling at danger all around, afraid, hand stiffly clamping the muzzle of his gun. Suddenly as she watches, his knees buckle and in slow motion he sags to his knees and flops backward, head clattering against a column of stone. Chloe stares, expecting blood to run from his split head. He lies in the dust, still clutching the gun.

She stares, heart pounding at a new level to see death so close up. Terror pumps blood and other chemicals and strange substances into her body like coffee drunk all night. Frightened people have been known to move cars—little puny people.

Is he really dead? She leans forward closer to the aperture of the booth, fixing him with her eyes, trying to reanimate him with her eyes. She cannot remember having heard a bullet. She draws her veil more tightly around her. Perhaps he is breathing. Something about him seems to stir or live, though he lies inert. He is in some way different from the dead man they pulled from the cave.

As the hot sun rises rapidly in the sky, the shadows grow deeper, mistily blue; cool, long columnar shadows stripe the atrium of the ancient palace. Once it had a roof and walls and was cool, but for centuries it had baked under this sun. She watches the Iranian youth. The flies begin to gather on his face, too horrible for words. Then one hand flutters but cannot move to his face. Not dead. She thinks of the man of the cave. If the boy is alive perhaps he can be helped. She will have somehow to help him. But she sits without moving.

She will have to use her judgment. She isn't sure she has been called on before to use her judgment. Certainly not in a matter concerning her death. But whether she now stays here or moves, in which direction moves, how clearly understands the temper of the men out there, will affect whether she dies or survives. Her heart speeds up smoothly, into a stronger mode; her mind is clear. She clearly sees that she knows nothing about the men out there, has been too idle to learn.

Flies. She thinks of films and photos, Africa, flies on the eyes of children there, India too, the camera shaking with disgust, the little starved children too weak to lift thin arms and brush the flies away. India, the flies, they must be worse there, the cow dung, the heat, but she has never been to India, has only seen photos, has only seen photos of dark little Middle Eastern fighters, why not find homes for them, who cares, it's all desert.

The flies still crawling slowly over the face of the boy lying there. She cares. She cannot bear it. She is not free of self-congratulation, to have found the unbearable, but still.

She figures she can creep down there, wrapped in black, and brush away the flies. She hears no shots for the moment, and anyway the shots are not meant for her. Not meant for women. Who would shoot her? They don't even know her. Mankind: why visited with flies? Is he dead? But he stirs, hand too weak to brush away the flies clustered blackly on one spot over the eye, as if drinking his tears, and now crawling on his lips.

Chloe feels faint, the heat, the horror of these flies. It is her duty to prevent them. She has the notion, brief and incomplete, that this is as much as she ever could do, and that she will not have another chance, ever, to be heroic, never to be in an open lifeboat, never lost leading others to safety, never to be called up in any way except now. Doubled over as if in pain, without thinking further of the shooting, she creeps down the ladder.

She could somehow, perhaps, drag him into the ladies' toilet. She tries to repudiate a sense of virtue as she wraps herself closely and approaches him. Is he a soldier of the Shah? A member of the marauding party, a defender of Persepolis, or a despoiler? Anyway, she is going to save him from death from heat and flies. Looking upward and all round in case the guns are pointing, she takes him by the foot and drags him a foot or two into the shade. She has been expecting him to be as heavy as a marble god. Instead he is as light as a starved person. She moves him without difficulty and without consequence. She kicks at the gun and it falls away from his hand and lies in the dust.

Getting him through the ladies' room door is harder, as he begins to waken, and tries to impede his progress by clutching at the bare ground. Once inside he lies back, perhaps unconscious again. She remembers how she had felt once, falling out of a swing. She had had the wind knocked out of her. This was not the same.

Inside, she wets her veil and dabs it at his forehead. The eternal duty of women. He stirs. She thinks of the man of the cave, and of the blood on Hugh. The eyes of this boy flutter open for a moment, then he swoons again. Perhaps he has just fainted in the sun, for there is no mark, no blood, except where he must have struck the column. She has not heard a shot. He struggles to sit up, and leans against the wall, eyes rolling back in a scary, mortal way, mouth open. He looks at her without alarm or understanding. On his sleeve he wears a packet of pink velvet, held on with elastic, a prayer or talisman. She puts her hand to her lapis beads.

Then she realizes someone is knocking at the door. She stops breathing, hand lifted in mid-air. She listens. They knock again. "Chloe," someone whispers. "Chloe, are you in there?"

She doesn't answer. Who is it? Who knows her name? The sound of her name frightens her even more than a nameless summons. Now someone is looking not just for people but for her. Her mind races, realizations jammed together in a half second.

"Chloe, help," says the whisper. Yes, appeal to her womanly helpfulness. Chloe, help. She doesn't move. Is it an American voice? Is it Abbas come back? From a whisper you cannot tell. The soldier is looking at her, wondering if she will answer and betray him. He wears an expression of dread. She shakes her head. Why isn't she answering, screaming, flinging herself gratefully toward the door imagining rescue, imagining the welcoming arms? Not so fast, she is thinking, and then hears footsteps, more confusion outside, and no one whispers after that.

Now outside were harmless-sounding soft spats of gunfire,

absorbed by the immortal stones. What had the sounds been of
Alexander's men, what was the sound of Macedonian fury,
Sassanian fury? We perish each alone, thinks Chloe; she feels
she had seen the point, and that was the point and she wouldn't
forget it. Sassanians, Achaemenians, Americans, what was the
difference?

The soldier looks at her with great surprise, and then he
looks around the ladies' toilet, with evident dismay, causing
Chloe to wonder if she had brought him in here in violation of
some severe Islamic stricture, thereby jeopardizing his soul.
He gets to his hands and knees, shaking his head like a dazed
horse, then stands. Chloe covers her face and turns away.

"Do you speak English?" she says. She watches him over
her shoulder.

She feels his anxious stare, feels him move toward the door,
hears the door open and him steal fearfully out. From outside
she hears another shot or two, and the noise of the airplane
taking off rises above them.

Chapter Thirty-one

FOUND AND LOST

> *For some we loved, the loveliest and the best*
> *That from his Vintage rolling Time hath prest,*
> *Have drunk their Cup a Round or two before,*
> *And one by one crept silently to rest.*

With the shadow and the sound of the plane in the sky, things changed in Persepolis. As after a play, people stepped out into the open spaces, walking normally. Where Dick had imagined there was no one at all, he now saw many people—Iranian women in shawls, workmen, men wearing the vaguely military clothes worn just now by people who had been shooting each other. It was still not clear whether these were newly arrived soldiers of the Shah or rebels, whether they had found a truce or had never been opposed, or whether one faction had been driven off entirely. No one seemed to have cleared off except the Americans in the airplane. People emerged from ditches and looked up into the sky, watching after the plane, letting the sun fall on them. A woman stretched aside her veil and squinted up into the sun. Like cave dwellers after a long siege, they communicated an air of relief and deep breathing. Here and there a man had fallen. Quite near him in the court of the Apadana sat a dead man, his arms flung loosely around a column.

In the ladies' toilet, Chloe was encouraged by the matter-of-fact sound of activities in the courtyard. She opened the door and peered around, less worried about her friends than she had been a moment ago. Things seemed calm. How one clings to the appearance of things and wants to believe, she thought. But surely it is all right now, even if you can't tell why it is all right or what has changed.

Moving outside, she heard her name being shouted in

chorus; it sounded like Dick and Sugar Dunham. Chloe
Chloe Fowler! Ned Henderson! for they were calling for hi
too.

To be safe, she thought, she should return to her vantag
point in the projection booth and look down again. She cre
carefully up the ladder. From here, where she had felt immune
safe, removed, like a battle commander, she could see
panorama of soldiers and vehicles, and their own forlorn ca
still parked where they had trustfully left them yesterda
evening—the hospital station wagon and Abbas's BMW.
the firing, people had fallen. Soldiers were gathering someon
up from quite near their car. In the shade of one of their truck
lay a row of men, and a woman was giving them water. Th
battle was only minutes over and already a woman was o
there giving water. The soldiers laid the person they had jus
moved alongside the others. He was wrapped, was the fac
wrapped? She felt especially uneasy about this figure, lying s
close to their car, in case it was Hugh who might have rashl
run out there, or Abbas or Dick, or even fat Dr. Dunham in
panic, unused to Iran. The distant woman waved the edges
her veil over them, like a black flag of death, though no doub
she meant only to fan them. It was already eleven o'clock. Th
thought sprang unbidden to Chloe that if you didn't eat fc
twenty-four hours you would lose half a pound.

Now she saw Dick and Hugh with Sugar Dunham.

"Where were you, Chloe?" they cried as she came up, an
she explained how she had huddled through the night, ha
hidden, had watched.

"I was locked in a tool shed," Dick said.

Hugh said nothing.

"Where were you?" Chloe asked.

"I hid in a drain," he said.

"When we saw the guys with the guns, everybody scattere
except me," said Dick. "I just stood there like a schmuck.

"I think the others were in the museum," Chloe said. '
think they had them locked in there."

Sugar Dunham gathered Chloe in a motherly embrace
"Honey, you sure you're all right?" she said.

"Where's Junie?" Dick asked.

"She was in the museum with us," Sugar assured him. "She was just the most amazingly brave."

"Junie! Fred Dunham! Ned Henderson!" they called, as they walked through the ruins toward the ceremonial steps, making their way quickly, trying not to look at a dead man or at the clusters of Iranian fighters who stood about, or sat on fallen columns and paid no attention to them. Dick saw the man he had been locked in the shed with, now walking with his stout wife, her head in a devout veil. The man raised his thumb to Dick. Dick wished he would offer him a cigarette.

"Are you all right, Chloe?" Hugh asked.

"Of course," she said.

They descended the staircase. The eyes of the Assyrian immortals under their curled coiffures seemed indifferent to the modern disruption. Clasping their spears they marched along unchanged. At the ticket booth an old man was setting out piles of currency and postcards, while, slumped in the booth, a boy sobbed. There was the important sound of new trucks approaching, and, in the air, the distant sound of planes.

Ahead of them, near Abbas's car, they suddenly saw a small lavender figure, lying or crawling.

"It's Junie!" cried Dick. Yes it was. Chloe remembered the lavender dress.

Hugh and Dick rushed forward. Sugar Dunham clung to Chloe, and they crept forward more timidly. Now they could hear, from somewhere, a terrible wail. It came from the huddle that was Junie. Dick and Hugh were lifting her to her feet. Junie screaming, screaming, a sickening sound to Chloe, for she had an idea what it must mean.

Junie's screams, they could see as they came closer, had been drawn by a bloodstain on the ground. Chloe hadn't realized blood would be so thick, a gelatinous film embedded with fine pebbles and dust, not yet dried in the sun.

"They shot him, they shot him," Junie was saying, her voice breaking with hiccuping sobs. She had dropped to her knees again, kneeling beside the stain while Dick and Hugh clung helplessly to her elbows. When Dick picked her up again, her knees were engraved with gravel. Her hand was sticky red, where she had put it in the puddle of blood.

Chloe looked away—away from the stain and across th
vacant desert, feeling sickness stir in the pit of her stomach

"Just get in the car, honey," Dick was saying. "Come or
Junie, let's sit in the car." Junie's hysterical grief rathe
silenced the rest of them. Chloe was not sure why Junie wa
claiming all the grief. She gave Junie a Kleenex and tol
herself that one bloodstain did not mean, necessarily, anyon
they knew.

Great dramas, your perspective on life, your life altered fc
all time and at the end you have to get into a car and driv
home, Chloe thought as they climbed into Abbas's BMW.

"Well, I don't have the keys," Dick Rothblatt said. "Abba
has the keys."

Hugh got out again and stood by the car, looking around
The Hendersons were waddling toward them, waving a scar.
"You could go with the Hendersons," said Hugh, leaning i
the car, looking at Junie, whose distress seemed the mo.
palpable, outside control, though it had subsided to sobs an
murmurs in the throat. Maybe she had been raped, mayb
terrible things had happened to her in the night. She, Chlo
had merely seen, but she had seen—she enumerated the horror
in her mind—the flies clinging to the eyes of a wounde
person, seen men shot and fall. Seen the thick puddle of blooc

The thick puddle of blood seemed to have nothing to do wit
Abbas, was perhaps not his, perhaps life did not seep out alor
with it. You bled, you cut your finger and bled and still yo
lived. You got your period and lived.

But the bleeding had begun. Emblematic, shaped like
continent, the spreading stain through the pebbles along th
hard earth. The Hendersons, approaching, stepped around i

"A nasty few hours," said Dr. Henderson. "Is your car a
right?"

"We don't have the keys," Hugh said. "Dr. Mowlavi ha
the keys, and we don't know where he is. We'll wait for hi
here for a while."

"Dr. Ames, we brought him, we should take him back. B
where is he?" said Mrs. Henderson.

"We'll keep an eye out for him. He must be somewhere
You go on," Hugh said. Dr. Henderson's face brightened. H

unlocked the doors of the hospital station wagon and motioned the ladies to get in. "There will be a locksmith or someone at the hotel; we'll ask there." But he made no move to start the car.

"Hotwire," said Dick. "I don't know how to do it," turning back to the BMW.

"No," said Hugh, "neither do I. Look, I'll have a look around for Abbas, and meet you at the Darius. You have to go there anyway to collect the bags." Hugh and Dick exchanged glances. It was, it struck Dick, a glance newly communicative, informed by a shared awareness, an unspoken agreement to silence, something they both knew and nobody else knew, whatever. It was a look he had exchanged with Abbas, too, when mention was made of the body in the desert. It struck him that he had not had this sort of relation with Hugh before. They were friendly colleagues, but they had not been in collusion. Now they were in collusion. They had seen Abbas run toward the shooting, toward the men, and they, American men, had not run.

If they had dashed out after Abbas to save the relics of Persepolis, then they would all have been shot, Dick told himself. But they could have helped, could have taken on Richard Dare, could have thought of something. Impulsive Abbas, running out into the path of men with guns. Dick felt uneasy. All those movies you saw as a kid, you knew it was supposed to be you running in a zigzag pattern through the line of fire to save something. Dick could see that Hugh knew— something in his glance showed a shade of rue, that it was supposed to be him.

No need to tell Chloe or Junie about this notion, since there was nothing to tell, strictly speaking, about that moment of hesitation more agonizing in retrospect than at the time. In memory it stretched out, emblematic of all betrayals and treachery. Hugh, Dick felt sure, would also not tell.

Hugh would not tell Chloe, his lips against her breast, murmurs against her throat, telling her other things. Chloe lying under him, he could imagine them—quite involuntarily, no voyeur he, why did the scene present itself to him in this voyeuristic form? The others were still talking excitedly.

"We found ourselves face to face with Dare," Hugh said. "Abbas ran out at that point. He was excited, he saw they were stealing things. We sort of stood there."

"There is blood on the door handle. Somebody's bloody hand," Junie sobbed. Dick thought there was something accusing in her tone. That was unfair.

"Were you trying to find me?" Chloe asked. "Was it you who called me, in the bathroom?" For it had struck her.

"No, we were near the stairs."

"Well, he must be alive, or he would be here lying dead, isn't that right?" said Junie suddenly, straightening up. No one said that people could have carried him away. Chloe did not say she had seen some people carry someone away, for, after all, who knew whom they carried?

"Maybe he's here; why are we assuming the worst?" said Dick.

Why had she told them about the whisper at the door? It might not have been Abbas. It might even have been Richard Dare, trying to trick her to come out. Help, Chloe, the voice had said, and of course she had not helped. Helped do what? It had frightened her to hear her name. But it was all so vague, so strange, there was nothing to tell, really.

They sat fitting the little pieces together. Except she did not tell them it could have been Abbas at the bathroom door. Richard Dare, stealing artifacts, bringing guns! It became a story; they wove it together sitting in the hot car waiting for Abbas to come walking up with the keys. "Look here," said Dr. Henderson from the station wagon, "the rest of you get in. I don't think you should sit here in this heat."

"I agree," said Hugh. "Let's get out of here."

"Abbas . . ." cried Junie.

"If he's okay he'll come out here and here's his car, and he has the keys. I don't see that there's any way of knowing where he is," said Hugh. "I think we'd just better leave."

"Jesus, a BMW," said Dick. "I hope it's okay."

"I know he's dead," said Junie. "We can't just leave."

"My dear, the sooner we talk to the authorities," said Dr. Henderson.

They crowded eight in the station wagon. Chloe and Junie, being smallest, had to sit on the flat shelf in back, where the body of the man had lain. The carpet seemed invisibly stained. Junie, no longer crying, now took off her glasses and wiped them. Dr. Henderson still did not start the car.

"Where were you? Where was the Iranian family?" asked Chloe.

"Where were you?"

"In the museum. They just rounded up everyone and locked us in the museum," said Dr. Dunham.

"We were in love," said Junie, beginning again her hysterical weeping. "I loved him." The others looked at her in shocked amazement. Hers was not ordinary grief; she seemed to be saying she and Abbas were in love.

Chapter Thirty-two

PEBBLES

YESTERDAY This Day's Madness did prepare;
TO-MORROW's Silence, Triumph, or Despair:
Drink! for you know not whence you came, nor why;
Drink, for you know not why you go, nor where.

Maybe he's not dead, thought Chloe. People we know aren't dead, not until they're old, why assume the worst? She felt tired, that was all, and unable to assess the possibilities or the meanings of things. Mrs. Henderson began in the front seat to hum. The wish to tell her to shut up began to give Chloe a headache. Dr. Ames came up, excited, and began to go over it all again: "The men at the entrance with guns, we were all herded into the museum, I tried to get out through the window, we probably won't really know what was going on till we read it in the newspapers. . . ." Hugh, Dick, and Dr. Henderson stood in front of the car muttering; she couldn't hear them. It was hot in the station wagon. They sat a long time and unaccountably she dozed off. When she woke, it could only have been a moment, her head jerking up as though someone had pulled a string, they were in front of the Darius Hotel. Hugh told them to get out and go in to get their bags. His the voice of an exasperated tour director. Maybe he had directed the whole thing? Why was he now hurrying them away? All at once she felt ready to die of thirst.

Military vehicles were parked in the parking lot next to a French tour bus with people piling out of it. In the lobby a confusion of soldiers and tourists stood in subdued groups while a voluble man negotiated something at the desk. Hugh, consulting with another clerk, reported that they, Chloe and the others, were expected to check out as if nothing had happened,

280

as if they had slept in their beds, made love on fresh sheets, paid for drinks beside the orange-scented pool. Chloe had an Ancient Mariner's impulse to tell the new people what had just happened to them but they were all speaking French.

"But it was Persepolis we came to see," the tour guide was screaming.

When they had finished at the desk, Chloe bought a Pepsi in the gift shop, and Hugh bought two bottles of water. He carried them back to the car, but he didn't get in with the others as they climbed in.

"Somebody—I'd better stay, find out what's happened. You go on. I'll do something about Abbas's car," he said. He did not say, I will find the body of Abbas, but that was what Dick knew he meant. For an instant he was inclined to volunteer to stay and help but he was unable to overcome his reluctance. His stomach crawled to think it could be true that Abbas lay dead out there someplace. Abbas had gone for help, was all; he would turn up. Anyway Junie needed him, poor girl, she looked near collapse, an odd bruised blueness under the surface of her pale skin, as if she had been beaten, or fallen against something. Eyes red-rimmed like a mouse's. It struck him that today her eyelashes were white. Ordinarily they were black. Despite her disdain for makeup, she must put mascara on them; she must even sleep in it. That touched him.

"You had nine shirts done at the Tehran Hilton and you said you weren't there," cried Chloe all at once to Hugh. He looked surprised at this sudden accusation.

"Well, that's true," he said, after a pause. "I was there. I wasn't supposed to tell anyone."

"You just thought no one would notice the shirts, not notice that you didn't turn up for ten days!"

"Well, I didn't think I had to account to all of Shiraz for my whereabouts," Hugh snapped, an unaccustomed note of asperity in his voice. He stepped away from the car window.

"Me in Shiraz by myself, the Iranians totally paranoid about where you were," Chloe was going on, unable to stop herself. Dick thought it was an inopportune time for this. Should he slap her? Why did he have this impulse lately to slap women?

"Maybe I should stay here with you," he said to Hugh but

Hugh's expression seemed to indicate that he would do better going back to manage these hysterical women.

Chloe's head under the low station-wagon roof grows hot with the heat of the metal; the ruts in the road jar. She tries to fix her mind on the tragedies she has witnessed, especially on the gory corpse she saw from far away. But she can only see it in the way she sees the future of her life, from far away through the wrong end of a telescope, the figures tiny and bright, like the brightness of the blood across a light-blue shirt—short-sleeved, ironed— who ironed for him?

Her mind does not grip tragedy firmly from both sides as if it had ears or handles, tragedy too insubstantial and it turns the minute she thinks about it into a thought about some inferior thing, some material circumstance, the hot trickle of sweat between her shoulder blades, her dress sticking to her back. Dead, she says to herself, and grows as still as she can within herself to try to hear the reverberations, the terrible resonance of this horrendous word, to try to experience its effect on her, on anyone, inside her, but it slips down inside as neatly as a small pill, doesn't choke, slips down without impediment, not a hot burning pill or anything. Just "dead." Dead, dead, dead, just echoing like mere words in any empty tunnel, echo chamber, like inside a barrel at the funhouse. How strange to think of that, of stepping into the spinning barrel of the funhouse, remembering herself as a child, not dreaming of death or of anything. But had that been the moment, long ago and forgotten, when, stepping into the spinning barrel, she had first had an intimation of death? And was death a spinning and a stumbling? *Abbas* is dead she says, and still gets not enough effect, not the effect she knows there should be; maybe it's she who is dead.

In the landscape, in the very air, a sense of menace and animation. Trucks full of soldiers roll along the highway. Soldiers stand at the crossroads, milling around. Up from the horizon two military jets bolt straight into the sky, making twin tracks behind themselves, like rails; the shriek of the engines seems upon them.

"Those must be from Shiraz," somebody says.

"Something else is going on," Dick says. "Something general. It must be."

"War, or civil war," Chloe says. "Or revolution."

Viewed from that perspective, things seem too calm. There are only two trucks of soldiers, two airplanes in the sky.

As they watch, the airplanes, before their astonished eyes, drop like stones out of the sky and disappear. They must have crashed, but miles away, so that there is no sound and no flames show. Then, as the party heads toward Shiraz, two plumes of smoke rise in the northern sky.

Planes falling on villages. Dick's stomach crawls to think of the molten metal, the bodies. He is thinking of General Ben and his ideas of saboteurs—someone, perhaps, from the hospital. Or it is just Iranian maintenance. How could you know? He thinks of the poor men in the planes, or would they have ejected? Was there something that he, Dick Rothblatt, could have or should have done?

News of the fighting at Persepolis had not reached the Azami Compound, and, thinking them all safe at the Darius, no one was concerned for them—but all in the compound were, in fact, in a flurry of departure and change. Yesterday there had been a significant riot near the university, with hundreds of students arrested, and another in Tehran, where thousands in the streets had been fired on by soldiers, and more than four hundred people were dead. These events were described by people dashing down the hospital corridors or across the grounds. Dr. Ali Yazdi was pacing in the garden of Villa One, waiting for the tourist party to come home. He believed that the Americans should all leave without further delay. Probably, he explained, at this moment there would be no difficulty getting planes to Tehran and thence out of the country. Even if their tickets were for some other day, he was sure the airlines would make every effort to get them on planes. It seemed to Dick and Chloe that he feared to be compromised by their presence as much as he feared for their safety.

"No danger—not, I think, to you—but it will be better until the political situation calms if all foreigners leave—all the foreigners are leaving from town—the American consul I think is advising it to all."

They stood in the garden. No one had mentioned Abbas, but Dr. Yazdi, or someone, would have to be told. Told what? Chloe looked up at her windows in Villa Two and thought it was strange that they were open, the turquoise sash so pretty and inviting in the sunshine. Dick began the account of the marauders. Chloe did not think she could bear to hear it, and so wandered toward her own apartment.

"Hugh stayed behind to try to find him," Dick was saying. Or his body, he was thinking.

"This is an extraordinary story," cried Dr. Yazdi. "The treasures of Persepolis, you tell me! And Abbas swept away! We will telephone the Darius. But he'll turn up, of course. Abbas is a 'survivor,' as you say."

"Do you have someone who could help us with the plane reservations?" Dick asked. "Who all am I talking about?"

"You and Dr. Monroe, Mrs. Fowler of course, the Dunhams, Dr. Ames, let me see—the Hendersons. The others I have already been on to, the Schwartzes, the Freys. Oh, and not forgetting Dr. Fay, you want to make her reservations too. She was not with you in Persepolis?"

"She's gone to her apartment," Dick said. "She is very upset by the whole thing."

"Who would imagine, her seeming so strong. And little fragile, flowerlike Mrs. Fowler, though she did look pale, came through brilliantly. What an experience!"

"Maybe I'll gather up the plane tickets, then I'll know what I'm talking about," said Dick. "I'll get everybody's tickets and come to your office."

"Hurry, my dear fellow, and then we'll go down to the ticket office in person, for I doubt that we'll get through by phone."

*   *   *

Chloe was thinking she'd better go to the American consulate and ask about her passport. Failing that, maybe they'd let her on the plane anyway. They wouldn't want American women stranded in Iran; they'd just say go ahead. Then, once away, she could chance the consequences of arriving in the United States. Passport lost, had already applied, danger in staying. It sounded all right. The worst that could happen was Ellis Island for a few days. She climbed the stairs to her apartment, and was surprised to find Linda Farmani coming out of it. Evidently she possessed a second key. Her heavy hair was down like a charwoman's; her mouth was colorless in her pale face.

"I'm moving in here. After you leave, of course—I've been bringing in my things," she said. Her face wore the same jittery expression it had worn when Vahid was taken away, and she bit fitfully at the corner of her lips. If this were America, you'd think she was on speed, Chloe thought.

"But you're leaving Villa One? Have the Yazdis put you out?" Chloe asked, not at all surprised that the Yazdis would do such a thing.

"The Yazdis? No, no, but I can't stay there. Villa One is for the head of the hospital." Chloe saw that Linda had piled her things on the bureau.

"Americans are being advised to leave at once, doesn't that apply to you?" she asked Linda.

"I suppose," Linda said, absently moving toward the door. Chloe walked downstairs with her, to go to the consulate.

In the street things were much the same as before. People idled along, cars screeched, animals brayed. Was it her imagination that people drew back from her as she came toward them, or turned to look at her? She adjusted her veil more carefully to cover her hair.

The consulate was shut. A penciled note on the door announced it would be open after lunch, but it was now after two. She dawdled outside for a while, but was too excited to sit there and felt too strange to bear sitting still. She'd come back, she could telephone. She wished she had bought a rug. *Abbas* is dead, she kept telling herself; without effect.

Gathered in her shawl, she crouched on the steps of the

consulate and waited. People passed by. As she watched more closely she saw that their steps were quicker than before, and their eyes were looking far ahead. An intangible aura of change was palpable in the dusty, scented air, as on the day it becomes autumn, and people are heard to say that the weather has changed. One day it is suddenly autumn. Their quickened steps had the animation of squirrels preparing for winter. Or was she imagining this? A rich Iranian woman in a kelly-green gabardine suit stepped smartly by in her high-heeled snakeskin shoes. Two little boys racing by on small bicycles suddenly wheeled and tossed a small stone into Chloe's lap.

She heard them giggling wildly as they pedaled away, around the corner out of sight. Did they know she was American? She nestled her face in the folds of black cloth. She was thinking, all at once, of caves collapsing, as by a shudder of the earth, or bombardment, little stones like this pouring down into laps, onto heads, and finally the earth itself shuddering down and filling up the cave rooms, burying the idols and pillars, and blocking all the tunnels and escapes.

Chapter Thirty-three

THE LOVED ONES

> *Alike for those who for* TO-DAY *prepare,*
> *And those that after some* TO-MORROW *stare,*
> *A Muezzin from the Tower of Darkness cries,*
> *"Fools, your Reward is neither Here nor There."*

In his apartment, Dick packed, not at first noticing the letter from Marla, rather a fat envelope, which distressed him when he saw it; he knew it meant papers to sign, probably house papers. He flung his socks into his bag and snatched up the letter.

It's a wonderful young couple with a darling baby.
I'm just happy it's someone I can feel glad is in our
house and loves it the way we did. They're just starting out, so they had some difficulty with a bank loan,
so they're going to pay me directly, as I don't need
the whole cash sum right now. They'll pay $350 a
month and more later when they can. He's a talented
artist, and she is a potter.

Dick read the papers over again, heart pounding. Sold. And there was nothing about interest or the term of the mortgage. He couldn't believe that anyone would let her sell without taking interest, but it didn't say. He couldn't believe that his house—huge, magnificent—could be sold to some flaky young artist with no money and no collateral; there must be more to it, and she was being vague this way to torture him. She was as clear to his mind as if she had been present, small lines at the upper lip, hair lighter than when she was younger, anxious eyes full of a kind of abashed reverence for art, which she was always too tense to try, didn't take painting classes like other

287

women. Also didn't bake for the bake sales at the children's schools when they were little; something about the idea of it seemed to frighten her.

One thing about Junie, she was not afraid to try things. It was strange that he couldn't remember him and Marla being happy; he couldn't remember them being passionate. All their love-making—years and years—had coalesced into the routine and automatic practice that continued, practically to the day of their divorce. But they must have once been happy and passionate. You get this amnesia, he thought, to insulate yourself from the poignancy of the end, the disappointment, the metaphysical lesson. A picture came to his mind of Junie, grabbing for Abbas's cock and saying, "My roommate's away." How and when could she and Abbas have fallen in love—that serious, that solemnized emotion requiring endless dreamy talk?

Then he thought for some reason of Chloe Fowler: what he admired in her was her independence of mind, and yet this quality, shared by both Marla and Junie too, had not caused Chloe to turn away from normal female pastimes, like Junie, or to become, like Marla, belatedly assertive. It was Chloe's independence of mind that seemed to enable her to support the nominal confines of a traditional role. She didn't appear confined. Once she had told him that when she thought of working in an office, or as a doctor like Junie, visions of misery and desiccation swam before her eyes, like the roots of an uprooted plant. Dick loved the idea of Chloe cheerfully planted and blooming. She would be a pot of marigolds, or something slightly more tender, a trail of lobelia. Marla would be something like a zinnia.

Abruptly, he gathered up his ticket and passport and walked over to Junie's apartment to collect hers. He found her sitting, tear-stained, on the lumpy sofa in her apartment, staring at her hands. "Hi," she said, with a pitiful quaver. Her two front teeth, he noticed, were really rather large, like a chipmunk's.

"Dick, tell me, no shit, are you mad at me?" Mad that she loved Abbas?

"No, honestly not, Junie. No shit," he said, smiling as reassuringly as he could. He wondered if they had actually made love and if so whether she had been more responsive with Abbas. But did not ask. He remembered Dave Weigandt, the surgical resident she'd been living with before him, and imagined her saying, "You're not mad, Dave, no shit?"

"You could stay here, Junie. Linda Farmani is staying, others are. Abbas is going to show up. You should wait for him." Just to show he was forgiving.

She sighed. There was about her the faint odor of fever, that sweet, tired smell.

"I hate Iran. I can't wait to get out of here," she said.

"Get me your ticket and passport. I'm getting us on the first plane possible out of Shiraz, then in Tehran we'll take it from there."

She sighed and stood up, and aimlessly rifled her top bureau drawer. "He's dead, I know. I touched his blood."

The stone had not hurt Chloe. She got to her feet and began to walk back to the compound. Just inside the gate she heard the familiar barking. In the confusion of their return, she had forgotten about Rustum. Here he was looking apprehensively at her, as if he believed himself responsible for her dereliction these two days. What had he done? His tail beat frantically. It curved around in an unpleasant arc so that the tip really touched his back. It should have been bobbed—he looked like the sort of dog whose tail would normally be bobbed at home. He watched her intently. He must be hungry. She saw from his eyes that he was now a perfectly socialized young dog, had learned all the dog lessons of adoration and dependence, and had none of the acumen of the wild.

"I can't leave Rustum," she said to Dick as he came up.

"Oh, don't be silly," said Dick vehemently.

She was going to be silly. She felt suddenly certain of that. She knew all the things there were to be said against transporting an ugly mongrel dog to America in a time of crisis, but she didn't care.

"I've ruined him. He doesn't know how to live in the wild." Jeffrey hates dogs, was her thought, and then her thought: but of course it doesn't matter!

"He'll learn quick enough," Dick said.

"The other dogs wouldn't accept him. Probably they'd kill him." Though in fact she knew nothing of dog society.

"They don't let dogs into the U.S. You can't just bring them in from anywhere."

"I'll get a certificate. They can put him in quarantine. You get a vet, a certificate." Without Jeffrey, she could have a dog. The children should have a dog.

"I'm not going to help you with this, Chloe," said Dick curtly. Like other men, he must despise women, Chloe supposed, despise their odd obsessions, their inconvenient whims, lack of business sense, and lack of propriety. All the same, she wasn't going to leave this poor Rustum, and she had a lovely sense of rising on a tide of irrational determination, afloat. Not going to leave Rustum.

"Just get me your airplane ticket and passport. I'm going now to see about the reservations," said Dick. He could not forbear adding, "I was surprised about you and Hugh. I hadn't realized."

"What about it?" said Chloe, with an edge to her voice, a warning tone. They climbed her stairs. Could it be, she was thinking, or was it imaginary, that the thick stench of cat piss she smelled now had been here all the time? Could it be she had got used to it?

"Well," he said, "it's none of my business. I only said I was surprised. I mean, felt made a fool of, a little, all that walking you home et cetera, guarding your virtue."

"And now you don't think of me as virtuous?" Chloe said, meaning to take a light tone, to turn this conversation aside. She had never doubted that she was virtuous—not bad, at least. Her parents had never made her feel herself to be bad.

"Virtue is a funny thing to call it," Dick said, with a laugh that Chloe found suddenly infuriating; she felt an ire worthy of Junie rising in her cheeks and earlobes.

"Oh, Dick, I cannot believe you believe that chastity and virtue are the same thing," she snapped. "Anyway, your life is one of candor and aboveboard, right?"

"My relationship with Junie was perfectly obvious."

"At least Hugh is approximately my own age," Chloe continued. "Anyway, you were trying to conceal your relationship with Junie. Deceit, subterfuge. All that business of coffee with me in the mornings, then she'd happen to stroll by."

"Keeping up appearances is not the same thing as deceit," Dick said.

"Isn't it?"

"Not at all. You keep up appearances to spare the feelings of others. We're in a modest Islamic country. Junie's conduct would be disapproved of. To say nothing of yours, I might add."

"My conduct!" screamed Chloe. "Oh! How can we even speak of this, with Abbas dead, and . . .''

Tears came to her eyes, the first tears she had shed. It was as if her tears had dried up in the hot desert air. "How can we bicker about sexual propriety when our friend is dead?" she said.

"Did Jeff find out about Hugh? Is that the problem?" Dick asked.

"Jeffrey does not know about Hugh, there's no connection. And I have not discussed my relationship with Jeffrey with Hugh," said Chloe.

"I think Abbas will turn up," Dick said. "There are a thousand explanations."

In Chloe's apartment she found her airplane ticket. Dick stood by, his heart crowded with random urgent subjects, things he wanted to talk to Chloe about. It was as if the plane were on its way, winging toward them, about to sunder them. "Junie and Abbas really were in love," he said. "I had no idea. It took me completely by surprise."

Chloe felt, unmistakably, the twist of the knife. Why was Dick being so unkind? Did Abbas love Junie?

"I never knew it," Dick went on. She forced a sympathetic smile. He did not seem to mean to wound.

"Well," she said, "do you mind very much?"

"Not really, I guess," Dick said. "But nobody likes to be taken by surprise. She could have told me, we're friends, after all. Or Abbas could have told me. I feel like a fool, hanging around to claim my—my rights—from time to time. I thought I was being supportive. Instead I was acting like a pig. They were in love and she was planning to stay with him in Iran, together to reform Iranian medicine. Sweet, no?"

"Oh," cried Chloe, tears flooding down her face. To think of it, hopes and life destroyed. "Poor Abbas, all that tragedy in his life and just when happiness had begun again." How like life that was, she thought. "The bloom is gone and with the bloom go I," said the Koran.

"Poor Junie too. She's completely collapsed. I had to give her Valium."

"It's just terrible," cried Chloe, the thought popping into her reluctant mind that it was deceitful of Abbas to sleep with her when he was in love with Junie. Of course she was prettier than Junie? But not nearly so young. How she detested herself for these frivolous thoughts. Why was she cursed with a nature that could not grasp the tragic and went on with egotism and vanity in spite of her conscious wishes?

"Well," Dick said, getting up and crossing to his rug, which he began to roll up. "Well, shit." She could not tell, really, what he was feeling. He made it into a tidy roll, and tied it with string.

"Abbas was so nice," Chloe said, hearing her ordinary voice, feeling the inadequacy of her emotions and power to explain them. "Junie can—can take comfort that he died for Iran, in a way." How could she be saying such fatuous things?

"Oh, shit," said Dick. "She's not his widow."

They were interrupted by a thumping and shuffling on the stairs outside Chloe's room. Dick went to the door and looked out, then stepped outside.

"Oh, here, let me help," Chloe heard him say. He reappeared carrying a large playpen. Linda Farmani came in with a shopping bag and baby Henry.

"I don't mean to be pushing you out," she said.

"You'd better fly out with us," Chloe said. "We don't have tickets—I don't even have a passport. The idea is that if we go to Tehran somebody will get us out."

How can two people be in love who are never even together? she was thinking. Had they ever made love? Well, undoubtedly, who knew when or where, it doesn't require special equipment or a lot of time. She could understand how Junie might not tell Dick, she wouldn't want to wound him, him going through the thing with Marla, female treachery on every hand, he'd even seemed upset to realize about her and Hugh.

"Don't be silly, I'm going to stay," Linda said. "Vahid will be released. Now with the changes, they'll release him. And anyway, where would I go? Back to L.A.? Back to Detroit?"

"I think she was basically attracted to the idea of service to Iran," said Dick, coming in with boxes. "Of course, Abbas is an attractive guy, too."

"Have you ever been to Detroit?" Linda's voice carried an unfamiliar note of hysteria.

"No, no," said Chloe.

"It's the murder capital of America, after Atlanta. Or rape. The black girls especially, they'd be missing from gym one day, or come back with a bandage on their heads, oh she got raped, people'd say. It was usually their fathers. There are good neighborhoods around Detroit, though. Grosse Pointe. Beautiful houses with weeping willows. When I was little it was the weeping willows I envied, I wanted a large lawn and weeping willows, I don't even know what the houses were like inside. Vulgar, I guess. Auto executives. But now it's the murder capital too. We don't have that here. I almost got raped once in Los Angeles; I never told Vahid about it."

"Everyone almost gets raped," said Chloe.

"Did I hear you say you don't have a passport?" Dick said. "Is that possible?"

"That kind of thing doesn't happen in Iran. They respect women. And there aren't any blacks. I know it sounds prejudiced, but I like it better without them."

"It's not only possible," said Chloe. "I don't have one."

"You'd be prejudiced too if you grew up in Detroit."

"What happened to your passport?" Dick shouted.

Chloe sighed and could not reply.

"I'm just plain afraid of them," said Linda. "Plenty of things that happened."

"Let me take my stuff out of the bureau, so you can get settled," Chloe said, thinking what a bigot Linda was.

"I like the turquoise color," said Linda, touching the painted window sill. "I wasn't sure when I first saw it. Or I could go back to L.A.? Maybe I could set up a business decorating for Iranians, there's enough of them there. I could do real estate, that's what I did before. I've thought about L.A., but of course I can't do anything until Vahid comes home. I had a condo in

L.A., before Vahid and I got married. I sold it, like a fool. They say you can't touch anything in L.A. now.''

"God knows why," said Chloe.

"Well, it's got the climate. And things are happening there, that's where it's at," Linda said. She gazed tragically out the window toward Villa One, and rearranged the interval between two of the pots of geranium.

At the thought of Los Angeles palm trees and restaurants that look like drive-ins with Rollses parked in front, Chloe felt her misery, diffuse except where it involved Abbas, focus on at least one of its components, her reluctance to return to certain things, especially automobiles and streets with no one walking on them. America in general. Of course no one *had* to live in L.A.—people could move. At least she could live in San Francisco. People more or less got what they wanted. But why was there an L.A.?

"But I don't know anyone in L.A. now," Linda said.

"I didn't turn your husband in," cried Chloe. "Really, how could I? I don't know why people thought so. I'm only me. And I think it's rotten of them to put you out of Villa One, that's your home, after all, Dr. Yazdi is a terrible person, he . . ."

"The Yazdis? No. It's Bahram and Noosheen. Bahram is the new head. He's well known to be a moderate—I suppose they think he will placate the dissidents. There are new ministers, changes, every day. He's trying to get some moderates in there, but of course it's too late now."

"Noosheen!" cried Chloe. "Is it possible? She's here?"

"Yes, she came home yesterday. She was at her brother's in Tehran."

"Well, *she* has my passport," said Chloe, too relieved to wonder why Noosheen had not used it. "I better go find her. Does she know we're back?"

"I don't know," said Linda.

"Does she know about Abbas?"

"I don't know."

Chapter Thirty-four

UNHAPPY COUCH

What! out of senseless Nothing to provoke
As conscious Something to resent the yoke
Of unpermitted Pleasure, under pain
Of Everlasting Penalties, if broke!

Chloe rushing to Villa One found Noosheen supervising the unpacking of her boxes. She was wearing chador, which, when she flung her arms out to embrace Chloe, swept over Chloe like a Dracula cape, and she wore some sort of familiar scent, American—Charlie, maybe. Her face was bright with a new animation.

"Oh, Chloe, thank heaven you are safe. News has come about the horror at Persepolis. Terror is everywhere. In Tehran, even here. But you are safe!"

Chloe's relief at seeing Noosheen safe soured a little into anger, but her heart was thankful. She took it as a personal sign of forgiveness that she was not to be tortured with something terrible happening to Noosheen for which she would be at fault; this time she was not to be punished for her meddling in the lives of innocent, vulnerable, desperate people. But she felt cross, angry at Noosheen for having caused her this fear.

"Thank heaven I am able to see you," said Noosheen. "It makes me heartbroken to think that you are leaving, my dear friend and mentor."

"But I thought you were in India," cried Chloe. "How come you're here?"

"There are still no chairs, let us sit out here in the garden," Noosheen said. They sat in the bushes, among the geranium pots. "Well, as you see—I am not. It didn't work out. How grateful I will be forever for your help, as a true friend. That I will never forget."

"Did you try? Didn't you try?"

"Oh, yes, I tried," she said. "I dressed in Western clothes and went to the airport. Sunglasses, careful makeup, everything. But then there was a problem in your passport. You had no resident visa."

"Of course I did," Chloe said. "Stamped in. I got it in San Francisco."

"No, it was not there. And so without it I could not leave. I was not properly in so I could not get out. They said I would have to go to the American Embassy and get them to help me get a resident visa, I don't know what, but I knew I could not go on fooling them. It is one thing to slip out at the airport, another to sit in the embassies. No one would believe me for long."

"That's impossible. All my stuff was in order," Chloe said.

"If I was a man they'd put me in jail, that's what they told me," said Noosheen. "Ah, well! 'No mischance chanceth but by God's permission.' "

"May I see?"

Noosheen handed her the passport, and Chloe leafed through it. It was perfectly true, there was no visa. On second glance she could see that a page had been cut out; the pages jumped from 4 to 7. Had Noosheen done this herself? Or who? Her passport had been lying right in her bureau drawer, unused except when she took it to the bank to cash traveler's checks. But of course someone had come in and rifled her bureau drawers. Hossein could have done it any time. Now how was she going to get out? She threw it down, no worse off than before, no better off, but then she picked it up again and put it in her purse.

"What did you do then?" she asked.

"My brother and sister-in-law had brought me to the airport. They took me home again. I was not quite truthful to them: I told them Bahram had done many bad things to me."

"So they were helping you?"

"Yes, but now I think it was all for the best, because in Tehran things are changing very fast, and it helped me to understand some things I had not understood before."

"Like what?" asked Chloe.

" 'Empedocles on Etna.' I could understand it completely. It applies to our modern world, it applies to Iran; that is the test of great poetry, that there is always meaning, at any era, don't you agree? Where Empedocles says we are becoming slaves, 'And we shall feel our powers of effort flag, And rally them for one last fight—and fail; And we shall sink in the impossible strife, And be astray for ever.' The Koran says this too. That is Iran. The way we are going we might as well jump into the crater.''

"What will happen?''

" 'We shall fly for refuge to past times, Their soul of unworn youth, their breath of greatness.' Arnold. We are on the eve of a great spiritual renaissance here, I believe it. I could see the signs—in Tehran they are everywhere. There is a leader at hand. The common people believe he is the Twelfth Imam. I don't believe that, of course, but what if it were true?''

Now Chloe was feeling, she realized, besides relief to see Noosheen, that it was rather mercurial and unreliable of Noosheen to have come back so contentedly and quickly. She, Chloe, might have been condemned forever to a troubled conscience and a life of concern for someone who like the wind changed directions or lost interest, like a child. She should have seen that Noosheen was a restless child.

"What will you do?'' Chloe asked.

"Well, there isn't much I can do, of course. What can a woman do? But there are things at the hospital, and the children, and there is something—I am translating poetry. There are certain poems of Matthew Arnold that I think will be an inspiration to others in the cause, only I am not putting his name on. Oh, I am not putting my name, no fear, it's just that I am afraid a Western poet would not be well received, so I am putting 'Ancient Persian Manuscript.' I am sorry you cannot judge the translation. I would like your opinion.''

"What is the text?'' asked Chloe.

"Well, it is from 'Rugby Chapel.' I will copy it out, with my translation, so that when your Farsi gets better . . .''

"Oh, I'll never learn it now,'' said Chloe. Now she would

never learn Farsi. She was, she knew, herself the restless child.

"The Twelfth Imam is

> 'Not like the men of the crowd
> Who all round me to-day
> Bluster or cringe, and make life
> Hideous, and arid, and vile;
> But souls temper'd with fire,
> Fervent, heroic, and good,
> Helpers and friends of mankind,' "

quoted Noosheen.

"You heard the bad news about Abbas?" Chloe asked, scarcely daring to ask for fear she had not, for fear she would have to tell Noosheen herself.

"Yes, oh, yes. I am so full of sorrow. My brother Abbas."

"If he is dead, it was some kind of guerrillas who killed him. It was the people who believe in the Twelfth Imam. Not exactly helpers and friends of mankind."

"It was Americans, that's what I heard," said Noosheen. "My poor Abbas, he was a martyr. His memory will live always, a martyr who died to save the treasures of our heritage. But one other terrible thing I have to tell you. They found the body of that old man, Hossein."

"Really? What happened?"

"It is so horrible. It is a thing that has happened before. He was attacked by a pack of dogs in the street, late at night. He had been stealing things from the laboratories at the hospital! Think of it. To sell, I imagine, poor man. They found him this very morning, half eaten up. And the wild dogs also attacked a guest from Texas who was staying at the Cyrus. They fell upon him, but he was able to fight them off. He is in the hospital."

Chloe heard herself utter a horrible giggle; despite tears flooding to her eyes again.

In the evening she ate with Junie and Dick in the hospital cafeteria, the usual chelo kebab and canned peas. Hugh came in. His face was sunburned and strained. They had no need to ask him what he had found.

''There were a number of men killed. Boys. They had taken the bodies to the village. For their mothers to come and get them, I don't know. I brought him back. I've seen Ali Yazdi.''

They guarded their faces from signs of weeping. Junie's face seemed less her own than the face of a tragic woman in a poster against war or starvation. In her grief, Junie was all women, but Chloe felt, uneasily, that her own face was unchanged. There was some lack of connection between her face (given to smiles, even radiance) and her heart. Hugh and Dick passed the cruet of salad dressing, estimated the chances of getting a plane out of Shiraz in the morning; their faces were tired but manly and unchanged, hearts inscrutable. Around them, nurses in their little veiled caps and thin men, off duty, in argyle pullovers, a normal mutter of Iranian speech, no edge of panic or sadness. They hadn't heard.

Alone in her room, Chloe packed her other bag. The first, packed before dinner, stood at the door. Matched bags of French nylon from La Bagagerie. She was sorry to leave her books, especially *Sassanian Pottery,* the standard work by Professor H. Raban. She hesitated over it. A heavy, rare work printed in 1937. If there was going to be more trouble in Iran, there would be students involved, and they might burn the library, or the Shah might shut the university down. She put the book in her suitcase, thinking that this might preserve it for civilization, and of course she would return it later, at the right time, for she had complete reverence for the sanctity of the library book.

Dead. How awful that she couldn't keep from thinking of her own situation when someone was dead and she ought to keep thinking of that. But how? It was not enough to recite, ''How sad.'' She couldn't find sufficient thoughts to capture in words the hard, pincerlike feeling, deep down inside her windpipe. Someone dead whom she had loved—had she? Whom did she love? Everyone? Anyone? How to keep from thinking of herself, the real object of such questions. It was of love, large, universal, she ought to think, and of large, universal death.

She hears a tap below her window, and, thinking it would be Hugh, calls down that the door is open. She hears footsteps, is surprised when Dick, not Hugh, comes in.

''I couldn't sleep,'' he says. ''Anyway, tomorrow will be—

I wanted to say goodbye, in case tomorrow, in the confusion . . .''

Chloe sighs. ''It's hard to know what to say. It's a sad way to leave. Is Junie very sad?''

''Very,'' Dick says. ''Of course.'' He pauses, stifling the little tone of querulousness he can hear piercing the solemn tone he is attempting. ''How could they have been in love? They—Junie was always with me. When were they ever together?''

Chloe feels, deplores in herself, an unreasonable interest in the same question. What does it matter? Yet if one is to understand anything, you have to try to understand it all. Dick reconsiders. There were endless hours, whole nights, Junie had not been with him.

''Do you care about that part?'' Chloe asks.

''As I said, I feel like an idiot. That said, I guess not. I feel so bad about what happened, that doesn't leave much room. Anyway, Junie and I aren't in love exactly.''

''I understand,'' Chloe says. She smiles her smile. ''Would you like some tea? Or there's some beer. We should drink it up.''

''Beer, thanks,'' he says. She crosses the hall to the kitchen. The Dunhams can be heard striding around, talking, in their quarters. Their three suitcases stand in the hall, as if they expected porters and limousines.

''Chloe,'' says Dick when she comes back. ''I hope it works out with you and Jeff.'' He won't, he thinks, mention Hugh. Covertly he examines the room for signs of Hugh, but there aren't any.

''Well, it won't,'' says Chloe firmly, though she doesn't plan to admit that Jeff has found Another. A certain righteousness in her expression suggests that Dick is being callous to talk of trivialities like marital discord and the future. Yet when but in the atmosphere of death is one more inclined to think of the future? He wishes they would fall into each other's arms in a comforting way.

''I'll come see you,'' he says. ''I come to San Francisco a lot. I have two former fellows who work at Moffitt Hospital; they often invite me.''

''Yes, be sure to,'' Chloe says. ''It's sort of like the end of camp, isn't it? Everyone says they'll keep in touch.'' But there had been death. They sought for a more dignified comparison than camp. He takes off his glasses and puts them in his shirt pocket. Chloe bustles fitfully around the room. When men take off their glasses they mean to kiss you. Yet she doesn't move forward. When Dick has gone, she notices the Koran lying on the table, a repository of gnomic revelation and gnostic wisdom, like the I Ching. She'd asked the I Ching things before. She opens the Koran and sticks her finger on a verse:

> But for the offenders we have got ready the fire whose
>   smoke shall enwrap them.
> And if they implore help, helped shall they be with
>   water like molten brass
> Which shall scald their faces. Wretched the drink! and
>   an unhappy couch!

Chapter Thirty-five

NINE SHIRTS

Chloe stayed awake as long as she could, waiting for Hugh, who did not come. In the night she dreamt of a rug. Waking later she could not remember whether the rug in her dreams was a real rug she had seen somewhere or an ideal rug, concocted of the imagination, born of a rich dinner, or of a belief in beauty. Paisleyed shapes in deep, bitter colors glowed on a forest field. The shapes were confused in the dream with the tastes of fruit whose peelings had been boiled to obtain the colors; and with the cries of snails or sea creatures similarly sacrificed, and the sacrificed fingers of little children tying the knots. As you walked on it, this cacophony of life cried up. It was the rug of life.

When she woke, the bareness of her room without Dick's rug struck her with sadness. The room had recovered its cell-like ugliness, yet she was attached to it now. She was glad to think it would remain in Linda Farmani's hands and that Linda liked the arrangement of flower pots. It is a charming room, really, she thought.

It remained to find a kennel or box for Rustum. Ordinarily she would have asked Hossein. Only with this thought did she remember what she had heard about the poor old man's fate. She tried to imagine it. She tried to imagine the last thoughts of the sad old creature, but she couldn't. She wondered if he had had a family, and whether anyone would miss him. She had planned to put out all her rials, to leave them lying on the table for him to find.

She set out looking for boxes, first at the back of the hospital, then at the vegetable market, where she found a serviceable wooden crate full of the leaves broken off cauliflowers, and managed to indicate that she would like to buy it. Had Rustum been with the dogs who killed Hossein, she wondered? If he had tasted human blood, would he now crave it, as leopards and tigers were said to do? Would he be a safe pet with children? She pulled the crate after her along the road.

The plane was to leave at noon. Ali Yazdi arrived in the road inside the gates with the hospital station wagon and two taxis. The foreigners began to assemble. Little outposts of baggage were established on porches. People stood in the road. Chloe came out on her doorstep with nails to fasten up the crate, once she got Rustum inside it. On the top she had painted her name and address with turquoise paint.

He came when she called him, his gait happy, and trustfully allowed her to lift him inside. He had barely enough space to turn in. She put some scraps of food inside, but he ignored them, and whimpered when she nailed down the lid. She was thinking of coffins, comforted that the flight to Tehran was only a short one, and she would probably be able there to get a proper cage from the airline.

She was obliged to ask Ali Yazdi if he would take Rustum in the station wagon. She was obliged to smile at him.

"Of course, dear lady, since you choose to rid us of one of our canine pests," and he bowed in his suave way. "We will be sorry to see you all go," he said as they drove along the flowered corridor to the airport. His insinuating manner was gone now, and in its place an expression of scowling purposiveness, as if he wouldn't wait for them to go. Chloe looked back at her window, its bright turquoise color, its geraniums, all symbolic of solitude, industry, and peace.

The airport was crowded with Western dependents, and had a certain cheerful, far from panicked air, with dozens of blond tots, materialized out of the secret back gardens of the American district, chasing around the dirty waiting room. The mothers stood in clusters, chattering excitedly, festooned with travel bags, backpacks, and huge shoulder purses. Iran Air had put on a special extra flight, with special open seating, so all had relaxed, and no one pushed or shrieked.

Noosheen came to see Chloe off. "I will send you a copy of my thesis," she said. "When I write it. 'Say not thou of a thing, "I will surely do it tomorrow" without "If God will." ' " She giggled. "The Koran. This is not goodbye. When you come back, perhaps I will still be living exquisitely in Villa One!" She hugged Chloe.

"Oh, I'm sorry to be going," cried Chloe, greatly surprising herself by this utterance. What about her children? What about real life?

"At home they will be so happy to see you," Noosheen reminded her.

"Oh, yes," Chloe agreed.

Hugh Monroe had not arrived, and Chloe began to feel worried, though no doubt he was attending to last-minute things. She began to see significance in the fact that he had spent the night in his own apartment. Was he sulking because of Rustum? But that would be more like Jeffrey. When Hugh did arrive, as the people began to surge toward the check-in counter, he explained that he had gone to see whether Loyal Cooley was well enough to travel.

"But he really isn't," Hugh said. "In another few days, perhaps. It's too bad to leave him, but he's a pretty sick man."

In his cage, Rustum began to whine and snarl, so that nearby people drew their children to them.

"This is Chloe trying to expiate her imperialist guilt," said Hugh. "Are we going to travel the whole way with that noise?"

"Dick gave me some phenobarbital for him," said Chloe, resolved not to be drawn into bickering about Rustum.

"I doubt they'll let you check in with him," Dick said, though he did see a few other animal cages among the assembled luggage. "They will," said Chloe, for some reason much surer that Iran Air would agree to take Rustum than that it would take them, at last, or that the plane, when it came, would fly. Dick's rugs, wrapped in sheets and tied with rope, looked like bodies. Junie had bought a small rug and three enormous round brass trays. Amid this welter of desperately assembled possessions stood Hugh's neat suitcase and expensive briefcase, discreetly black.

"Well, back to Tehran," she said, when they had got on the plane, and she was sitting in between Junie and Hugh, uncomfortably consigned again by her smallness to the middle seat. Hugh's long legs stretched into the aisle. Junie pressed her face against the cold glass of the porthole window and sighed. The plane rose high above the desert. Chloe thought of the jet airplane crashes but did not torment the others with her horrid imaginings.

"What were you doing at the Royal Tehran Hilton?" she reminded Hugh when they were airborne. "You said you weren't even there." It seemed to her that Junie's closed lids stirred with a flutter of interest, and Dick, behind them, leaned forward to hear.

"Well," said Hugh, "it was supposed to be secret. A few days before I was scheduled to leave Rochester, I got a call from the dean asking me to go a few days early to Tehran, to see an important patient. 'Important patient' was exactly how he put it, with no extra significance, no reverently lowered voice, just an important patient, so that it could have been a rich Iranian businessman, anything, but then I also got a call from the State Department, giving me a contact number. So it was pretty obvious.

"His own doctors thought he might have malaria, that's all I was told, and to go to the Hilton and somebody would be in touch. So I left London—I'd been lecturing at Hammersmith Hospital—a few days early, and when I arrived in Tehran, someone was in touch, a Dr. Moshir, who met me at the airport and drove me to the hotel. He explained that someone else would be in touch. There was still no indication of the identity of the patient and from this guy no discussion of the case, but he was a doctor, and I had guessed."

"The Shah?" said Dick.

Hugh nodded. "I got to Tehran I guess eight at night, had dinner, and went to bed. In the morning I got a phone call: someone was coming for me. It was all a little cryptic, a little solemn, but not per se mysterious. Around noon someone rang up from the lobby. I went down. Three people, including this same Dr. Moshir. One drove, the other guy sat in front, I sat in the back of an old Peykan with the doctor, and he explained that the patient was the Shah, that they were a bit puzzled by certain things about his case, they appreciated my having a look, there were reasons for secrecy. If people thought his health was frail there would be panic, etc. So—of course I thought it would be interesting to meet the Shah. We went to the medical school, the Shah came there, through the back way, and I was given an examining room and instruments, and was told that the lab facilities were at my disposal."

"What was he like?" Chloe said, gratified that her lover was as important as this.

"The Shah? A regal character, not tall but erect, smiling, affable but remote. Extremely courteous in his replies when I took the history. He appeared ill—jaundiced and anemic, and had fever, but I didn't think he had malaria. He, his doctors and other attendants, emphasized that there must be no discussion whatever of his case. I had to promise not to mention that I had seen him and to keep the whole thing confidential. To emphasize this, they took my passport, saying they'd fix it so that my arrival dates coincided with my original travel plans. In fact they hadn't stamped my passport at the airport, though they'd looked at it; the authorities must have been watching for me.

"Anyhow, I was told to return to the Hilton, and wait to be contacted by a French doctor presently in Iran, who had also seen the Shah and wanted to discuss the case. The examination and lab work took two days, during which I saw the Shah twice—I saw her, too, the Czarina, whatever she's called. A nice woman, rather overdressed.

"Anyway, the next day, this Frenchman, Dr. Juneau, called, said he was in Shiraz but was coming to Tehran. We would meet, was that all right? By now I was overdue in Shiraz, and sworn not to admit that I was in Iran at all, so I said yes, please by all means hasten to Tehran, or I could come to Shiraz, which I was planning to do anyway, and we could talk there. He said he'd check into that possibility and call me back. But he didn't. Several days went by."

"You were just stuck there?"

"I began to hassle Dr. Moshir. He said they didn't know what had happened to Dr. Juneau, and, finally, that I might as well go along to Shiraz but to remember the extreme secrecy of my mission. This was all conducted with an air of urgent concern, not only about the health of the Shah, which indeed was a matter of concern—he clearly seemed to me to be a very sick man—but for the political consequences if it became known he was sick. They didn't spell out the consequences, I suppose they didn't know them, but no one was to have even the faintest suspicion. When the Shah left the clinic he left the back way, collar turned up, in a little car. It was interesting, all right. And now they appeared to be greatly concerned about the whereabouts of the French doctor. They seemed to have fears for his safety. That was not too reassuring to me, as you can imagine. I got the idea that there might be people out to get Dr. Juneau, why not me too? But why? Then the business of the guy jumping me in the compound and going through my stuff; obviously they were looking for the history. That's when I went again to Tehran. There I found that Dr. Moshir had disappeared and no one would talk to me. I couldn't get through anywhere. I went to the medical school where I'd been, and it was more or less just people rushing around. They seemed too disorganized to worry that I might now talk and spill the beans somehow or not cooperate. No one seemed to know anything."

Oh, really, thought Chloe, this all seems preposterous. I don't believe him.

"Who called for me?" It occurred to her again. "At the bathroom door? At Persepolis?"

"Not I," said Hugh.

"It must have been Abbas. Or Richard Dare." It occurred to her again that if she had let him in perhaps he would not have been killed. What had he wanted? Still, it could have been Richard Dare.

"What was your diagnosis?" Dick asked Hugh.

"I didn't make a diagnosis. Some sort of neoplasm, I guessed. All I did was rule out malaria."

"What was she wearing?" asked Chloe.

"Who?"

"The Empress!"

Chapter Thirty-six

BAD NEWS

There was the Door to which I found no Key;
There was the Veil through which I might not see:
Some little talk awhile of ME *and* THEE
There was—and then no more of THEE *and* ME.

The plane landed shortly at Mehrabad Airport and taxied toward the giant passenger building. The passengers stood in the aisles and pushed each other, and lifted down their packages; they broke from the plane and swarmed across the tarmac, ignoring the little buses that stood to receive them. Inside the terminal, at the Iran Air counters, extra clerks, with unusual efficiency, handled the long, agitated line of foreigners and Iranians who were buying tickets, and uniformed officials traveled along it assuring people that extra flights were being added so that all might depart. Even so, the waiting rooms were a pandemonium of weeping and shrieking, and the floors were strewn as thickly as a stadium with paper cups, cigarette packages, and plastic sacks.

There were no flights directly to San Francisco, but Chloe was able to book a flight to Los Angeles via Rome. The ticket clerk did not ask to see her passport. Rustum would cost two hundred dollars extra, and was transferred to an Air Iran metal cage. Sensing freedom, when his box was opened he tried to bolt, but was captured by a glaring Hugh. Hugh, Dick, and Junie were able to get on a flight together to New York via London. Now Chloe for the first time felt the reality of their parting, felt keenly her own reluctance to tell them goodbye and make her way alone. What would she and Hugh say to each other? What did she want to say?

She did not feel as worried about the irregularity in her travel documents as Hugh and Dick did. Surely the Iranians wanted

them to leave? But Hugh insisted that he go with Chloe in a taxi
to the American Embassy in downtown Tehran to get some sort
of paper that would ensure that she could leave the country.
"Probably they can give you some special diplomatic status, or
a duplicate passport, something like that."

"If not, I could just stay here. I could stay at the Hilton. I'd
be all right, while I waited for clearance," Chloe said.

"You could, and I'm sure it's perfectly safe. Or we could try
bribing someone at the airport. I'm sure it'll be all right," he
said.

Taxis were abundant outside the airport terminal, the drivers
milling and calling out. Carefully, as they had learned, they
chose one and agreed on the price to downtown Tehran and
back. The driver, a dark, round-shouldered man, wore a vivid
knitted cap of red and green. "The American embassy! Of
course I know it," he cried, grinning vivaciously. "We will
try! We will go as close as we can!" The car lurched into an
ominously heavy stream of traffic, portending a slow trip into
town. Chloe saw for the first time the ugliness of Tehran, all
rectangles of cement block, cement, treeless. She thought of
beautiful Shiraz.

"Alone at last." She smiled at Hugh, leaning against his
strong shoulder, suffused, all at once, with the pangs of
sadness that had been deferred by the business of packing and
flying here. "It's over, or almost over. That feels strange. I
feel awfully sad."

"You'll feel better when you're safely on the airplane,"
Hugh said. "Safely airborne with a gin martini. You have a
resilient nature."

"Gin? I never drink gin," Chloe said. "Anyway, I won't.
I don't really want to leave. I don't know. Going back. Missing
you. And I feel disappointed, in a way, I don't know why. Oh,
Hugh." She sighed. She understood her fear of going back.
The future seemed so unpatterned, so like a vast dance floor,
flat, immense, and she a wallflower in an ugly dress, visited
with depressed longings, restless self-depreciations, desire,
desires for events unspecified. She tried to imagine being
married to Hugh, with new rooms to paint. It was just possible
to feel an interest in that, and to imagine painting the door sills
and lattices of Hugh's charming Cape Cod house, or so she

imagined it would be, with the turquoise blue of safety and haven. But of course he hadn't asked her, and anyway she knew she ought to try to imagine something more independent and resourceful, like digging potsherds in Egypt or Jordan.

"Well," said Hugh abruptly, in a tone of unfamiliar petulance, "what about me?"

Caught by surprise, Chloe's attention shifted, stirred, focused on Hugh. "What do you mean, what about you?"

"You'll pick up life as if nothing happened, you've never once said you're sorry to leave me. After all I have to go home alone, just when, just when . . . I'm in love with you, Chloe, it's hard to just pack it all in."

His expression was puzzled, as if he were not quite getting at what he meant. Chloe's heart jolted out of its track of contemplation of herself in the little Cape Cod kitchen, which she could easily picture, teak, with Mexican tiles and built-in ovens, and a kitchen clock, and herself glancing at the clock, Hugh late. He is speaking of love!

"I know you've been married twice," she said. Hugh's glance was puzzled at this non sequitur.

"Where did you get that idea?"

"Everybody says so," she said.

"Tha-that's r-r-ridiculous," Hugh said, an uncharacteristic stammer making her suppose he was lying.

"Oh, Prophet! Speak to thy wives, and to thy daughters, and to the wives of the Faithful, that they let their veils fall low," said the taxi driver suddenly to the stalled traffic.

"It's more than even love," said Hugh. He stared out the window, averting his face, the nature of his emotion completely unclear to Chloe, but rippling the muscles in front of his handsome ears. It appeared from his silence that he could not explain. "It's okay for you, you'll go home as if nothing had happened, you'll pick up your life. But you haven't even asked me how I feel. In fact no one ever does ask. You never ask. I'm just useful. I do everything, not that I mind, but it's I who make reservations, arrangements, it's I who have to hunt for Abbas and, you know, see him and drive him back, and I get beaten up and lied to and stranded in Iranian hotels or sneaking around in the dark all the time to visit you, and getting up at five in the morning, did you think I liked that? Okay, okay,

d like staying with you, it was worth it, but still . . .'' She
w to her surprise that a tear stood in his eye, at his pitiable
t.

She was stricken. His accusations were perfectly true: she let
m do everything and didn't try to understand him. Was it
cause he was so tall? She was struck speechless with the
morseful conviction of her own callousness. She had no
tion of his real nature and in fact had been rather suspicious
f it. And he had no notion of her real nature, and if he had he
ouldn't like her. He didn't realize that she was meddling,
ceitful, and useless; wasn't aware of her unnatural lack of
robity, deficient maternal feeling, her repellent pragmatism
d moral indolence. Didn't know how she had meddled in the
fe of Noosheen, or slept with Abbas. If she were to confess
er deeds, his disappointment didn't bear thinking of. It would
e kindest, since they were to part, to leave him with some
lusions, some kindly feelings. And now, it seemed to her, she
d not want to leave him at all, for she saw that in comparison
her own frivolity and superficiality he had depths she had not
scerned before. All this self-reproach flashed before her, as if
e were drowning, and, being unfamiliar to her, had a toxic
ffect of silencing her.

Hugh was wiping his glasses. Chloe's remorse grew. For an
stant she could imagine Hugh transparent, like one of those
emonstration mannequins, all the organs and structures seen
side—Hugh, usually so opaque, now revealing the complex-
y of his innards, emotions of various colors running up and
own little pipettes and coiled tubes. She had made no effort to
nderstand. What on earth did Hugh mean by love, anyway?

"Bad women for bad men and bad men for bad women; but
irtuous women for virtuous men!" said the driver suddenly.

I must be a bad person, she was thinking. It had never before
ccurred to her as plainly as this that she was perhaps a bad
erson. An unfaithful wife, a neglectful mother, making no
ontribution, making no one happy. Whereas Hugh was good.
er panic and misery made her speechless. It had never before
her life occurred to her she might be bad. And yet in time he
ould leave her, she thought. As with Jeffrey, did this matter?
oes she love him?

Her mind whirled. Was it necessary to decide on your own

character? No. Yes! It was necessary to take herself serious
as a moral agent. It mattered, in the fabric of the worl
whether a person was good or bad. How terrible! She saw th
answer and she was bad.

"But I do love you," she said. "I would have thought it wa
obvious." Despite herself, a quarrelsome note sounded in he
voice.

"Well, I'm sorry I'm so obtuse," said Hugh.

"Oh, I'm sorry. Of course I love you," said Chlo
apologetically.

"Of course I understand that Jeffrey—that you have you
life . . ." said Hugh, in his normal, courteous tone.

"When we get home," said Chloe, "do you think tha
things will be different? Or the same? I guess I mean that w
won't know till we get home."

"I suppose," said Hugh, not sounding convinced.

No, that's not right, she wanted to say. Let's decide th
future right now, and abolish all uncertainty. The world ha
neither joy nor certitude nor light.

"I know I'm not a fascinating person," Hugh began agair
"But if . . ."

So intent upon herself—how would she know? Perhaps h
was. How she had failed him.

"Chloe, when we get home can we talk about the future
What will happen?"

"Oh, Hugh, of course."

All at once they realized the car had stopped. They were i
the mouth of a narrow street, stucco balconies overheac
clothing draped from the balconies. Hugh opened the ca
window and stuck his head out, looking apprehensively aroun(

"Is blocked off," the driver said. "They got many stree
blocked off." He began to back the car. Hugh and Chlo
looked around them. An odor of saffron. At the end of th
street, a man waved his arms. It appeared that they would hav
to do something here, were being menaced and impeded.

On the main street, at each of the four corners stood th
familiar trucks of the army, stuffed with soldiers squatting o
the flat beds. Chloe felt Hugh's body grow tense. She dre
away from him. The driver began again to back his car, thi
time around one of the trucks, turned around and starte

rward in a direction exactly opposite to the one they had been
•ing. Around the next corner people came into view, walking
large parties in the street. The driver stopped to let some of
em pass, then drove a short distance on the curb. Something
ud clattered against their car.

"What's going on?" Hugh asked the driver.

"There will be another protest today," he said. He stopped
,ain, the car obstructed by another crowd. Women in black
ils, their faces uncovered, glared at them. Some boys carried
sign. All were walking in one direction, rapidly. People had
ized the streets from automobiles. Other cars were stopped;
eir drivers shouted from the windows.

The din and murmur of collective anger began to beset the
r at first distantly, as one approaches the sea through calm
nks of whispering grass, drawn by the growing roar. They
ere drawn to the roar. The driver seemed to point the nose of
s taxi at it. The sound excited, it warmed the blood. Flocks
people in black or white, little boys and girls.

"What do they say?" Chloe asked the driver.

"They are saying, 'Death to the Shah,' " he said. "They
e going to the Jaleh Square. The square is near the embassy.
m not sure we can get there."

"Are we far?" asked Hugh.

"Not far. You can walk there. I think it is better."

"But how will we get back?" Hugh asked.

"Oh, I will wait for you, of course." He leaned out the car
indow and spoke to someone in the street. He laughed. "Yes!
ere will be a million people in Jaleh Square!" he said.

"Yes! Let's walk, let's see!" said Chloe.

"I don't know," said Hugh. The car had stopped. People
alked toward them down the street. They seemed like those
ts in Africa that would walk right over the car, unstoppable.
e noise grew, people working themselves up; little boys,
ipping and dancing, cried, "Death to the Shah!"

"I will stay right here," said the driver. "You must walk to
e end of this street, then across the square, then you will see
e building on your right. That is the embassy of America."

"He won't wait for us, will he?" Chloe said, clinging to
ugh's arm as they alighted. He stepped along swiftly, here
d there pushing someone.

"No," he said. "We have to make this fast. We'll just siz
up the situation."

They took a few more steps, clinging, people pushing pa
them. Someone took Chloe's shoulder and squeezed it in
cruel pinch, then walked on without looking. People did n
look at them. The faces were angry. Chloe thought of the Lo
Angeles peace march and saw that this was different. Thes
faces were sullen, as the faces of the police had been. In Lo
Angeles the marchers were happy but the police were full o
rage. Here, too, angry soldiers, up ahead, waving the peopl
by. She grew afraid, but it was thrilling. What can happen
you as your feet tread along the ground, the ground is th
ground, others are simply others, there were no guns or knive
they would not be pushed. There were women, wearing white
in numbers, like beehives of nurses, arms linked like chums
Old mullahs in black robes, white-bearded, wandered along
When Chloe stumbled on the broken pavement, Hugh clutche
her. They were swept along in the torrent of people wh
erupted from every doorway, every alley, every car stuck o
the street as surely as if in thick mud.

"I didn't feel it, before, did you, in Azami Compound? N
even on the streets," cried Chloe. "This anger—I never fe
this; no one ever said." Her body sang in response to the hu
and din of the rising voices.

"Yes, of course, each time I took someone's hand, someon
sick. Their thin, dry hands, something in their silence. I've fe
it all along," said Hugh.

"It's funny that you never mentioned it," said Chloe.

"They're rising up," said Hugh. "I didn't think the
would."

"And the Shah will just shoot them. That's the difference
Lyndon Johnson couldn't shoot us—in the sixties, that wa
different, but here . . ."

"Yes, this is different," said Hugh.

"But it's the same, too," said Chloe. "People by marchin
can bring a tyrant down."

"They haven't brought him down," said Hugh.

"They will! Don't you feel that?" cried Chloe, joyful
think that people had power over their lives and the course o
things. Power after all, palpable here.

"They are cruel, they are still a cruel people," said Hugh.
"Chloe, I think we should turn back. We aren't going to get
rough. The embassy won't be open in all this."

"Just to the edge of the square, then," said Chloe, knowing
ugh was right. The throng, the shouting multitude would
event them from crossing the square. But she wanted to see
e whole sea, the whole black and white sea to the horizon of
gns and shouting people, and the fists, for the fists went by
em, pounding in the air, people chanted, and above them
ey saw cameras, television films being made. Would they be
 television, on NBC, say? Chloe Fowler and Hugh Monroe,
ms embraced, marching against the Shah? She laughed
oud. It did not seem that she could ever go back to San
ancisco. Here you were a part of history.

"How lucky we are to see this," cried Chloe. "Let's just go
 the edge of the square!" They pushed ahead until it was
possible to go further; the people ahead of them had stopped,
d people crowded up behind them, so no one else could fit
to the square. At the feeling of people pressing from behind,
hloe began to grow afraid. She could imagine being trampled.
e could not see over the heads of the tallest. It was as if an
lipse had occurred. People jostled her, she felt their elbows,
lt a gentle but insistent pushing from behind.

"Hurry," said Hugh, "turn back!" But to turn back was to
uggle against a beating surf. Thrusting their arms before
em, they turned to push through the crowd. Sometimes
ople stepped aside. Others, like inanimate objects, had to be
shed, rocked back on bare heels, on their plastic sandals,
raight-armed. Hugh, bigger than the Iranians, went first,
shing along. "Excuse me, excuse me," he said.

"Pardon me," Chloe said, "excuse us, we have to get
ack." With difficulty, from among the maze of alleys, they
und the little street where they had left the taxi. To their
rprise, it was still there, its driver standing on its hood to
atch developments along the street. He greeted them with a
gor that surprised them, that surprised perhaps the man
mself. He was invigorated by the exciting marching, singing,
outing. He leapt from the hood to the ground. "Back to the
rport!" he cried. "Yes?"

"Is that possible?" Hugh asked.

"Get in, get in," he said, starting his engine already, an speaking to people outside the car. People hammered on th top of the car and leaned in to grin, but they did not seer unfriendly.

"How thrilling," said Chloe to the driver. "Thousands people."

"Yes," he said.

"The Shah will have to pay attention," she said.

"Yes," said the driver. "It is not so good for foreigners, think. But I will get you safely to the airport and peace be you. 'Let him then who will, believe, and let him who will, an infidel.' The words of Mohammed."

"Thank you, brother," said Hugh, which Chloe great admired. She would not have thought to call the man brothe

Women thrust leaflets at them. Some were in Farsi. One, English, said:

A Verse for Our New Leader Beloved Ayatollah Khomeini:

> *Then, in such hour of need*
> *Of your fainting, dispirited race*
> *Ye, like angels appear,*
> *Radiant with ardour divine!*
> *Beacons of hope, ye appear*
> *Languor is not in your heart,*
> *Weakness is not in your word,*
> *Weariness not on your brow.*

It seemed to Chloe that these were the words of Matthew Arnold.

As they drove into the airport, Hugh began to take Chloe his arms, but was constrained by the muttering of the driver, b some sense that his political or religious zeal would b inflamed or offended by any emotional desperation or eroti display. They clung furtively. Would this be their last embrace Chloe wondered? Except for a polite, perfunctory kiss as the took their respective planes? He to London–New York; she Rome–Los Angeles? "Oh, Chloe," he murmured into her ear

"Oh, Hugh," she said, thinking of the rushing and desperat winds of change.

Chapter Thirty-seven

DEPARTURE LOUNGE

Ah, Love! could you and I with Him conspire
To grasp this sorry Scheme of Things entire,
Would not we shatter it to bits—and then
Remould it nearer to the Heart's Desire!

Dick Rothblatt was waiting on the pavement by the taxi stand, anxiously scanning the flood of arriving cabs, looking for Chloe and Hugh. "Thank God," he said. "We heard a rumor they were going to close the highway between here and Tehran."

They told him of what they had seen there. "Crazy Chloe of course wanted to plunge into the throng," said Hugh in a way that Chloe saw meant that he was concerned about her. One danger, that without a correct visa she could not get out, was unresolved. She was still in danger of being kept in Iran.

How can I imagine being in danger? I've had no experience of that, she thought, resentfully, although she had had fear enough in the past few days to learn in. But it had not really stuck. It was still hard to imagine a country keeping you in when it wanted you to go. Surely Iran would say to her, Go.

Inside the terminal waiting room, Junie and Dick were encamped with Dr. Ames in a corner section of plastic chairs, with coats and bags thrown over empty chairs to reserve them for Chloe and Hugh. The drugged Rustum lay apathetically in his new metal cage, as if knowing he stood no chance against it, but he stirred feebly when he heard Chloe's voice.

The loudspeaker called the arrival of another plane from Shiraz. They watched the passengers straggle in, loaded with baskets and sacks, wearing layers of clothes—people none of them had ever seen before, residents of Shiraz—businessmen and schoolgirls, people with money. Conspicuous among them was Zareeneh Yazdi, wearing a sumptuous dark calf-length mink, despite the sweltering weather, and enough gold chains to coin a statue. She waited at the end of the gangway for her daughter, a plump, dark-haired, sallow little girl of eight, who tottered down the steps clutching a teddy bear and two rag dolls. The beaming Hendersons were right behind. Zareeneh waved at Chloe and the others, and rushed over to them.

"Thank heavens I am here on time," she said. "I have this for you." She opened her bag and thrust a paper at Chloe. It was the torn page of her passport, with the exit visa stamped on it. Chloe stared at it and at Zareeneh. Various explanations rushed to mind to explain this. Had Dr. Yazdi taken it? Why was Zareeneh returning it? They had parted? Political differences?—Why was it being delivered in this way?

"Ali found it. It was in Vahid Farmani's desk." She smiled. Now she took the teddy bear and dolls from her little girl and put them carefully in an opaque plastic bag. She put the plastic bag on a chair of its own, threw her coat over it, and settled herself on the chair next to it.

"Are you leaving, Zareeneh?" asked Dick.

"Oh, it is so sad. I cannot believe it is really necessary but Ali says we must not be foolish. He is foolishly staying another moment, there is so much to do at the hospital, and to help Bahram settle in."

"Where are you going?" asked Chloe.

"I? Oh, I am going to Geneva," she said.

Now, two hours before the time of departure, with no problems indicated on the manifest of departing flights, other concerns began to preoccupy each traveler. Dick began to think of the necklace in his pocket. Chloe at the sight of Rustum lying drugged in his cage began to worry about him, that someone would protest that the space he would take might be taken by a person, though surely animals traveled with the luggage, and a person couldn't travel in there. Zareeneh Yazdi began to rustle nervously among her hand luggage, with sudden fears, it appeared, that she had left things behind. Her face would be transfixed an instant with panic, she would dive into a bag, hands groping inside, find or not find what she sought, highly anxious, all the time smiling. Her little girl indifferently read a book.

"They can see that it goes there, Chloe, the numbering matches, the paper matches," said Hugh, fitting the pages of her passport together. Perhaps it's illegal to use a torn passport, she thought.

"They're so legalistic. Think of the Erdmans. They look for reasons to put you in jail," she said. They looked without success at the newsstand for some glue to stick it with.

"Maybe something like toothpaste?" suggested Dick. "Zareeneh, do you have any glue?"

"No, I'm sorry," she said.

"And what is this?" Dick can imagine them saying when they see his necklace. "A national treasure. Do you know what the penalty for that is, sir?"

"I have some Scotch tape," says Zareeneh.

"That's probably okay, we'll just be up front about it, and tape it in," says Hugh.

"It all boils down to whether they want you to go. They can always find a reason to keep you," Zareeneh says.

"If for some reason they don't let me go," Chloe says, "promise me you'll take Rustum. Promise." She says it to anyone, but no one volunteers to believe this request has been to him. "It would only be, you know, a few days. I would have to wait here and get it straightened out. Then I'd come and get him."

They look at Rustum. Asleep he looks more attractive than when awake, but he is still a nondescript dog, and when awake rather rambunctious, and they cannot imagine him being welcome in America, either officially, by the American customs, or by Jeffrey, when she gets him home.

It was delicate. There would be something proprietary, something official, about agreeing to take Rustum; it contained some implication for the future, some implied obligation, connection, continuity. Dick watched Hugh with close attention. Hugh was just shaking his head over Chloe's silliness, and made no commitment.

"They'll let you take him back to the Hilton while you make

your arrangements," he said, laughing. "You have to deal with this yourself, Chloe."

Chloe fell silent, wearing, Dick saw, a sulky expression.

"We could take him," Dick said, "as far as New York, but you'd have to collect him there."

"My plane goes to Rome–Los Angeles," said Chloe wretchedly. "But thank you, dear Dick." She was surprised and touched by the difference between a true friend and a so-called lover like Hugh, when it came to hard sacrifices.

"Jeff will be crazy about him," Hugh went on, in the same disagreeable tone he had been using to Chloe, and which Dick resented, though she appeared not to notice it. Dick was also struck by Hugh's reference to Jeffrey, as if he didn't realize that Jeff and Chloe were splitting up. Perhaps there was some new development, or perhaps—it struck him that she had said as much—Chloe hadn't confided in Hugh her marital problems? He was somehow rather pleased at this notion, that Chloe had confided in him but not in Hugh. Well, she could have all kinds of reasons for not wanting to involve Hugh—not wanting to put him on the spot, maybe, or not wanting to get further involved.

Chloe put her mended passport in her purse. Rather dazed at this unexpected delivery from the presumably last hurdle, except for the arrival of the aircraft itself, she sat down and wrote postcards to the children. But her thoughts brimmed and flooded. I'm escaping, Chloe thought, but the idea came without the swell of relief and gratitude she had expected. She felt, instead, illicit and unfinished. She thought of her Sassanian beaker, her work table. She had finished nothing, left nothing behind, and was returning to nothing, or so it seemed, over the weeks, over the oceans. Men could start over in the Yukon. She should have been a man like that, leaving lives and people behind, going off on dog sleds into wild places. She could do that now; she could go anywhere, Los Angeles, Detroit. But she knew she wouldn't, because of her prudence and indolence. She'd go back to San Francisco and put up an undignified fight for the house, or Jeffrey would have changed his mind and she would just accept that things were as before. And Hugh . . . In his pocket airplane tickets: Tehran–London, London–New York. What were they going to say about the future?

How do you profit from experience, anyhow? Can you bank

it, get interest, watch it grow? You grow sadder and wiser or older and wiser, but the corollary to wiser is always something undesirable.

She must contemplate, commit herself in some way, take some action worthy of all this, but what? When she took actions, they were usually wrong. It had never been too bad, drifting along, but it was, she now felt, no longer possible. She'd changed, even if she didn't know how. What on earth did she feel, what should she do, about Hugh?

Dick thinks of smoking. They all sit, subdued and anxious, in the encampment of plastic chairs in the corner, away from the cloud of cigarette smoke that dominates with its fatal miasma the center of the great waiting room. Near them, abject, exhausted women slump in the chairs, cradling limp babies, their knees surrounded by bundles. Men smoke in little groups and pace together from window to wall, uttering little barks in their strange language.

Dick, checking in his pocket for the antique necklace, finds Marla's letter, and for lack of anything else to read, pulls it out and continues reading.

. . . one thing about you being all that way is, it
really helps me to think things out on my own. You've
always been such an influence on me, not always for
the best if I let my temper get the better of the
situation! But you have always made me stand on my
own two feet for better or worse, and that was
something as I see now I needed to get through. Now
that I've been . . .

Dick casts his eye over the rest of the page to see if it switches to the subject of real estate. Apparently not. Relaxed, he skims along; more in the same vein, Marla's usual vein— no mention of the kids. She's gotten a dog. As he reads, inattentively, a sudden chill strikes him. He backtracks a paragraph.

I wonder if in some ways it wasn't the house that
caused the trouble between us, and now that I'm set-

tled in the apartment I feel so much freer to think.
I've been thinking about all you said before you left
about reconciliation. I know people never change, but
maybe I've been wrong in thinking it was you (or me)
who ought to change when it's just dramatic how not
having the house and all those memories and responsibilities . . .

He can see her, alone in her apartment, writing this. Dick
shivers. What is he reading here? He reads hurriedly but
carefully on. His hand begins to shake like an old drunk's.
Reconciliation? What is the emotion that accelerates his heart?
Fright, he realizes. He is appalled. All that he had wanted, had
thought, is now being offered and he is appalled.

All at once, with a clattering of numbers in the board above
them, their flights are posted and they are being advised to
check in. Airline clerks and customs officials come in, in
military throng, and array themselves behind counters between
this room and the international departure lounge behind them.
All round, people line up to pile their luggage on the counters,
pushing it slowly along toward the dark little men with
mustaches, carrying guns.

Chloe and the others assemble their suitcases. Chloe feels
the creep of apprehensiveness, Dick feels himself sweat. Will
the customs people be instructed to look for artifacts? The
necklace burns in his pocket. He has never been searched
bodily except once in Israel. Up ahead at the customs counter
people are emptying their pockets in front of expressionless
soldiers; men paw around in the satchels and string-wrapped
cardboard boxes. Dick thinks maybe he'd better put the
necklace in the suitcase after all. He unzips the suitcase and
plunges the necklace into the center of dirty clothes and things
thrust in unfolded. How horrible if they open the bag and all
this dirty laundry comes springing out.

Chloe is indifferent, has nothing to hide but her shards, and
doesn't think they will care about those. When her turn comes,
the men seem to see her indifference and to feel, therefore,
indifferent to her, contenting themselves with a cursory glance
at her ticket and her passport, loose leaf and all, and wave her
on. She is only a woman. Her feeling is not entirely of relief.

They wave Junie on in. They take a moment with Dick. They look in the suitcase with the necklace, look at the necklace and wave him on in. He doesn't know whether to be relieved or disappointed that they didn't think it valuable or genuine. It is Hugh they stop; they look over his papers and call a superior, a soldier from the sidelines. Chloe and the others watch anxiously from the safe, the international, side of the departure lounge, with Hugh technically in Iran.

"It must be the stamp; it didn't get stamped when I came in," he says across to them. "Because of . . ." He looks grim—indeed, frightened, Chloe thinks, and very reasonably. Officials confer. Hugh glares helplessly at them, and over at Chloe and Dick. At another counter, men are opening Zareeneh's bags one by one, and shaking out the beautiful clothes, and feeling in the linings.

If they don't let Hugh out, I'll stay with him, Chloe thinks. But would they let her back in to Iran?

Anyway she isn't really worried. They are Americans, aren't they? Leaving where no one wanted them to stay. Poor Zareeneh, she thinks; even if you didn't like Zareeneh, her bras being lifted out, shaken out, by soldiers. Anyone can see the good things are in the teddy bear, that was so obvious. But the guards don't see it. The daughter hugs the teddy bear and the two rag dolls. At last they wave her in. Zareeneh is compelled to repack in view of everyone. At other counters, other Iranians repack in view of everyone.

At last Hugh comes through, like a cork popping out, stuffing his passport away, sighing. His face is shiny. "That had me worried," he says.

"Did they just say 'go ahead'?"

"They called someone."

"Thank God," says Junie in a shrill, rapid voice. "Thank God we're getting out of this awful place. I never thought we would. I really never thought we would. Did you? Did you really, in your heart, Dick?" Dick imagines Junie becoming hysterical, slapping her. Maybe he just wants to slap her.

"In Persepolis I didn't think we'd get out. After that I did," Dick says.

"It's going to get very interesting here," says Hugh, "but I'm just as glad we won't be in on it."

I don't know, thinks Chloe. "I don't know."

"You don't seem happy, Chloe," says Dick.

"No, I'm not. I feel—I feel—it didn't turn out very well, did it? This visit to Iran."

"I don't know. It turned out," Dick says, "as well as could be expected. Except for Persepolis."

"Which wouldn't have happened if it hadn't been for us. But that isn't what I mean. It's more—I don't know. I just feel that now I know how to be good. But I'll never have another chance. We're just going back to America, where I'll never have another chance to be good."

Now they sink lethargically into new chairs, subdued by the growing weight of private reflections, the corrosive sadness of parting and change. Yes, thinks Chloe, her thoughts turning to home, it was wrong of me to stay with Jeffrey. I didn't love him enough. Marriage is an ancient contract with universal rules, rules always the same despite local differences—fidelity and cooperation and affection—all those things I never gave. She feels ashamed to have imagined she was specially exempt from the ancient marriage rules.

She realizes that she has thought of her children, in the past few days, hardly at all. Now, all at once, she is able to picture them again, staring at her gravely as out of a photograph—Max's rather large ears, Sara's golden braids. She is overcome with her sudden sense of them as separate from herself, and of how it is impossible, just by knowing things herself, to spare them the pain of having large ears or of knowing the things they know, or of having horrible thoughts—thought by them already, no doubt—which she doesn't know, and doesn't want to know, their brains deep as the universe with atoms of thoughts not hers. Maybe everything is electricity, she thinks. Braces, she thinks of, and of their touching little clothes and of how sweet they were as babies.

It's true you don't give your children enough time, enough thought, she thinks; they are there for you to feel tender toward but do you knit for them or paint murals on their walls, or play games, even if you don't like games?

How wrong of her it has been to judge Junie, poor Junie, who worked so hard and made a contribution, even if her mind isn't subtle; she is young, for one thing. People shouldn't judge Junie until they can make a contribution themselves. She will make a contribution. She will try to make a contribution. Does she want or deserve Hugh?

What's he going to say to Marla? Dick wonders, mind leached to perfect blank idiocy. How can it be that he can't begin to imagine the idea of going back to Marla? Maybe it has always been the house he loved, the house as surely as any beloved child keeping them together with its needs of paint and cleaned-out gutters and a kind of cornmeal compound to be spread in the garage to soak up the oil that dripped from Marla's Civic.

Maybe Abbas was really in the Savak, thinks Chloe. It's true that he was always around. She wonders if he had told Junie what had happened between them. Such inconsiderate indiscretion seemed hardly imaginable, but it would explain Junie's hostility.

It's wise of Chloe not to jump into anything with Hugh, thinks Dick. One thing at a time. He thinks she is being rather brave, considering her situation, a woman facing divorce, approaching middle age, no job skills. He can't imagine Chloe doing social work, sitting behind a desk with a little sign MARLA ROTHBLATT on it, in that greenish painted room, papers all around, sullen Hispanics outside the door. Couldn't imagine her acquiring that certain tarnished, exasperated look that Marla had developed since doing social work; it wouldn't work for Chloe. But she'd have to do something.

How pretty Chloe is, tired and flushed, little dry creases beginning at the corners of her eyes, delicate dry skin, will wrinkle early probably. She would like the necklace. He will give it to her. Had they seen it was an ancient artifact and yet let him take it? Or seen that it wasn't an ancient artifact and he'd been swindled. Try not to mind whichever way it turns out. It doesn't matter, better if it's fake, in a way, then you can take it out and give it to Chloe, a souvenir, even if not valuable. Who else would appreciate it?

Like survivors of summer camp, ardors endured together, tender camaraderie—will they vanish like the friends from summer camp? Will they endure like survivors of a massacre? Chloe wonders, looking at Dick, at Hugh, soon to return to Rochester, New York, at the powder-white Junie, her face pinched and cocktail-waitressy; she wasn't pretty really, just had bloom on her side, had had bloom, but it would come back, but she was too thin, like one of those West Virginia women, a miner's wife maybe, it's an Anglo-Saxon type, thin and pitiful.

But Junie is a doctor, Chloe reminds herself; she's lucky to have something like that.

Hugh just nodding off, a handsome man in his early forties, thinking of what? drowsy in an airport, rumpled.

Dick paces, passes near the jostling caviar queue. Chloe notices again his jouncing walk, off the balls of his feet, like a fighter; he must have practiced it sometime when he was young, walking around his bedroom; now he just walked that way.

Even if I am bad, thinks Chloe, it isn't too late to be better. Or is it? And in what does better consist?

She should have been nicer to Jeffrey. Probably all he needed was kindness to have been a nice person. Probably he *was* nicer, perfectly nice with his new love. It was all her fault, she has never loved him enough. She sees that Hugh, immersed in the *Herald Tribune*, steals glances her way, of an uncertain character.

She has, for a moment, a sensation of perfect indifference to her personal fate; she will marry or not, will divorce, will suffer illness and die; she is for an instant serene in knowing that it will all happen as it will happen. Her mind, as usual, takes another turn on this. It is the Eastern lesson. She has learned something after all. Kismet, and after all could the universal will have anything so very bad in store for her? Anything worse than for other people?

It is hard to believe so.

Chapter Thirty-eight

BELUGA

Indeed, indeed, Repentance oft before
I swore—but was I sober when I swore?
And then and then came Spring, and Rose-in-hand
My thread-bare Penitence apieces tore.

Junie appeared to sleep. It seemed to Chloe that she was not asleep, but didn't want to talk. Whenever anyone came near her eyelids screwed down tighter. Thus she did not see, though Chloe and Hugh saw, a man who kept gazing strangely at her and making little movements toward her, only to retreat each time as if he were being jerked on a line. Finally he came decisively forward. Junie opened her eyes alertly, as if he had come to hurt her, and indeed his expression was hostile and wary.

"Excuse me," he said, speaking in a strongly French accent. "Excuse me, but I think, is it possible? that you are wearing my watch?"

Junie stared at him, looked down at her wrist.

"I don't know," she said, "am I?"

"May I?" He took her wrist and peered closely at the watch.

"Oui, bien sûr," he said. "Could there be another, see the Navaho band, a Patek Philippe, même modèle. But this is very strange. Perhaps you would give the explanation to the officials of Iran, for I am going to call them."

Dick and Hugh tensed and drew closer, protectively. "What's the problem?" Hugh said. "Maybe you could explain?"

"Certainly. This is my watch, stolen from me in Shiraz and under circumstances which I have been protesting."

"Dr. Juneau?" said Hugh, after a moment. "Are you by any chance Émile Juneau?"

327

The Frenchman looked startled at this mention of what wa
evidently his name.

"I'm Hugh Monroe," said Hugh. "We were to meet."

"Monroe? Mon dieu. I have been telephoning to you a
Shiraz."

"The watch came from a dead man in Shahpur's Cave.

Dr. Juneau looked pained at the grisly history of his watch
"Ah, yes, the cave," he said, indignation swelling his eyes

"Won't you sit down?" Hugh asked.

This is too much, thought Chloe. We're supposed to believ
anything. Junie happening to sit there, happening to wear
watch. "Some coincidence," she remarked, with asperity, t
Hugh.

"Not really," he said, "when you consider every Wester
person in Iran must be in this airport today."

She hadn't thought Junie was connected to Hugh's game
That was a surprise.

The doctor sat with formal bearing on the edge of th
waiting-room chair. "I was, as you know, on a particula
mission," he said, hesitating delicately and glancing at th
others, seeking to know from Hugh whether he should con
tinue.

"I've told them all about it," he said. "Plenty of thing
have been happening to me, too."

Dr. Juneau leaned forward and spoke in a low voice
"Understood. Alors—the Shah has been our patient sinc
1974, when we saw him in Paris. He was diagnosed at tha
time as having lymphoma. He was treated with cyclophospha
mide and did very well. In our view he had an excellen
response and we attended a long-term remission, if not
cure."

"Oh, I see, a lymphoma," said Hugh. "This wasn
mentioned in the history. I suspected something—perhap
cancer of the pancreas, but in fact there was very little evidenc
of that. In fact, he had no lymphadenopathy."

"That is interesting," said Dr. Juneau. "He originall
presented with mild anemia and hepatosplenomegaly. Wha
was the blood count now?"

Hugh hitched his chair nearer the doctor and they began t

onverse in numbers. "The chest x-ray showed no abnormalies," said Hugh.

"Anyway, now he falls ill again, and we are called. I fly from aris with the old medical records, and proceed to Shiraz, where he Shah is staying, I am told, in his summer palace. I descend t the Cyrus, that hotel there. The very night of my arrival, and am half dead with jet lag, is that not what you call it?"

"Yes," they said.

"I telephone you, we speak. Suddenly some men appear in ay hotel room. They have guns. They search my room, vidently looking for the medical records. But here is the mazing true intervention of fate, for in fact I have left my riefcase on the plane."

"What if someone had found it?" Hugh asked.

"I was not worried about that, for in fact there is another ame, of course, on the dossier. We always referred to him as ouis."

"Who were these people?"

"My belief was that they were Iranians connected with the anians in Paris and that there had somehow been a leak in aris about my mission. The Iranians in Paris oppose the hah."

"And these were their colleagues?"

"I suppose. But in any case they fall into a fury when they nd no dossier in my room, and now turn their guns on me. hey oblige me to dress and leave the hotel with them. I am indfolded and treated cruelly.

"We drive some distance out of town—at least, I could not iy longer hear the sounds of Shiraz—and I am put in a hut. ther men come, and I am brutally tortured." He drew his reath at the memory. He appeared quite recovered, bore no iarks or bruises.

"They want to know about the Shah's health?"

"Exactly. Naturally I tell them. I do not feel it is information vital it is worth losing an eye or an ear for. Would you?"

"Of course not," Hugh agreed. "He is probably suffering a currence of the lymphoma—it would explain the fever and undice. But I didn't make that diagnosis." He seemed quite sappointed with himself.

"And as I did not see him, I cannot be sure, but that is m
presumption too. They hoped, of course, malaria."

"But what did they do then?" asked Chloe.

"I am left in this place, with a guard, for an unknow
length of time, perhaps several days. Then new men come
apparently Russians. After a great deal of most alarmin
consultation among them I am put into a car and driven sti
further into the countryside. It is late evening, not yet entire
dark. With one man I am made to climb a path appalling
slanted?"

"Steep," said Chloe.

"Yes. We walked I noticed more than one hour. And that i
fact is when this man, this Russian, took my watch. Believ
me, I understood what that portended. Although I am ver
weak—the torture—I had very little to eat—I am on my guard
We go together into the cave, and here I am planning to brea
away and run, or else to push him, when by good fortune h
slips himself and crashes down the rocks." He paused
dramatically. "I threw rocks at him. Then I ran up out of th
cave, then down the steep path—I am half dead myself befor
I get to the bottom, and fall in a faint, am found by som
villagers, and taken to a hospital. That is all."

The others murmured, stirred. Junie had taken off the watc
and handed it to him.

"We found the man still alive, it must have been the nex
day. But he died soon after," Dick explained. "We nev
found out who he was."

"And we never found out what happened to him," Hug
said. "He was put into the morgue at the hospital, and the
when I looked, he wasn't there."

"No," Dick said, "he never was in the morgue, Abbas an
I buried him. Vahid Farmani told us not to put him in th
morgue. He said to take him to the American embassy, to th
police—we did all this, no one would take him. So we had
bury him—it was hot . . ."

How puny men are, frail and mortal, their bodies have to b
hurried into the ground, thought Chloe crossly. She thoug
this a disappointing story but Hugh was laughing. "How ne
and tidy," he said. "What if we hadn't met? We'd never hav
known."

"Well, I would have written to you at Rochester. I know who you are," said Dr. Juneau.

Only men like secrets and intrigue, thought Chloe. Why is it women are always blamed for it? She, it seemed to her, only wanted things to be simple. She had almost got hold of simplicity. It was like a dream that you forget. It slips away. In the noise of the loudspeakers, under the flashing lights of the notice board, she felt some vestige of understanding trickle and slip away, increasing her panicked sense of loss and dread.

As they had been speaking, an animated line had formed near a customs window whose purpose they could not quite discern, and Dick got up to draw nearer and find out, in case it was something they needed to get stamped or cleared.

"It's caviar," he reported. "You buy government-produced caviar right there. That's what all the fuss is about."

"We must get in line," cried Dr. Juneau, leaping to his feet. "It is excellent, the Iranian caviar. Me, I always take some back. Do not neglect to do so!"

"Will my things be all right here?" asked Zareeneh Yazdi at the same moment. "I am going to get my caviar. Will you keep an eye?"

"Sure," they said.

"I always like to take it to people; they're always so glad to get it. Our Iranian caviar is better than Russian," she said.

I have to think what I'm going to do, Chloe thought. She could picture her plane landing in San Francisco, Jeffrey—no, he'd go home unannounced in a cab—no, what if the woman friend was there; anyway she didn't have a key, she'd have to call him. But what time of day was it going to be? She had to decide what course of action to take next. She could not go drifting along as she always had done, she had to make decisions, had to take herself seriously. It mattered what she did. Her insides felt like the sawdust of this floor. Did she have any American money to pay for the taxi?

"Do you by any chance have a cigarette?" asked Dick of Zareeneh, walking along with her to the caviar line, out of earshot of the others. He didn't want to buy a whole pack, then he'd just smoke the whole thing. He didn't want to smoke in front of Junie or Chloe. Guilt and self-contempt made the first drag seem better.

A conga line of caviar seekers had developed, each perso
clinging paranoiacally to the person in front. Dick was severa
people behind Zareeneh, and she was twelfth. Dr. Juneau wa
just behind her. Dick counted the line twice. Each transactio
seemed to take an inexplicable length of time. The person a
the head of the line came away with a stack of sma
paper-wrapped packages. It must have been five hundre
dollars' worth of caviar. Dick looked in his wallet.

"Iranian currency only, no credit cards," Zareeneh calle
back to him.

"Could you save my place?" Dick asked the well-dresse
man ahead of him in line. He thought he would go back and as
the others if they wanted any caviar and suggest, if they ha
Iranian money, that this was a good way to spend the last of i
The man did not say yes, but he smiled in a friendly way.

"It's two hundred touman a package, two thousand rials. A
package is two hundred fifty grams," he told the others. "Th
line is long but we could take turns standing there."

Caviar, thought Chloe. So emblematic of all luxury, a
desire. She didn't want any.

"It would just spoil by the time I got it back to California,"
she said.

"No thanks," said Hugh, "but you can have my touman."

"Come and spell me on line, will you, if I don't come bac
in twenty minutes?"

"On line," thought Chloe. So New York, such a sill
expression.

Luxury, desire. She imagined she would never feel the nee
of these. She felt permanently flat, going home. It was lik
heaping caviar on flat, stale crackers, what a waste of the ric
mystery of flavor. Iran, Persia. The rebels would have horse
guns, they would rise up, you could see from the faces, th
thrilling faces, the fists, that they would rise up.

Even women. They would rise up. The Shah would ki
them, but he couldn't kill them all. Some would have rise
who could not be killed. She herself would be in California
Junie—Junie, staring at the *New England Journal of Medicin*
in her lap—was she feeling this flatness too? Let Jeffrey go t
the divorce court, Chloe thought; she was not going to bothe

Why did they not post the departure for their plane?

"I'll feel better when we get on the plane," said Hugh, pacing. Has he forgotten that they are getting on separate planes? Is he eager to leave her?

"Why would they keep us? They don't want us here," said Chloe.

"Not us," said Junie. "Not us, we're harmless enough."

"Jesus, I hope they don't run out," thinks Dick, watching the line, worried at the size of the plastic sacks full of packages of caviar that people carry off. The stacks in reserve, piled high behind the woman at the counter, are shrinking. Again he counts the people ahead of him. Zareeneh is nearly the next up; she would tell him if there was a problem, or anything special you had to do. Did you have to show your passport or your ticket? "I don't want to get caught up in this," he thinks, but he is, he can tell, from the crawling unease of his stomach each time the woman turns and takes from behind her off the dwindling stack one, two, six, nine tins of caviar.

Now a man is screaming, he is ahead of Zareeneh, and she looks round at Dick, her large black eyes rolling in fright. The man is screaming, "But my plane is leaving, don't you understand? I don't have time to change the money. Look, French francs, if you don't want dollars, francs."

"I can spell you now if you want," Chloe says to Dick, coming up behind him. But he'd got interested in this altercation up ahead.

"Thanks, I'm okay. Are you going to get some?"

"No," Chloe says.

"Deutsche marks, then? Look, take this." The man tears off his watch. "Take this, Rolex, look."

"Is that an American?" asks Chloe.

"I don't think so," Dick says. "He has some kind of accent."

"Thank God," says Chloe.

"Can you come here, please," the man is shouting at someone sitting near their own encampment among the chairs.

"Please, sir, there are others waiting," they hear Zareeneh saying.

"Look, have you got rials?" says Dick to Chloe. "If I could

borrow some? Could you go ask Junie how much she has?"

"I left mine," Chloe says. "I'll go ask Junie." Hugh comes back in a minute with Junie's rials, and is fishing in his wallet for his. He hands his money to Dick.

"How's it going?" he asks.

"It's useless; if this guy gets the money, he's going to take it all," says Dick miserably. "And if he doesn't take it, Zareeneh will." The man is piling banknotes on the counter in front of him, counting them. Three other men standing to one side are handing him banknotes. A tremendous pile of reddish bills grows on the counter.

"Do you want me to help you stand in line for a while?" asks Hugh.

"No, it's okay," says Dick, unhappily aware of the cigarette burning between his fingers. Hugh doesn't seem to notice it. Dick looks around for an ashtray. The floor is a sea of cigarette butts.

"Unhappy Iran," says Hugh, in a melancholy tone.

Without looking down, Dick drops the cigarette and steps on it, "Yeah, we're getting out just in time."

"They're going to be boiling Americans in oil pretty soon. I feel kind of bad about Cooley."

"This son of a burned father," hisses Zareeneh, "wants all the caviar in Iran."

"It's been kind of fun, in a way, hasn't it? Though it doesn't seem very appropriate to say so. If you could have seen them in the streets . . ."

Dick reflects, without saying so, that he too would have thought it fun to have Chloe Fowler for a lover.

"Chloe finds riots exciting and fun. Her everyday life must be kind of boring. Jeff . . ." Hugh pauses, sighs. "Jeff's okay, but he's never been a particular friend of mine. He's very much a surgeon."

Dick perfectly agrees with this term of opprobrium.

"Of course she's devoted to her children," Hugh says, his tone increasingly morose. Dick understands that Hugh is trying to confide in him, or bring it all out in the open, but he finds himself unwilling to respond. If Chloe hadn't told Hugh that she was leaving Jeffrey, then it wasn't up to him to betray her confidences. How did things stand between them? It was impossible to tell. It looked as if they planned to go their separate ways. But always, in the affairs of heart of one's friends, it's best to say nothing, he knew that much.

"That's a thousand, count it," says the man ahead of him.

"Dust on his head!" says Zareeneh, bitterly.

The caviar clerk begins slowly to count the leaves of money. It seems to all the other people in line as if she counts with particular deliberation, even hate. Is there no limit per customer? Could this heap of money compel all that caviar? Zareeneh is sending them dark, flashing looks, as if enjoining them to kill the man.

"Maybe there's a limit per customer," says Dick.

Behind them people begin to mutter and push. Dick feels a hard elbow in his back. Just as well that Junie and Chloe aren't here, if things get rough, he thinks.

"We'll miss Chloe too. It's unusual to get to know a woman without her husband. Some of them are quite nice." He means a joke, a touch of innuendo, but Hugh doesn't smile.

"For Christ's sake hurry," screams the caviar customer. "My plane's leaving." His friends have deserted his side and are sprinting toward a departure gate.

"We don't have much time either," Hugh says. They watch the methodical clumsiness of the woman's fingers. Does she hate this man only, or does she hate all of them? Will she treat Zareeneh with gracious celerity?

"Oh, for God's sake," moans the man, in agony, his head swiveling first to look at his bolting friends, then at the way the money seems to stick to her fingers. Now she turns, lifts down some packages from the shelf behind her, and begins to put them into a big plastic sack. Dick finds that he is holding his breath. He turns and irritably pushes back at the man behind him so rudely shoving.

Now, with a terrible animal moan, the customer snatches up the plastic sack and dashes across the waiting room, leaving the huge wad of money and another dozen tins waiting to be packaged. The implacable woman begins again to count the money. Zareeneh steps briskly up to the counter and raps on it with her jeweled fist. She smiles and opens her purse, speaking in rapid Farsi. The woman begins to assemble packages.

"Sixteen! She's taking sixteen!" whispers Dick to Hugh.

"Maybe I'll buy some for Chloe," Hugh says. "She'll be
sorry if she doesn't get some." He hands Dick some touman
notes. Behind them, actual shouting has begun, and the
pushing intensifies. Dick now notices with surprise that the line
extends clear to the restrooms. Are these all passengers for the
London plane?

"Hurry," says Zareeneh to Dick. "The plane will be
leaving."

"Stupid bitch," thinks Dick bitterly, as if we can hurry. As
if we can help this. He tries not to watch the next transaction;
it is too stressful.

"Would you watch my things?" Chloe says to Junie. "I'll go
see what's taking them so long. They've called the London
plane." She just wants to walk, is made restless by a stirring
of desire, for Iran, for Hugh, for something. Maybe they could
find a hiding place to make love in? But there isn't time.
Zareeneh Yazdi, her face moist in the hot room, smiles as she
comes toward Chloe with an immense plastic sack that says
Mehrabad Airport Caviar Shop. Triumph, relief, every last
obstacle overcome, says her expression. Chloe wanders up to
Hugh and Dick.

"Look at all these people, they're all Westerners, it's
disgusting," said Chloe, of the hysterical line.

"Some are Iranians," objects Hugh. "Zareeneh bought
sixteen packages."

"I've got three hundred dollars' worth of rials here," said
Dick. "Shall I just spend it all?"

"I always save enough for a gin martini on the plane," says
Hugh.

"I don't mind the danger. I would rather stay," said Chloe,
her stomach turning over with reluctance to hear them speak of
the plane, and gin and ordinary life.

"On airplanes is the only time I drink them," says Hugh.

She doesn't mind the danger; she thinks she had almost got
hold of something. But what? Why did she feel this inappropriate feeling of desire, this wish to be in Hugh's arms, or
someone's arms? She thinks of nymphomania. Maybe, like a
ghoul, like a vampire, once you see blood and hear guns that

changes you, that interests you. Can it be interest, not desire, that quickens the blood, quickens the breath?

Lucky Noosheen, thinks Chloe. I could stay with Noosheen and help her. But of course this is not a place you would want to stay, where people are shot before your eyes, and blood rolls out across the gravel, and the guns are being distributed to everyone, and little girls in villages are left to die.

"My life has been a flower, what do I know?" she says. Dick and Hugh look at her, not following her.

"What would you have, a terrible life?" asks Dick.

"No, of course not. Of course not," she says.

"It's okay," said Hugh, meaning to reassure her. "We'll soon be on the plane."

"Attention. All passengers to Rome, now boarding at gate seven," said the loudspeaker. Dick discovers that although there is now no danger of not getting up to the caviar window before they have to go, he is trembling. The man ahead of him is served. "Aha," says Dick happily, slapping his banknotes down on the counter in front of the caviar clerk. Her eyes, catching his for one instant, have the opaque glint of copper pennies. He will open a tin on the plane, he decides. Does Junie like caviar?

"One always feels so sad at the end of a trip," Chloe says.

"Do you?" asks Dick. "I don't. I'm always glad to get home." The woman is putting his packages in a large plastic sack. He recognizes the numbers as she counts in Farsi, "Panj, haft . . ."

"That's three thousand grams, that's three kilos," Dick says. "We can have a hell of a party with three kilos of caviar."

"No, I always feel sad," Chloe says. "Sometimes I begin to cry. I always have. Tears, sobs, as we land. Often. I thought that was the normal thing."

"You have it all wrong," said Hugh.

"Attention, all passengers to London on Iran Air flight 154, to London, Heathrow, all passengers should be on board, all on board please, gate six."

Chloe races along with Dick and Hugh, back to the luggage. Junie is standing, her coat over her arm. Dick fishes in his plastic sack and hands two packages of caviar to Hugh. Behind them, people in the caviar line have begun to scream.

I will try to be better, thinks Chloe. I'll try to be good.

"Hurry up, for God's sake," says Junie. "The plane's ready." They load themselves with bags and stagger toward the gates. Hugh puts Chloe's two cases under his arms. A row of airplanes stretches across the airfield, poised for escape. Eagerly hundreds of passengers throng toward the various gates of departure, men pushing wagons heaped with bags. I always have it all wrong, thinks Chloe. But how can I get it right? It had seemed that she was getting closer, but there is no time to think about it now, as she struggles along behind Hugh and Dick and Junie. They walk her to her gate and set her bags down.

"Call, Chloe, as soon as you get home," Hugh says. He gives her a kiss as fervent as is consonant with propriety. Dick kisses her. Junie kisses her.

"Yes, let us know that you're home safely," Dick says.

"Yes, yes, I will," she says, emotions sealing her throat against more words. Emotions, unnamable, tears starting. Going home alone.

Hugh hands Chloe the two tins of caviar. "One for you, one for Jeffrey," he says.

"Thank you," she says. "Thank you." Without looking back at them, she girds herself with her carry-ons and stumbles out across the hot concrete. The odor of Iran is gone, clove and straw; now it is of jet fuel. She crowds herself in among the people climbing up the metal steps.

She will eat both the tins of caviar herself, is her thought, settling in her seat. At least, she certainly won't give one to Jeffrey. This idea makes her feel a little better, though she is still as wretched as ever she has been in her life. All airplanes, all steps and bags and seats in the world are alike and she is home already. She fastens her seatbelt. Tears wet her cheeks. People will think they are tears of joy and relief.

About the Author

Diane Johnson is the author of six novels. Her collection of essays, TERRORISTS AND NOVELISTS, was nominated for the 1983 Pulitzer Prize and her biography of Mary Ellen Peacock Meredith, LESSER LIVES, was nominated for a National Book Award in 1973. A frequent contributor to the *New York Review of Books*, Ms. Johnson lives in San Francisco and teaches at the University of California at Davis.

SUPERIOR FICTION *from the* FINEST CONTEMPORARY AUTHORS